Nancy Drew™ & The Hardy Boys™

THE CASE OF THE MISSING ADULTS!

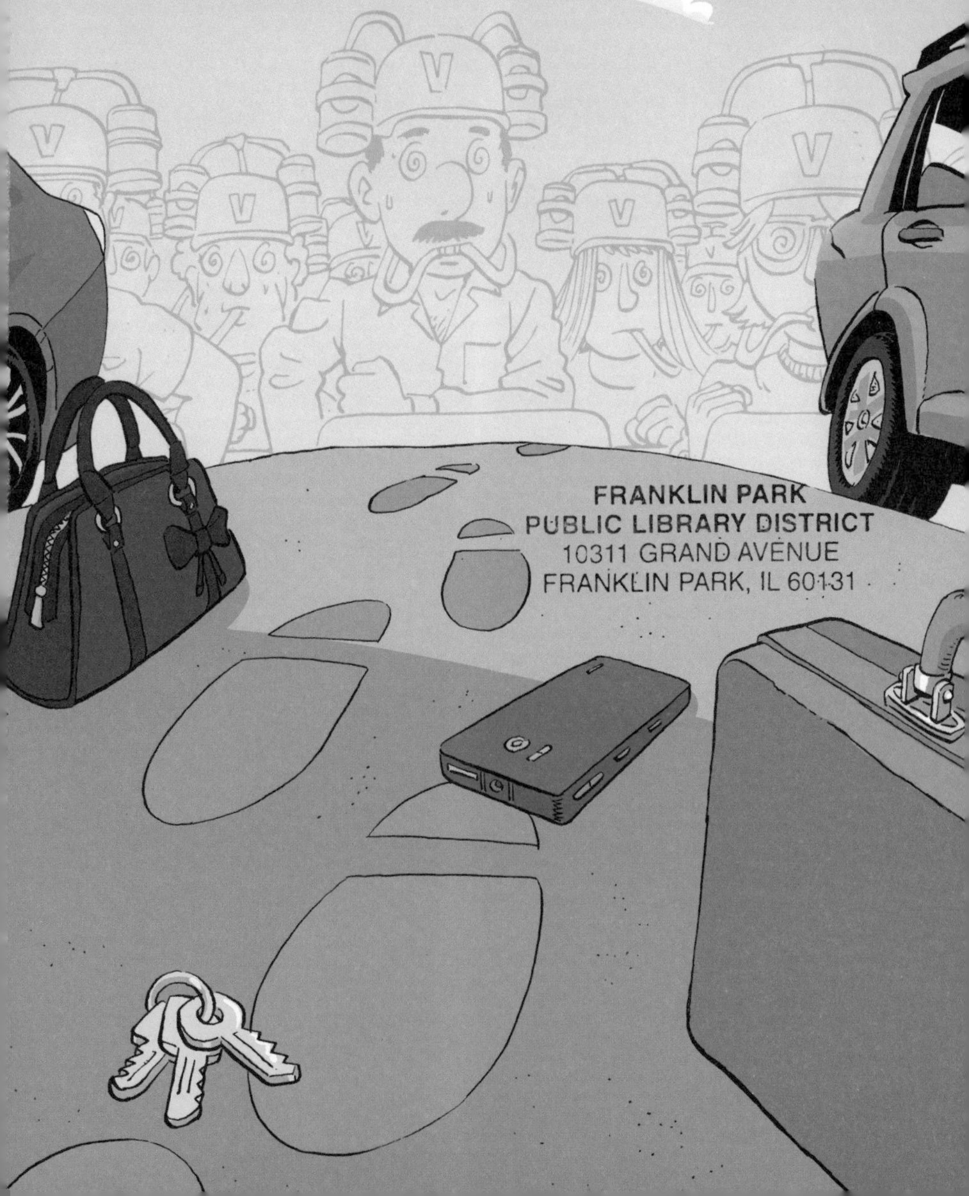
V

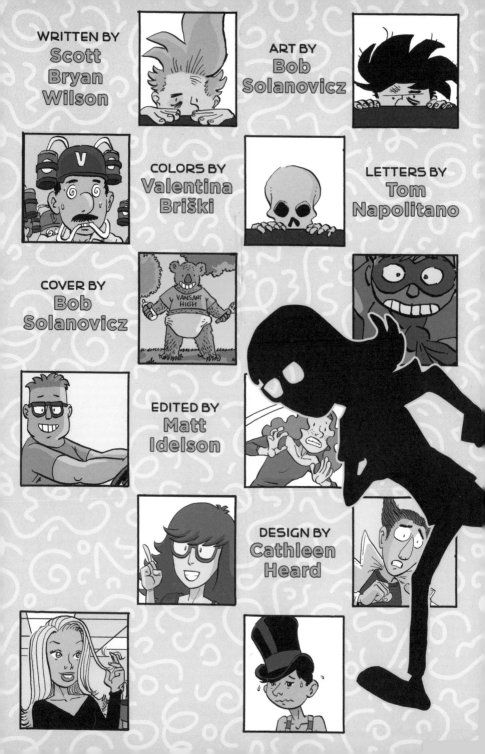

WRITTEN BY
Scott Bryan Wilson

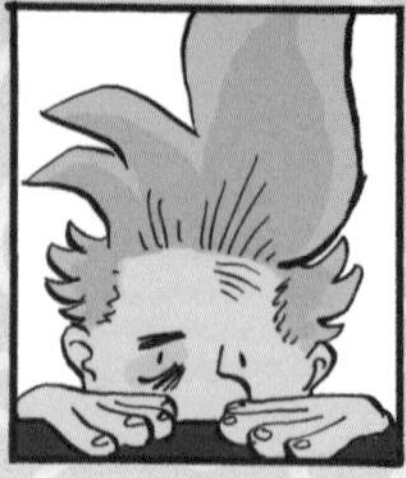

ART BY
Bob Solanovicz

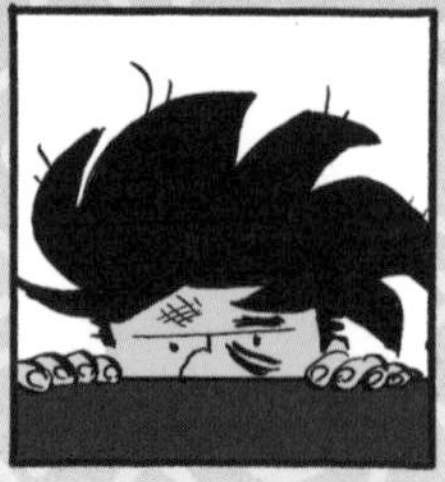

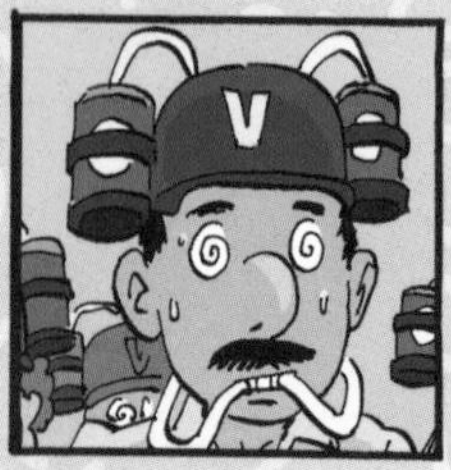

COLORS BY
Valentina Briški

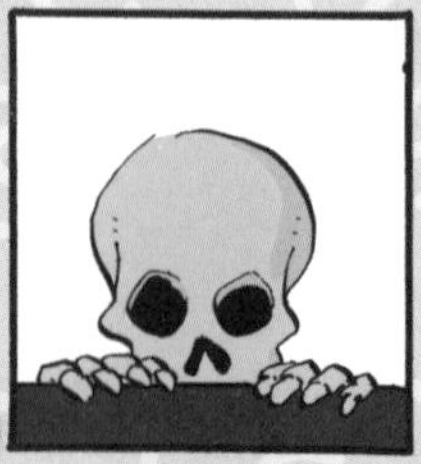

LETTERS BY
Tom Napolitano

COVER BY
Bob Solanovicz

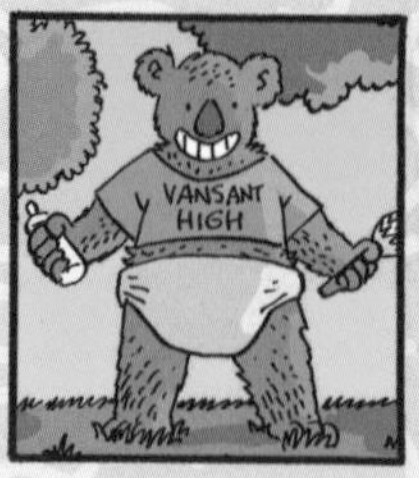
VANSANT
HIGH

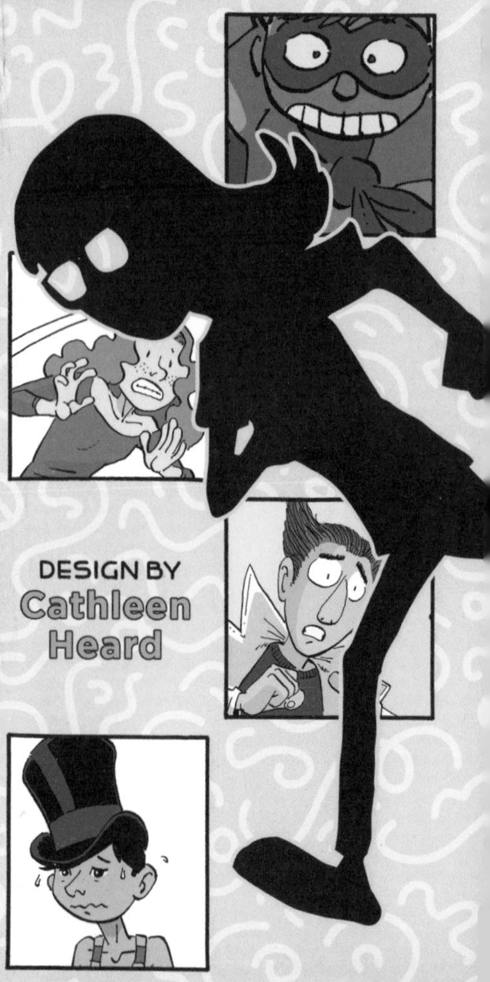

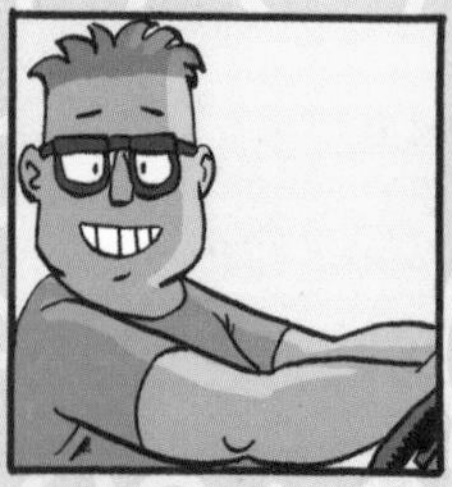

EDITED BY
Matt Idelson

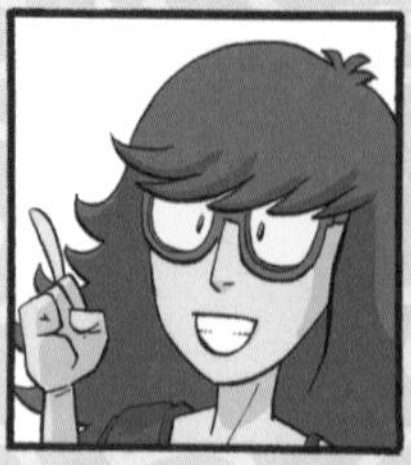

DESIGN BY
Cathleen Heard

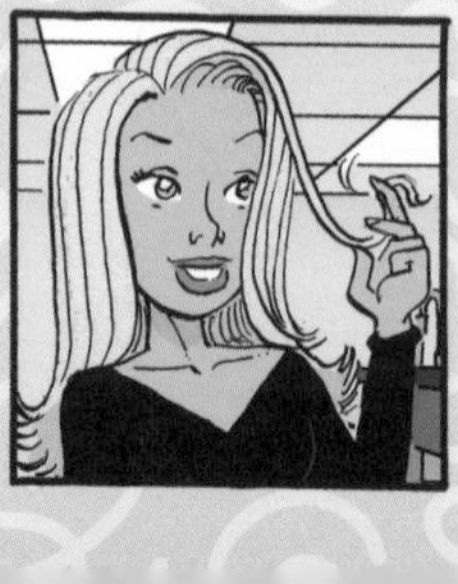

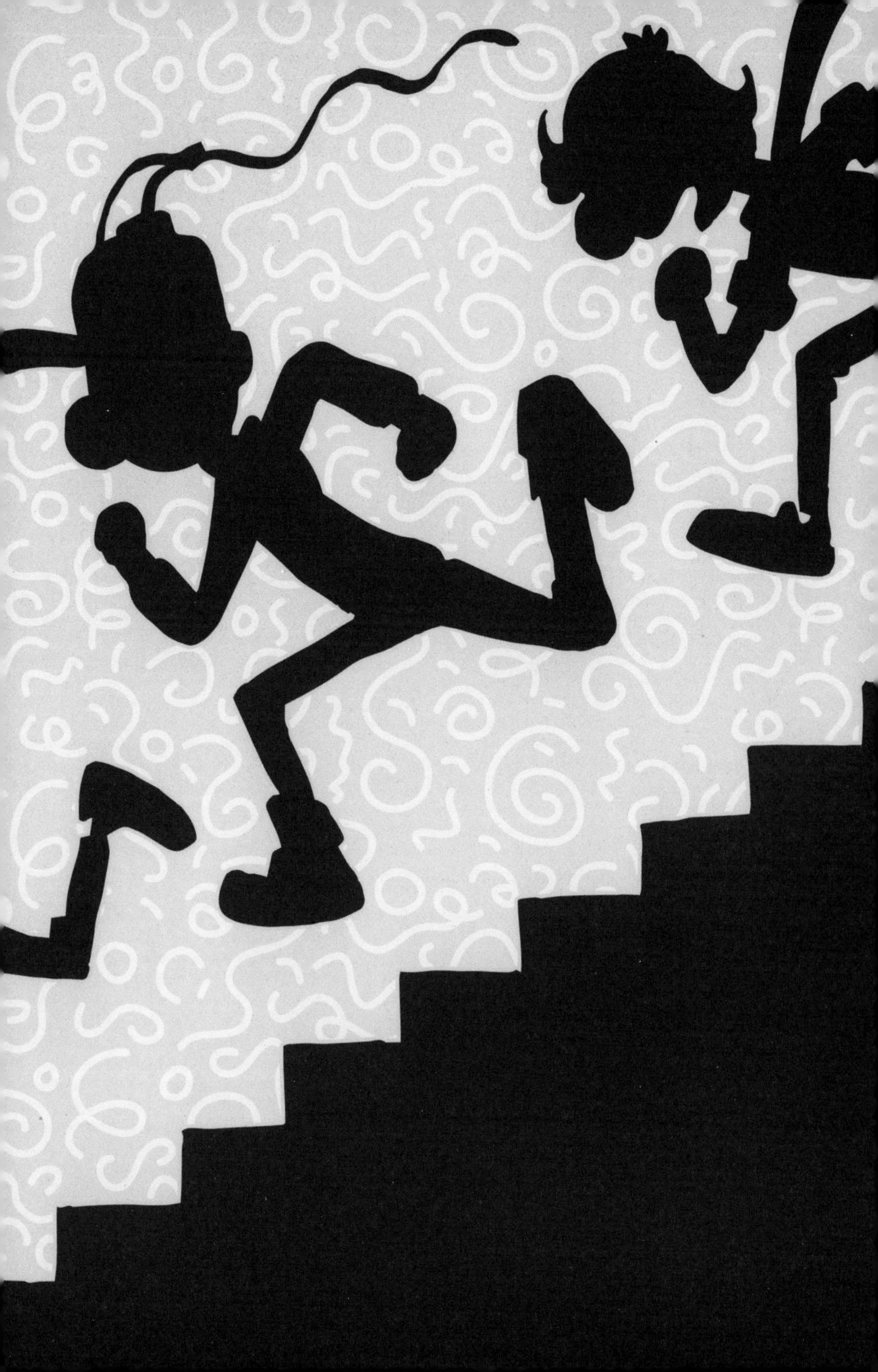

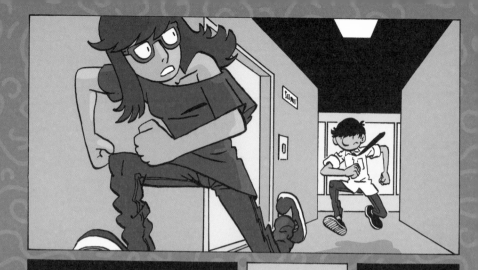

DYNAMITE

Online at www.DYNAMITE.com
On Facebook /Dynamitecomics
On Instagram /Dynamitecomics
On Twitter @dynamitecomics

Nick Barrucci CEO / Publisher
Juan Collado President / COO
Brandon Dante Primavera V.P. of IT and Operations

Joe Rybandt Executive Editor
Matt Idelson Senior Editor
Kevin Ketner Editor

Cathleen Heard Art Director
Rachel Kilbury Digital Multimedia Associate
Alexis Persson Graphic Designer
Katie Hidalgo Graphic Designer

Alan Payne V.P. of Sales and Marketing
Rex Wang Director of Consumer Sales
Pat O'Connell Sales Manager
Vincent Faust Marketing Coordinator

Jay Spence Director of Product Development
Mariano Nicieza Director of Research & Development

Amy Jackson Administrative Coordinator

For media rights, foreign rights, promotions, licensing, and advertising: marketing@dynamite.com.

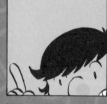

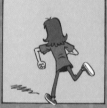

For Ellie,
Love, Dad

To Džuka,
who made it
possible, and to the
Studijo crew who
made it easier.

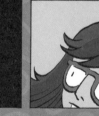

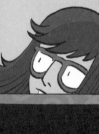

ISBN13:
978-1-5241-1178-6

First Printing
10 9 8 7 6 5 4 3 2 1

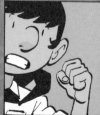

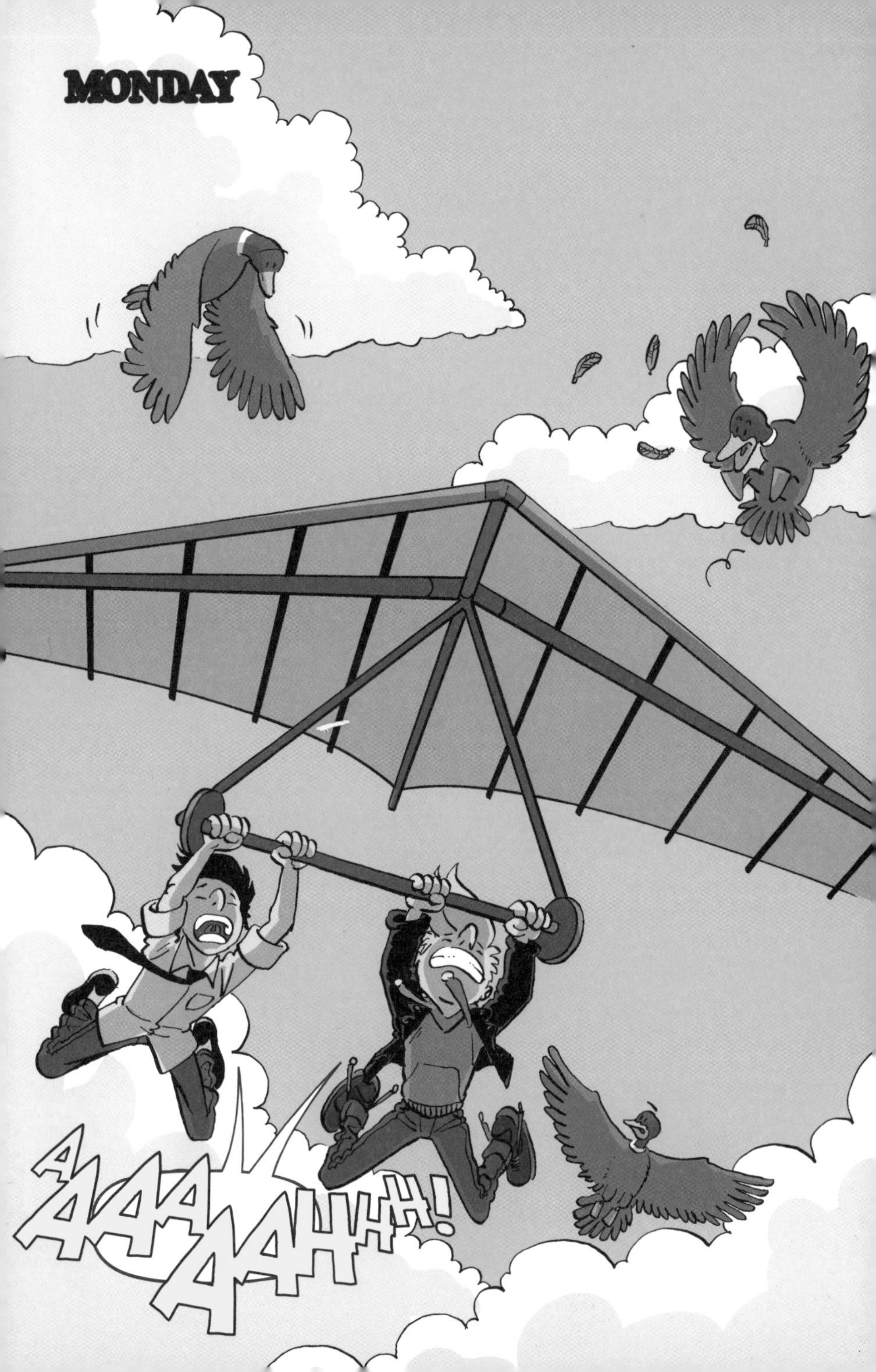
MONDAY
AAAAAAAHHH!

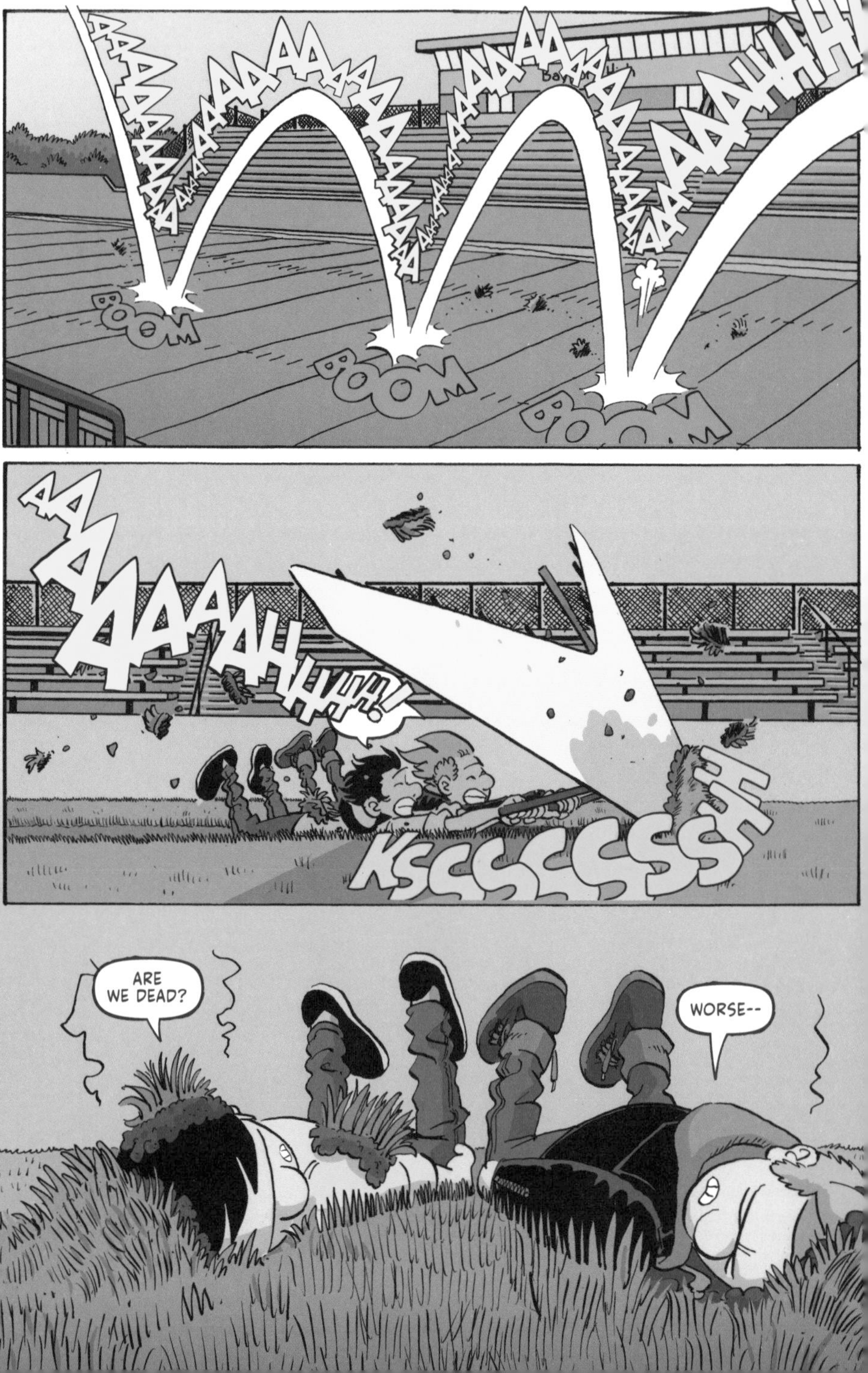
AAAAAAAAAAAAAAAAAAAAAAAAAAAAAAAAAAAAAAAAAAAAAAAAAAAHHH
BOOM
BOOM
BOOM
AAAAAAAHHHH!
KSSSSSSH
ARE WE DEAD?
WORSE--

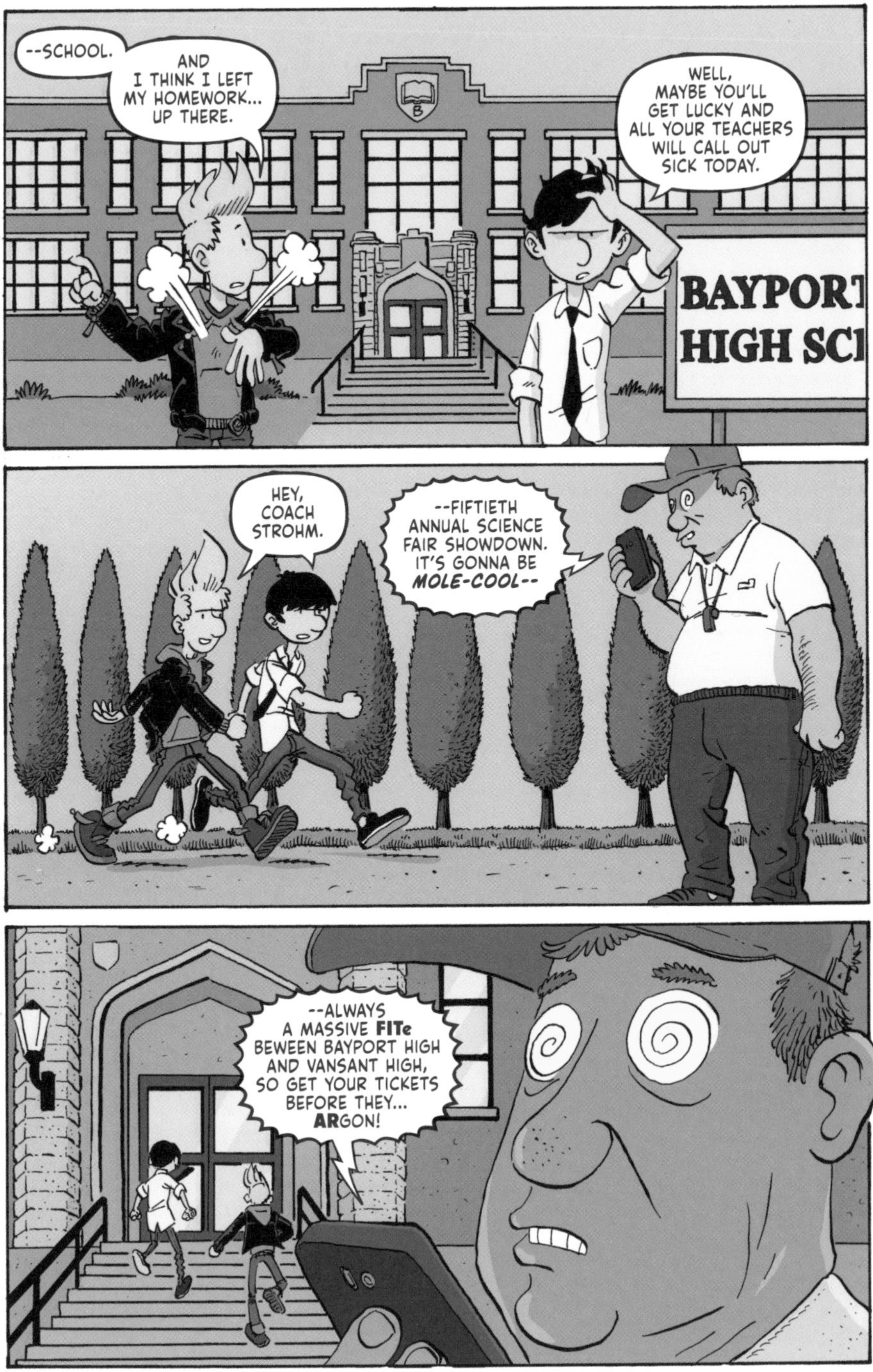
--SCHOOL.
AND I THINK I LEFT MY HOMEWORK... UP THERE.
WELL, MAYBE YOU'LL GET LUCKY AND ALL YOUR TEACHERS WILL CALL OUT SICK TODAY.
BAYPORT HIGH SC
HEY, COACH STROHM.
--FIFTIETH ANNUAL SCIENCE FAIR SHOWDOWN. IT'S GONNA BE MOLE-COOL--
--ALWAYS A MASSIVE FITe BEWEEN BAYPORT HIGH AND VANSANT HIGH, SO GET YOUR TICKETS BEFORE THEY... ARGON!

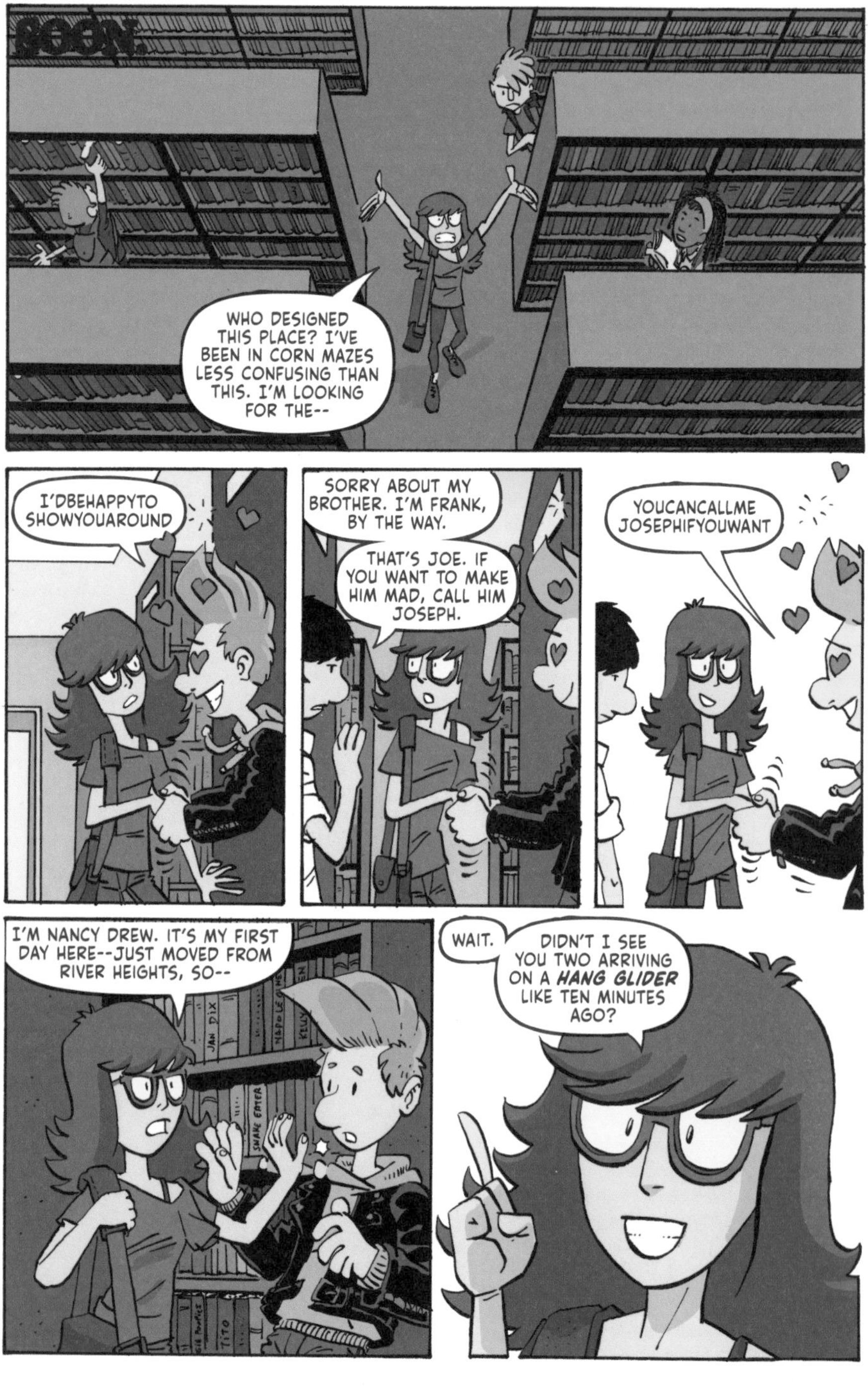
BOOM.
WHO DESIGNED THIS PLACE? I'VE BEEN IN CORN MAZES LESS CONFUSING THAN THIS. I'M LOOKING FOR THE--
I'DBEHAPPYTO SHOWYOUAROUND
SORRY ABOUT MY BROTHER. I'M FRANK, BY THE WAY.
THAT'S JOE. IF YOU WANT TO MAKE HIM MAD, CALL HIM JOSEPH.
YOUCANCALLME JOSEPHIFYOUWANT
I'M NANCY DREW. IT'S MY FIRST DAY HERE--JUST MOVED FROM RIVER HEIGHTS, SO--
WAIT.
DIDN'T I SEE YOU TWO ARRIVING ON A HANG GLIDER LIKE TEN MINUTES AGO?

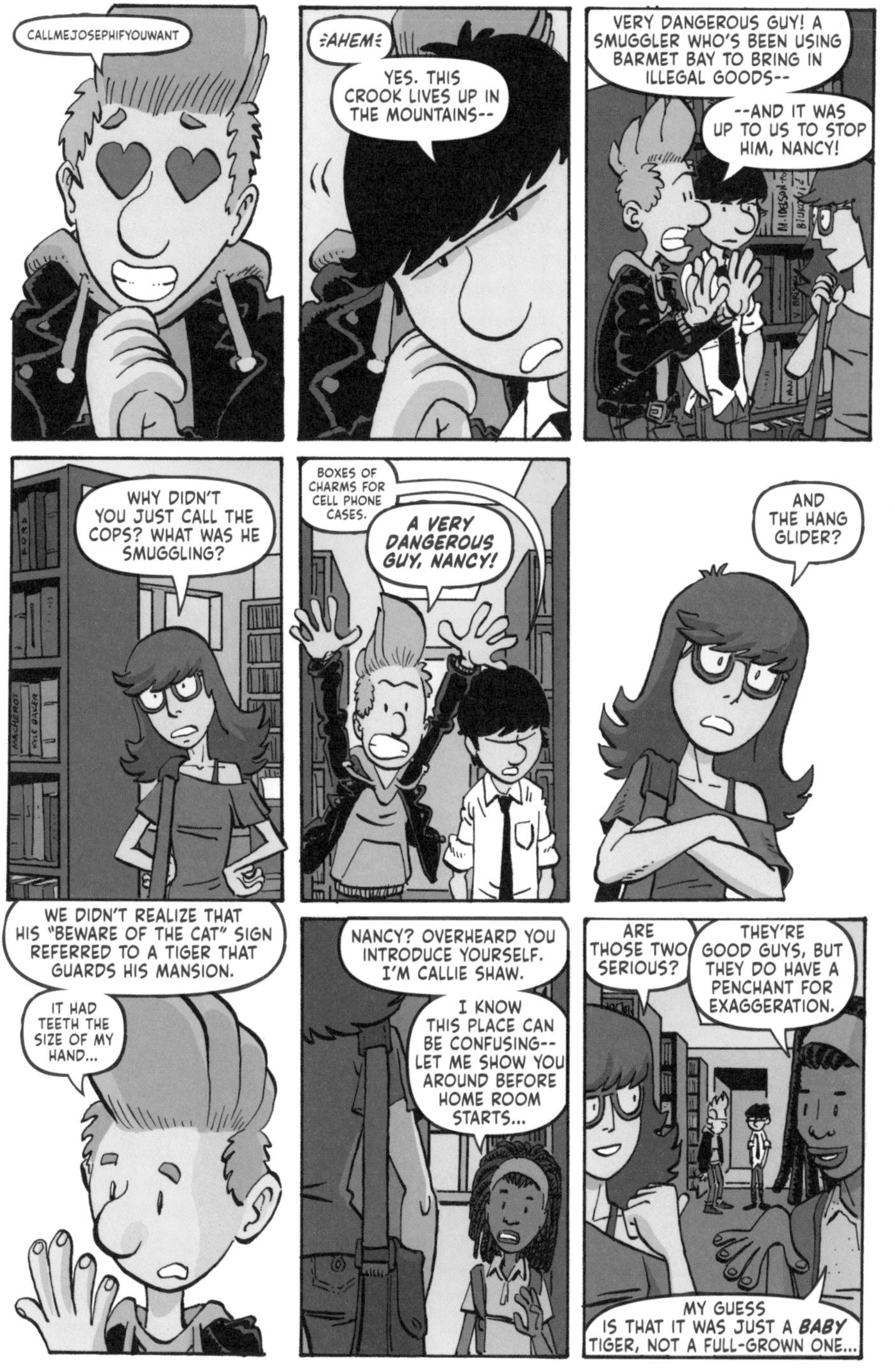
CALLMEJOSEPHIFYOUWANT
AHEM
YES. THIS CROOK LIVES UP IN THE MOUNTAINS--
VERY DANGEROUS GUY! A SMUGGLER WHO'S BEEN USING BARMET BAY TO BRING IN ILLEGAL GOODS--
--AND IT WAS UP TO US TO STOP HIM, NANCY!
WHY DIDN'T YOU JUST CALL THE COPS? WHAT WAS HE SMUGGLING?
BOXES OF CHARMS FOR CELL PHONE CASES.
A VERY DANGEROUS GUY, NANCY!
AND THE HANG GLIDER?
WE DIDN'T REALIZE THAT HIS "BEWARE OF THE CAT" SIGN REFERRED TO A TIGER THAT GUARDS HIS MANSION.
IT HAD TEETH THE SIZE OF MY HAND...
NANCY? OVERHEARD YOU INTRODUCE YOURSELF. I'M CALLIE SHAW.
I KNOW THIS PLACE CAN BE CONFUSING-- LET ME SHOW YOU AROUND BEFORE HOME ROOM STARTS...
ARE THOSE TWO SERIOUS?
THEY'RE GOOD GUYS, BUT THEY DO HAVE A PENCHANT FOR EXAGGERATION.
MY GUESS IS THAT IT WAS JUST A BABY TIGER, NOT A FULL-GROWN ONE...

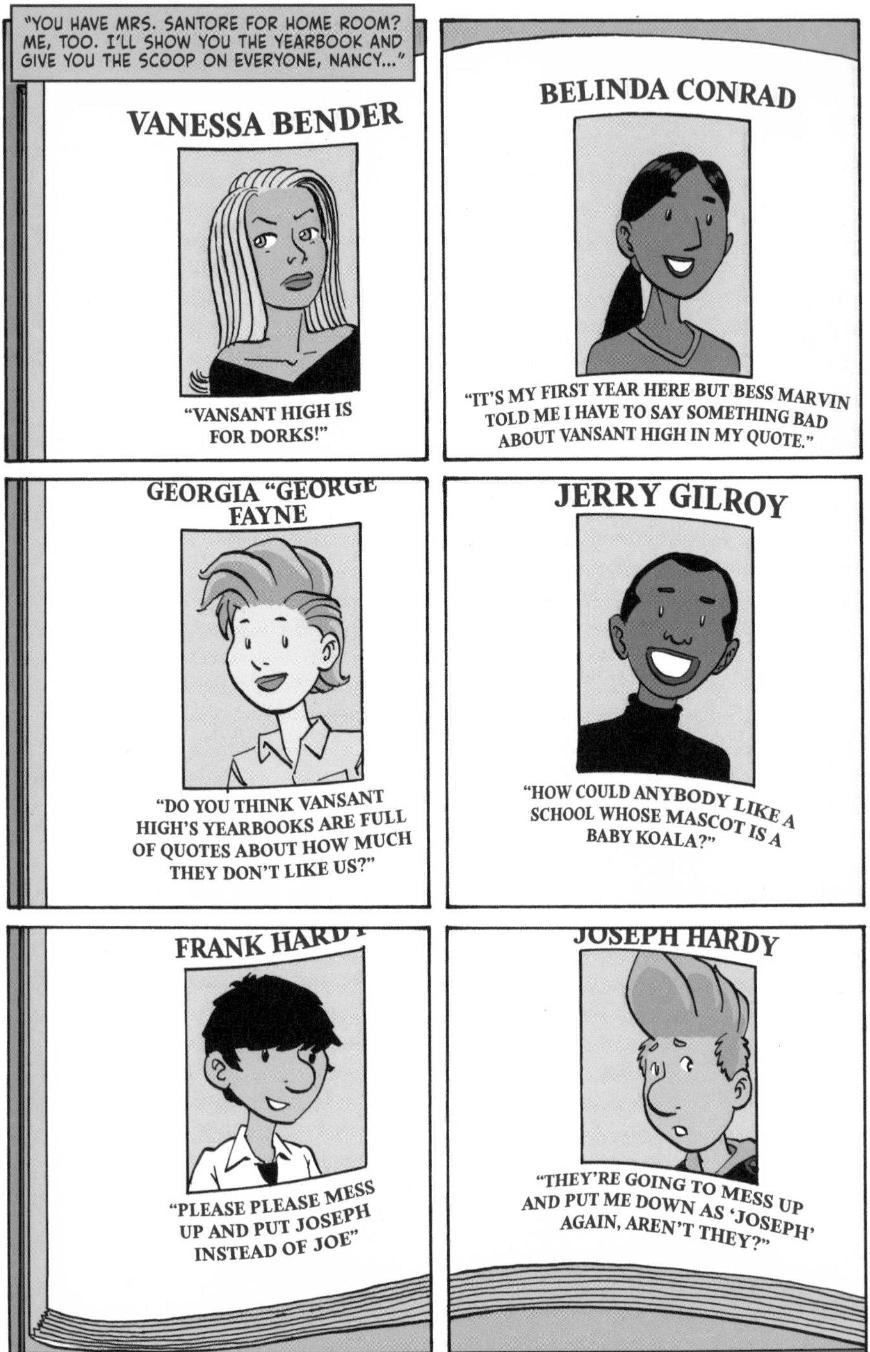
"YOU HAVE MRS. SANTORE FOR HOME ROOM? ME, TOO. I'LL SHOW YOU THE YEARBOOK AND GIVE YOU THE SCOOP ON EVERYONE, NANCY..."
VANESSA BENDER
"VANSANT HIGH IS FOR DORKS!"
BELINDA CONRAD
"IT'S MY FIRST YEAR HERE BUT BESS MARVIN TOLD ME I HAVE TO SAY SOMETHING BAD ABOUT VANSANT HIGH IN MY QUOTE."
GEORGIA "GEORGE" FAYNE
"DO YOU THINK VANSANT HIGH'S YEARBOOKS ARE FULL OF QUOTES ABOUT HOW MUCH THEY DON'T LIKE US?"
JERRY GILROY
"HOW COULD ANYBODY LIKE A SCHOOL WHOSE MASCOT IS A BABY KOALA?"
FRANK HARDY
"PLEASE PLEASE MESS UP AND PUT JOSEPH INSTEAD OF JOE"
JOSEPH HARDY
"THEY'RE GOING TO MESS UP AND PUT ME DOWN AS 'JOSEPH' AGAIN, AREN'T THEY?"

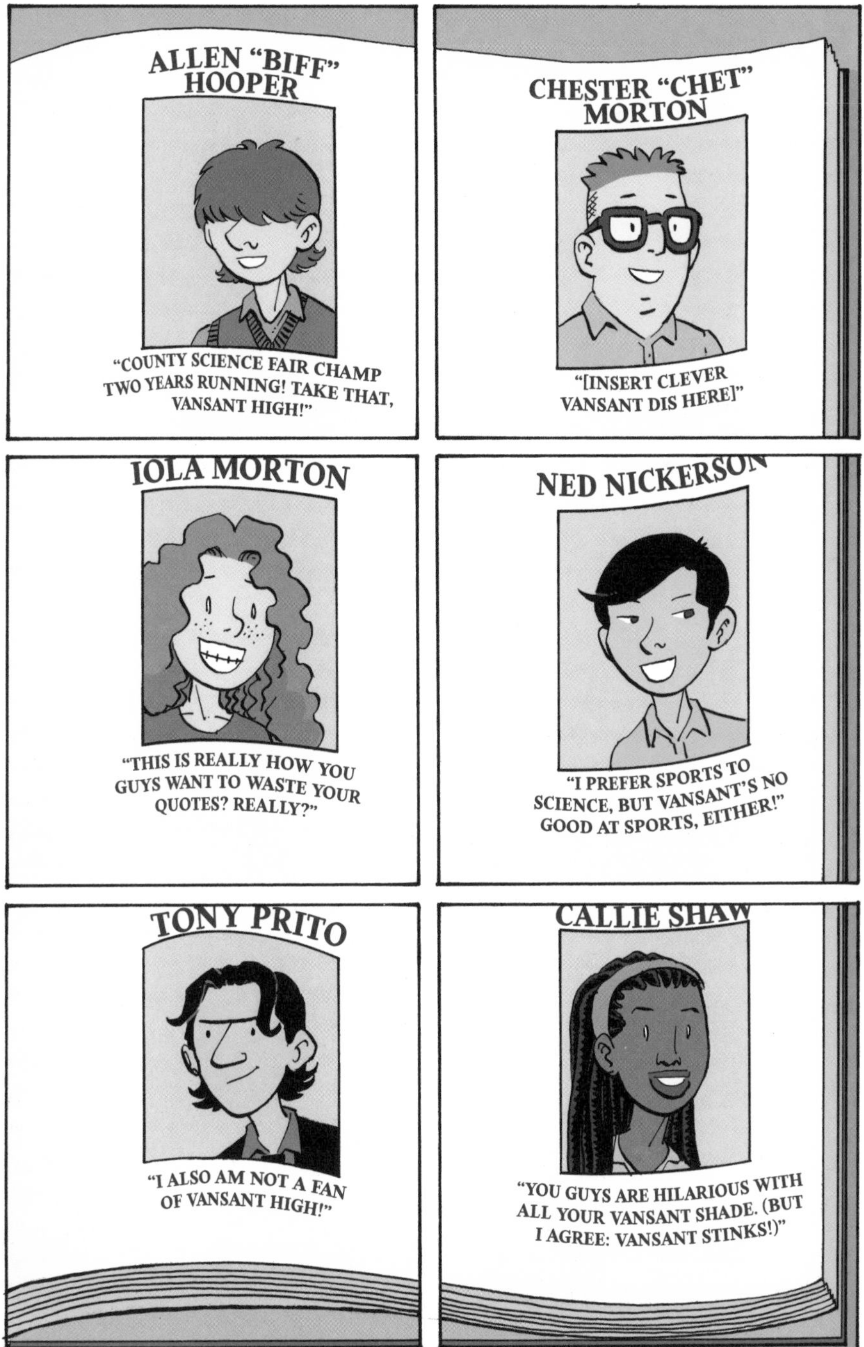
ALLEN "BIFF" HOOPER
"COUNTY SCIENCE FAIR CHAMP TWO YEARS RUNNING! TAKE THAT, VANSANT HIGH!"
CHESTER "CHET" MORTON
"[INSERT CLEVER VANSANT DIS HERE]"
IOLA MORTON
"THIS IS REALLY HOW YOU GUYS WANT TO WASTE YOUR QUOTES? REALLY?"
NED NICKERSON
"I PREFER SPORTS TO SCIENCE, BUT VANSANT'S NO GOOD AT SPORTS, EITHER!"
TONY PRITO
"I ALSO AM NOT A FAN OF VANSANT HIGH!"
CALLIE SHAW
"YOU GUYS ARE HILARIOUS WITH ALL YOUR VANSANT SHADE. (BUT I AGREE: VANSANT STINKS!)"

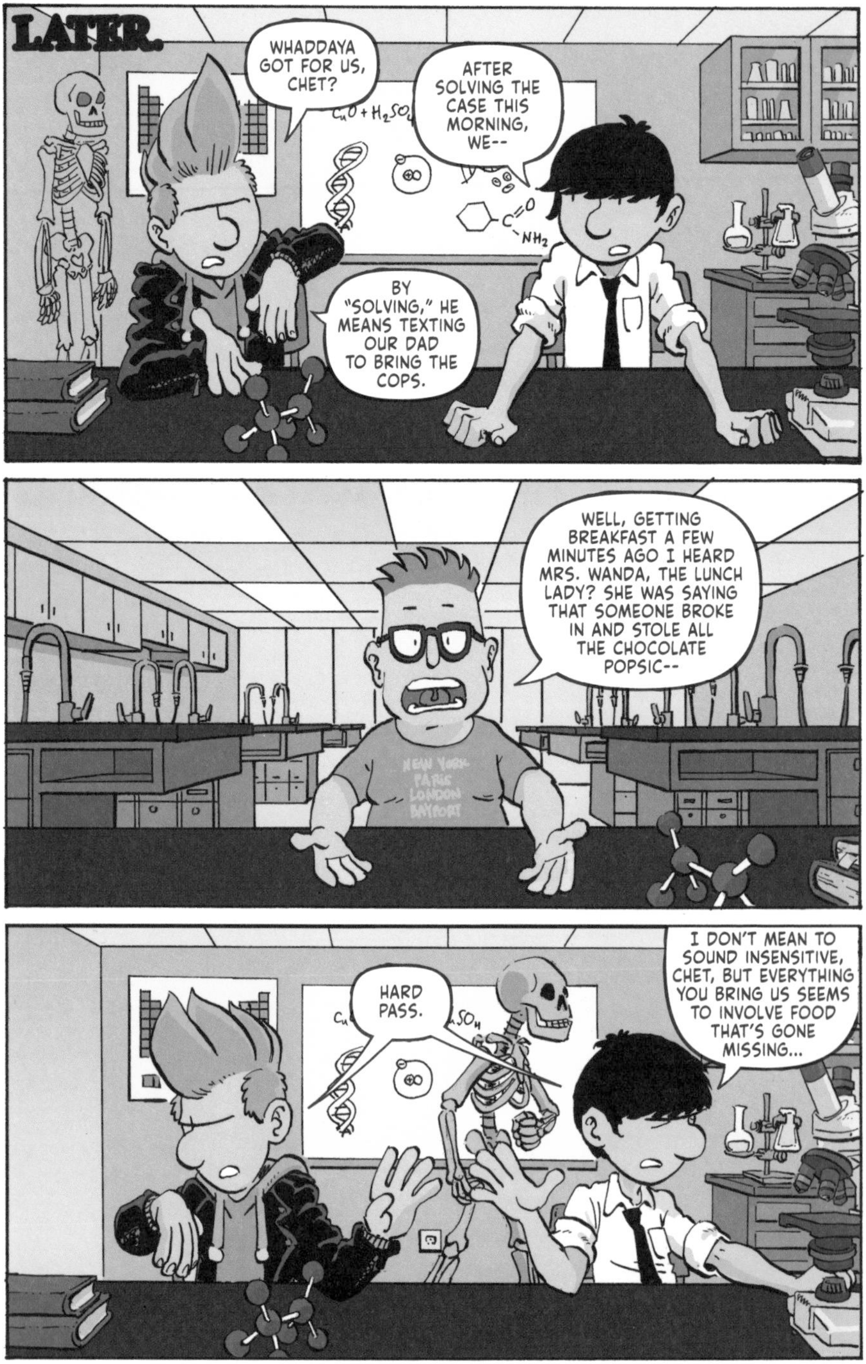
LATER.
WHADDAYA GOT FOR US, CHET?
AFTER SOLVING THE CASE THIS MORNING, WE--
BY "SOLVING," HE MEANS TEXTING OUR DAD TO BRING THE COPS.
WELL, GETTING BREAKFAST A FEW MINUTES AGO I HEARD MRS. WANDA, THE LUNCH LADY? SHE WAS SAYING THAT SOMEONE BROKE IN AND STOLE ALL THE CHOCOLATE POPSIC--
NEW YORK PARIS LONDON BAYPORT
I DON'T MEAN TO SOUND INSENSITIVE, CHET, BUT EVERYTHING YOU BRING US SEEMS TO INVOLVE FOOD THAT'S GONE MISSING...
HARD PASS.

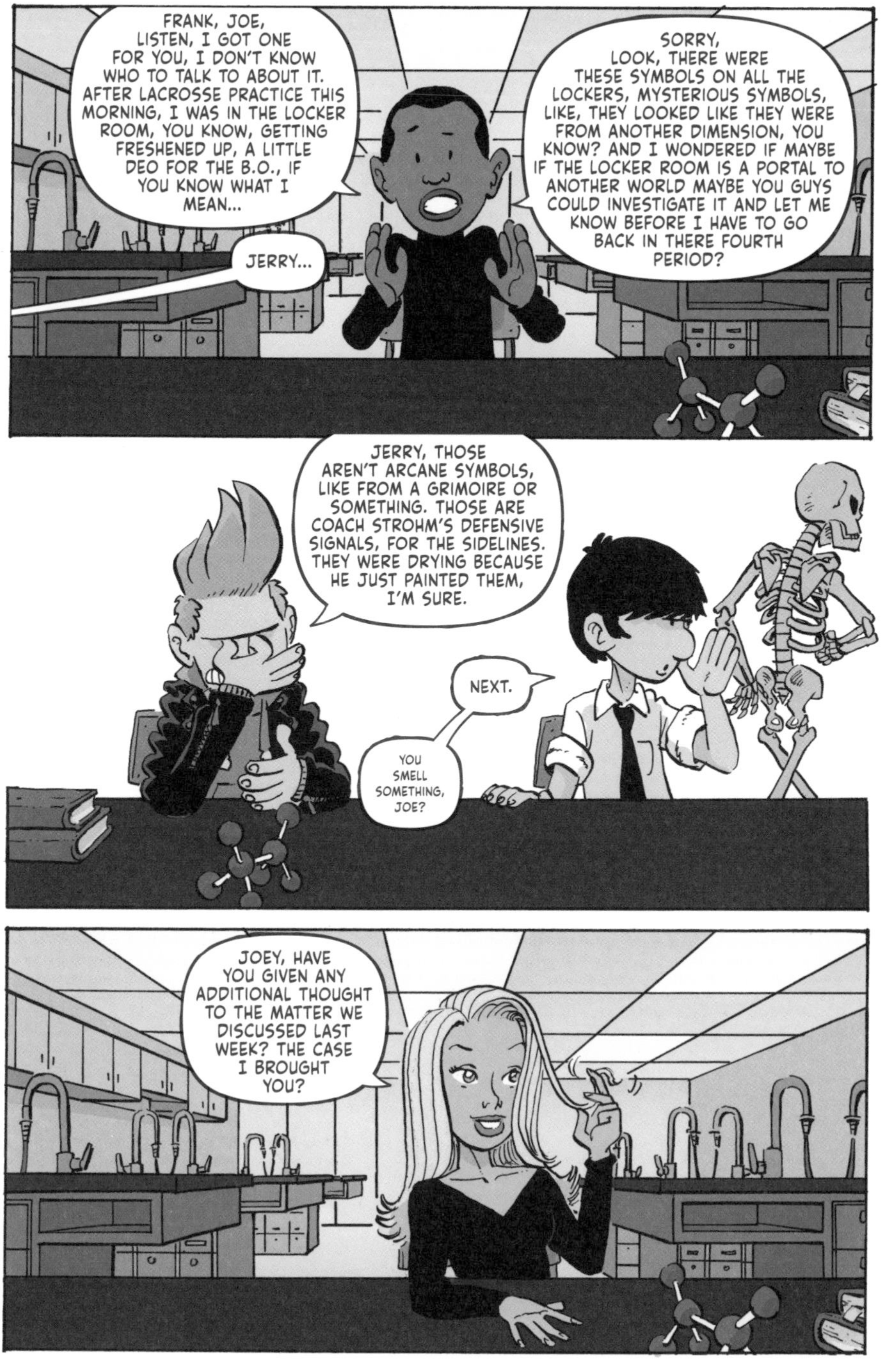
FRANK, JOE, LISTEN, I GOT ONE FOR YOU, I DON'T KNOW WHO TO TALK TO ABOUT IT. AFTER LACROSSE PRACTICE THIS MORNING, I WAS IN THE LOCKER ROOM, YOU KNOW, GETTING FRESHENED UP, A LITTLE DEO FOR THE B.O., IF YOU KNOW WHAT I MEAN...
JERRY...
SORRY, LOOK, THERE WERE THESE SYMBOLS ON ALL THE LOCKERS, MYSTERIOUS SYMBOLS, LIKE, THEY LOOKED LIKE THEY WERE FROM ANOTHER DIMENSION, YOU KNOW? AND I WONDERED IF MAYBE IF THE LOCKER ROOM IS A PORTAL TO ANOTHER WORLD MAYBE YOU GUYS COULD INVESTIGATE IT AND LET ME KNOW BEFORE I HAVE TO GO BACK IN THERE FOURTH PERIOD?
JERRY, THOSE AREN'T ARCANE SYMBOLS, LIKE FROM A GRIMOIRE OR SOMETHING. THOSE ARE COACH STROHM'S DEFENSIVE SIGNALS, FOR THE SIDELINES. THEY WERE DRYING BECAUSE HE JUST PAINTED THEM, I'M SURE.
NEXT.
YOU SMELL SOMETHING, JOE?
JOEY, HAVE YOU GIVEN ANY ADDITIONAL THOUGHT TO THE MATTER WE DISCUSSED LAST WEEK? THE CASE I BROUGHT YOU?

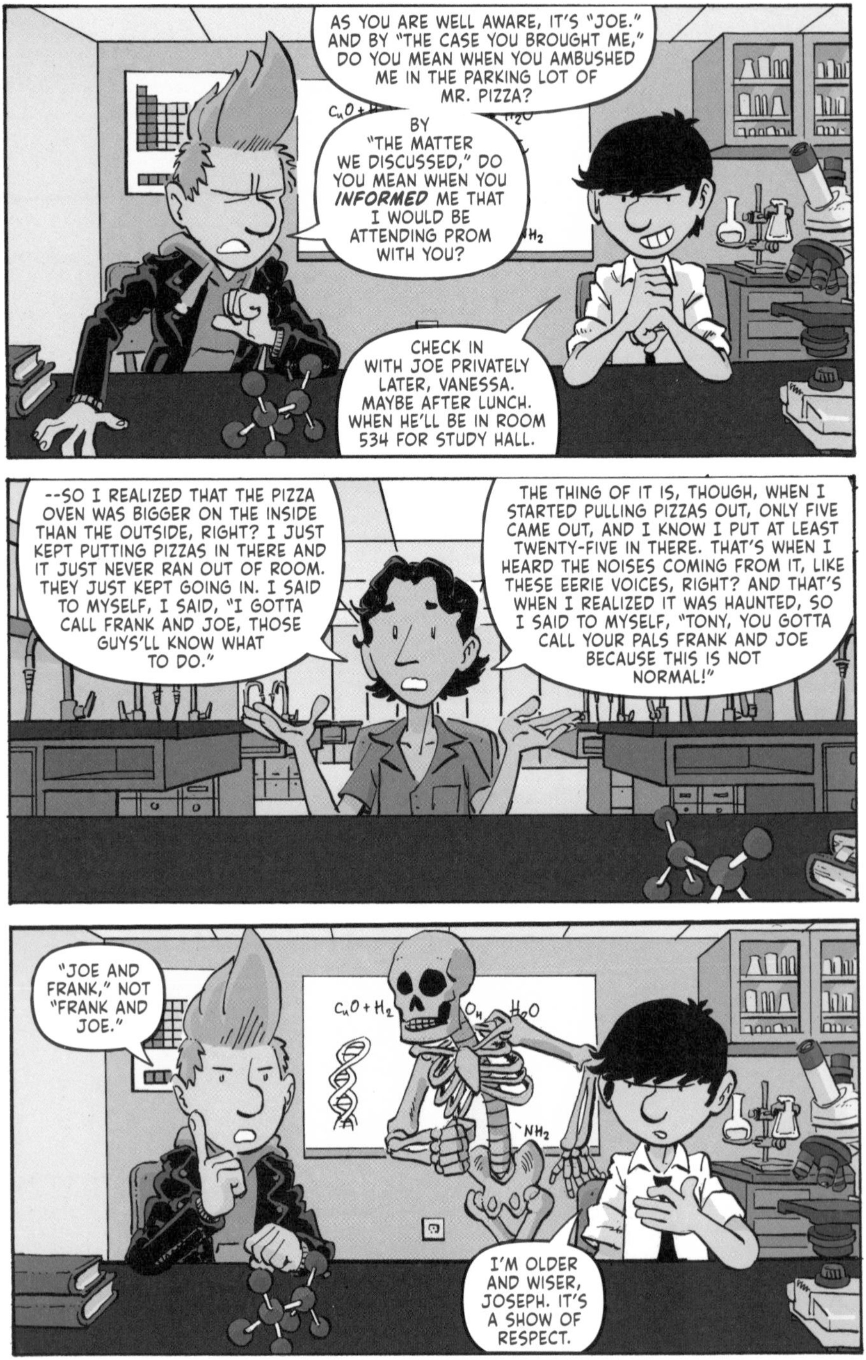
AS YOU ARE WELL AWARE, IT'S "JOE." AND BY "THE CASE YOU BROUGHT ME," DO YOU MEAN WHEN YOU AMBUSHED ME IN THE PARKING LOT OF MR. PIZZA?
BY "THE MATTER WE DISCUSSED," DO YOU MEAN WHEN YOU *INFORMED* ME THAT I WOULD BE ATTENDING PROM WITH YOU?
CHECK IN WITH JOE PRIVATELY LATER, VANESSA. MAYBE AFTER LUNCH. WHEN HE'LL BE IN ROOM 534 FOR STUDY HALL.
--SO I REALIZED THAT THE PIZZA OVEN WAS BIGGER ON THE INSIDE THAN THE OUTSIDE, RIGHT? I JUST KEPT PUTTING PIZZAS IN THERE AND IT JUST NEVER RAN OUT OF ROOM. THEY JUST KEPT GOING IN. I SAID TO MYSELF, I SAID, "I GOTTA CALL FRANK AND JOE, THOSE GUYS'LL KNOW WHAT TO DO."
THE THING OF IT IS, THOUGH, WHEN I STARTED PULLING PIZZAS OUT, ONLY FIVE CAME OUT, AND I KNOW I PUT AT LEAST TWENTY-FIVE IN THERE. THAT'S WHEN I HEARD THE NOISES COMING FROM IT, LIKE THESE EERIE VOICES, RIGHT? AND THAT'S WHEN I REALIZED IT WAS HAUNTED, SO I SAID TO MYSELF, "TONY, YOU GOTTA CALL YOUR PALS FRANK AND JOE BECAUSE THIS IS NOT NORMAL!"
"JOE AND FRANK," NOT "FRANK AND JOE."
I'M OLDER AND WISER, JOSEPH. IT'S A SHOW OF RESPECT.

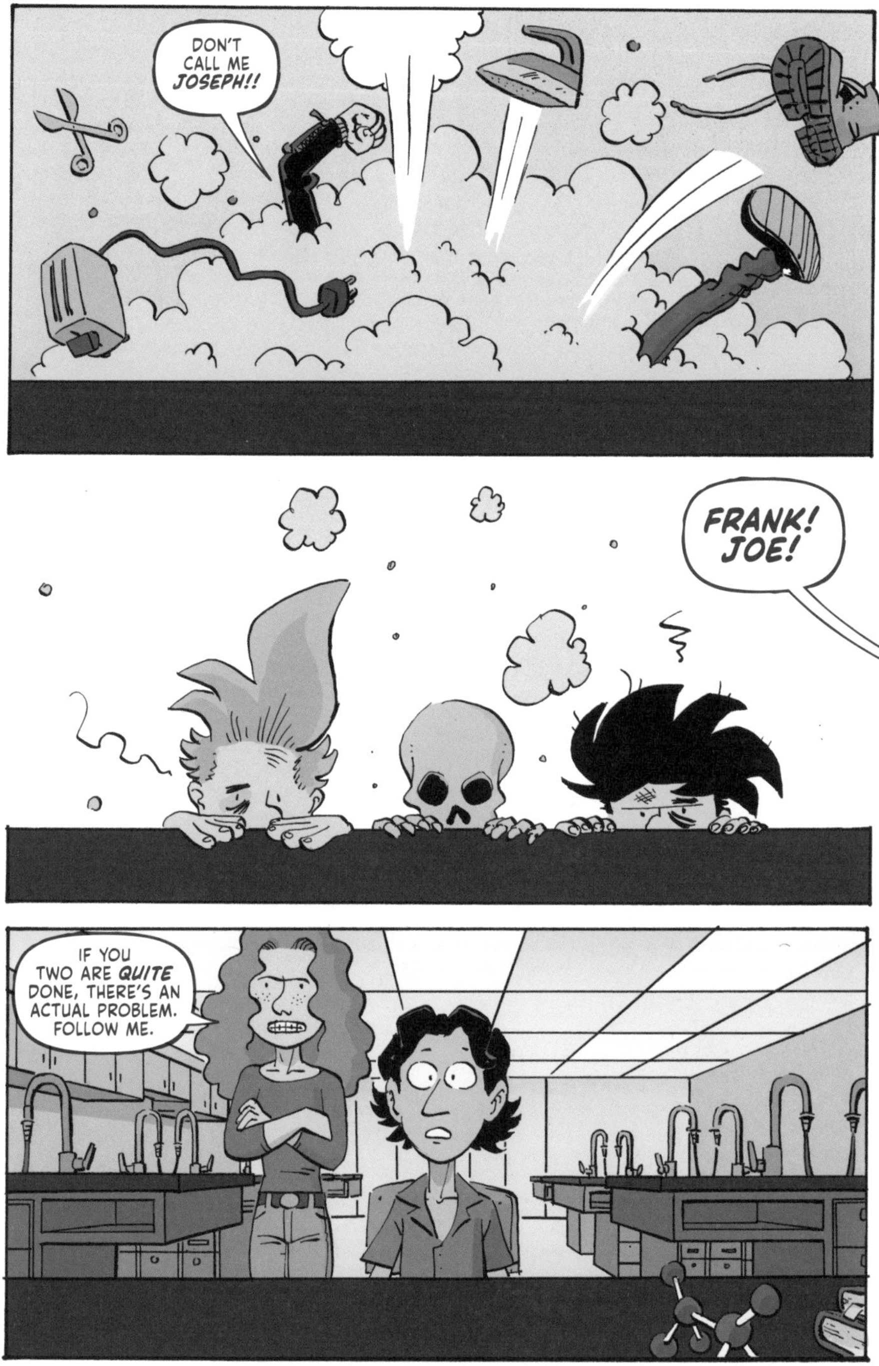
DON'T CALL ME *JOSEPH!!*
FRANK! JOE!
IF YOU TWO ARE *QUITE* DONE, THERE'S AN ACTUAL PROBLEM. FOLLOW ME.

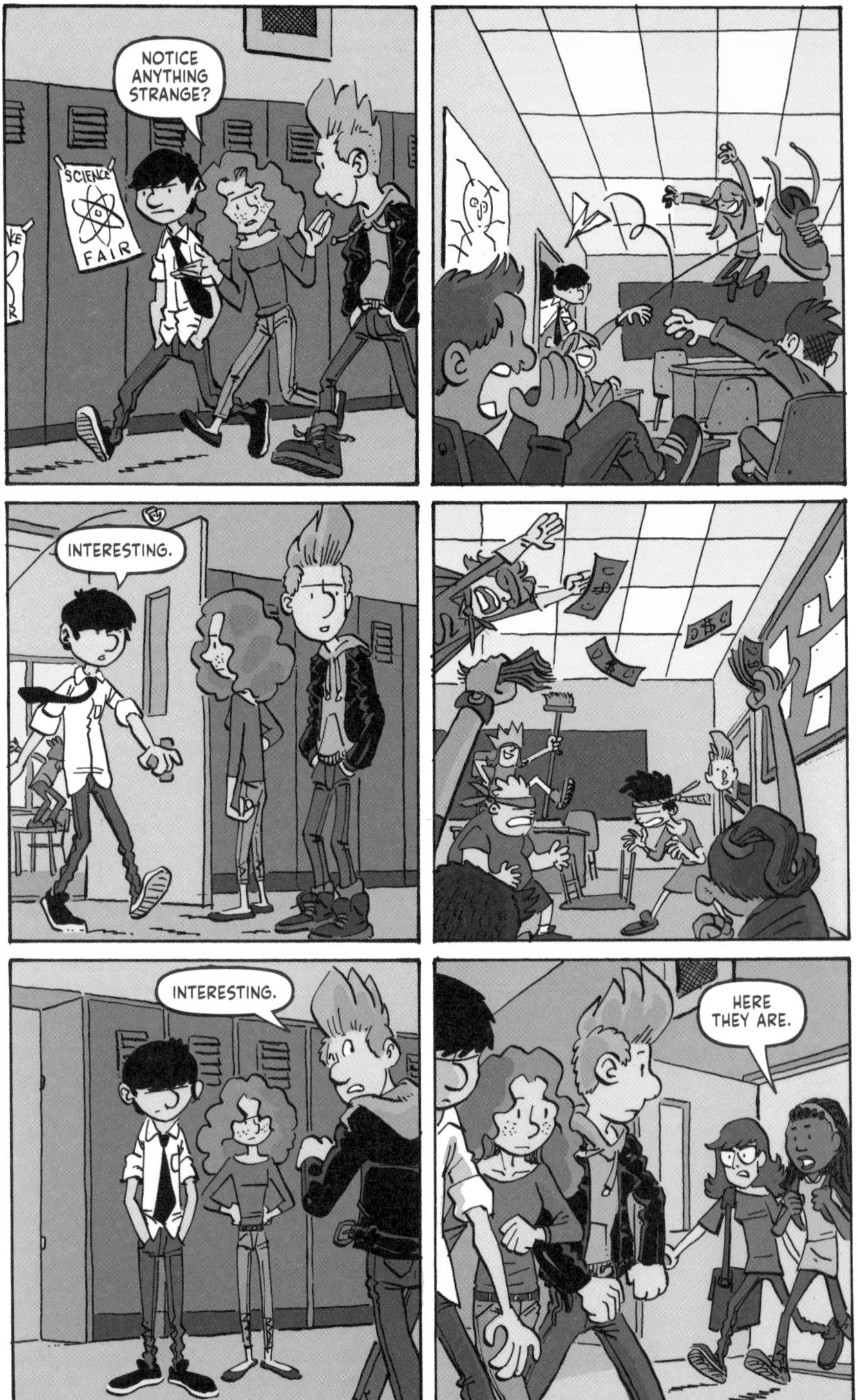
NOTICE ANYTHING STRANGE?
SCIENCE FAIR
INTERESTING.
INTERESTING.
HERE THEY ARE.

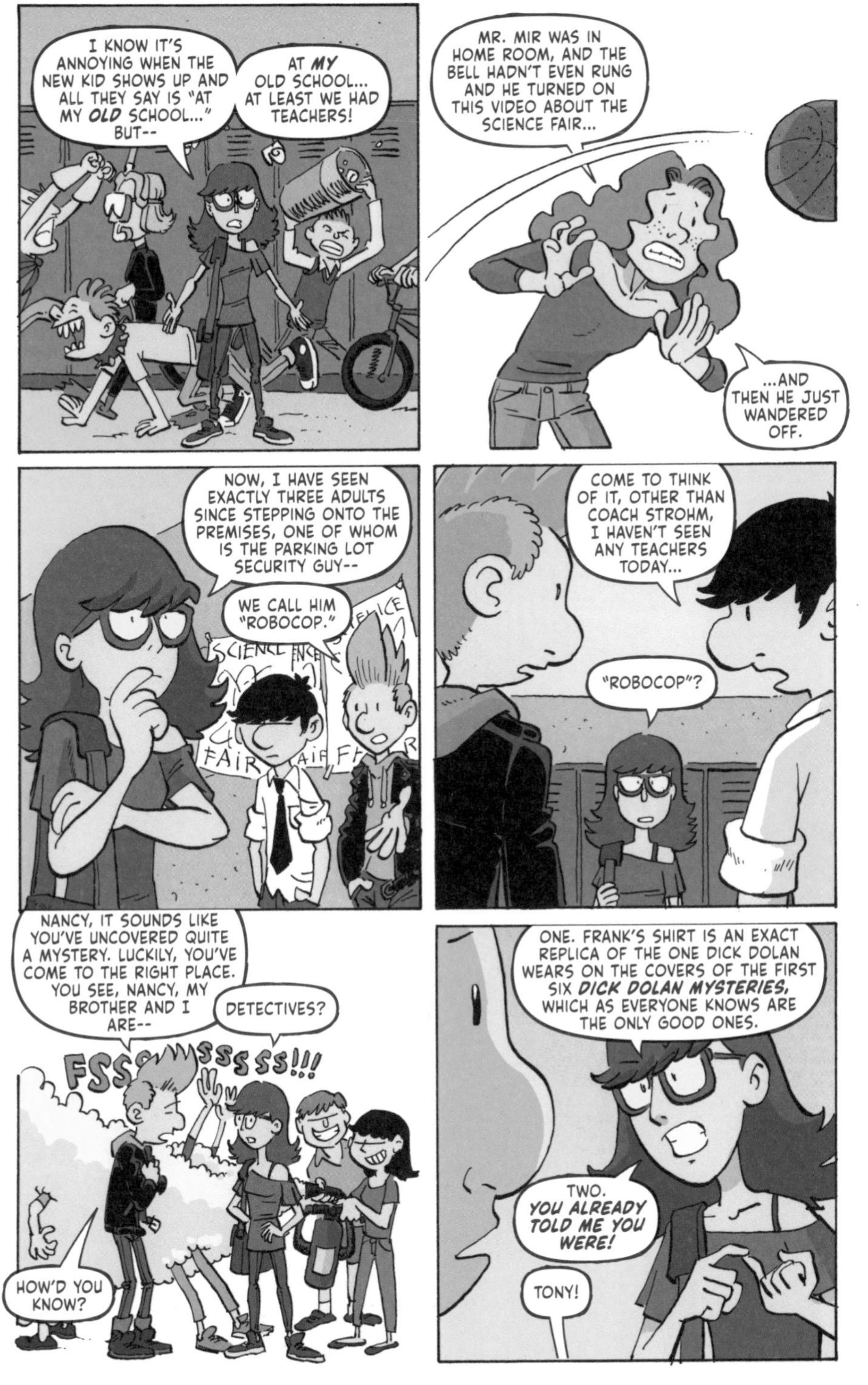
I KNOW IT'S ANNOYING WHEN THE NEW KID SHOWS UP AND ALL THEY SAY IS "AT MY OLD SCHOOL..." BUT--
AT MY OLD SCHOOL... AT LEAST WE HAD TEACHERS!
MR. MIR WAS IN HOME ROOM, AND THE BELL HADN'T EVEN RUNG AND HE TURNED ON THIS VIDEO ABOUT THE SCIENCE FAIR...
...AND THEN HE JUST WANDERED OFF.
NOW, I HAVE SEEN EXACTLY THREE ADULTS SINCE STEPPING ONTO THE PREMISES, ONE OF WHOM IS THE PARKING LOT SECURITY GUY--
WE CALL HIM "ROBOCOP."
COME TO THINK OF IT, OTHER THAN COACH STROHM, I HAVEN'T SEEN ANY TEACHERS TODAY...
"ROBOCOP"?
NANCY, IT SOUNDS LIKE YOU'VE UNCOVERED QUITE A MYSTERY. LUCKILY, YOU'VE COME TO THE RIGHT PLACE. YOU SEE, NANCY, MY BROTHER AND I ARE--
DETECTIVES?
FSSSSSSSSS!!!
HOW'D YOU KNOW?
ONE. FRANK'S SHIRT IS AN EXACT REPLICA OF THE ONE DICK DOLAN WEARS ON THE COVERS OF THE FIRST SIX DICK DOLAN MYSTERIES, WHICH AS EVERYONE KNOWS ARE THE ONLY GOOD ONES.
TWO. YOU ALREADY TOLD ME YOU WERE!
TONY!

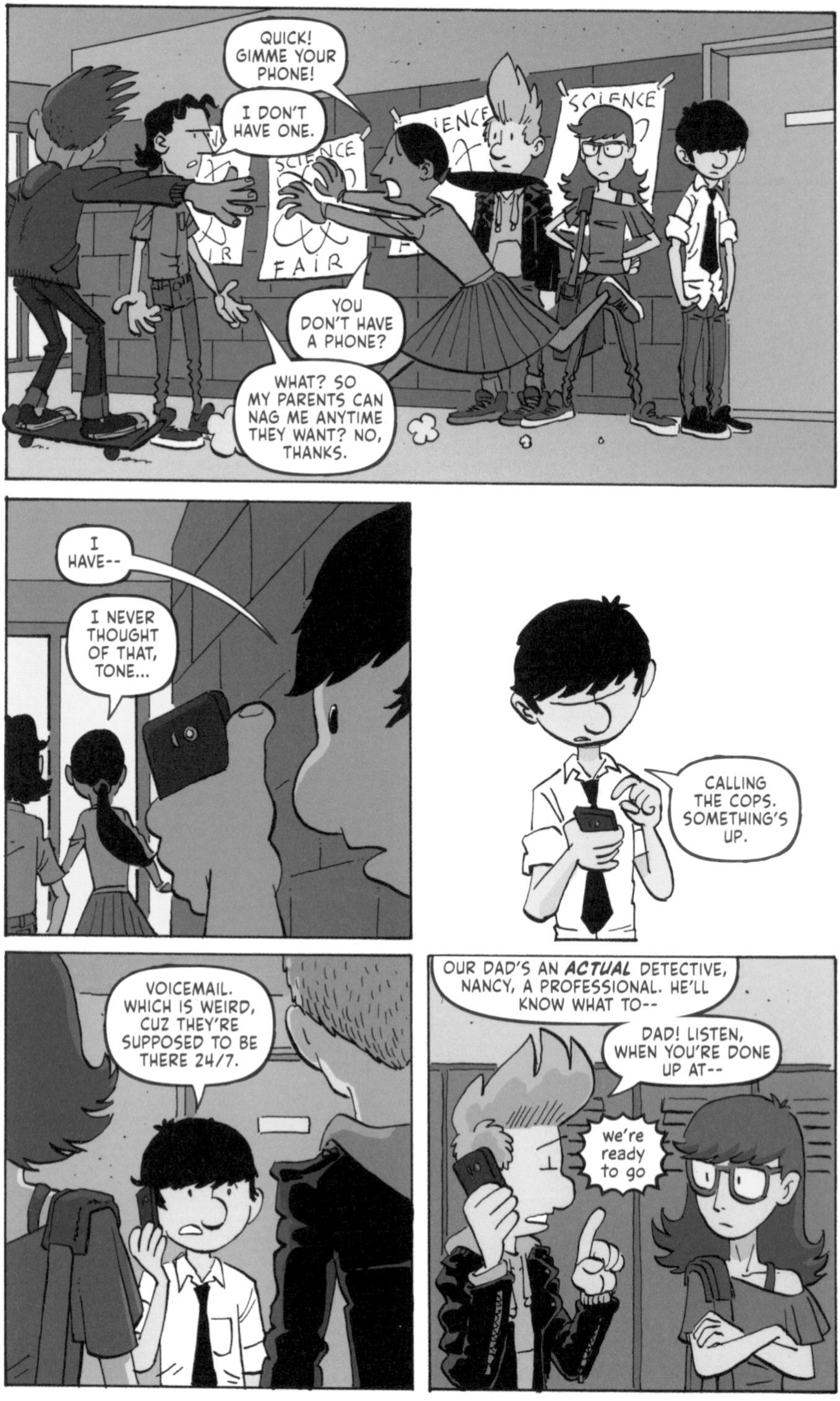

QUICK! GIMME YOUR PHONE!
I DON'T HAVE ONE.
SCIENCE FAIR
YOU DON'T HAVE A PHONE?
WHAT? SO MY PARENTS CAN NAG ME ANYTIME THEY WANT? NO, THANKS.
I HAVE--
I NEVER THOUGHT OF THAT, TONE...
CALLING THE COPS. SOMETHING'S UP.
VOICEMAIL. WHICH IS WEIRD, CUZ THEY'RE SUPPOSED TO BE THERE 24/7.
OUR DAD'S AN *ACTUAL* DETECTIVE, NANCY, A PROFESSIONAL. HE'LL KNOW WHAT TO--
DAD! LISTEN, WHEN YOU'RE DONE UP AT--
we're ready to go

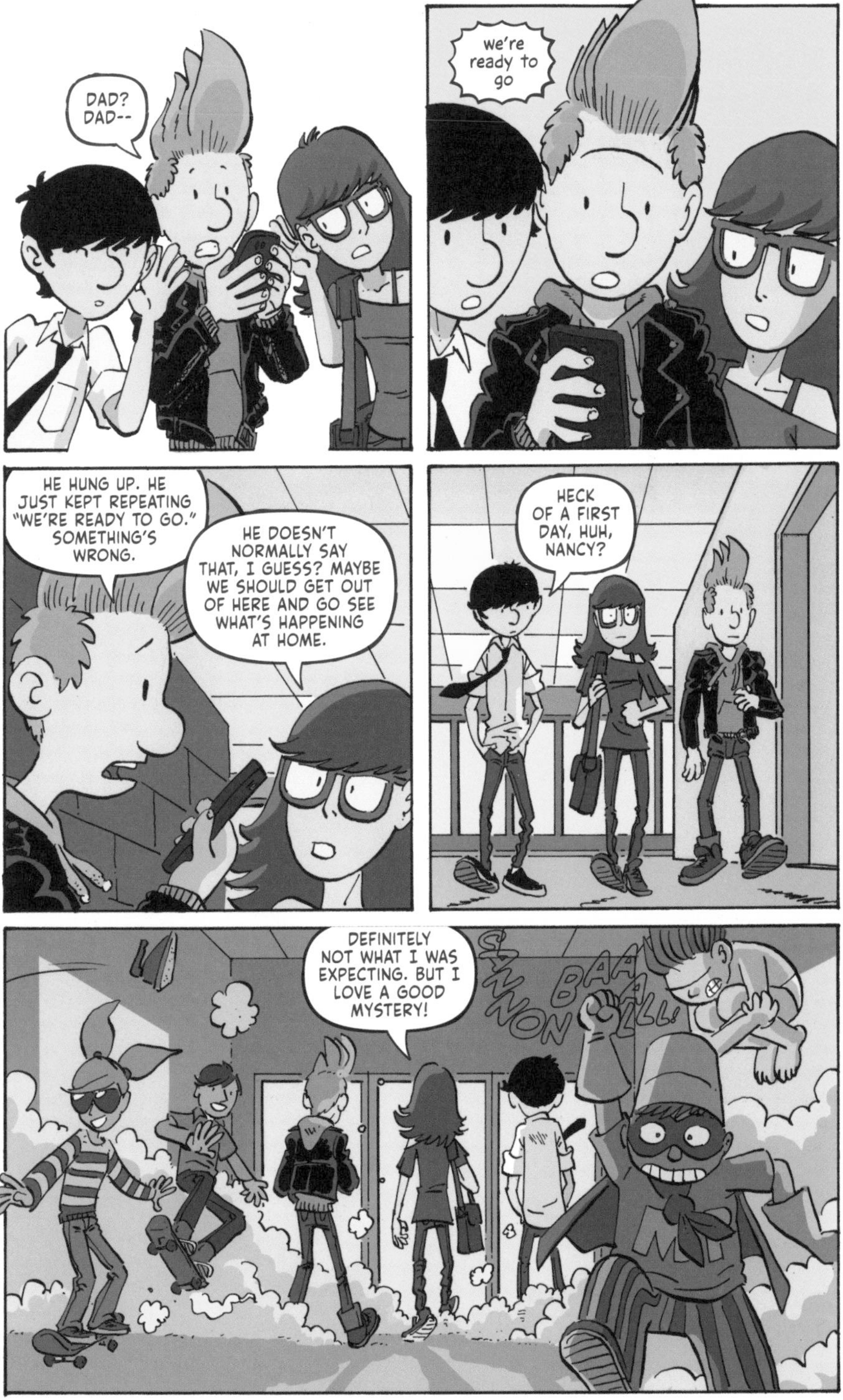
DAD?
DAD--
we're ready to go
HE HUNG UP. HE JUST KEPT REPEATING "WE'RE READY TO GO." SOMETHING'S WRONG.
HE DOESN'T NORMALLY SAY THAT, I GUESS? MAYBE WE SHOULD GET OUT OF HERE AND GO SEE WHAT'S HAPPENING AT HOME.
HECK OF A FIRST DAY, HUH, NANCY?
DEFINITELY NOT WHAT I WAS EXPECTING. BUT I LOVE A GOOD MYSTERY!
CANNONBAAAALLL!

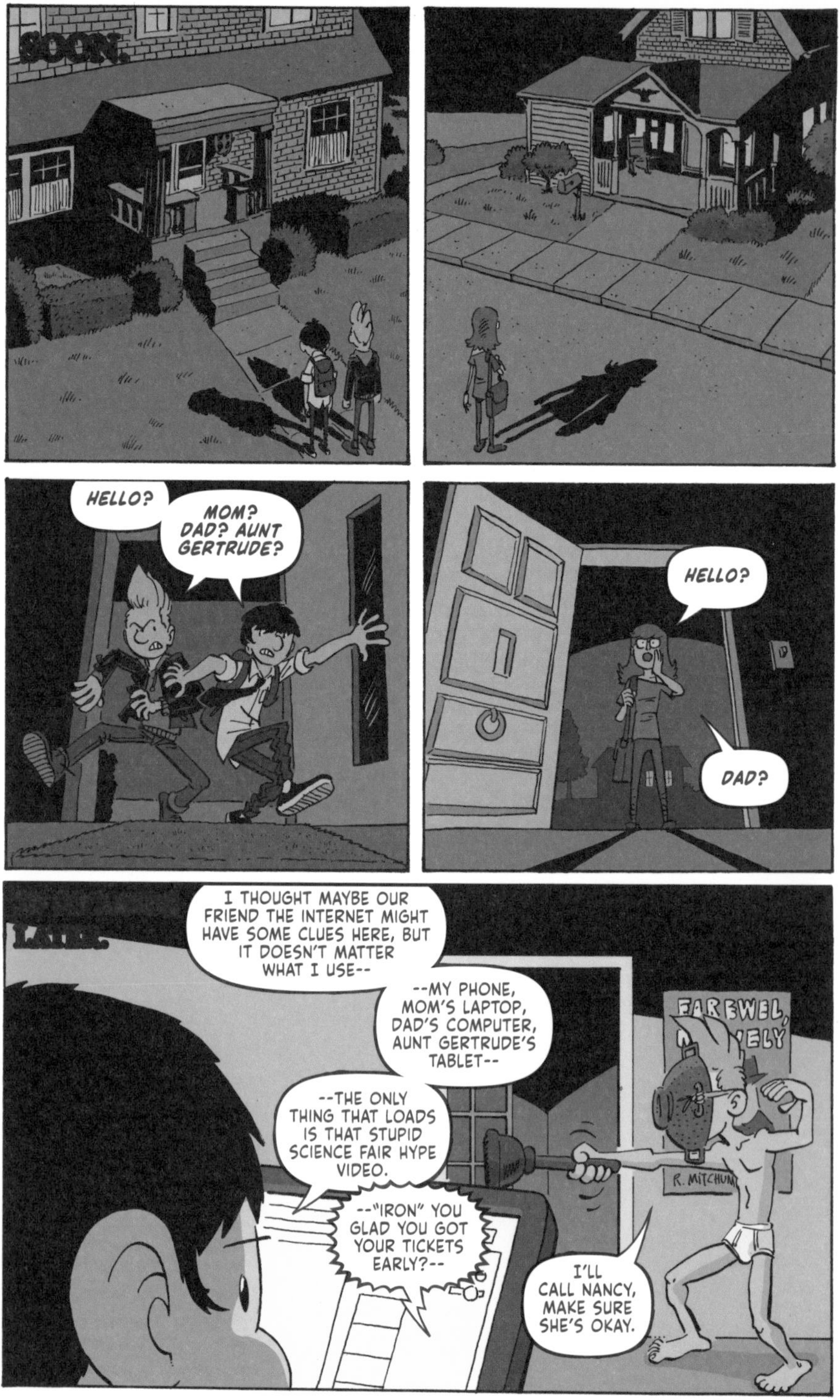
SOON.
HELLO?
MOM? DAD? AUNT GERTRUDE?
HELLO?
DAD?
I THOUGHT MAYBE OUR FRIEND THE INTERNET MIGHT HAVE SOME CLUES HERE, BUT IT DOESN'T MATTER WHAT I USE--
--MY PHONE, MOM'S LAPTOP, DAD'S COMPUTER, AUNT GERTRUDE'S TABLET--
--THE ONLY THING THAT LOADS IS THAT STUPID SCIENCE FAIR HYPE VIDEO.
--"IRON" YOU GLAD YOU GOT YOUR TICKETS EARLY?--
R. MITCHUM
I'LL CALL NANCY, MAKE SURE SHE'S OKAY.

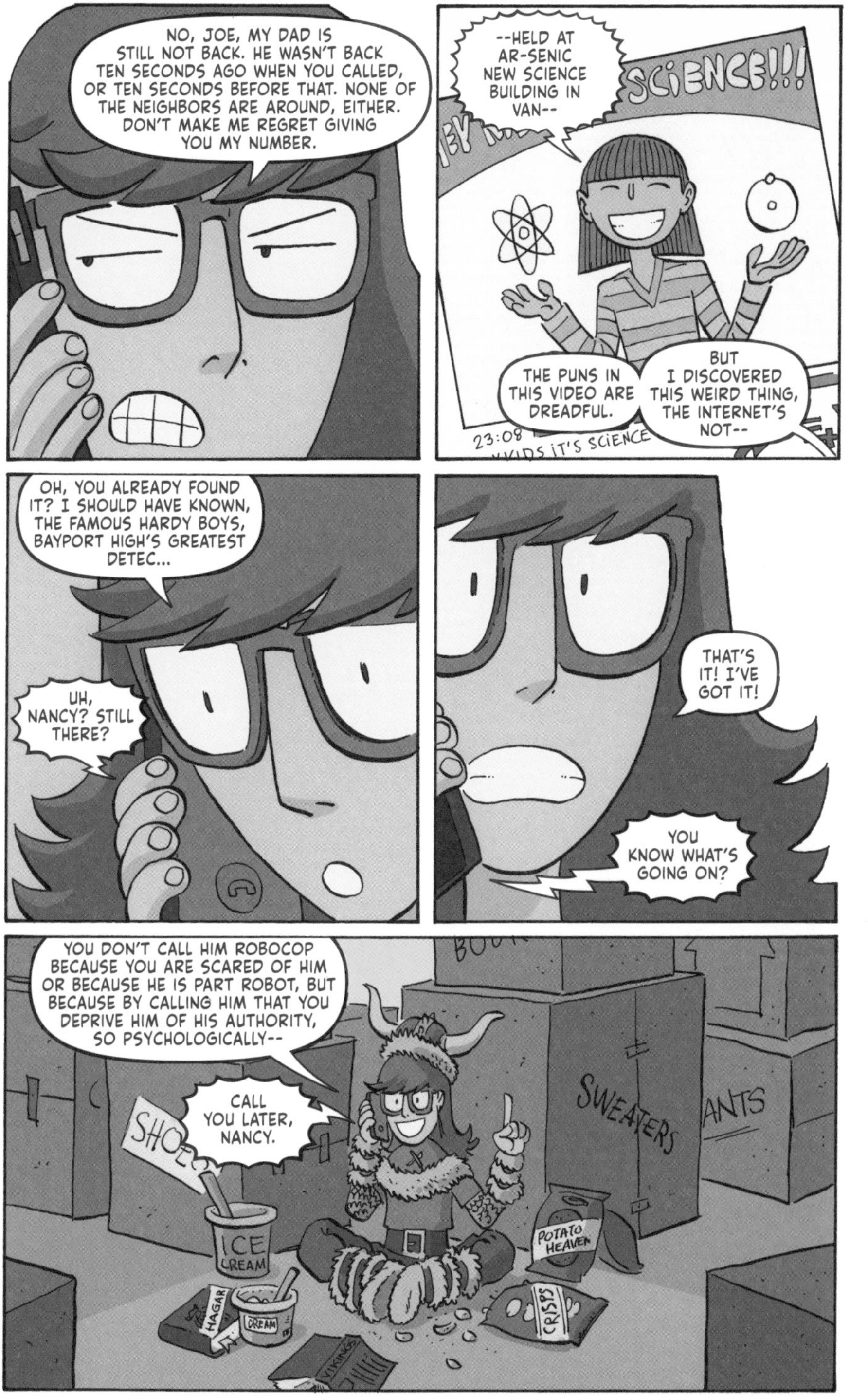
NO, JOE, MY DAD IS STILL NOT BACK. HE WASN'T BACK TEN SECONDS AGO WHEN YOU CALLED, OR TEN SECONDS BEFORE THAT. NONE OF THE NEIGHBORS ARE AROUND, EITHER. DON'T MAKE ME REGRET GIVING YOU MY NUMBER.
--HELD AT AR-SENIC NEW SCIENCE BUILDING IN VAN--
SCIENCE!!!
THE PUNS IN THIS VIDEO ARE DREADFUL.
BUT I DISCOVERED THIS WEIRD THING, THE INTERNET'S NOT--
23:08
KIDS IT'S SCIENCE
OH, YOU ALREADY FOUND IT? I SHOULD HAVE KNOWN, THE FAMOUS HARDY BOYS, BAYPORT HIGH'S GREATEST DETEC...
UH, NANCY? STILL THERE?
THAT'S IT! I'VE GOT IT!
YOU KNOW WHAT'S GOING ON?
YOU DON'T CALL HIM ROBOCOP BECAUSE YOU ARE SCARED OF HIM OR BECAUSE HE IS PART ROBOT, BUT BECAUSE BY CALLING HIM THAT YOU DEPRIVE HIM OF HIS AUTHORITY, SO PSYCHOLOGICALLY--
CALL YOU LATER, NANCY.
SWEATERS
ICE CREAM
POTATO HEAVEN
CRISPS
HAGAR
CREAM
VIKINGS

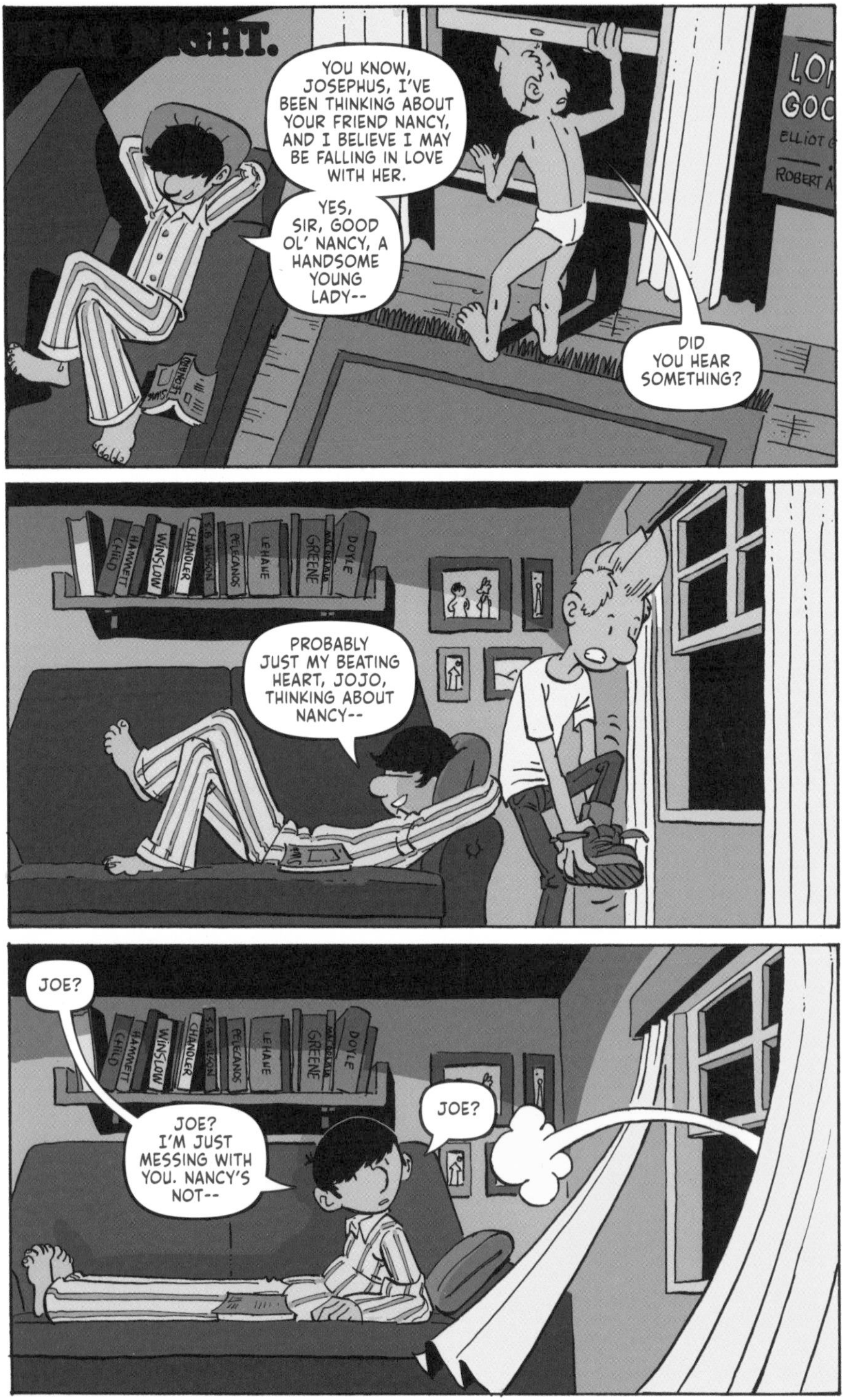

YOU KNOW, JOSEPHUS, I'VE BEEN THINKING ABOUT YOUR FRIEND NANCY, AND I BELIEVE I MAY BE FALLING IN LOVE WITH HER.
YES, SIR, GOOD OL' NANCY, A HANDSOME YOUNG LADY--
DID YOU HEAR SOMETHING?
CHILD
HAMMETT
WINSLOW
CHANDLER
S.A. WILSON
PELECANOS
LEHANE
GREENE
DOYLE
PROBABLY JUST MY BEATING HEART, JOJO, THINKING ABOUT NANCY--
JOE?
JOE? I'M JUST MESSING WITH YOU. NANCY'S NOT--
JOE?

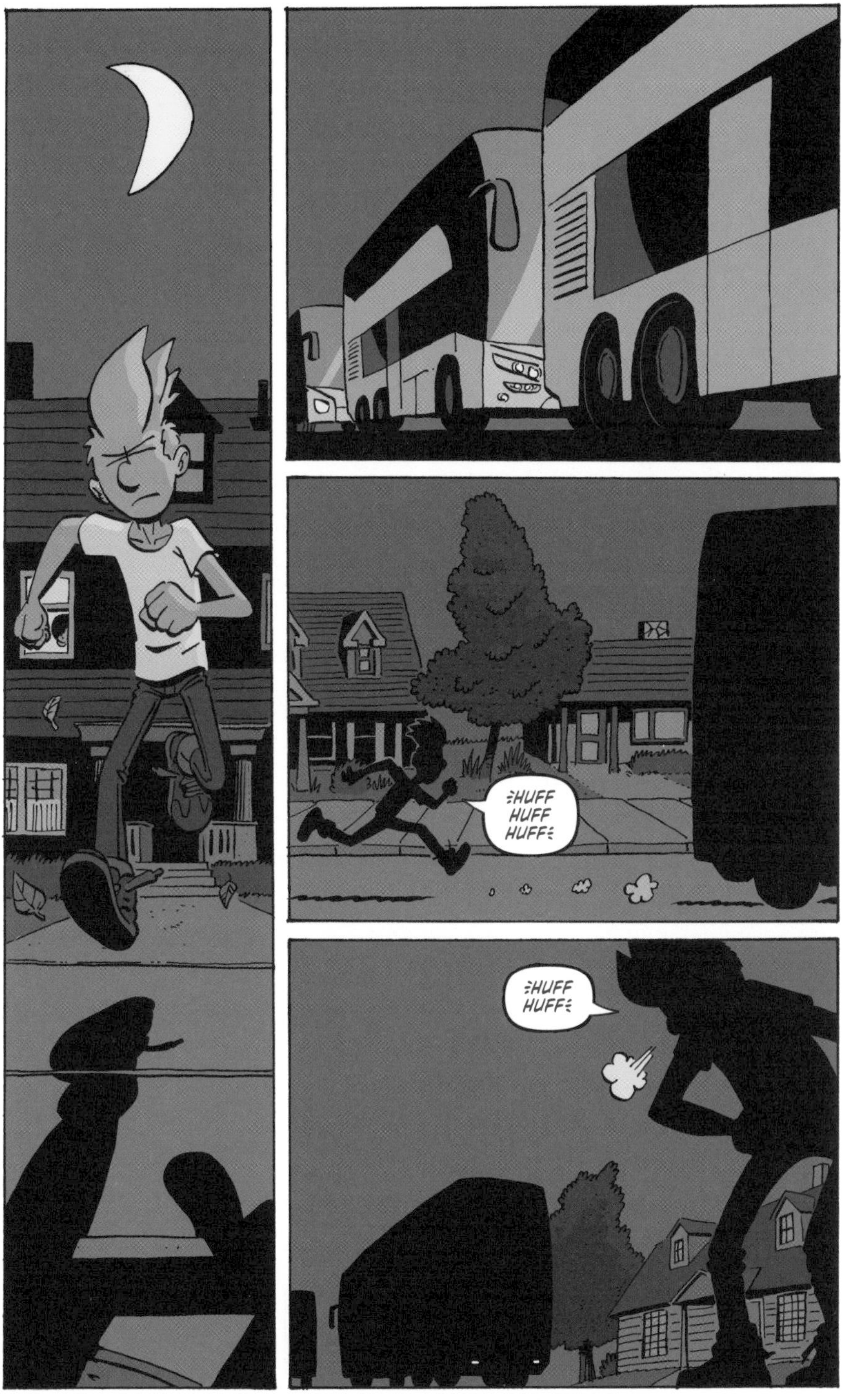
HUFF HUFF HUFF
HUFF HUFF

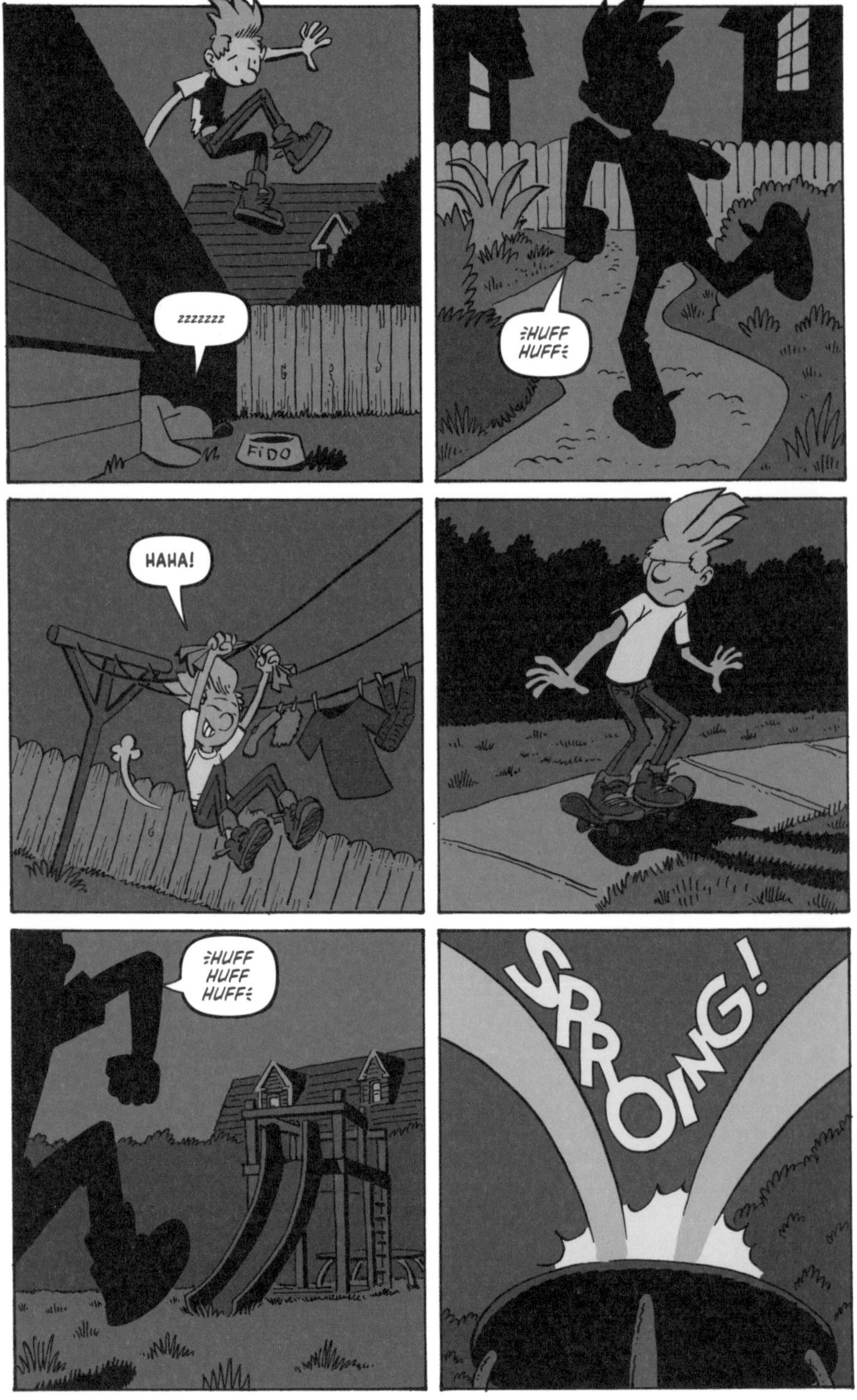
zzzzzzz
FIDO
HUFF HUFF
HAHA!
HUFF HUFF HUFF
SRRONG!

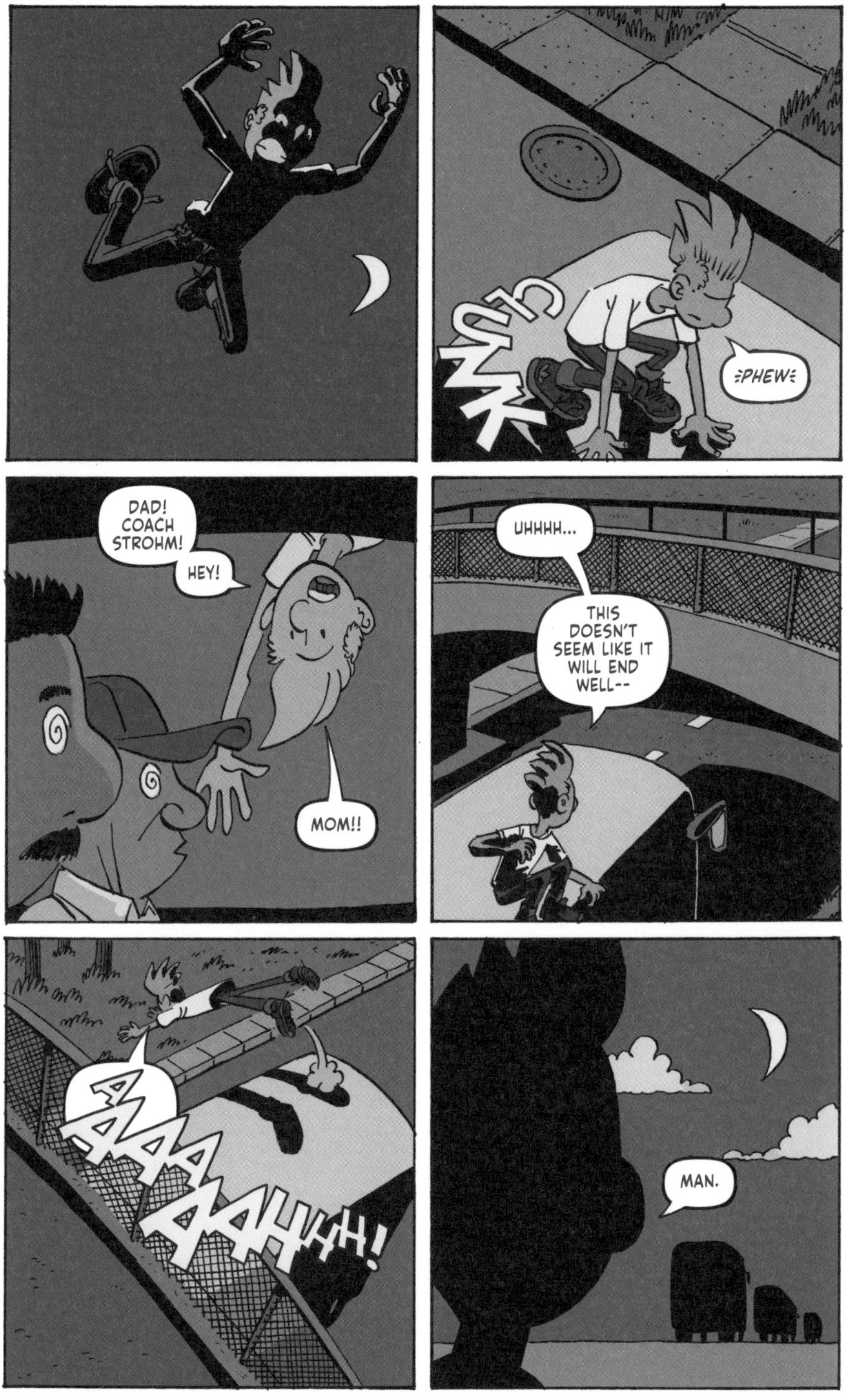

CLUNK
PHEW
DAD! COACH STROHM!
HEY!
MOM!!
UHHHH...
THIS DOESN'T SEEM LIKE IT WILL END WELL--
AAAAAAHHH!
MAN.

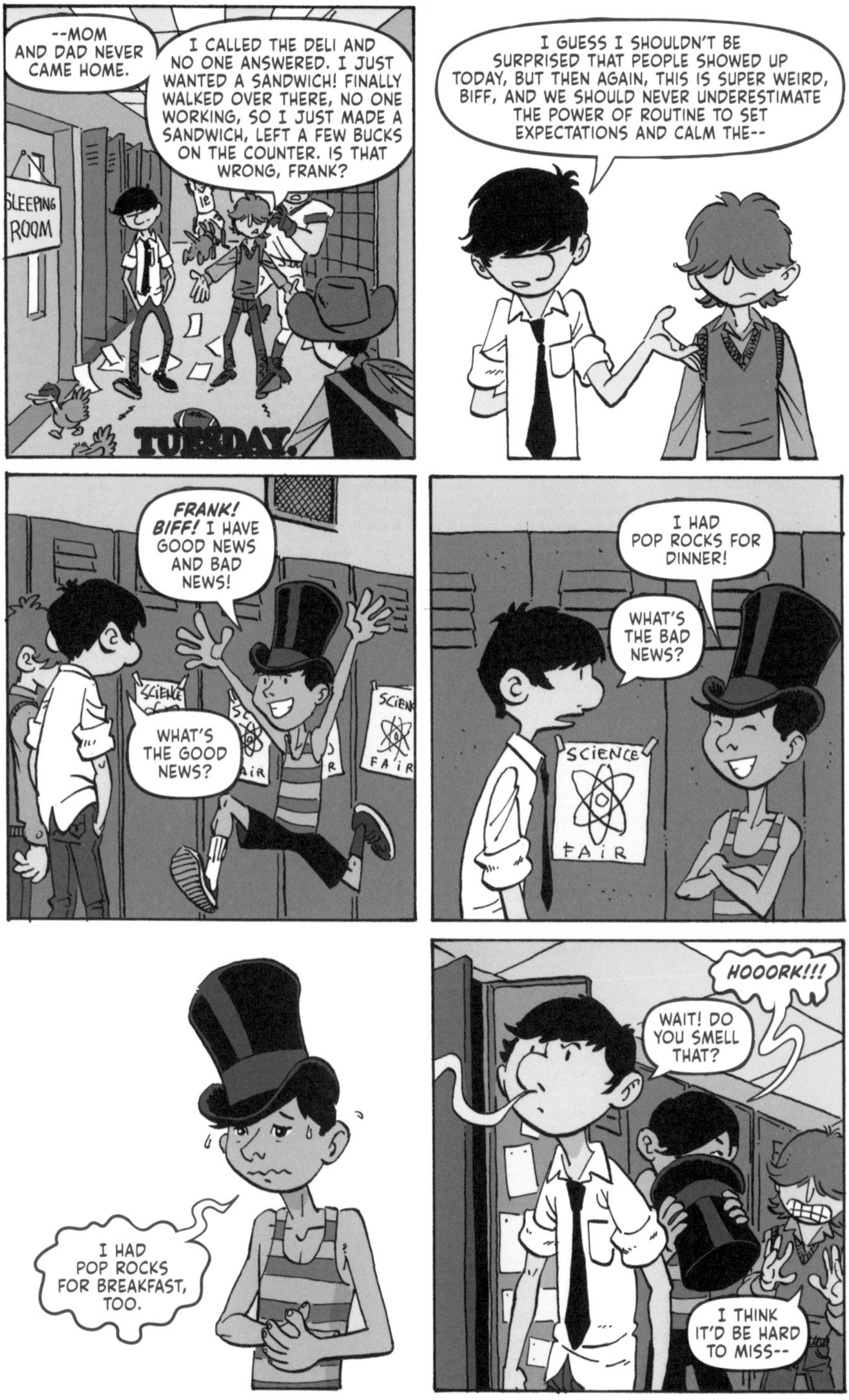
--MOM AND DAD NEVER CAME HOME.
I CALLED THE DELI AND NO ONE ANSWERED. I JUST WANTED A SANDWICH! FINALLY WALKED OVER THERE, NO ONE WORKING, SO I JUST MADE A SANDWICH, LEFT A FEW BUCKS ON THE COUNTER. IS THAT WRONG, FRANK?
SLEEPING ROOM
TUESDAY.
I GUESS I SHOULDN'T BE SURPRISED THAT PEOPLE SHOWED UP TODAY, BUT THEN AGAIN, THIS IS SUPER WEIRD, BIFF, AND WE SHOULD NEVER UNDERESTIMATE THE POWER OF ROUTINE TO SET EXPECTATIONS AND CALM THE--
FRANK! BIFF! I HAVE GOOD NEWS AND BAD NEWS!
WHAT'S THE GOOD NEWS?
I HAD POP ROCKS FOR DINNER!
WHAT'S THE BAD NEWS?
SCIENCE FAIR
I HAD POP ROCKS FOR BREAKFAST, TOO.
HOOORK!!!
WAIT! DO YOU SMELL THAT?
I THINK IT'D BE HARD TO MISS--

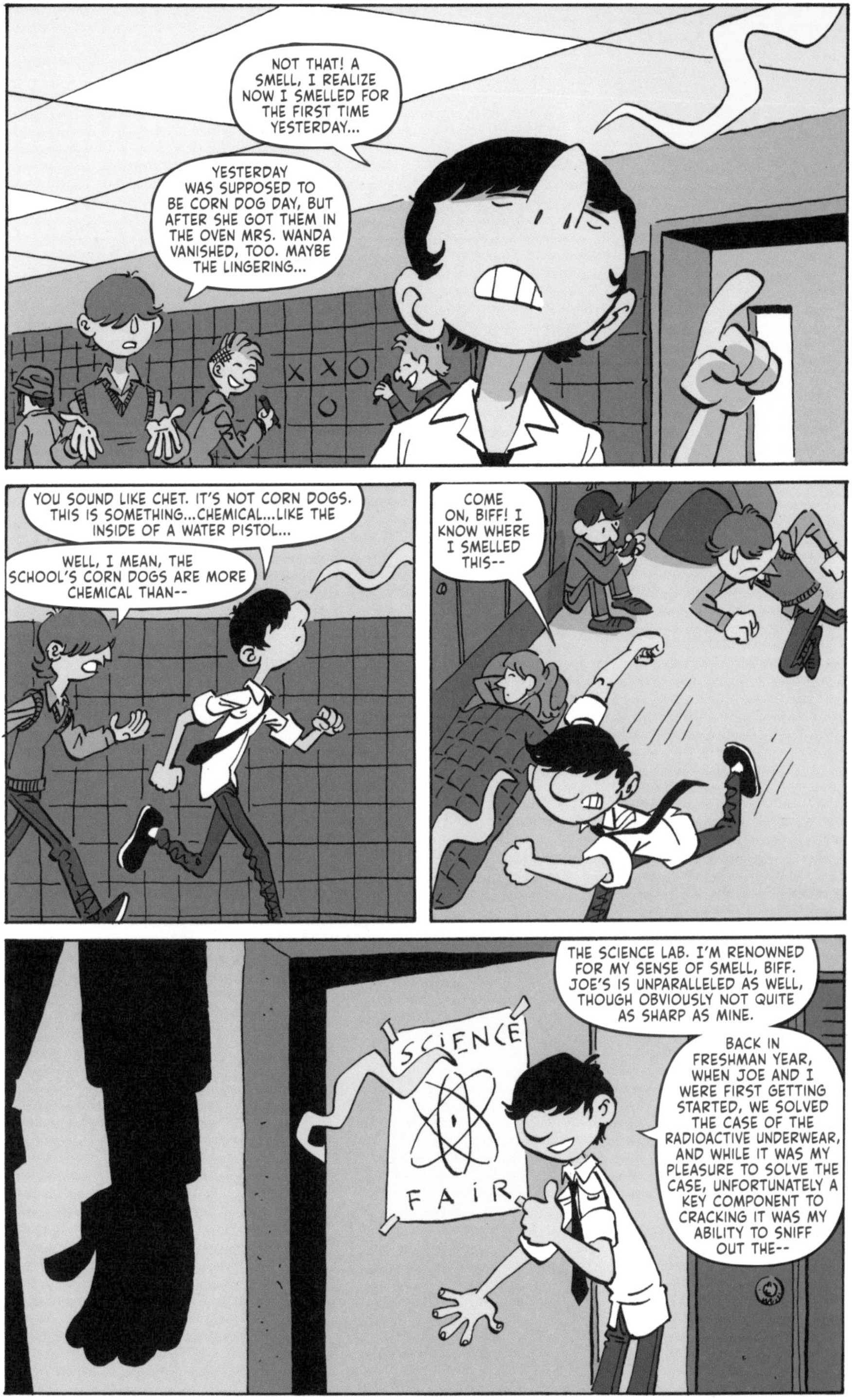
NOT THAT! A SMELL, I REALIZE NOW I SMELLED FOR THE FIRST TIME YESTERDAY...
YESTERDAY WAS SUPPOSED TO BE CORN DOG DAY, BUT AFTER SHE GOT THEM IN THE OVEN MRS. WANDA VANISHED, TOO. MAYBE THE LINGERING...
YOU SOUND LIKE CHET. IT'S NOT CORN DOGS. THIS IS SOMETHING...CHEMICAL...LIKE THE INSIDE OF A WATER PISTOL...
WELL, I MEAN, THE SCHOOL'S CORN DOGS ARE MORE CHEMICAL THAN--
COME ON, BIFF! I KNOW WHERE I SMELLED THIS--
THE SCIENCE LAB. I'M RENOWNED FOR MY SENSE OF SMELL, BIFF. JOE'S IS UNPARALLELED AS WELL, THOUGH OBVIOUSLY NOT QUITE AS SHARP AS MINE.
SCIENCE FAIR
BACK IN FRESHMAN YEAR, WHEN JOE AND I WERE FIRST GETTING STARTED, WE SOLVED THE CASE OF THE RADIOACTIVE UNDERWEAR, AND WHILE IT WAS MY PLEASURE TO SOLVE THE CASE, UNFORTUNATELY A KEY COMPONENT TO CRACKING IT WAS MY ABILITY TO SNIFF OUT THE--

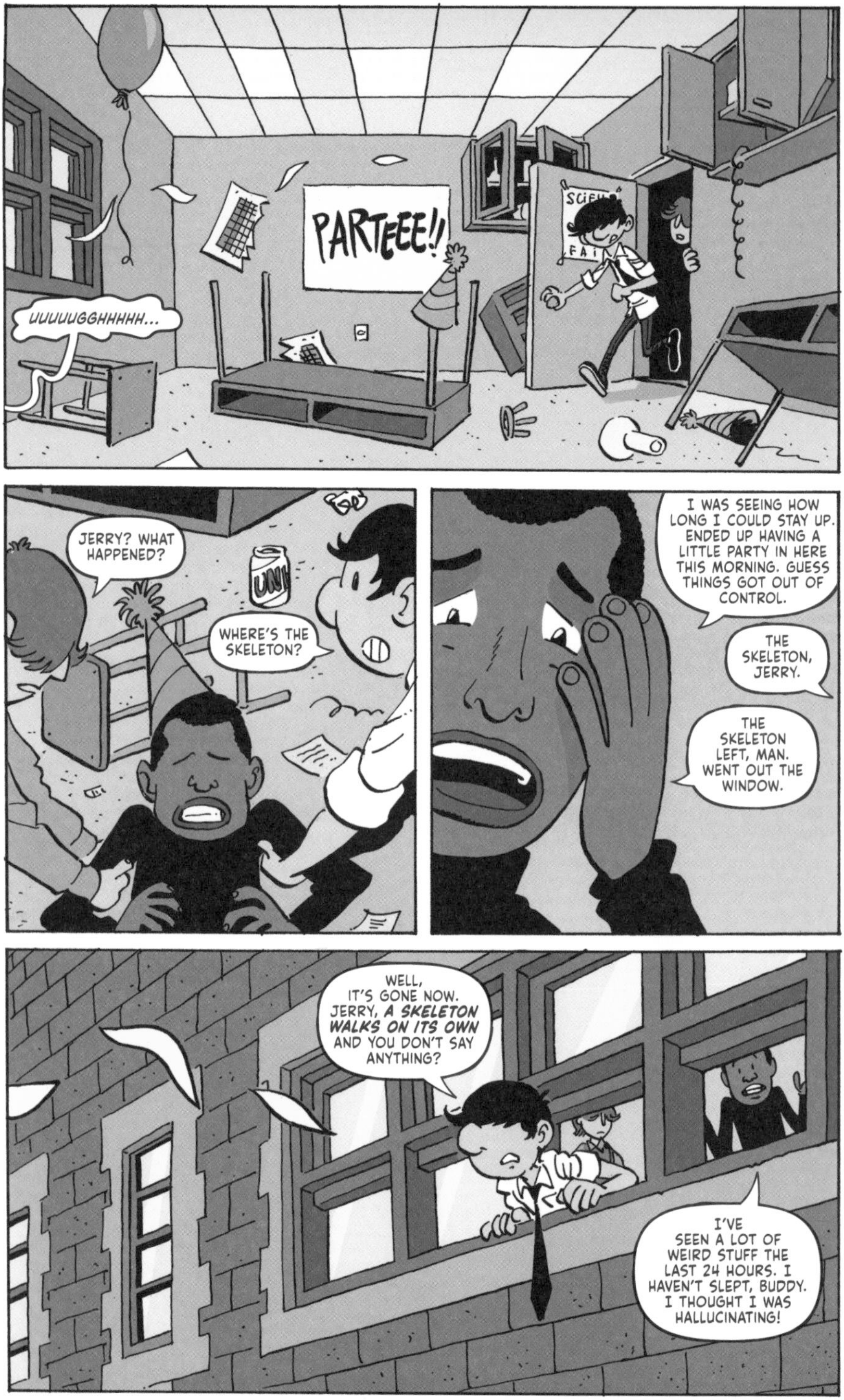
PARTEEE!!
UUUUUGGHHHHH...
JERRY? WHAT HAPPENED?
WHERE'S THE SKELETON?
I WAS SEEING HOW LONG I COULD STAY UP. ENDED UP HAVING A LITTLE PARTY IN HERE THIS MORNING. GUESS THINGS GOT OUT OF CONTROL.
THE SKELETON, JERRY.
THE SKELETON LEFT, MAN. WENT OUT THE WINDOW.
WELL, IT'S GONE NOW. JERRY, A SKELETON WALKS ON ITS OWN AND YOU DON'T SAY ANYTHING?
I'VE SEEN A LOT OF WEIRD STUFF THE LAST 24 HOURS. I HAVEN'T SLEPT, BUDDY. I THOUGHT I WAS HALLUCINATING!

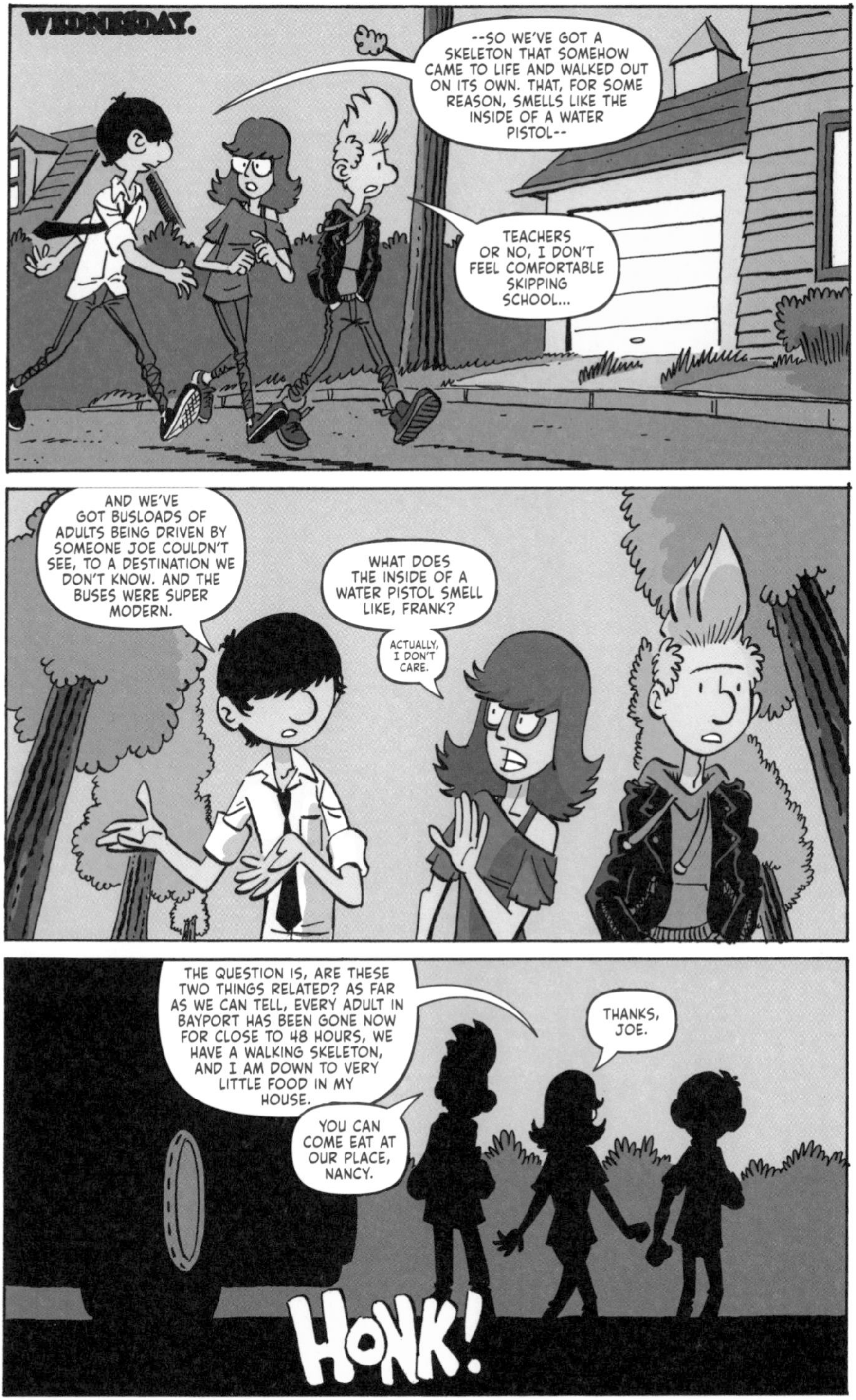
WEDNESDAY.
--SO WE'VE GOT A SKELETON THAT SOMEHOW CAME TO LIFE AND WALKED OUT ON ITS OWN. THAT, FOR SOME REASON, SMELLS LIKE THE INSIDE OF A WATER PISTOL--
TEACHERS OR NO, I DON'T FEEL COMFORTABLE SKIPPING SCHOOL...
AND WE'VE GOT BUSLOADS OF ADULTS BEING DRIVEN BY SOMEONE JOE COULDN'T SEE, TO A DESTINATION WE DON'T KNOW. AND THE BUSES WERE SUPER MODERN.
WHAT DOES THE INSIDE OF A WATER PISTOL SMELL LIKE, FRANK?
ACTUALLY, I DON'T CARE.
THE QUESTION IS, ARE THESE TWO THINGS RELATED? AS FAR AS WE CAN TELL, EVERY ADULT IN BAYPORT HAS BEEN GONE NOW FOR CLOSE TO 48 HOURS, WE HAVE A WALKING SKELETON, AND I AM DOWN TO VERY LITTLE FOOD IN MY HOUSE.
YOU CAN COME EAT AT OUR PLACE, NANCY.
THANKS, JOE.
HONK!

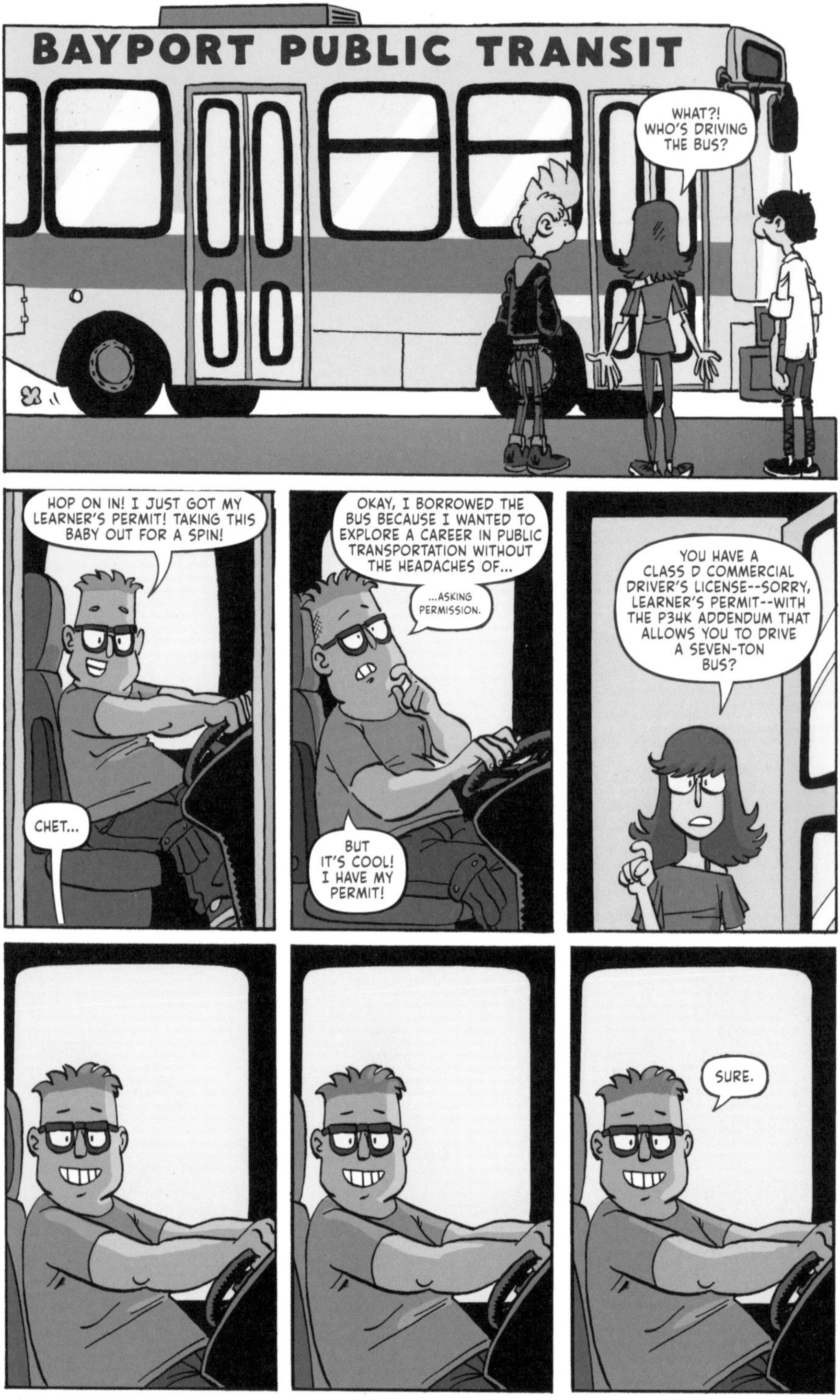
BAYPORT PUBLIC TRANSIT
WHAT?! WHO'S DRIVING THE BUS?
HOP ON IN! I JUST GOT MY LEARNER'S PERMIT! TAKING THIS BABY OUT FOR A SPIN!
CHET...
OKAY, I BORROWED THE BUS BECAUSE I WANTED TO EXPLORE A CAREER IN PUBLIC TRANSPORTATION WITHOUT THE HEADACHES OF...
...ASKING PERMISSION.
BUT IT'S COOL! I HAVE MY PERMIT!
YOU HAVE A CLASS D COMMERCIAL DRIVER'S LICENSE--SORRY, LEARNER'S PERMIT--WITH THE P34K ADDENDUM THAT ALLOWS YOU TO DRIVE A SEVEN-TON BUS?
SURE.

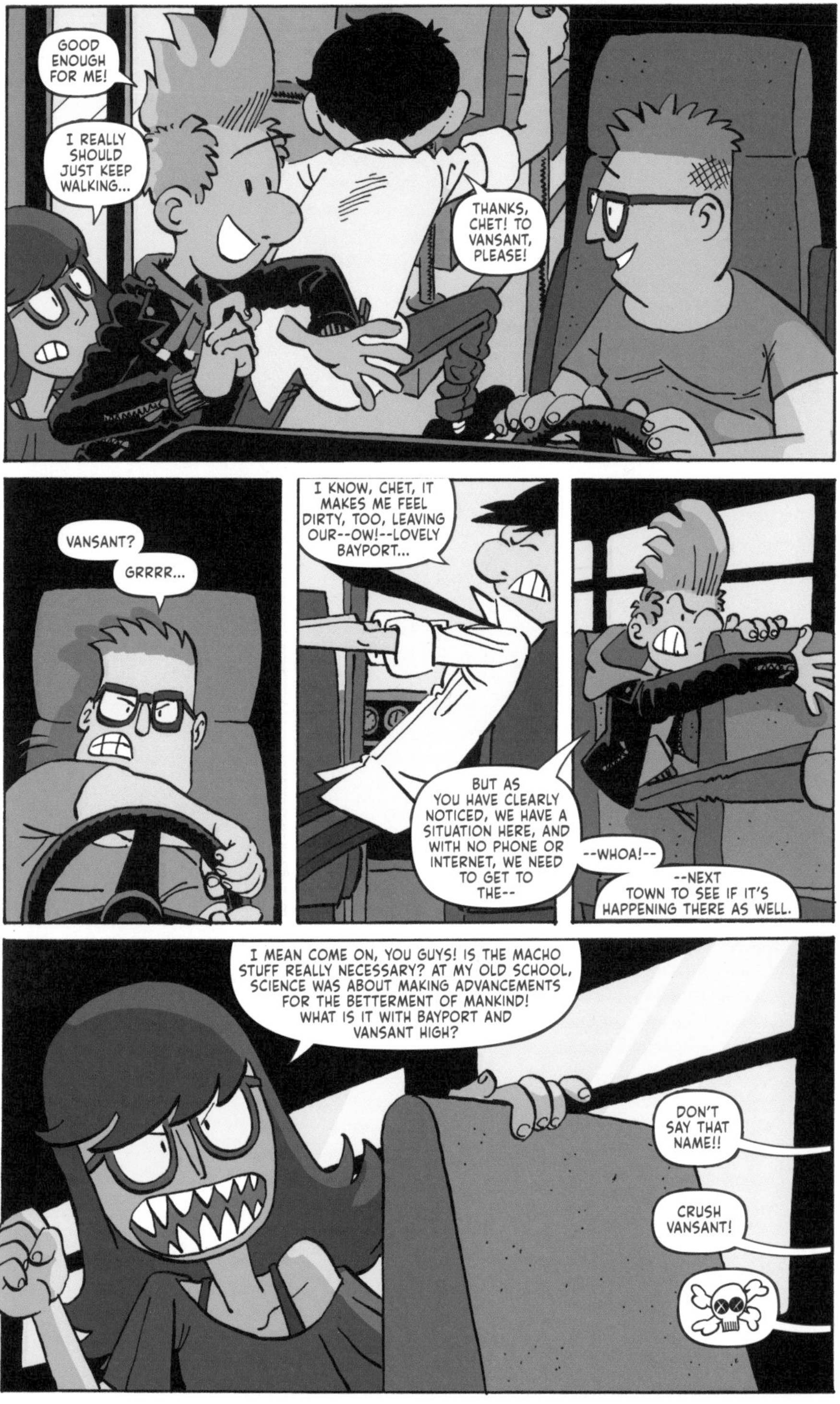
GOOD ENOUGH FOR ME!
I REALLY SHOULD JUST KEEP WALKING...
THANKS, CHET! TO VANSANT, PLEASE!
VANSANT?
GRRRR...
I KNOW, CHET, IT MAKES ME FEEL DIRTY, TOO, LEAVING OUR--OW!--LOVELY BAYPORT...
BUT AS YOU HAVE CLEARLY NOTICED, WE HAVE A SITUATION HERE, AND WITH NO PHONE OR INTERNET, WE NEED TO GET TO THE--
--WHOA!--
--NEXT TOWN TO SEE IF IT'S HAPPENING THERE AS WELL.
I MEAN COME ON, YOU GUYS! IS THE MACHO STUFF REALLY NECESSARY? AT MY OLD SCHOOL, SCIENCE WAS ABOUT MAKING ADVANCEMENTS FOR THE BETTERMENT OF MANKIND! WHAT IS IT WITH BAYPORT AND VANSANT HIGH?
DON'T SAY THAT NAME!!
CRUSH VANSANT!

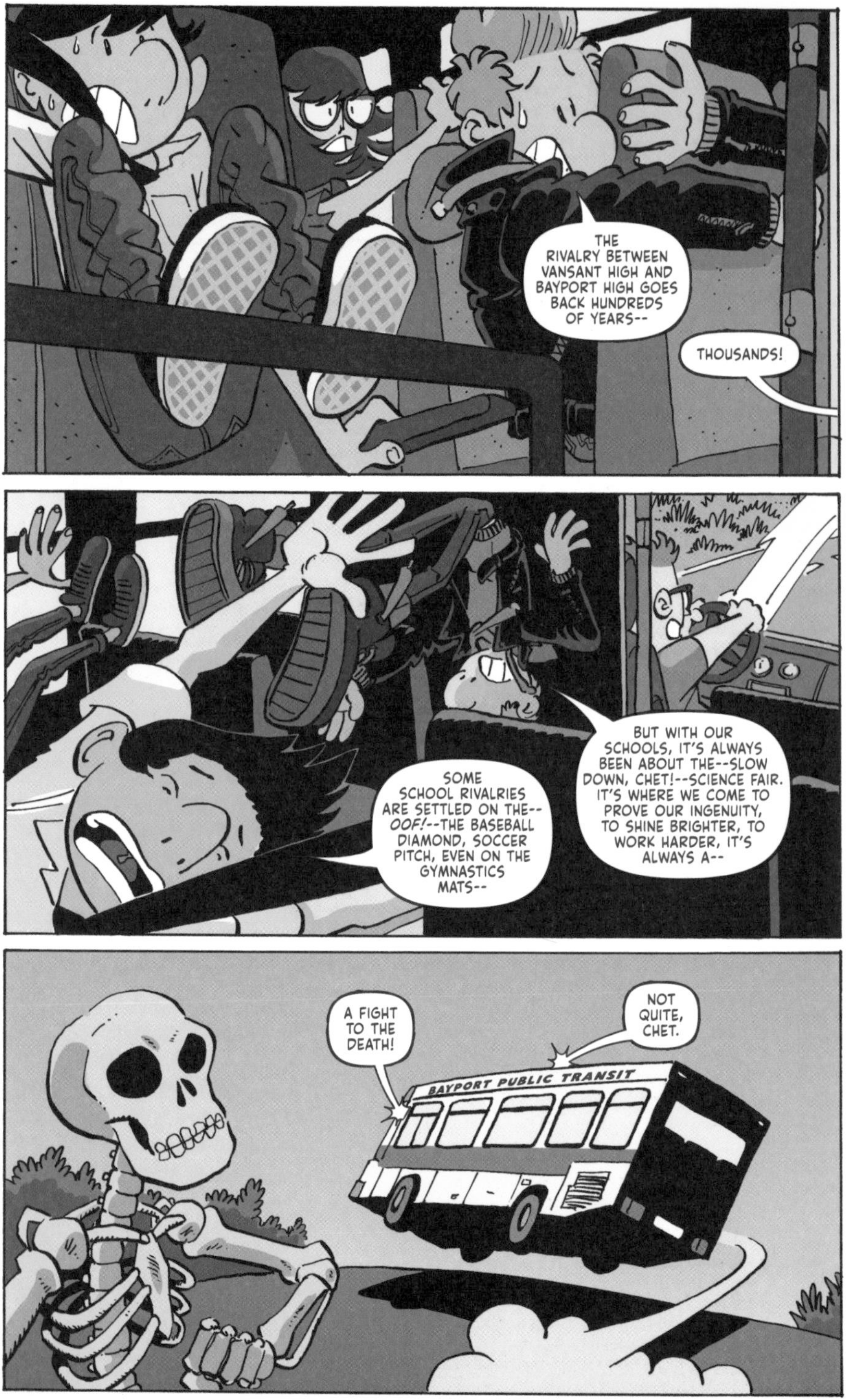
THE RIVALRY BETWEEN VANSANT HIGH AND BAYPORT HIGH GOES BACK HUNDREDS OF YEARS--
THOUSANDS!
SOME SCHOOL RIVALRIES ARE SETTLED ON THE--*OOF!*--THE BASEBALL DIAMOND, SOCCER PITCH, EVEN ON THE GYMNASTICS MATS--
BUT WITH OUR SCHOOLS, IT'S ALWAYS BEEN ABOUT THE--SLOW DOWN, CHET!--SCIENCE FAIR. IT'S WHERE WE COME TO PROVE OUR INGENUITY, TO SHINE BRIGHTER, TO WORK HARDER, IT'S ALWAYS A--
A FIGHT TO THE DEATH!
NOT QUITE, CHET.
BAYPORT PUBLIC TRANSIT

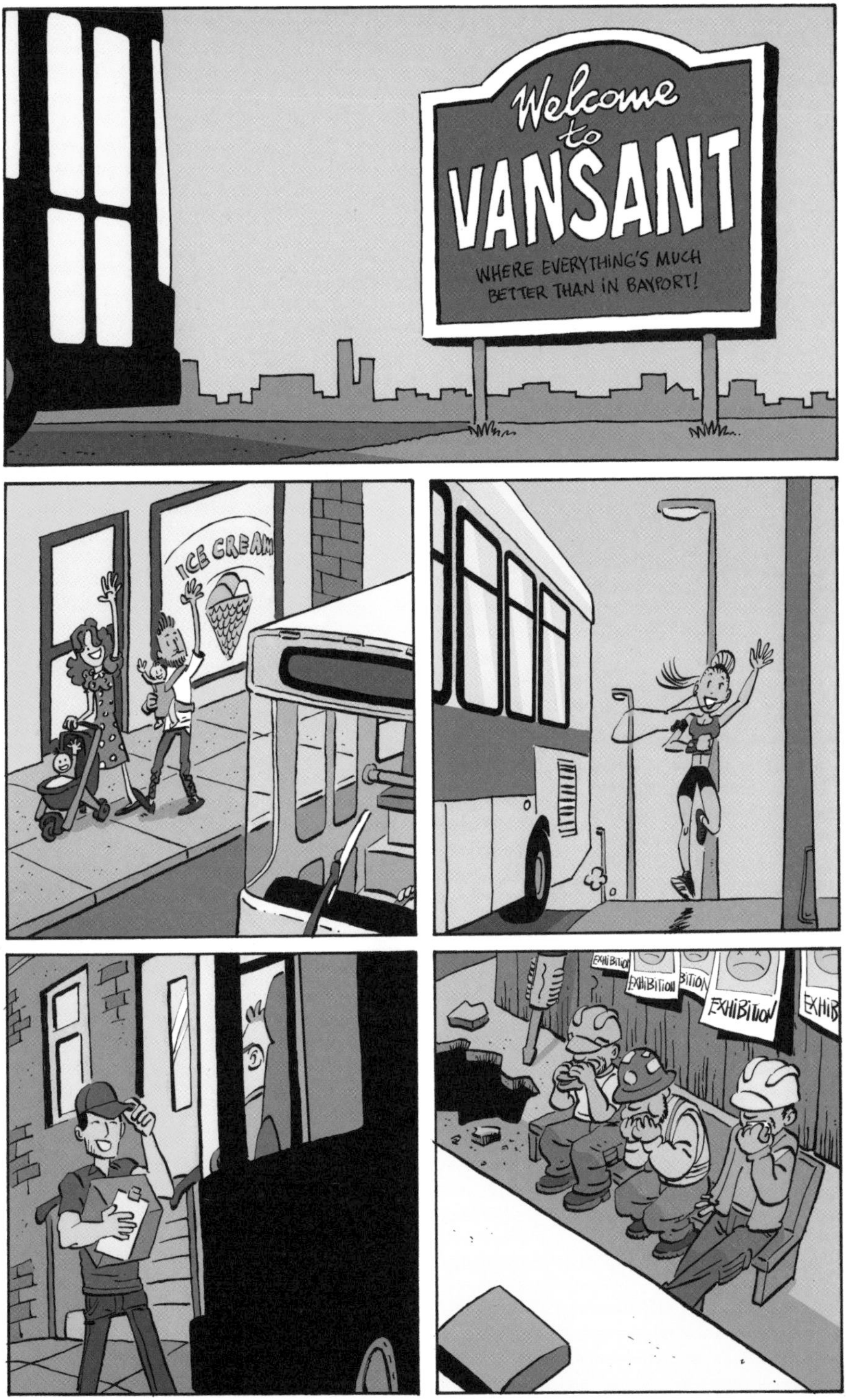
Welcome to VANSANT
WHERE EVERYTHING'S MUCH BETTER THAN IN BAYPORT!
ICE CREAM
EXHIBITION
EXHIBITION
BITION
EXHIBITION
EXHIB

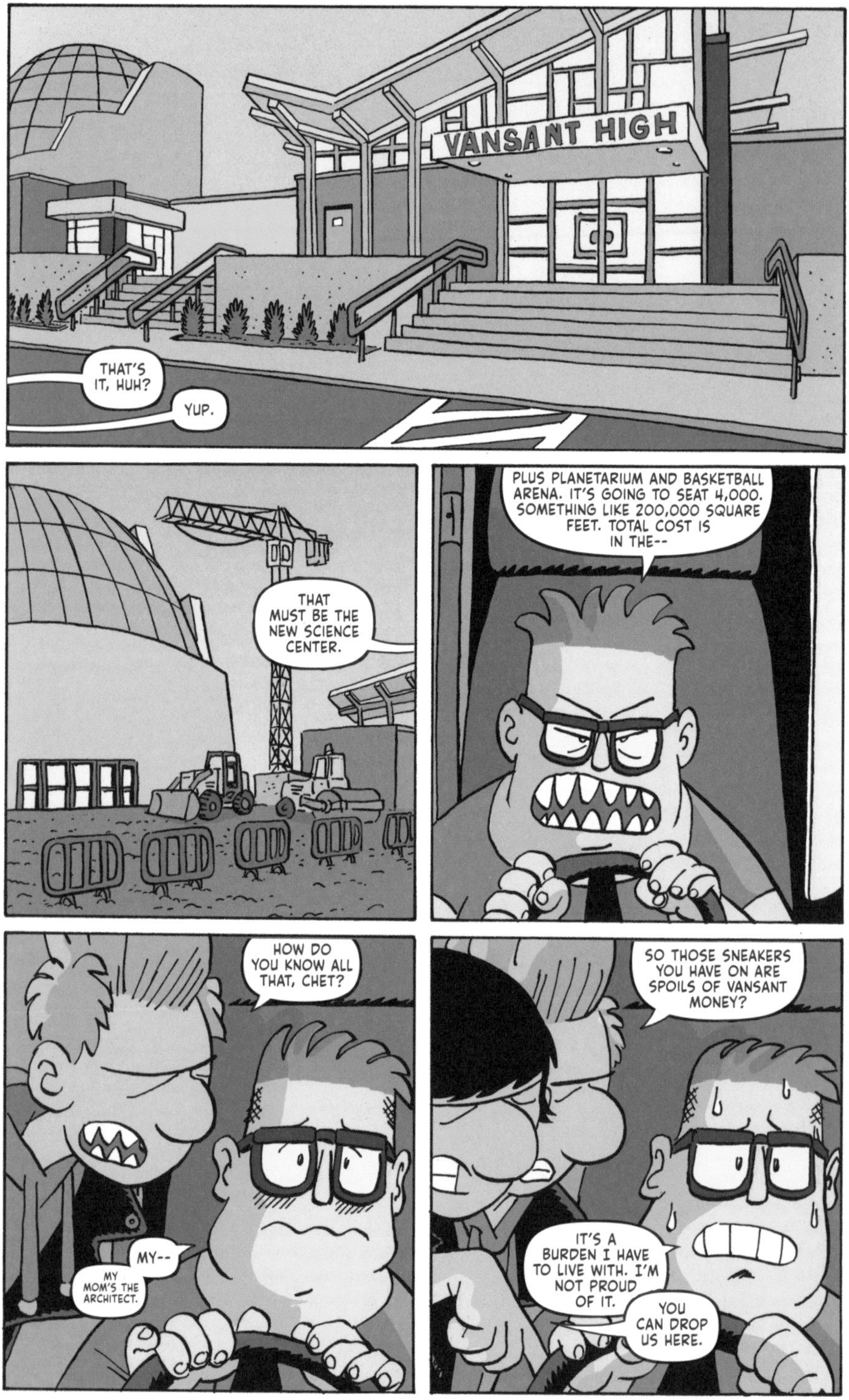
VANSANT HIGH
THAT'S IT, HUH?
YUP.
THAT MUST BE THE NEW SCIENCE CENTER.
PLUS PLANETARIUM AND BASKETBALL ARENA. IT'S GOING TO SEAT 4,000. SOMETHING LIKE 200,000 SQUARE FEET. TOTAL COST IS IN THE--
HOW DO YOU KNOW ALL THAT, CHET?
MY--
MY MOM'S THE ARCHITECT.
SO THOSE SNEAKERS YOU HAVE ON ARE SPOILS OF VANSANT MONEY?
IT'S A BURDEN I HAVE TO LIVE WITH. I'M NOT PROUD OF IT.
YOU CAN DROP US HERE.

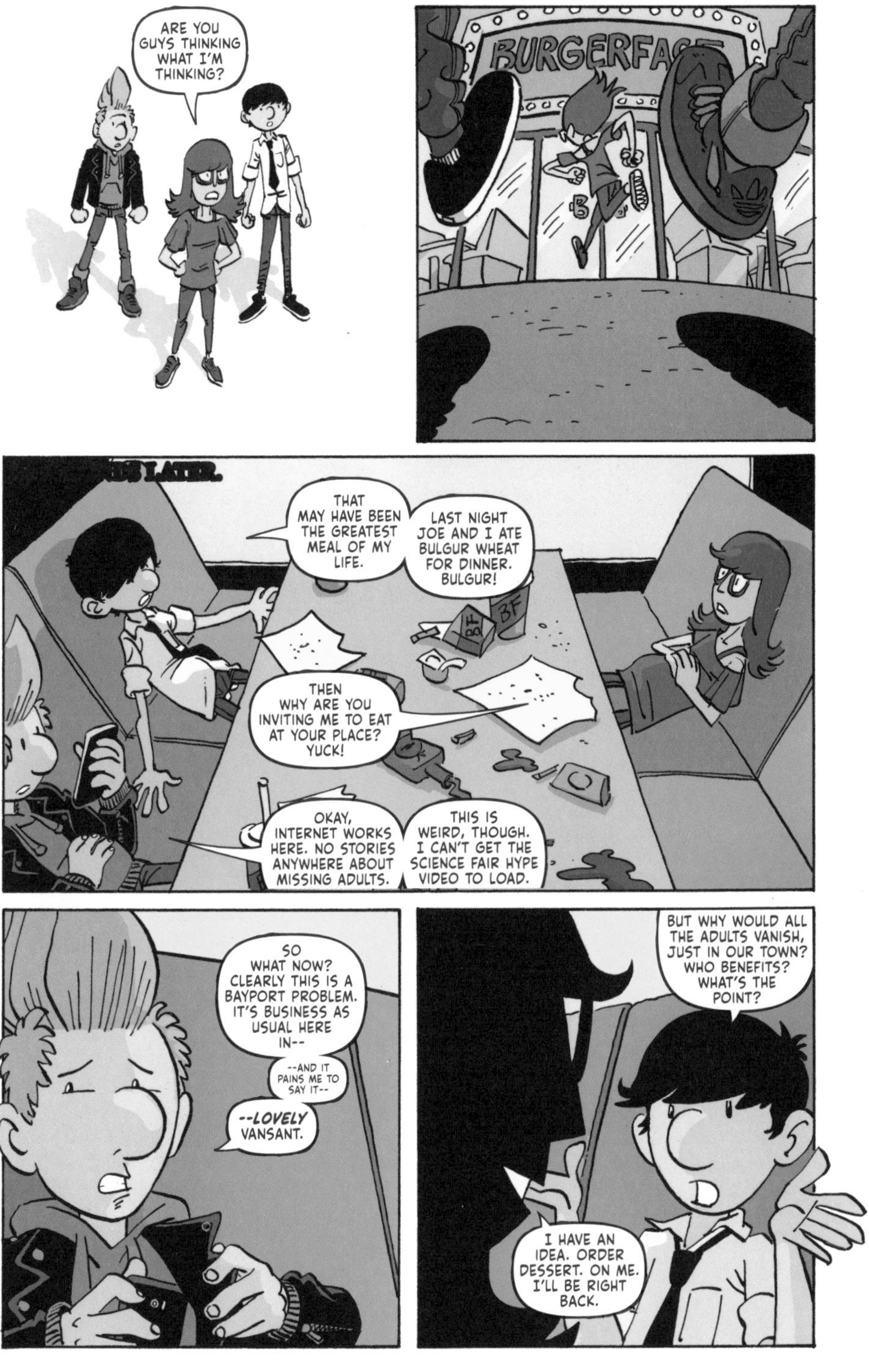

ARE YOU GUYS THINKING WHAT I'M THINKING?
BURGERFACE
LATER.
THAT MAY HAVE BEEN THE GREATEST MEAL OF MY LIFE.
LAST NIGHT JOE AND I ATE BULGUR WHEAT FOR DINNER. BULGUR!
THEN WHY ARE YOU INVITING ME TO EAT AT YOUR PLACE? YUCK!
OKAY, INTERNET WORKS HERE. NO STORIES ANYWHERE ABOUT MISSING ADULTS.
THIS IS WEIRD, THOUGH. I CAN'T GET THE SCIENCE FAIR HYPE VIDEO TO LOAD.
SO WHAT NOW? CLEARLY THIS IS A BAYPORT PROBLEM. IT'S BUSINESS AS USUAL HERE IN--
--AND IT PAINS ME TO SAY IT--
--*LOVELY* VANSANT.
BUT WHY WOULD ALL THE ADULTS VANISH, JUST IN OUR TOWN? WHO BENEFITS? WHAT'S THE POINT?
I HAVE AN IDEA. ORDER DESSERT. ON ME. I'LL BE RIGHT BACK.

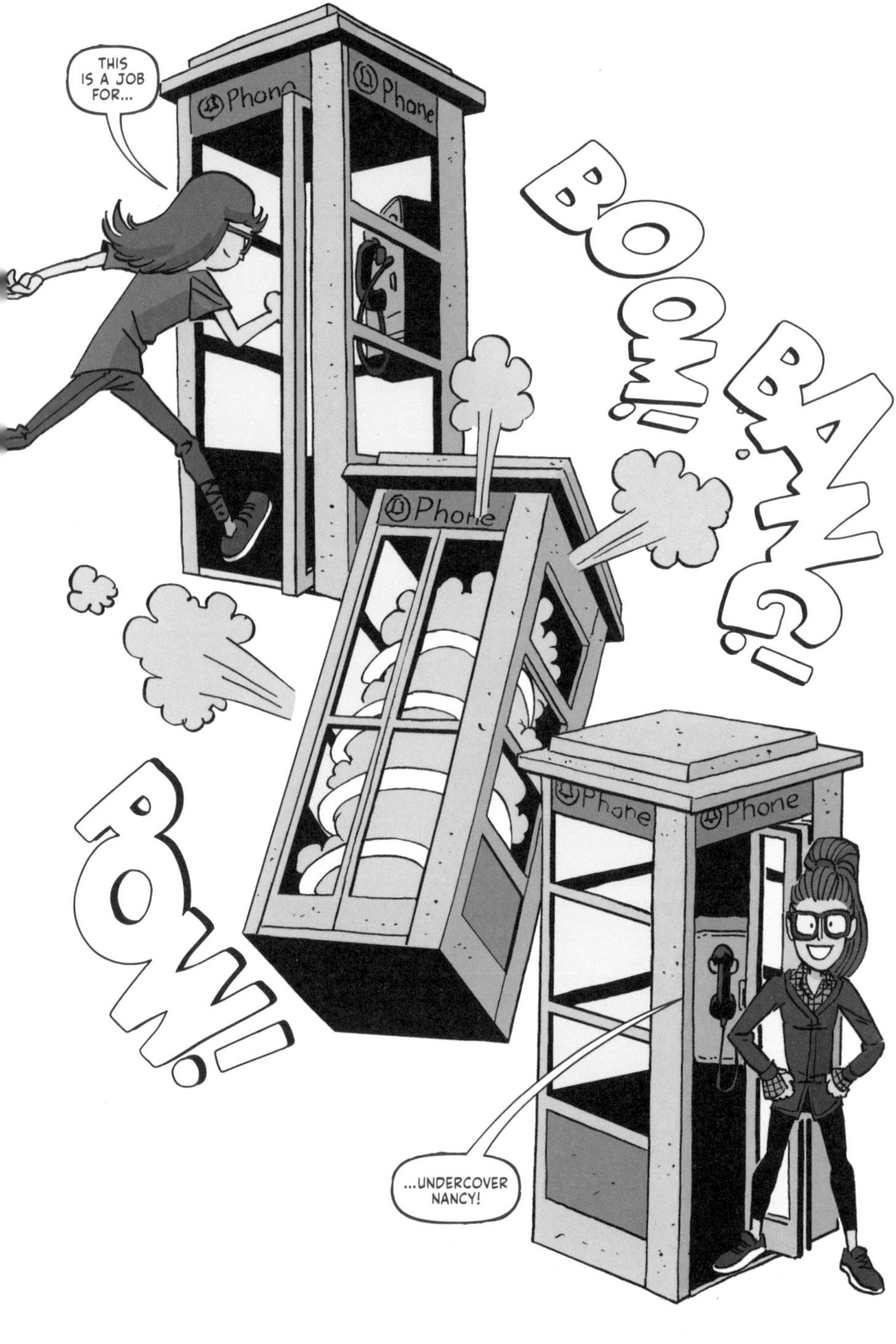
THIS IS A JOB FOR...
Phone
Phone
BOOM!
BANG!
Phone
POW!
Phone
Phone
...UNDERCOVER NANCY!

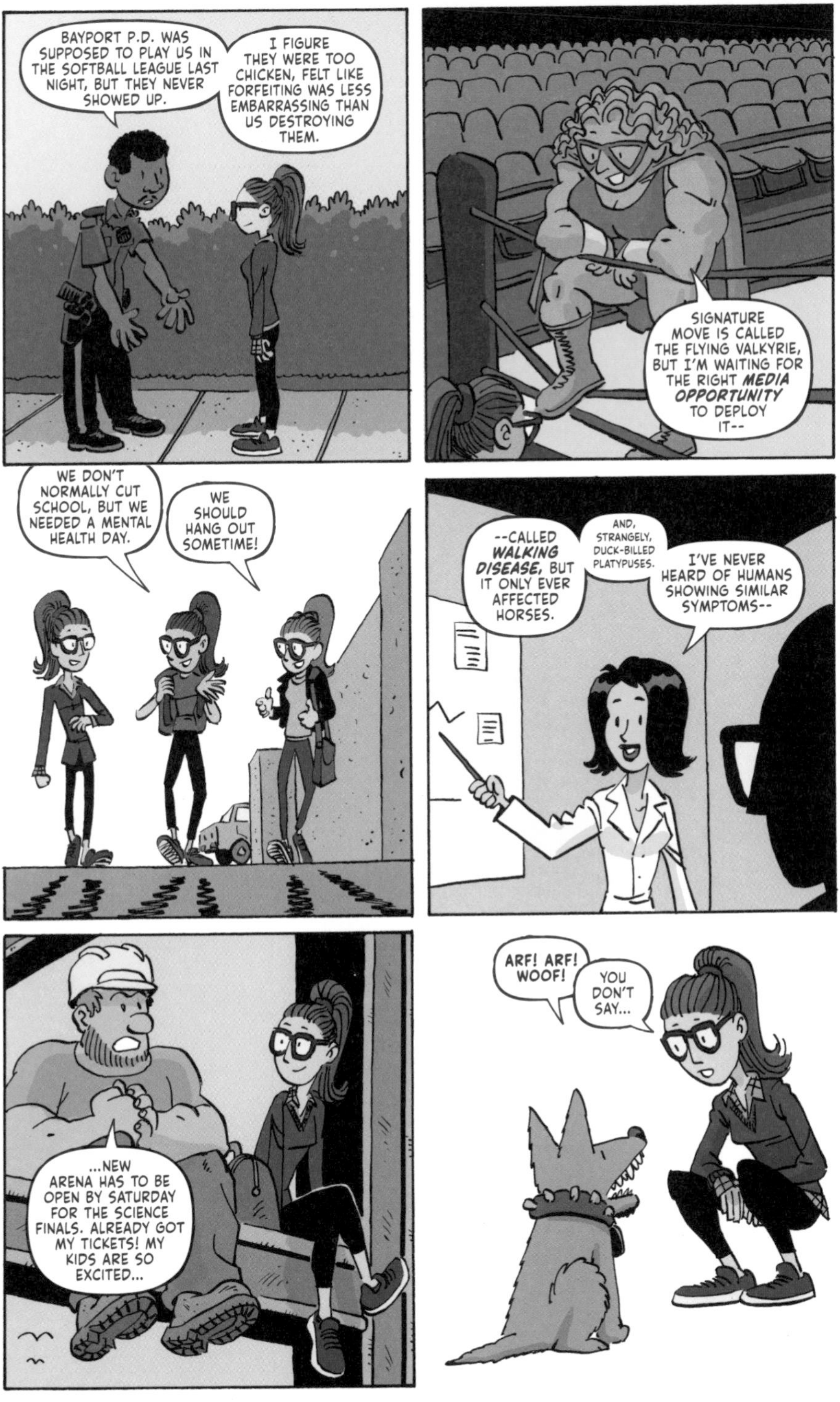
BAYPORT P.D. WAS SUPPOSED TO PLAY US IN THE SOFTBALL LEAGUE LAST NIGHT, BUT THEY NEVER SHOWED UP.
I FIGURE THEY WERE TOO CHICKEN, FELT LIKE FORFEITING WAS LESS EMBARRASSING THAN US DESTROYING THEM.
SIGNATURE MOVE IS CALLED THE FLYING VALKYRIE, BUT I'M WAITING FOR THE RIGHT *MEDIA OPPORTUNITY* TO DEPLOY IT--
WE DON'T NORMALLY CUT SCHOOL, BUT WE NEEDED A MENTAL HEALTH DAY.
WE SHOULD HANG OUT SOMETIME!
--CALLED *WALKING DISEASE,* BUT IT ONLY EVER AFFECTED HORSES.
AND, STRANGELY, DUCK-BILLED PLATYPUSES.
I'VE NEVER HEARD OF HUMANS SHOWING SIMILAR SYMPTOMS--
...NEW ARENA HAS TO BE OPEN BY SATURDAY FOR THE SCIENCE FINALS. ALREADY GOT MY TICKETS! MY KIDS ARE SO EXCITED...
ARF! ARF! WOOF!
YOU DON'T SAY...

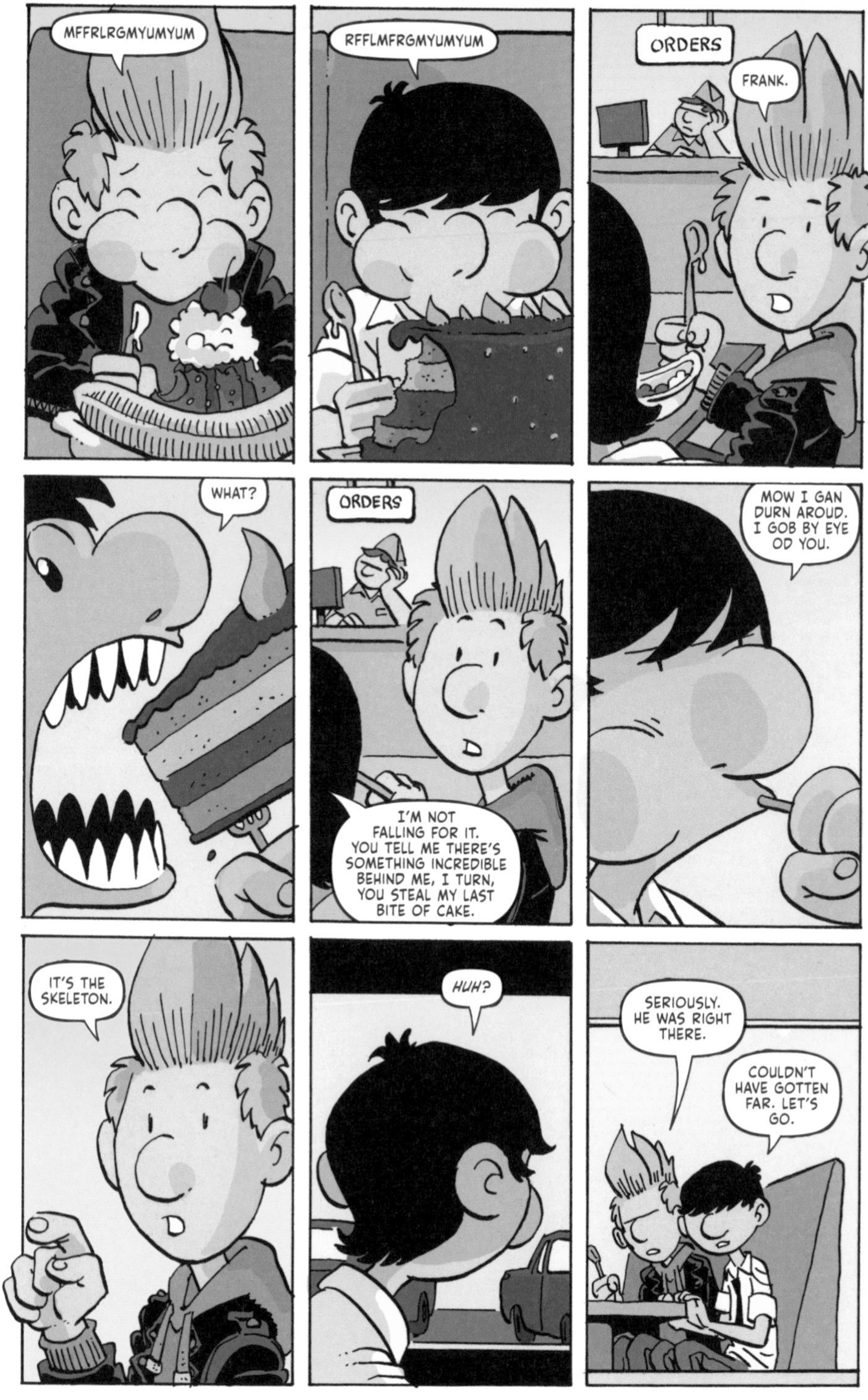
MFFRLRGMYUMYUM
RFFLMFRGMYUMYUM
ORDERS
FRANK.
WHAT?
ORDERS
I'M NOT FALLING FOR IT. YOU TELL ME THERE'S SOMETHING INCREDIBLE BEHIND ME, I TURN, YOU STEAL MY LAST BITE OF CAKE.
MOW I GAN DURN AROUD. I GOB BY EYE OD YOU.
IT'S THE SKELETON.
HUH?
SERIOUSLY. HE WAS RIGHT THERE.
COULDN'T HAVE GOTTEN FAR. LET'S GO.

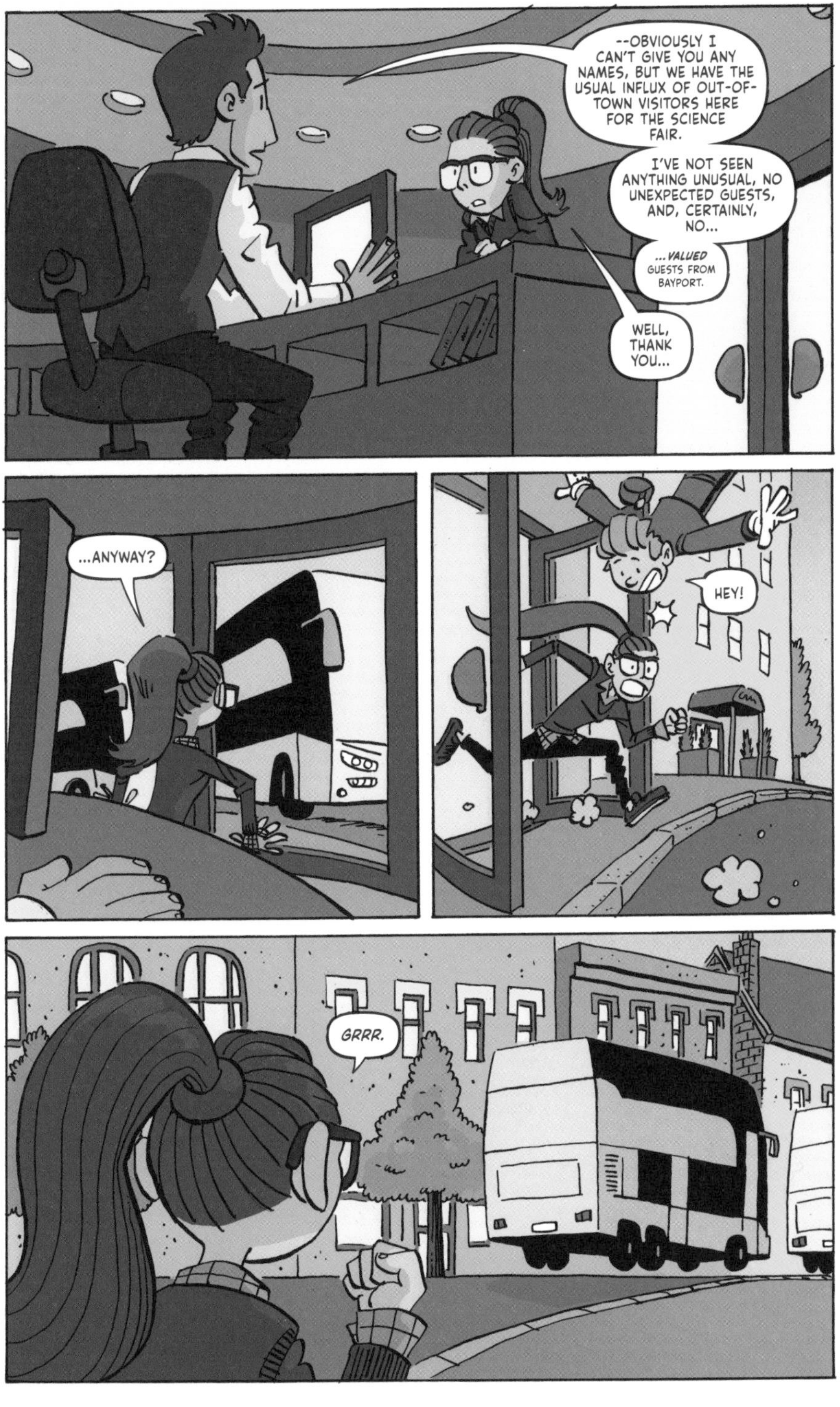
--OBVIOUSLY I CAN'T GIVE YOU ANY NAMES, BUT WE HAVE THE USUAL INFLUX OF OUT-OF-TOWN VISITORS HERE FOR THE SCIENCE FAIR.
I'VE NOT SEEN ANYTHING UNUSUAL, NO UNEXPECTED GUESTS, AND, CERTAINLY, NO...
...VALUED GUESTS FROM BAYPORT.
WELL, THANK YOU...
...ANYWAY?
HEY!
GRRR.

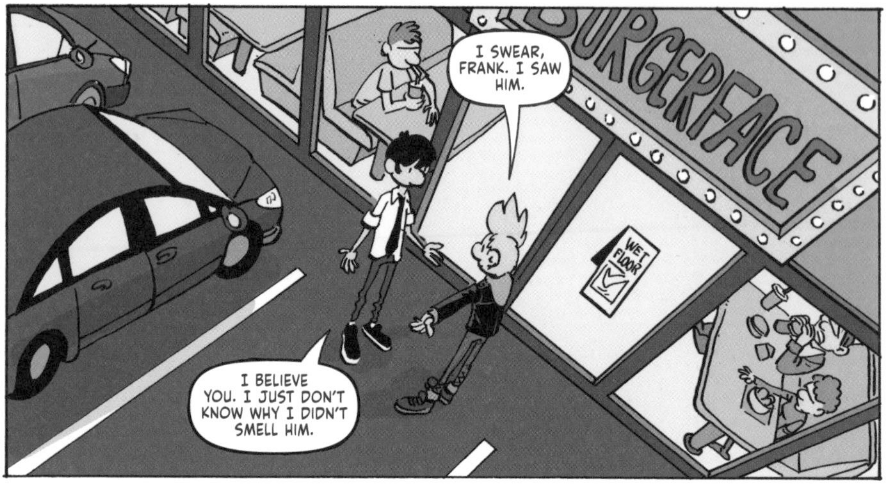
BURGERFACE
I SWEAR, FRANK. I SAW HIM.
WET FLOOR
I BELIEVE YOU. I JUST DON'T KNOW WHY I DIDN'T SMELL HIM.

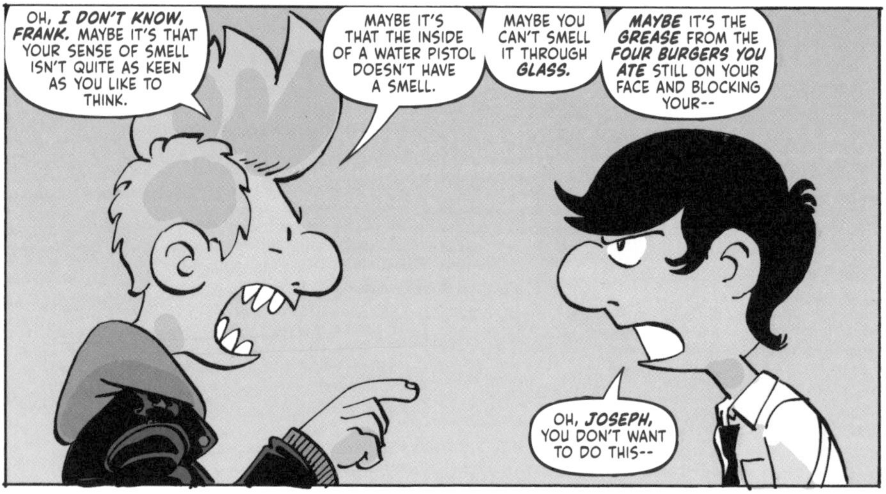
OH, ***I DON'T KNOW, FRANK.*** MAYBE IT'S THAT YOUR SENSE OF SMELL ISN'T QUITE AS KEEN AS YOU LIKE TO THINK.
MAYBE IT'S THAT THE INSIDE OF A WATER PISTOL DOESN'T HAVE A SMELL.
MAYBE YOU CAN'T SMELL IT THROUGH ***GLASS.***
MAYBE IT'S THE ***GREASE*** FROM THE ***FOUR BURGERS YOU ATE*** STILL ON YOUR FACE AND BLOCKING YOUR--
OH, ***JOSEPH,*** YOU DON'T WANT TO DO THIS--

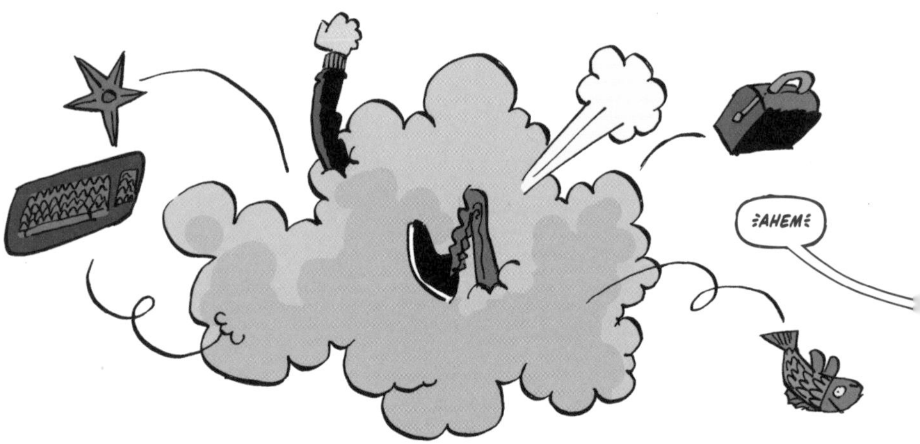
AHEM

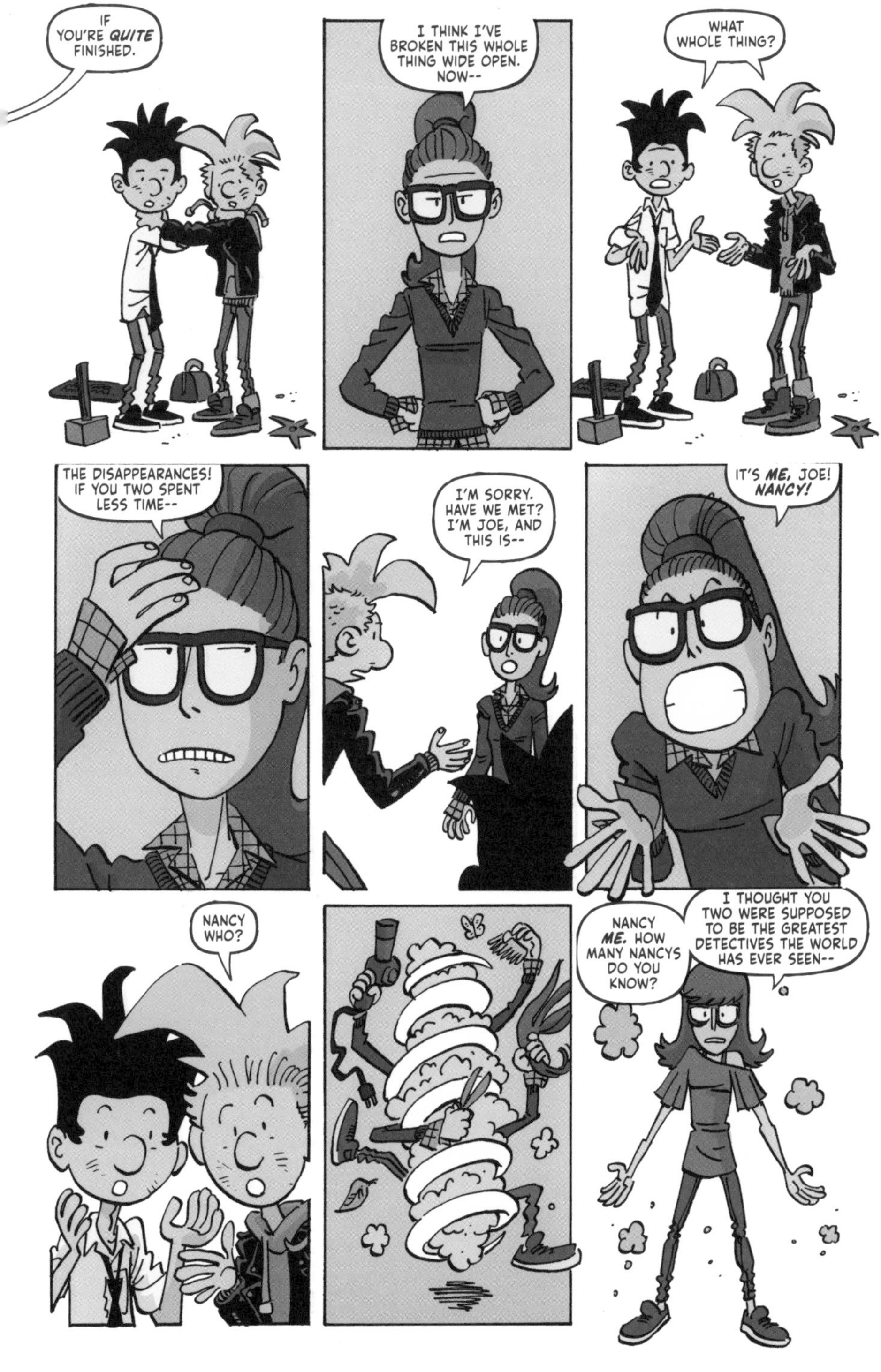

IF YOU'RE ***QUITE*** FINISHED.
I THINK I'VE BROKEN THIS WHOLE THING WIDE OPEN. NOW--
WHAT WHOLE THING?
THE DISAPPEARANCES! IF YOU TWO SPENT LESS TIME--
I'M SORRY. HAVE WE MET? I'M JOE, AND THIS IS--
IT'S ***ME,*** JOE! ***NANCY!***
NANCY WHO?
NANCY ***ME.*** HOW MANY NANCYS DO YOU KNOW?
I THOUGHT YOU TWO WERE SUPPOSED TO BE THE GREATEST DETECTIVES THE WORLD HAS EVER SEEN--

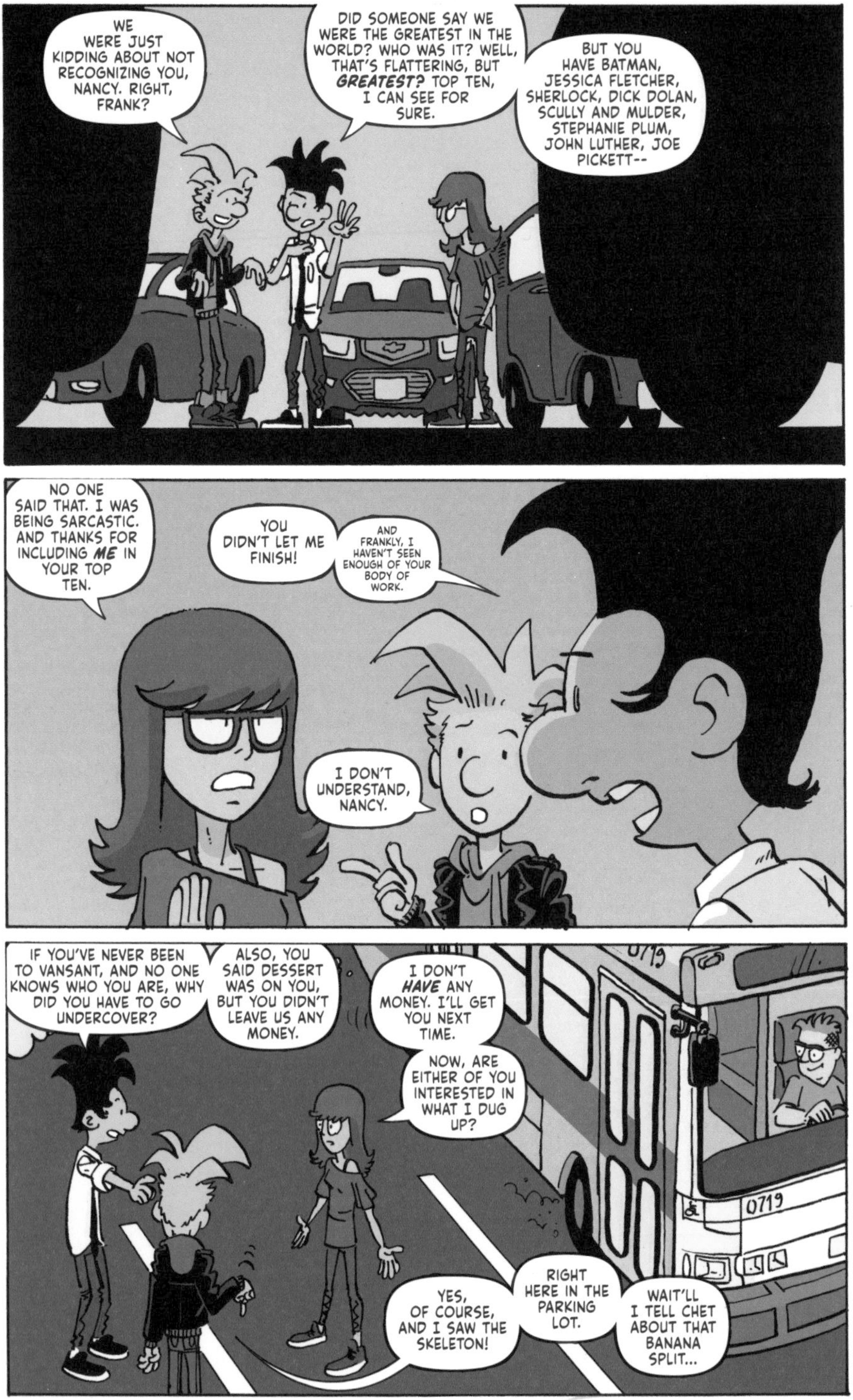
WE WERE JUST KIDDING ABOUT NOT RECOGNIZING YOU, NANCY. RIGHT, FRANK?
DID SOMEONE SAY WE WERE THE GREATEST IN THE WORLD? WHO WAS IT? WELL, THAT'S FLATTERING, BUT *GREATEST?* TOP TEN, I CAN SEE FOR SURE.
BUT YOU HAVE BATMAN, JESSICA FLETCHER, SHERLOCK, DICK DOLAN, SCULLY AND MULDER, STEPHANIE PLUM, JOHN LUTHER, JOE PICKETT--
NO ONE SAID THAT. I WAS BEING SARCASTIC. AND THANKS FOR INCLUDING *ME* IN YOUR TOP TEN.
YOU DIDN'T LET ME FINISH!
AND FRANKLY, I HAVEN'T SEEN ENOUGH OF YOUR BODY OF WORK.
I DON'T UNDERSTAND, NANCY.
IF YOU'VE NEVER BEEN TO VANSANT, AND NO ONE KNOWS WHO YOU ARE, WHY DID YOU HAVE TO GO UNDERCOVER?
ALSO, YOU SAID DESSERT WAS ON YOU, BUT YOU DIDN'T LEAVE US ANY MONEY.
I DON'T *HAVE* ANY MONEY. I'LL GET YOU NEXT TIME.
NOW, ARE EITHER OF YOU INTERESTED IN WHAT I DUG UP?
YES, OF COURSE, AND I SAW THE SKELETON!
RIGHT HERE IN THE PARKING LOT.
WAIT'LL I TELL CHET ABOUT THAT BANANA SPLIT...
0719

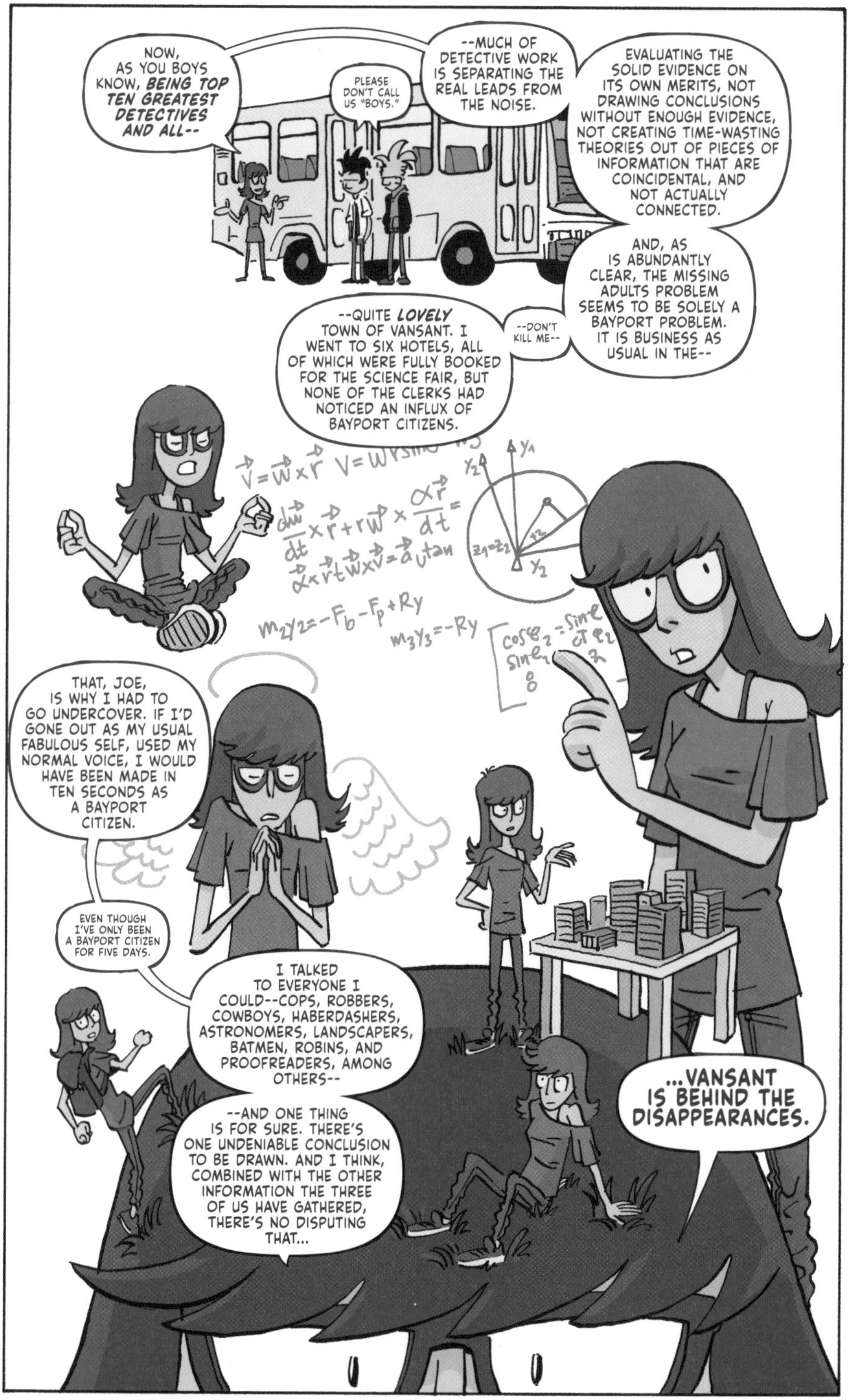

NOW, AS YOU BOYS KNOW, ***BEING TOP TEN GREATEST DETECTIVES AND ALL--***
PLEASE DON'T CALL US "BOYS."
--MUCH OF DETECTIVE WORK IS SEPARATING THE REAL LEADS FROM THE NOISE.
EVALUATING THE SOLID EVIDENCE ON ITS OWN MERITS, NOT DRAWING CONCLUSIONS WITHOUT ENOUGH EVIDENCE, NOT CREATING TIME-WASTING THEORIES OUT OF PIECES OF INFORMATION THAT ARE COINCIDENTAL, AND NOT ACTUALLY CONNECTED.
AND, AS IS ABUNDANTLY CLEAR, THE MISSING ADULTS PROBLEM SEEMS TO BE SOLELY A BAYPORT PROBLEM. IT IS BUSINESS AS USUAL IN THE--
--DON'T KILL ME--
--QUITE ***LOVELY*** TOWN OF VANSANT. I WENT TO SIX HOTELS, ALL OF WHICH WERE FULLY BOOKED FOR THE SCIENCE FAIR, BUT NONE OF THE CLERKS HAD NOTICED AN INFLUX OF BAYPORT CITIZENS.
THAT, JOE, IS WHY I HAD TO GO UNDERCOVER. IF I'D GONE OUT AS MY USUAL FABULOUS SELF, USED MY NORMAL VOICE, I WOULD HAVE BEEN MADE IN TEN SECONDS AS A BAYPORT CITIZEN.
EVEN THOUGH I'VE ONLY BEEN A BAYPORT CITIZEN FOR FIVE DAYS.
I TALKED TO EVERYONE I COULD--COPS, ROBBERS, COWBOYS, HABERDASHERS, ASTRONOMERS, LANDSCAPERS, BATMEN, ROBINS, AND PROOFREADERS, AMONG OTHERS--
--AND ONE THING IS FOR SURE. THERE'S ONE UNDENIABLE CONCLUSION TO BE DRAWN. AND I THINK, COMBINED WITH THE OTHER INFORMATION THE THREE OF US HAVE GATHERED, THERE'S NO DISPUTING THAT...
...VANSANT IS BEHIND THE DISAPPEARANCES.

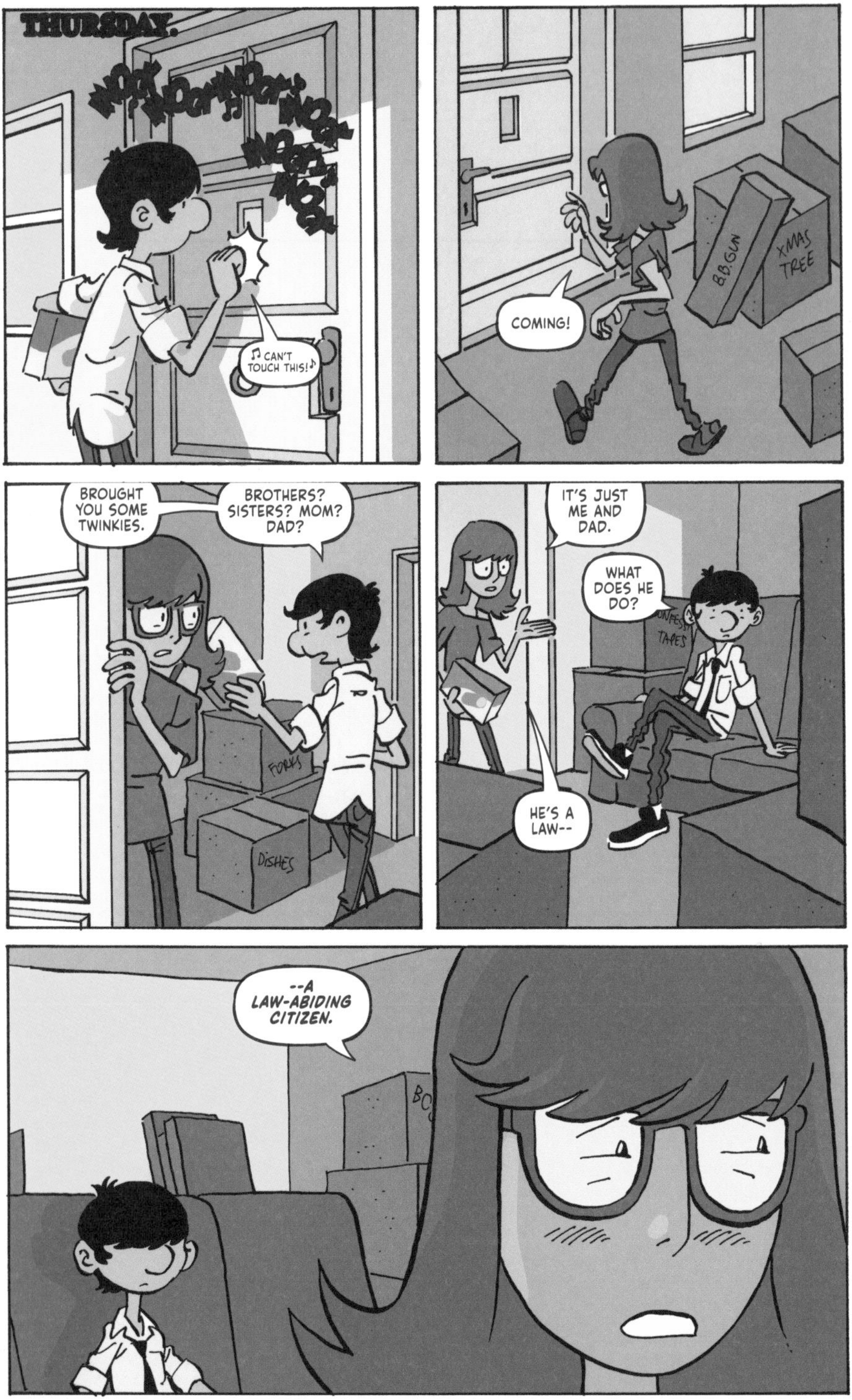
THURSDAY.
♫ CAN'T TOUCH THIS! ♪
COMING!
BROUGHT YOU SOME TWINKIES.
BROTHERS? SISTERS? MOM? DAD?
IT'S JUST ME AND DAD.
WHAT DOES HE DO?
HE'S A LAW--
--A LAW-ABIDING CITIZEN.
B.B. GUN
XMAS TREE
FORKS
DISHES
TAPES

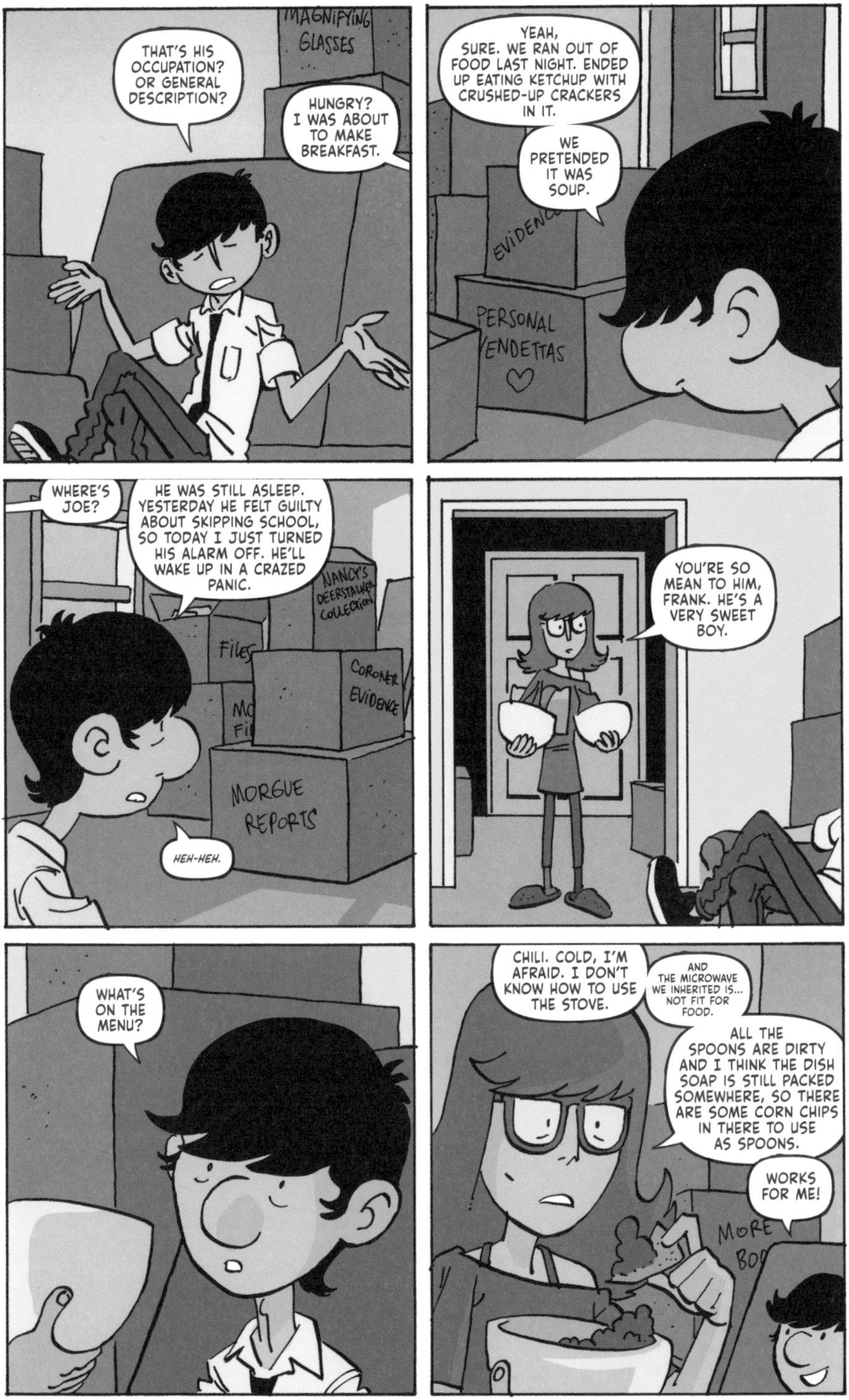
MAGNIFYING GLASSES
THAT'S HIS OCCUPATION? OR GENERAL DESCRIPTION?
HUNGRY? I WAS ABOUT TO MAKE BREAKFAST.
YEAH, SURE. WE RAN OUT OF FOOD LAST NIGHT. ENDED UP EATING KETCHUP WITH CRUSHED-UP CRACKERS IN IT.
WE PRETENDED IT WAS SOUP.
EVIDENCE
PERSONAL VENDETTAS
WHERE'S JOE?
HE WAS STILL ASLEEP. YESTERDAY HE FELT GUILTY ABOUT SKIPPING SCHOOL, SO TODAY I JUST TURNED HIS ALARM OFF. HE'LL WAKE UP IN A CRAZED PANIC.
NANCY'S DEERSTALKER COLLECTION
FILES
CORONER EVIDENCE
MORGUE REPORTS
HEH-HEH.
YOU'RE SO MEAN TO HIM, FRANK. HE'S A VERY SWEET BOY.
WHAT'S ON THE MENU?
CHILI. COLD, I'M AFRAID. I DON'T KNOW HOW TO USE THE STOVE.
AND THE MICROWAVE WE INHERITED IS... NOT FIT FOR FOOD.
ALL THE SPOONS ARE DIRTY AND I THINK THE DISH SOAP IS STILL PACKED SOMEWHERE, SO THERE ARE SOME CORN CHIPS IN THERE TO USE AS SPOONS.
WORKS FOR ME!

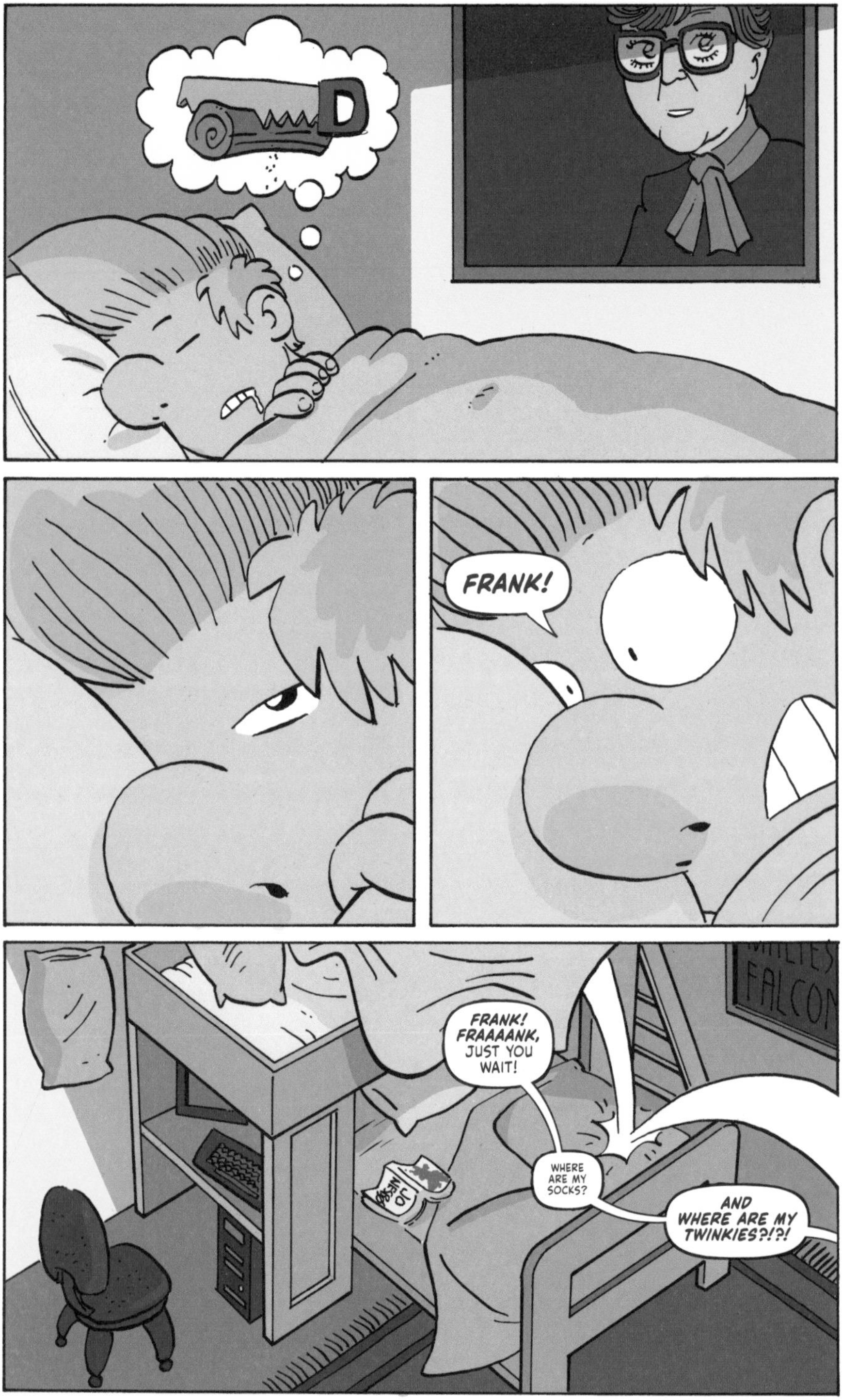
FRANK!
FRANK! FRAAAANK, JUST YOU WAIT!
WHERE ARE MY SOCKS?
AND WHERE ARE MY TWINKIES?!?!

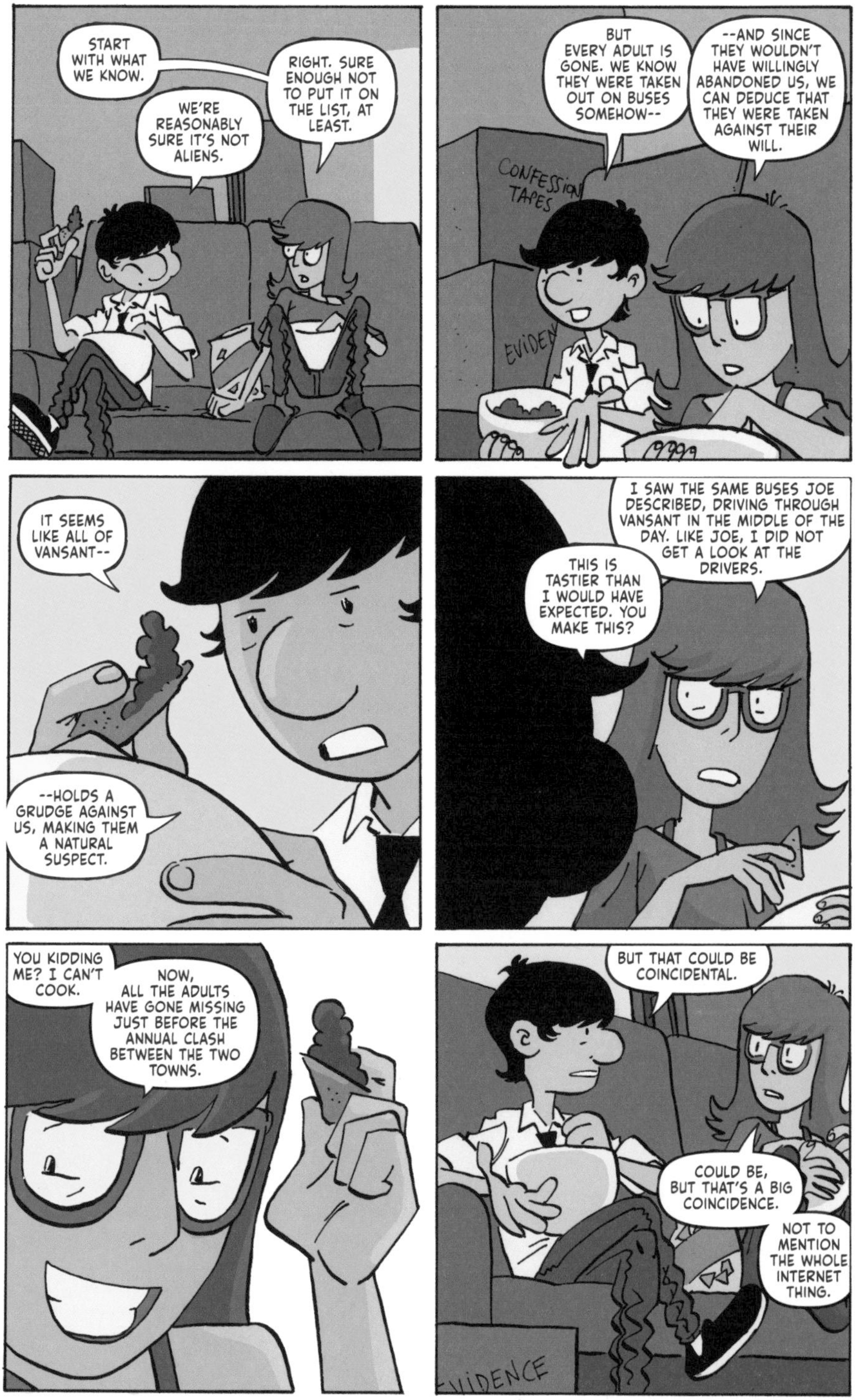
START WITH WHAT WE KNOW.
WE'RE REASONABLY SURE IT'S NOT ALIENS.
RIGHT. SURE ENOUGH NOT TO PUT IT ON THE LIST, AT LEAST.
BUT EVERY ADULT IS GONE. WE KNOW THEY WERE TAKEN OUT ON BUSES SOMEHOW--
--AND SINCE THEY WOULDN'T HAVE WILLINGLY ABANDONED US, WE CAN DEDUCE THAT THEY WERE TAKEN AGAINST THEIR WILL.
CONFESSION TAPES
EVIDEN
IT SEEMS LIKE ALL OF VANSANT--
--HOLDS A GRUDGE AGAINST US, MAKING THEM A NATURAL SUSPECT.
I SAW THE SAME BUSES JOE DESCRIBED, DRIVING THROUGH VANSANT IN THE MIDDLE OF THE DAY. LIKE JOE, I DID NOT GET A LOOK AT THE DRIVERS.
THIS IS TASTIER THAN I WOULD HAVE EXPECTED. YOU MAKE THIS?
YOU KIDDING ME? I CAN'T COOK.
NOW, ALL THE ADULTS HAVE GONE MISSING JUST BEFORE THE ANNUAL CLASH BETWEEN THE TWO TOWNS.
BUT THAT COULD BE COINCIDENTAL.
COULD BE, BUT THAT'S A BIG COINCIDENCE.
NOT TO MENTION THE WHOLE INTERNET THING.
EVIDENCE

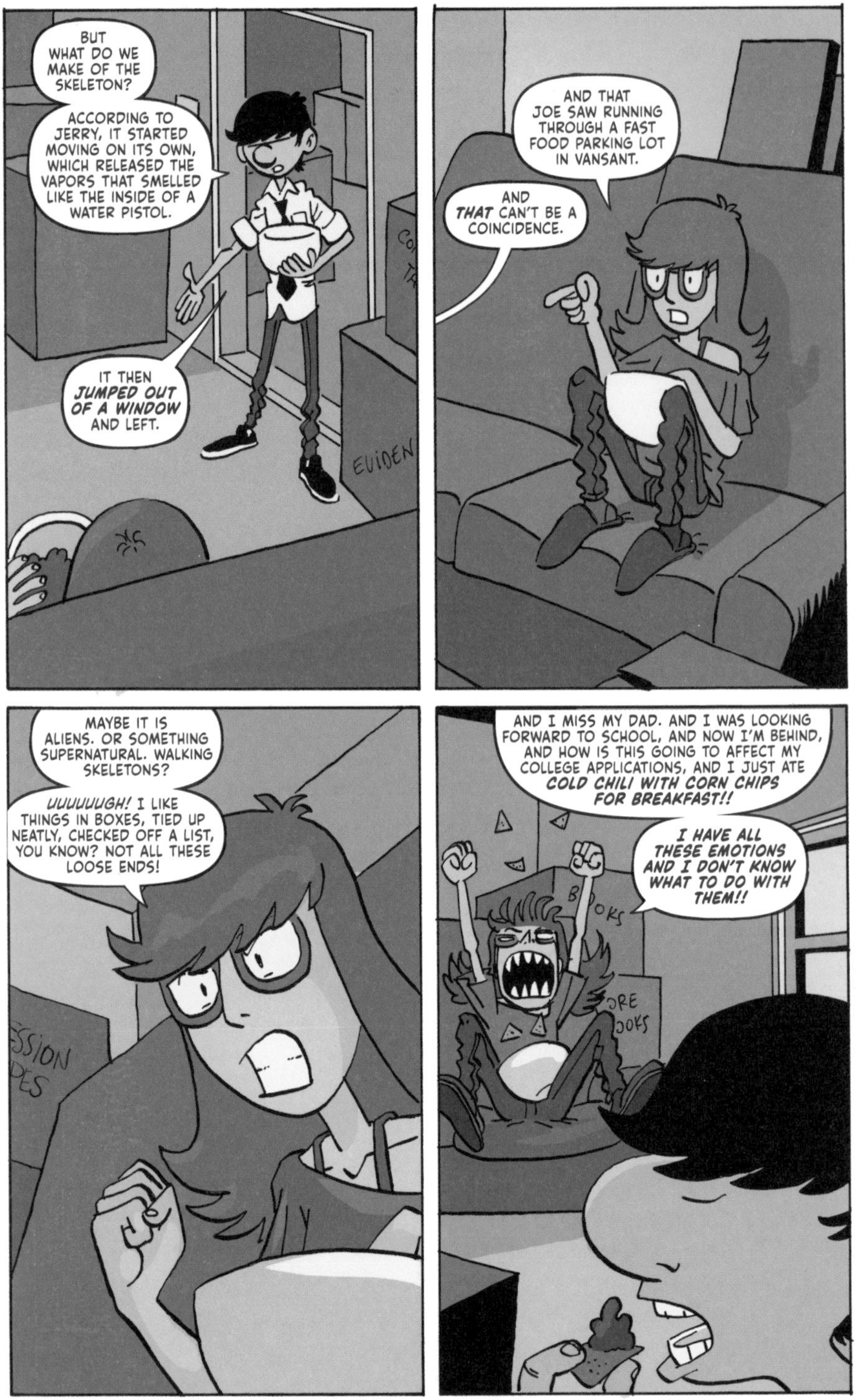
BUT WHAT DO WE MAKE OF THE SKELETON?
ACCORDING TO JERRY, IT STARTED MOVING ON ITS OWN, WHICH RELEASED THE VAPORS THAT SMELLED LIKE THE INSIDE OF A WATER PISTOL.
IT THEN *JUMPED OUT OF A WINDOW* AND LEFT.
EVIDEN
AND THAT JOE SAW RUNNING THROUGH A FAST FOOD PARKING LOT IN VANSANT.
AND *THAT* CAN'T BE A COINCIDENCE.
MAYBE IT IS ALIENS. OR SOMETHING SUPERNATURAL. WALKING SKELETONS?
UUUUUUGH! I LIKE THINGS IN BOXES, TIED UP NEATLY, CHECKED OFF A LIST, YOU KNOW? NOT ALL THESE LOOSE ENDS!
AND I MISS MY DAD. AND I WAS LOOKING FORWARD TO SCHOOL, AND NOW I'M BEHIND, AND HOW IS THIS GOING TO AFFECT MY COLLEGE APPLICATIONS, AND I JUST ATE *COLD CHILI WITH CORN CHIPS FOR BREAKFAST!!*
I HAVE ALL THESE EMOTIONS AND I DON'T KNOW WHAT TO DO WITH THEM!!

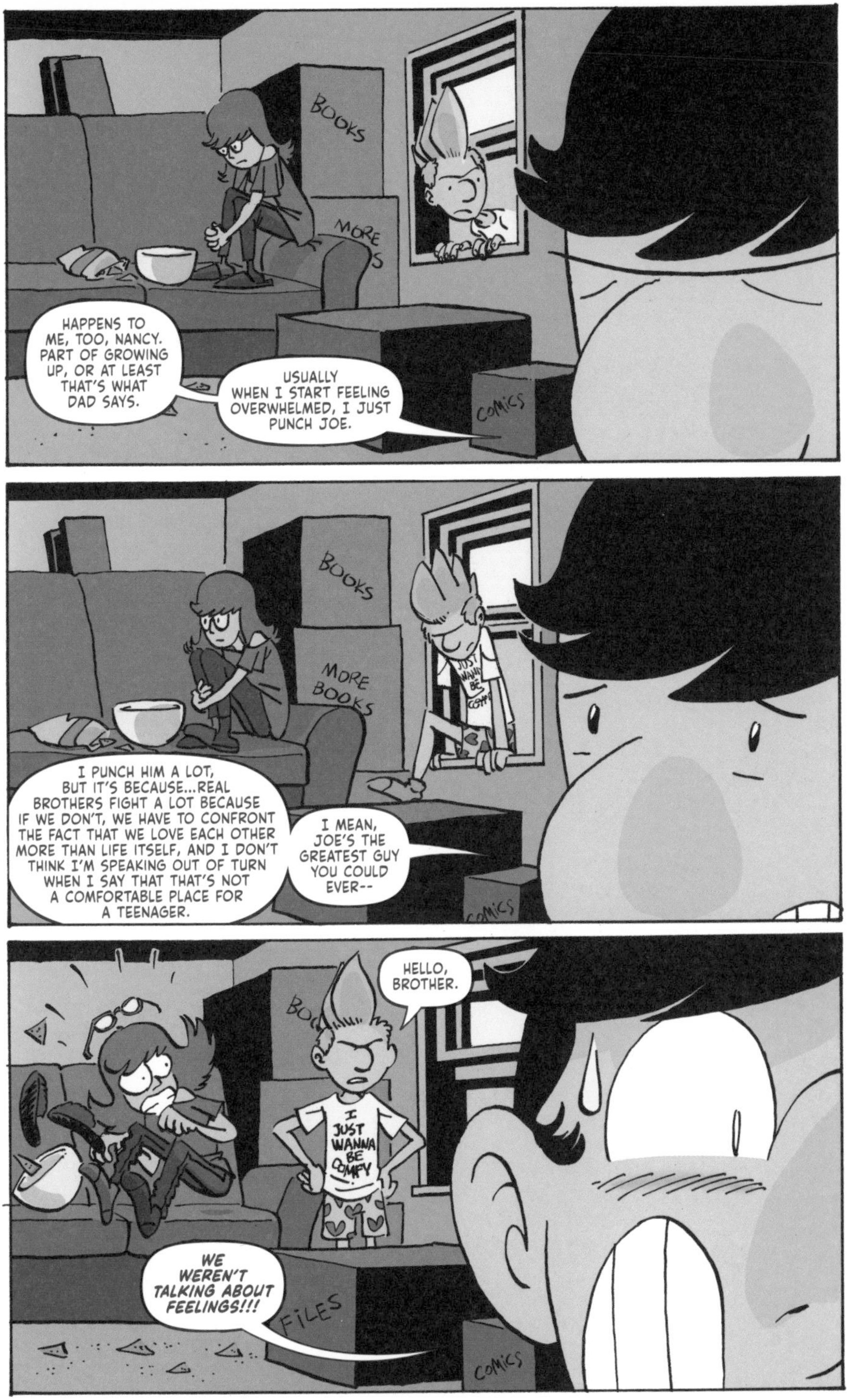
BOOKS
MORE
HAPPENS TO ME, TOO, NANCY. PART OF GROWING UP, OR AT LEAST THAT'S WHAT DAD SAYS.
USUALLY WHEN I START FEELING OVERWHELMED, I JUST PUNCH JOE.
COMICS
BOOKS
MORE BOOKS
I PUNCH HIM A LOT, BUT IT'S BECAUSE...REAL BROTHERS FIGHT A LOT BECAUSE IF WE DON'T, WE HAVE TO CONFRONT THE FACT THAT WE LOVE EACH OTHER MORE THAN LIFE ITSELF, AND I DON'T THINK I'M SPEAKING OUT OF TURN WHEN I SAY THAT THAT'S NOT A COMFORTABLE PLACE FOR A TEENAGER.
I MEAN, JOE'S THE GREATEST GUY YOU COULD EVER--
COMICS
HELLO, BROTHER.
I JUST WANNA BE COMFY
WE WEREN'T TALKING ABOUT FEELINGS!!!
FILES
COMICS

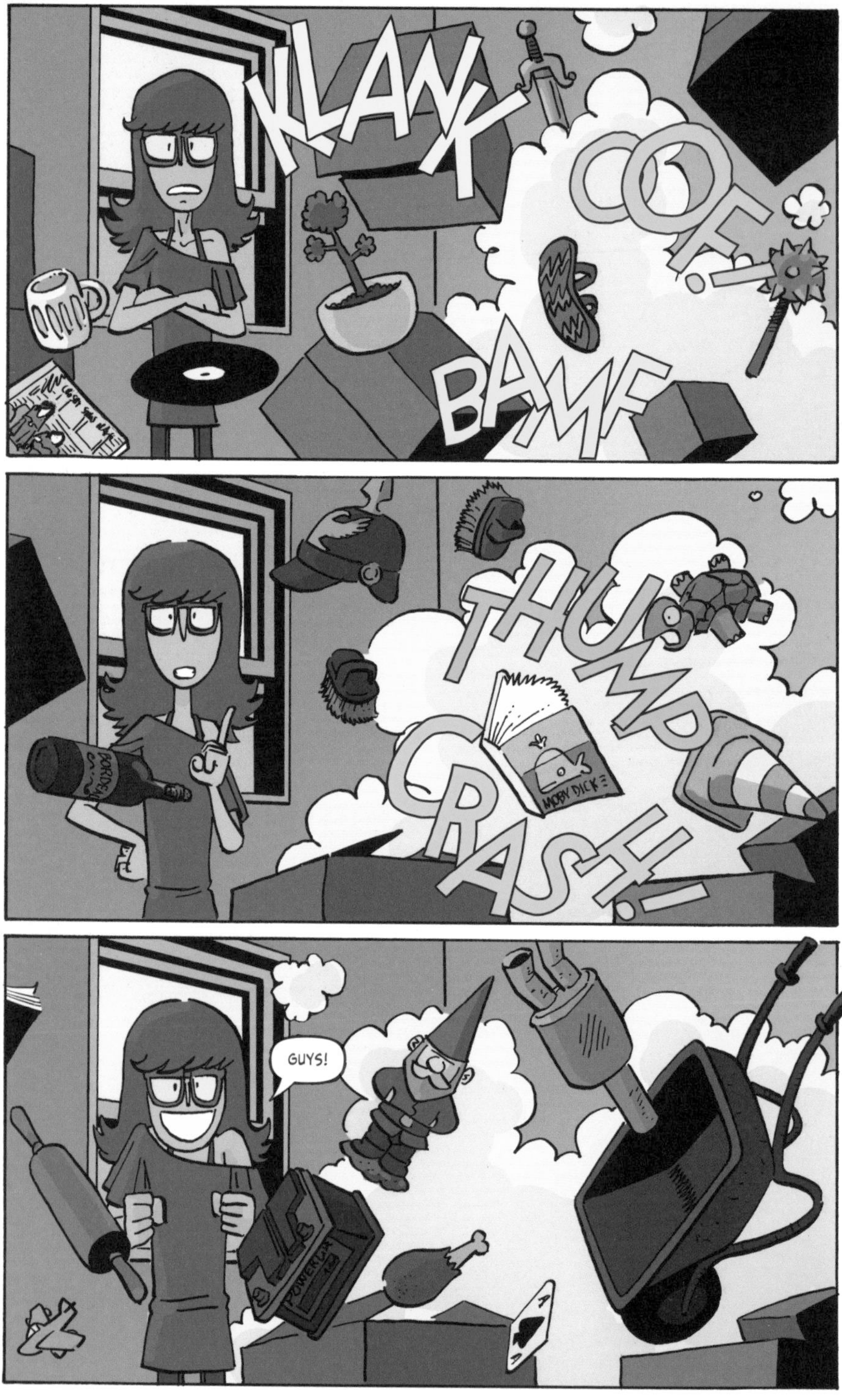
KLANK
OOF!
BAMF
THUMP
MOBY DICK
CRASH!
GUYS!

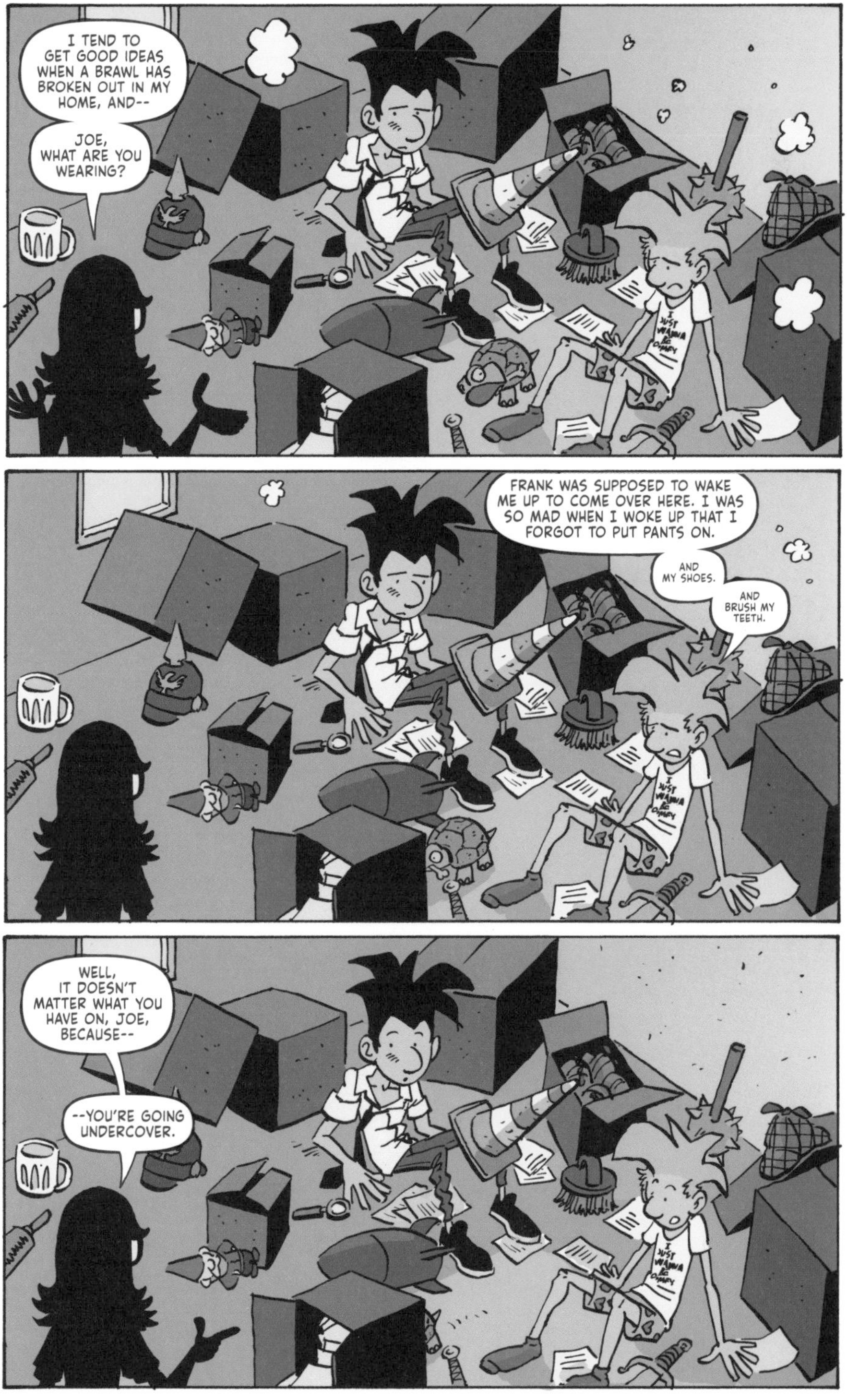
I TEND TO GET GOOD IDEAS WHEN A BRAWL HAS BROKEN OUT IN MY HOME, AND--
JOE, WHAT ARE YOU WEARING?
I JUST WANNA BE CHAPPY
FRANK WAS SUPPOSED TO WAKE ME UP TO COME OVER HERE. I WAS SO MAD WHEN I WOKE UP THAT I FORGOT TO PUT PANTS ON.
AND MY SHOES.
AND BRUSH MY TEETH.
WELL, IT DOESN'T MATTER WHAT YOU HAVE ON, JOE, BECAUSE--
--YOU'RE GOING UNDERCOVER.

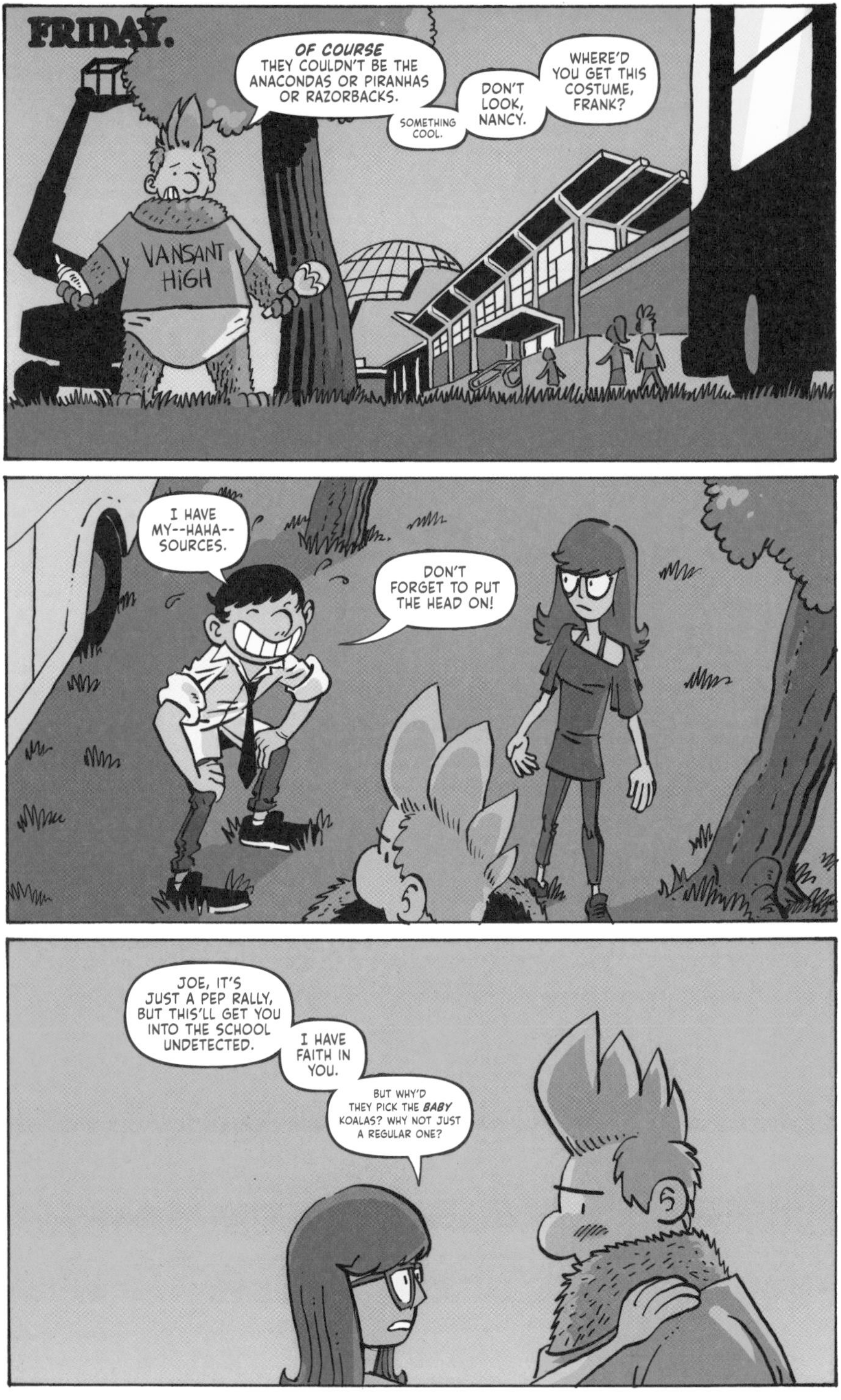
FRIDAY.
OF COURSE THEY COULDN'T BE THE ANACONDAS OR PIRANHAS OR RAZORBACKS.
SOMETHING COOL.
DON'T LOOK, NANCY.
WHERE'D YOU GET THIS COSTUME, FRANK?
VANSANT HIGH
I HAVE MY--HAHA-- SOURCES.
DON'T FORGET TO PUT THE HEAD ON!
JOE, IT'S JUST A PEP RALLY, BUT THIS'LL GET YOU INTO THE SCHOOL UNDETECTED.
I HAVE FAITH IN YOU.
BUT WHY'D THEY PICK THE BABY KOALAS? WHY NOT JUST A REGULAR ONE?

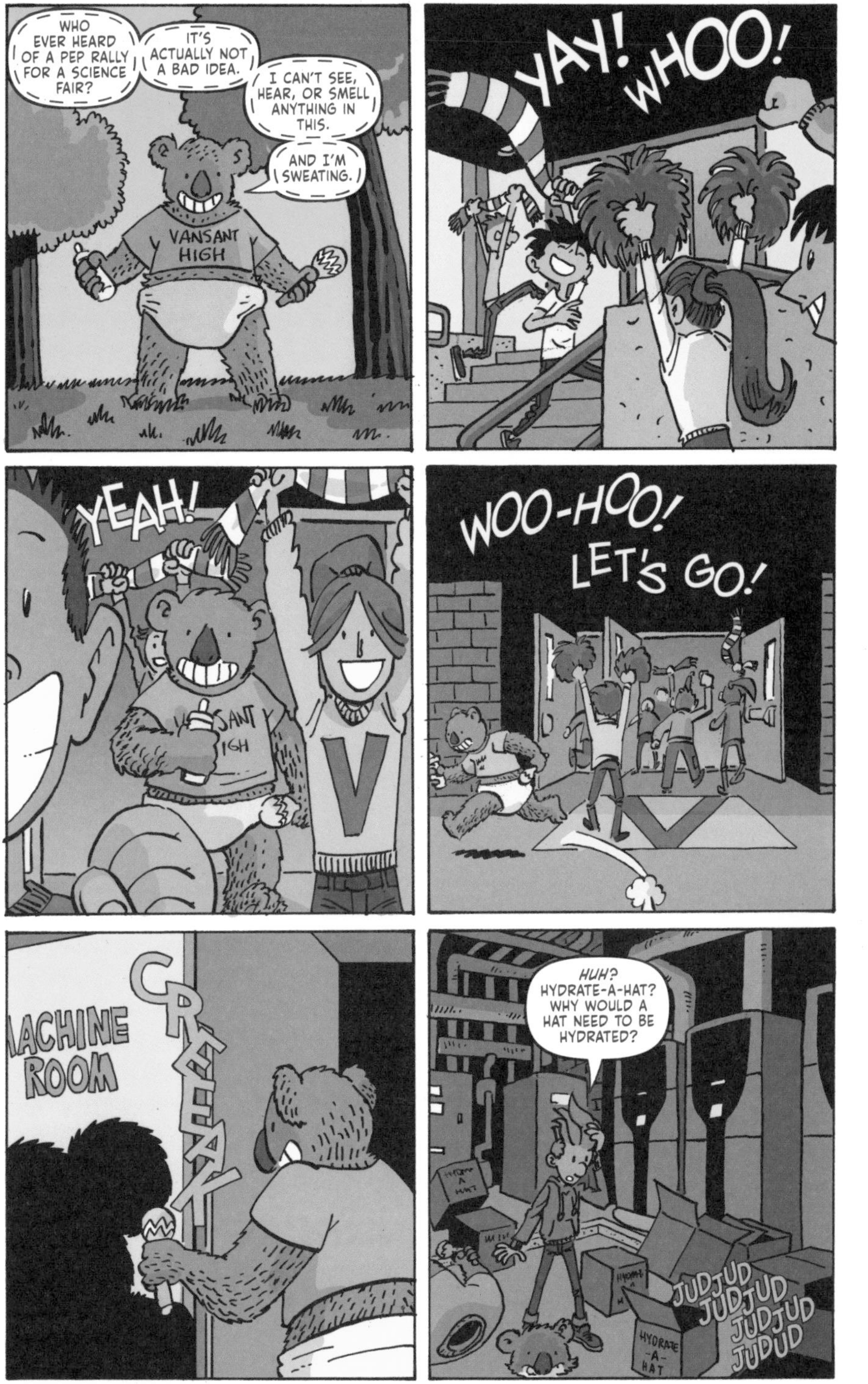
WHO EVER HEARD OF A PEP RALLY FOR A SCIENCE FAIR?
IT'S ACTUALLY NOT A BAD IDEA.
I CAN'T SEE, HEAR, OR SMELL ANYTHING IN THIS.
AND I'M SWEATING.
VANSANT HIGH
YAY!
WHOO!
YEAH!
V
WOO-HOO!
LET'S GO!
MACHINE ROOM
CREEAK
HUH? HYDRATE-A-HAT? WHY WOULD A HAT NEED TO BE HYDRATED?
HYDRATE -A- HAT
JUDJUD JUDJUD JUDJUD JUDUD

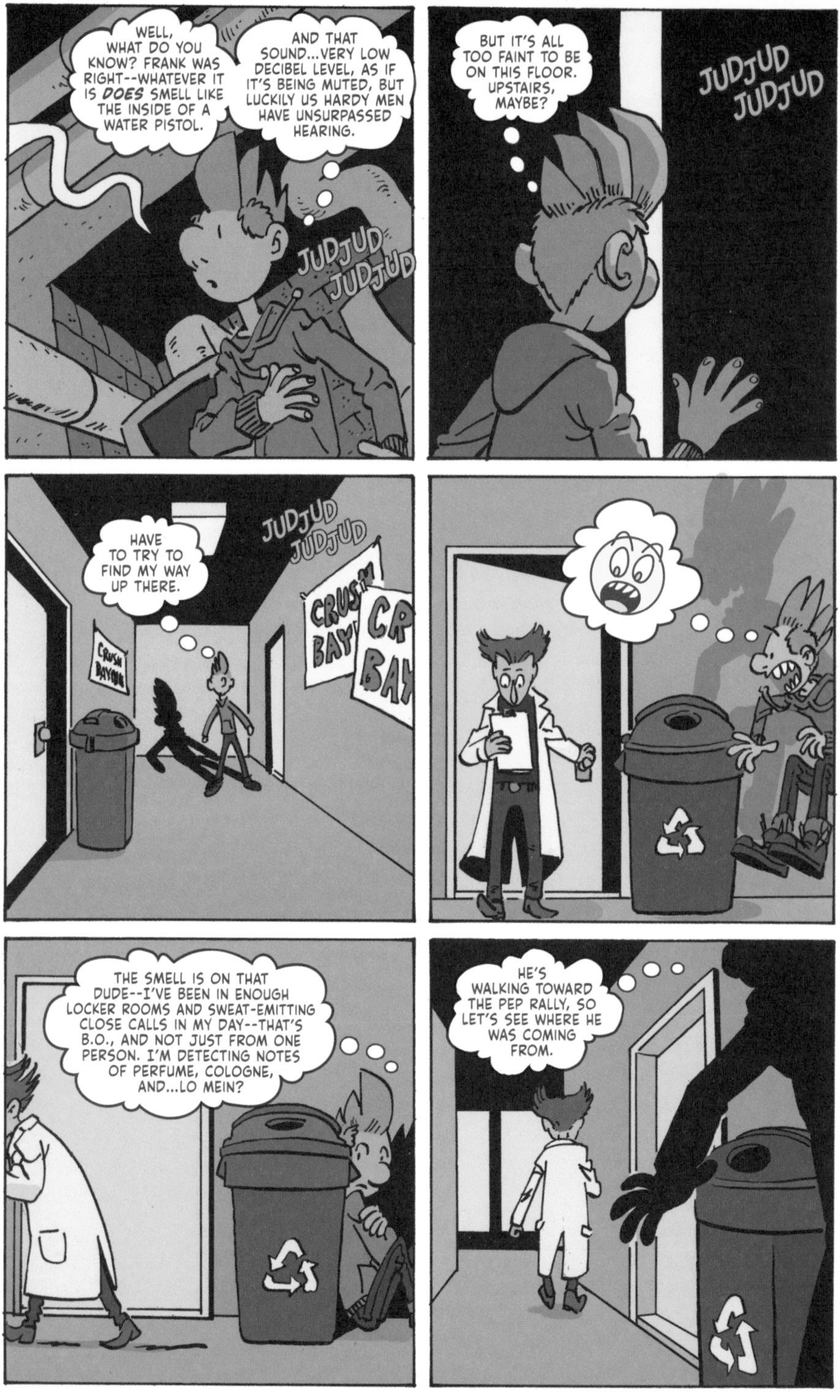
WELL, WHAT DO YOU KNOW? FRANK WAS RIGHT--WHATEVER IT IS **DOES** SMELL LIKE THE INSIDE OF A WATER PISTOL.
AND THAT SOUND...VERY LOW DECIBEL LEVEL, AS IF IT'S BEING MUTED, BUT LUCKILY US HARDY MEN HAVE UNSURPASSED HEARING.
JUDJUD JUDJUD
BUT IT'S ALL TOO FAINT TO BE ON THIS FLOOR. UPSTAIRS, MAYBE?
JUDJUD JUDJUD
HAVE TO TRY TO FIND MY WAY UP THERE.
JUDJUD JUDJUD
CRUSH BAYOU
THE SMELL IS ON THAT DUDE--I'VE BEEN IN ENOUGH LOCKER ROOMS AND SWEAT-EMITTING CLOSE CALLS IN MY DAY--THAT'S B.O., AND NOT JUST FROM ONE PERSON. I'M DETECTING NOTES OF PERFUME, COLOGNE, AND...LO MEIN?
HE'S WALKING TOWARD THE PEP RALLY, SO LET'S SEE WHERE HE WAS COMING FROM.

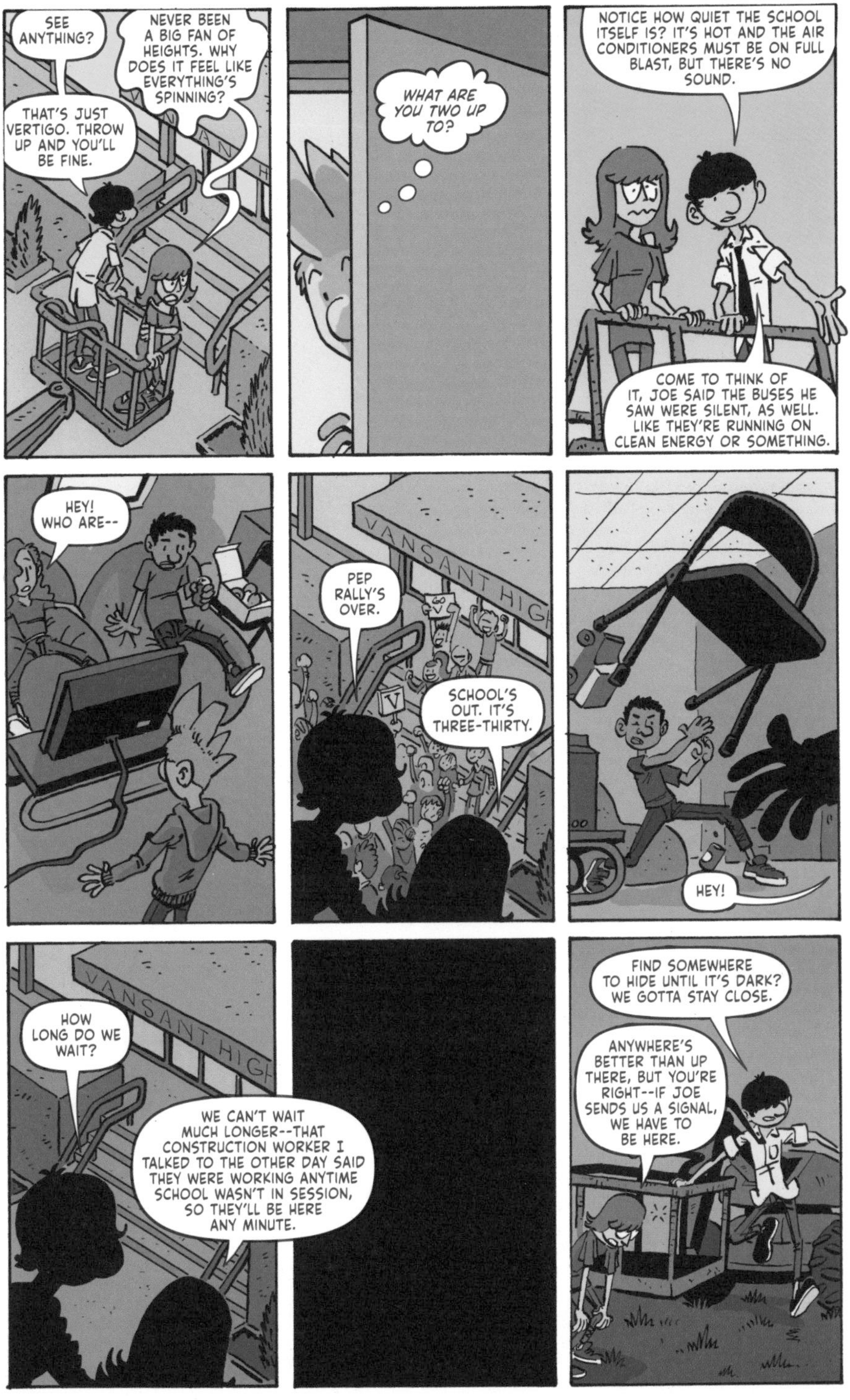
SEE ANYTHING?
NEVER BEEN A BIG FAN OF HEIGHTS. WHY DOES IT FEEL LIKE EVERYTHING'S SPINNING?
THAT'S JUST VERTIGO. THROW UP AND YOU'LL BE FINE.
WHAT ARE YOU TWO UP TO?
NOTICE HOW QUIET THE SCHOOL ITSELF IS? IT'S HOT AND THE AIR CONDITIONERS MUST BE ON FULL BLAST, BUT THERE'S NO SOUND.
COME TO THINK OF IT, JOE SAID THE BUSES HE SAW WERE SILENT, AS WELL. LIKE THEY'RE RUNNING ON CLEAN ENERGY OR SOMETHING.
HEY! WHO ARE--
VANSANT HIGH
PEP RALLY'S OVER.
SCHOOL'S OUT. IT'S THREE-THIRTY.
HEY!
VANSANT HIGH
HOW LONG DO WE WAIT?
WE CAN'T WAIT MUCH LONGER--THAT CONSTRUCTION WORKER I TALKED TO THE OTHER DAY SAID THEY WERE WORKING ANYTIME SCHOOL WASN'T IN SESSION, SO THEY'LL BE HERE ANY MINUTE.
FIND SOMEWHERE TO HIDE UNTIL IT'S DARK? WE GOTTA STAY CLOSE.
ANYWHERE'S BETTER THAN UP THERE, BUT YOU'RE RIGHT--IF JOE SENDS US A SIGNAL, WE HAVE TO BE HERE.

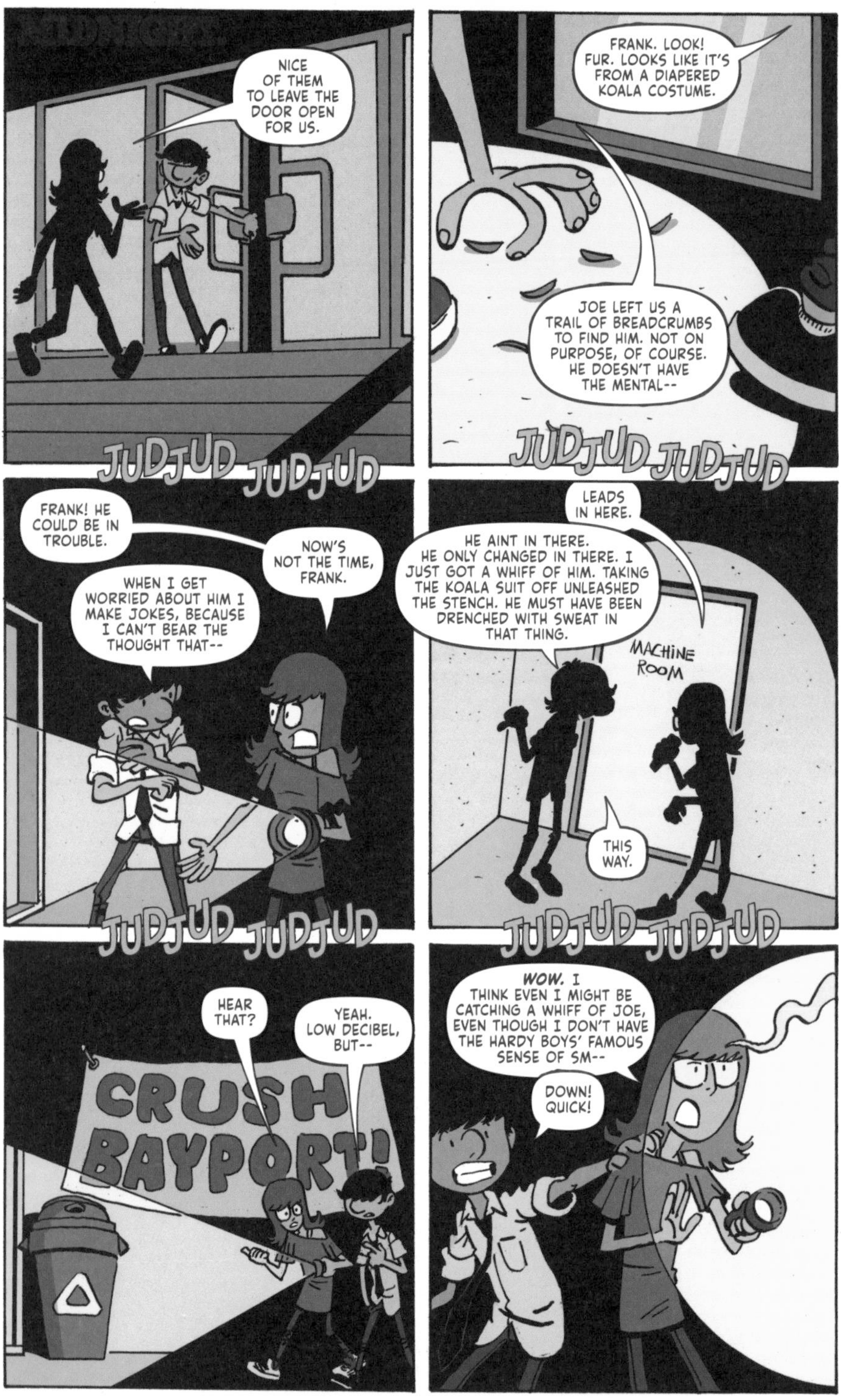
NICE OF THEM TO LEAVE THE DOOR OPEN FOR US.
JUDJUD JUDJUD
FRANK. LOOK! FUR. LOOKS LIKE IT'S FROM A DIAPERED KOALA COSTUME.
JOE LEFT US A TRAIL OF BREADCRUMBS TO FIND HIM. NOT ON PURPOSE, OF COURSE. HE DOESN'T HAVE THE MENTAL--
JUDJUD JUDJUD
FRANK! HE COULD BE IN TROUBLE.
NOW'S NOT THE TIME, FRANK.
WHEN I GET WORRIED ABOUT HIM I MAKE JOKES, BECAUSE I CAN'T BEAR THE THOUGHT THAT--
JUDJUD JUDJUD
LEADS IN HERE.
HE AINT IN THERE. HE ONLY CHANGED IN THERE. I JUST GOT A WHIFF OF HIM. TAKING THE KOALA SUIT OFF UNLEASHED THE STENCH. HE MUST HAVE BEEN DRENCHED WITH SWEAT IN THAT THING.
MACHINE ROOM
THIS WAY.
JUDJUD JUDJUD
HEAR THAT?
YEAH. LOW DECIBEL, BUT--
CRUSH BAYPORT!
WOW. I THINK EVEN I MIGHT BE CATCHING A WHIFF OF JOE, EVEN THOUGH I DON'T HAVE THE HARDY BOYS' FAMOUS SENSE OF SM--
DOWN! QUICK!

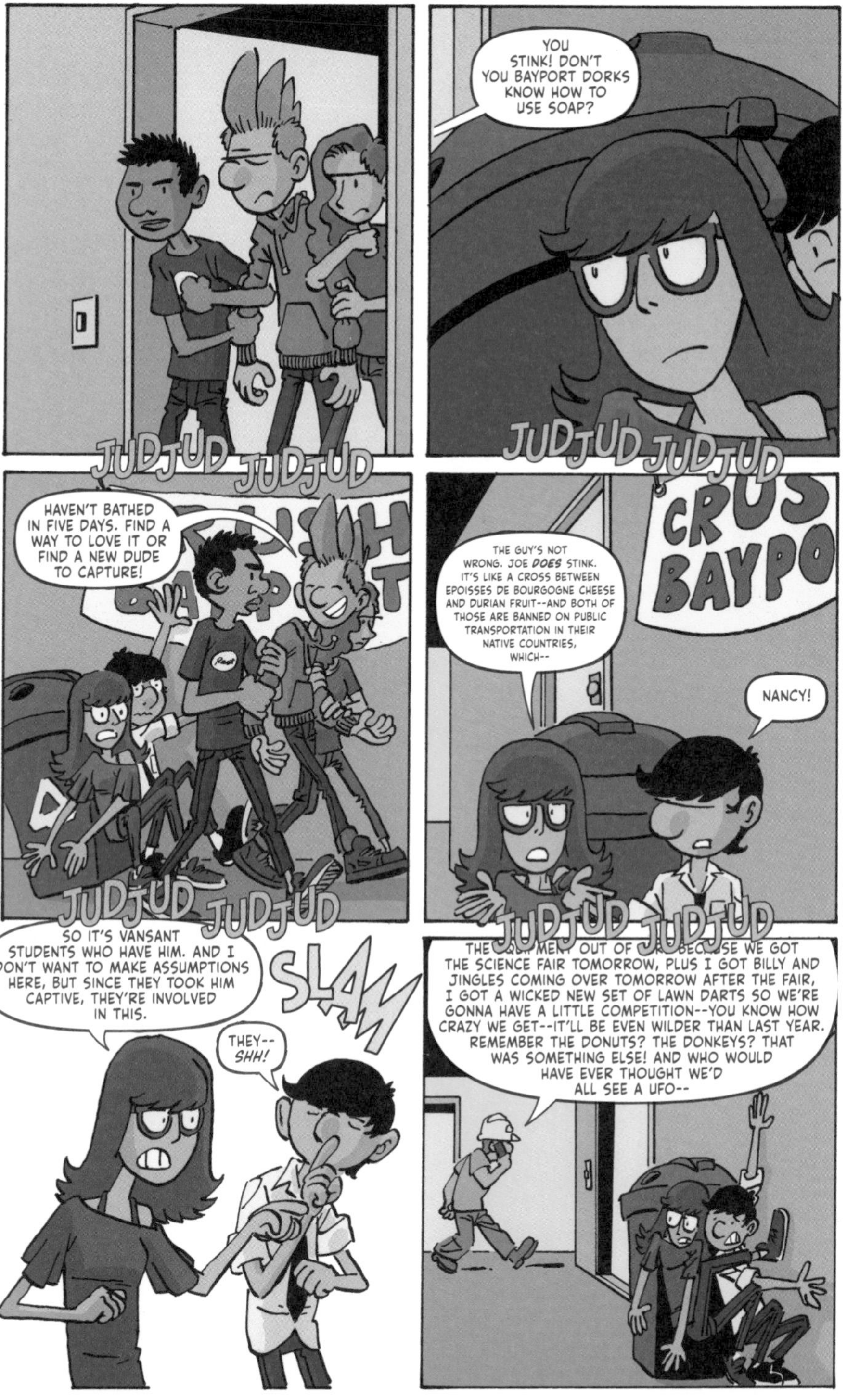
YOU STINK! DON'T YOU BAYPORT DORKS KNOW HOW TO USE SOAP?
JUDJUD JUDJUD
JUDJUD JUDJUD
HAVEN'T BATHED IN FIVE DAYS. FIND A WAY TO LOVE IT OR FIND A NEW DUDE TO CAPTURE!
CRUS
BAYPO
THE GUY'S NOT WRONG. JOE **DOES** STINK. IT'S LIKE A CROSS BETWEEN EPOISSES DE BOURGOGNE CHEESE AND DURIAN FRUIT--AND BOTH OF THOSE ARE BANNED ON PUBLIC TRANSPORTATION IN THEIR NATIVE COUNTRIES, WHICH--
NANCY!
JUDJUD JUDJUD
JUDJUD JUDJUD
SO IT'S VANSANT STUDENTS WHO HAVE HIM. AND I DON'T WANT TO MAKE ASSUMPTIONS HERE, BUT SINCE THEY TOOK HIM CAPTIVE, THEY'RE INVOLVED IN THIS.
SLAM
THEY-- *SHH!*
THE SCIENCE FAIR TOMORROW, PLUS I GOT BILLY AND JINGLES COMING OVER TOMORROW AFTER THE FAIR, I GOT A WICKED NEW SET OF LAWN DARTS SO WE'RE GONNA HAVE A LITTLE COMPETITION--YOU KNOW HOW CRAZY WE GET--IT'LL BE EVEN WILDER THAN LAST YEAR. REMEMBER THE DONUTS? THE DONKEYS? THAT WAS SOMETHING ELSE! AND WHO WOULD HAVE EVER THOUGHT WE'D ALL SEE A UFO--

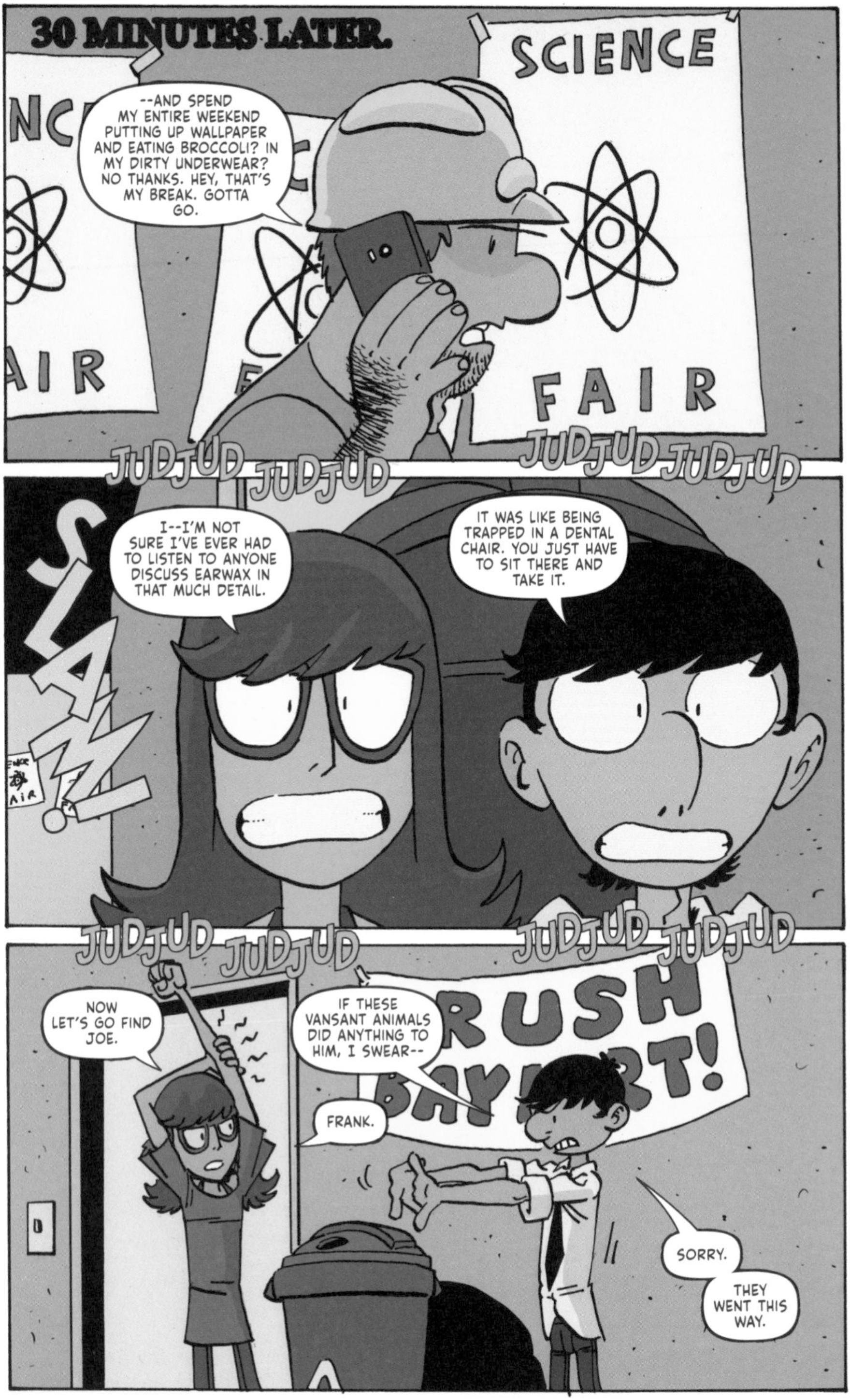
30 MINUTES LATER.
SCIENCE
--AND SPEND MY ENTIRE WEEKEND PUTTING UP WALLPAPER AND EATING BROCCOLI? IN MY DIRTY UNDERWEAR? NO THANKS. HEY, THAT'S MY BREAK. GOTTA GO.
FAIR
JUDJUD JUDJUD JUDJUD JUDJUD
SLAM!
I--I'M NOT SURE I'VE EVER HAD TO LISTEN TO ANYONE DISCUSS EARWAX IN THAT MUCH DETAIL.
IT WAS LIKE BEING TRAPPED IN A DENTAL CHAIR. YOU JUST HAVE TO SIT THERE AND TAKE IT.
JUDJUD JUDJUD JUDJUD JUDJUD
NOW LET'S GO FIND JOE.
IF THESE VANSANT ANIMALS DID ANYTHING TO HIM, I SWEAR--
FRANK.
SORRY.
THEY WENT THIS WAY.

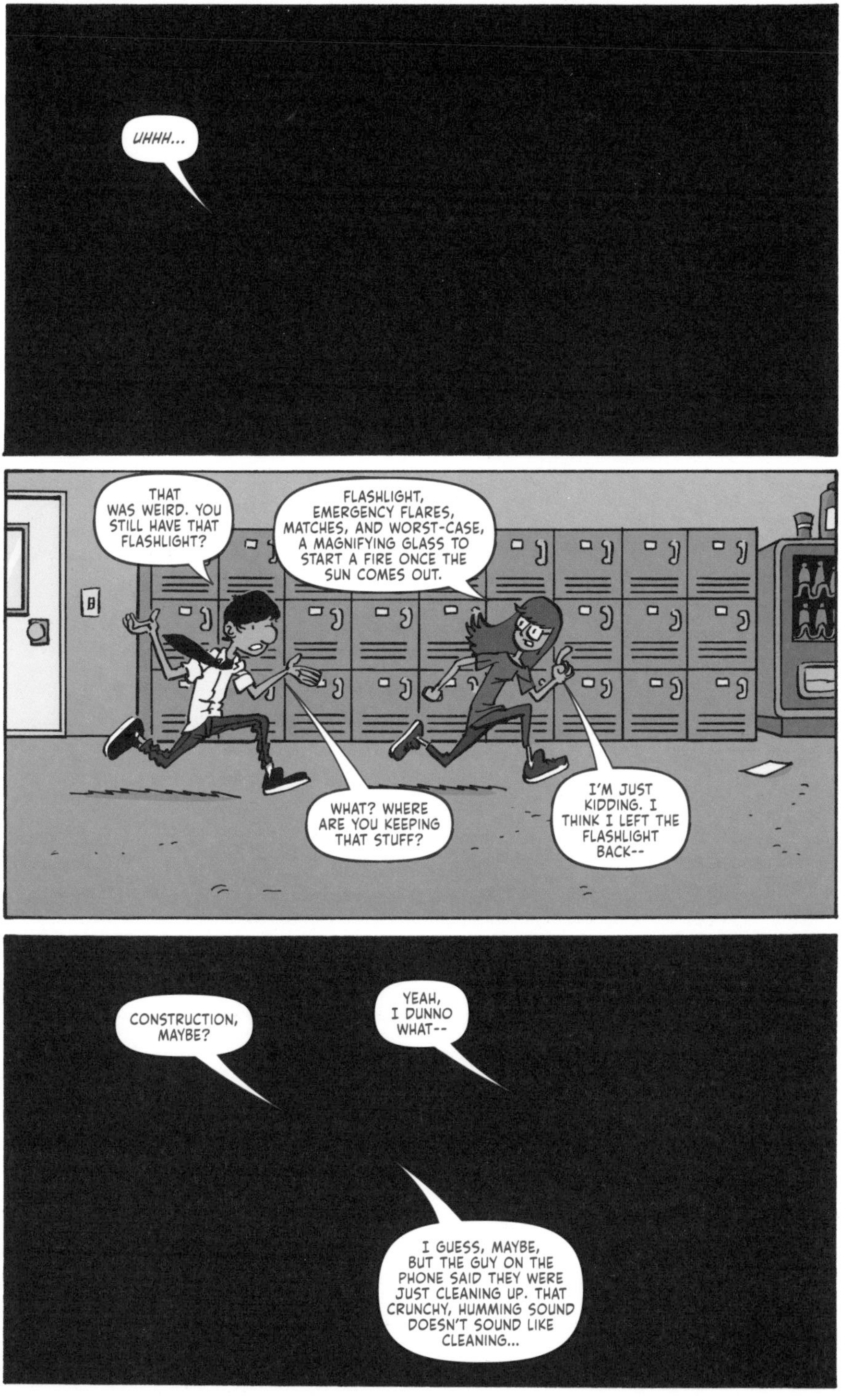
UHHH...
THAT WAS WEIRD. YOU STILL HAVE THAT FLASHLIGHT?
FLASHLIGHT, EMERGENCY FLARES, MATCHES, AND WORST-CASE, A MAGNIFYING GLASS TO START A FIRE ONCE THE SUN COMES OUT.
WHAT? WHERE ARE YOU KEEPING THAT STUFF?
I'M JUST KIDDING. I THINK I LEFT THE FLASHLIGHT BACK--
B
CONSTRUCTION, MAYBE?
YEAH, I DUNNO WHAT--
I GUESS, MAYBE, BUT THE GUY ON THE PHONE SAID THEY WERE JUST CLEANING UP. THAT CRUNCHY, HUMMING SOUND DOESN'T SOUND LIKE CLEANING...

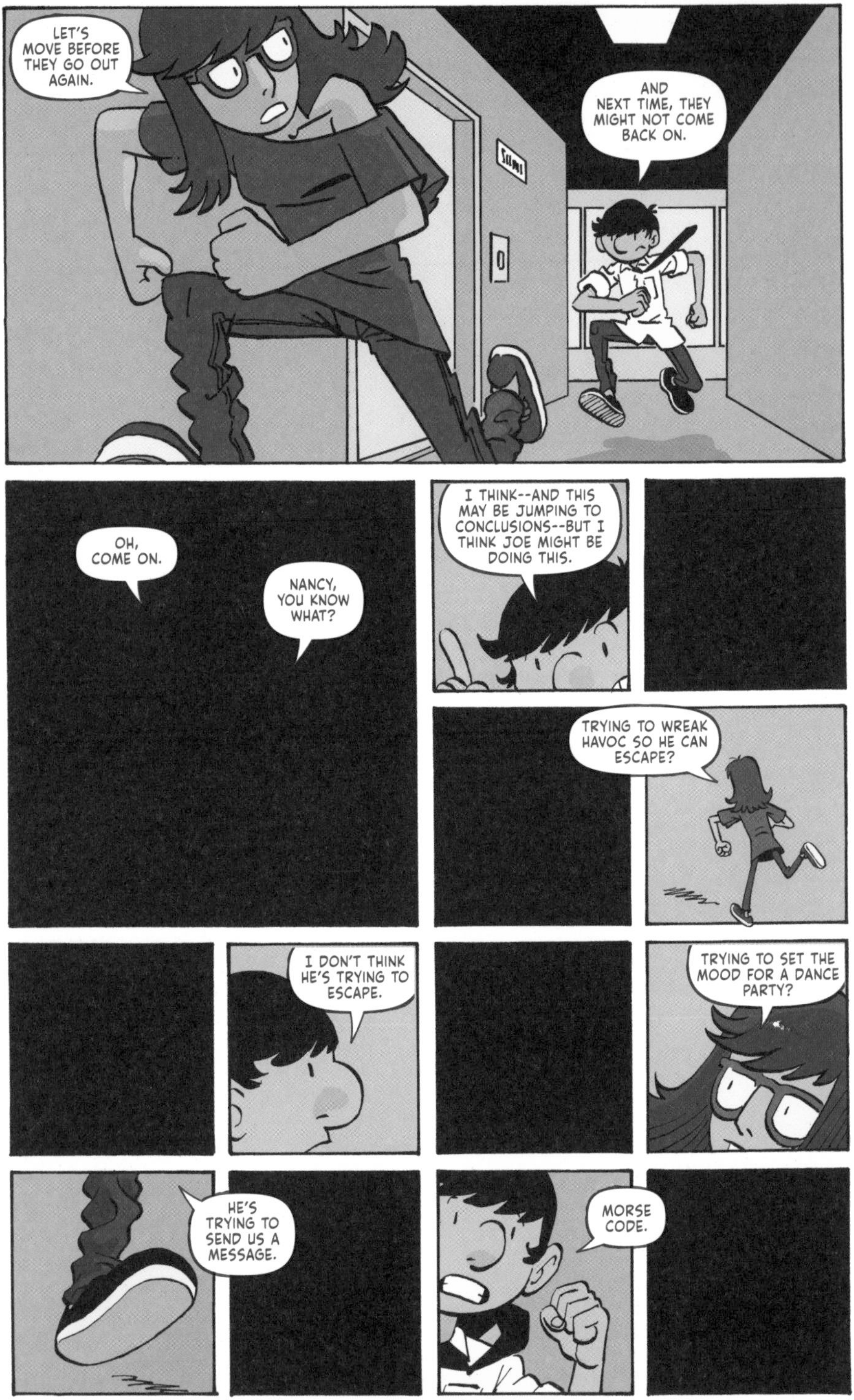
LET'S MOVE BEFORE THEY GO OUT AGAIN.
AND NEXT TIME, THEY MIGHT NOT COME BACK ON.
OH, COME ON.
NANCY, YOU KNOW WHAT?
I THINK--AND THIS MAY BE JUMPING TO CONCLUSIONS--BUT I THINK JOE MIGHT BE DOING THIS.
TRYING TO WREAK HAVOC SO HE CAN ESCAPE?
I DON'T THINK HE'S TRYING TO ESCAPE.
TRYING TO SET THE MOOD FOR A DANCE PARTY?
HE'S TRYING TO SEND US A MESSAGE.
MORSE CODE.

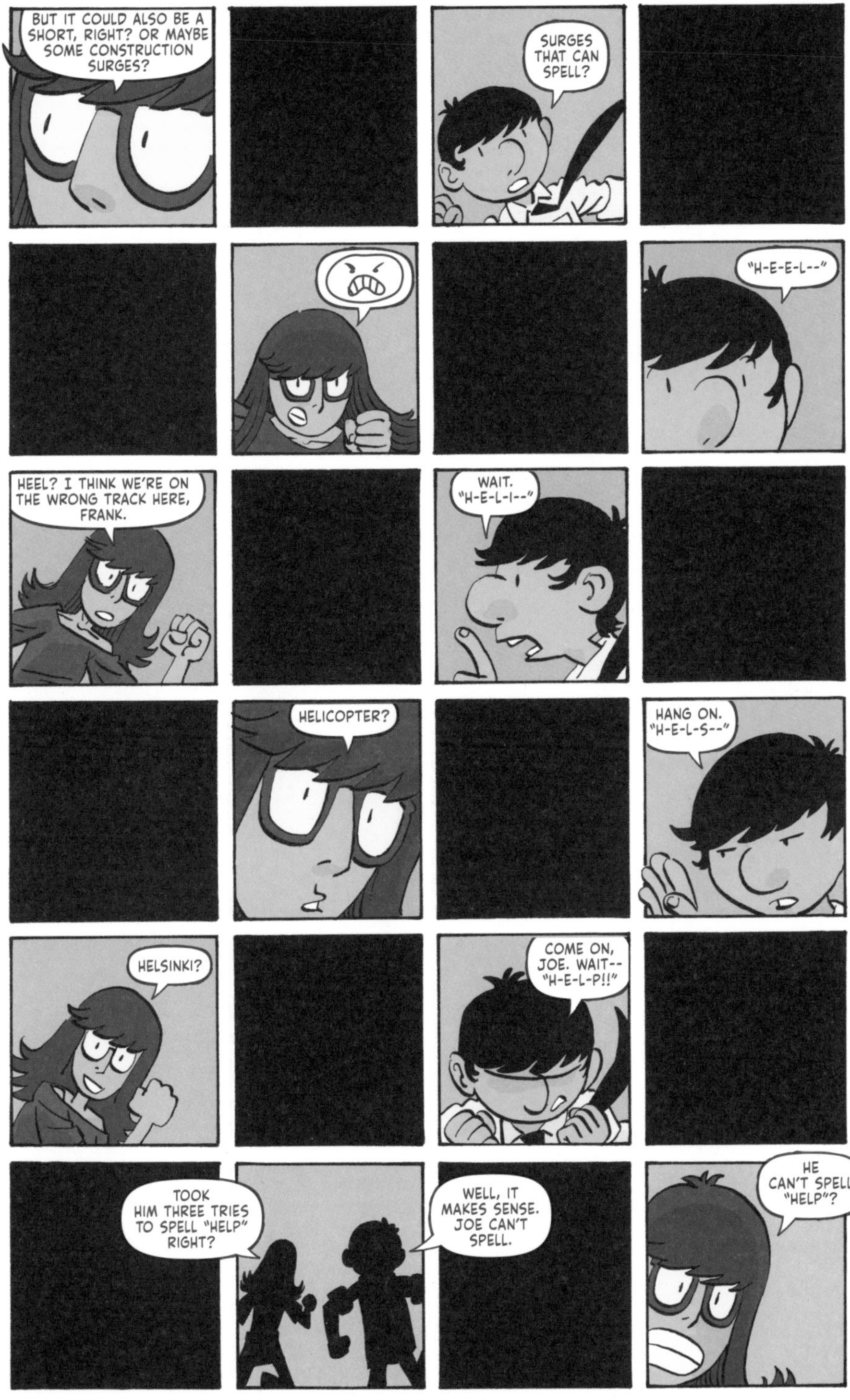
BUT IT COULD ALSO BE A SHORT, RIGHT? OR MAYBE SOME CONSTRUCTION SURGES?
SURGES THAT CAN SPELL?
"H-E-E-L--"
HEEL? I THINK WE'RE ON THE WRONG TRACK HERE, FRANK.
WAIT. "H-E-L-I--"
HELICOPTER?
HANG ON. "H-E-L-S--"
HELSINKI?
COME ON, JOE. WAIT-- "H-E-L-P!!"
TOOK HIM THREE TRIES TO SPELL "HELP" RIGHT?
WELL, IT MAKES SENSE. JOE CAN'T SPELL.
HE CAN'T SPELL "HELP"?

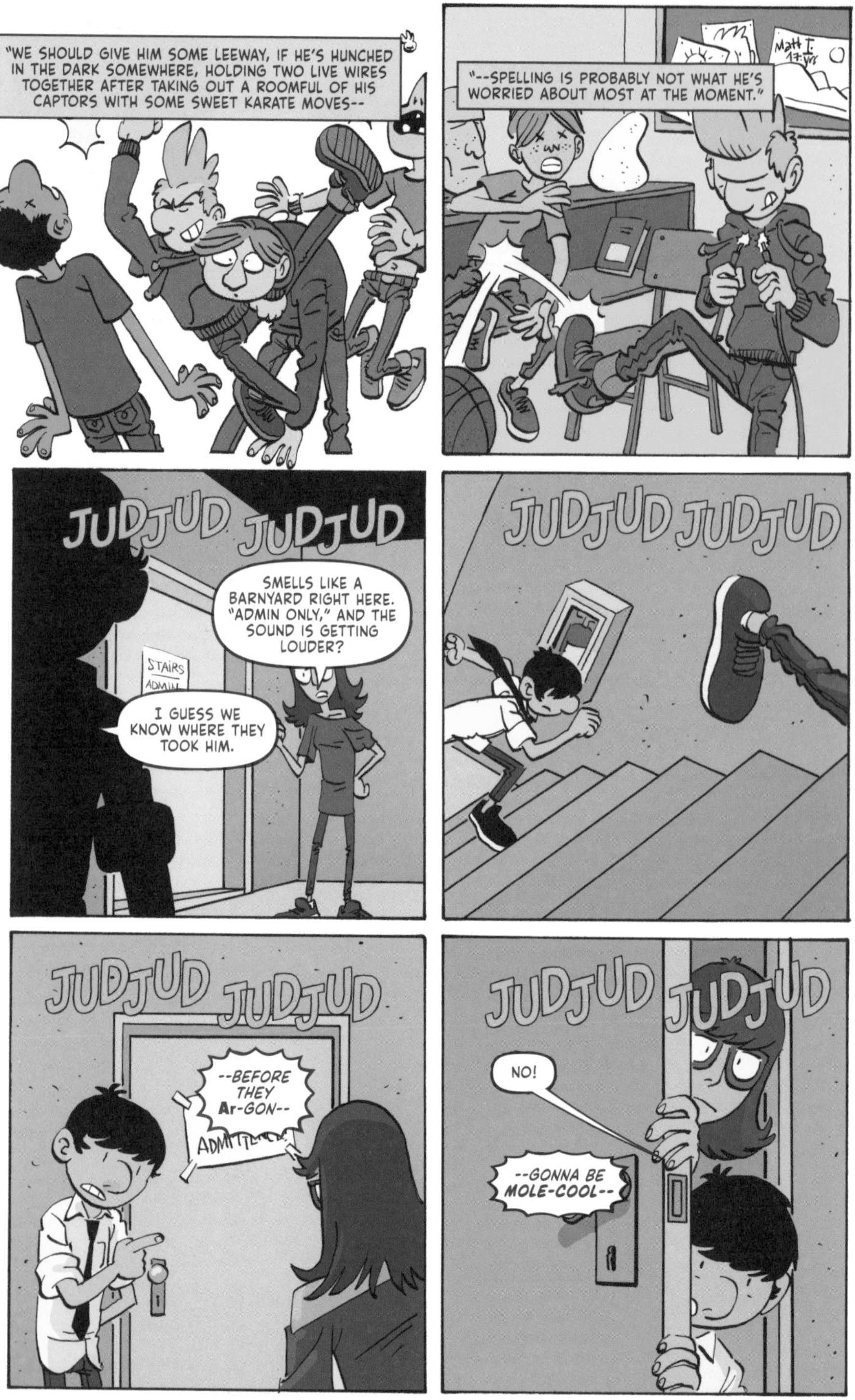
"WE SHOULD GIVE HIM SOME LEEWAY, IF HE'S HUNCHED IN THE DARK SOMEWHERE, HOLDING TWO LIVE WIRES TOGETHER AFTER TAKING OUT A ROOMFUL OF HIS CAPTORS WITH SOME SWEET KARATE MOVES--
"--SPELLING IS PROBABLY NOT WHAT HE'S WORRIED ABOUT MOST AT THE MOMENT."
Matt I. 17 yrs
JUDJUD JUDJUD
SMELLS LIKE A BARNYARD RIGHT HERE. "ADMIN ONLY," AND THE SOUND IS GETTING LOUDER?
STAIRS
ADMIN
I GUESS WE KNOW WHERE THEY TOOK HIM.
JUDJUD JUDJUD
JUDJUD JUDJUD
--BEFORE THEY Ar-GON--
JUDJUD JUDJUD
NO!
--GONNA BE MOLE-COOL--

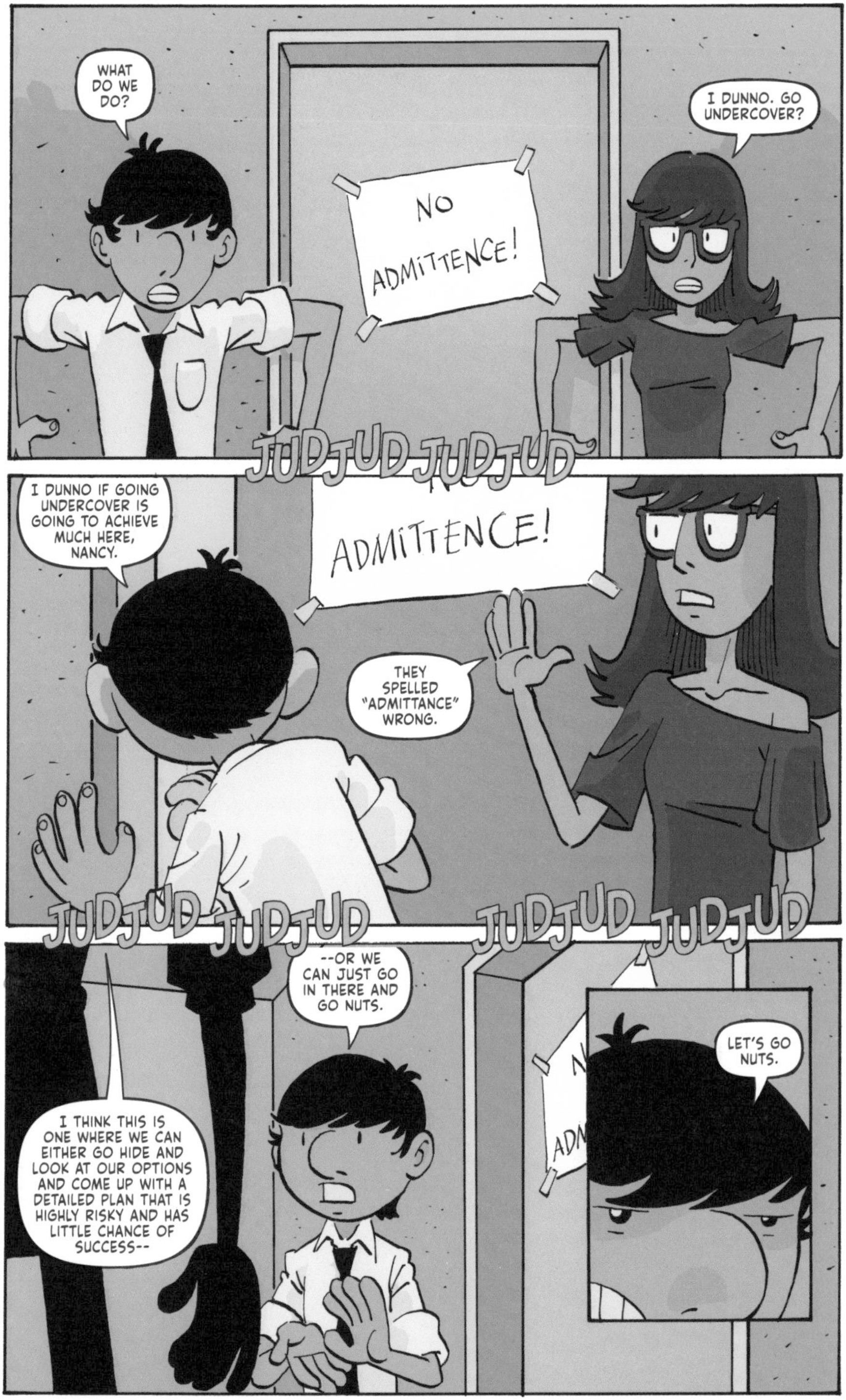
WHAT DO WE DO?
NO ADMITTENCE!
I DUNNO. GO UNDERCOVER?
JUDJUD JUDJUD
I DUNNO IF GOING UNDERCOVER IS GOING TO ACHIEVE MUCH HERE, NANCY.
ADMITTENCE!
THEY SPELLED "ADMITTANCE" WRONG.
JUDJUD JUDJUD JUDJUD JUDJUD
I THINK THIS IS ONE WHERE WE CAN EITHER GO HIDE AND LOOK AT OUR OPTIONS AND COME UP WITH A DETAILED PLAN THAT IS HIGHLY RISKY AND HAS LITTLE CHANCE OF SUCCESS--
--OR WE CAN JUST GO IN THERE AND GO NUTS.
LET'S GO NUTS.

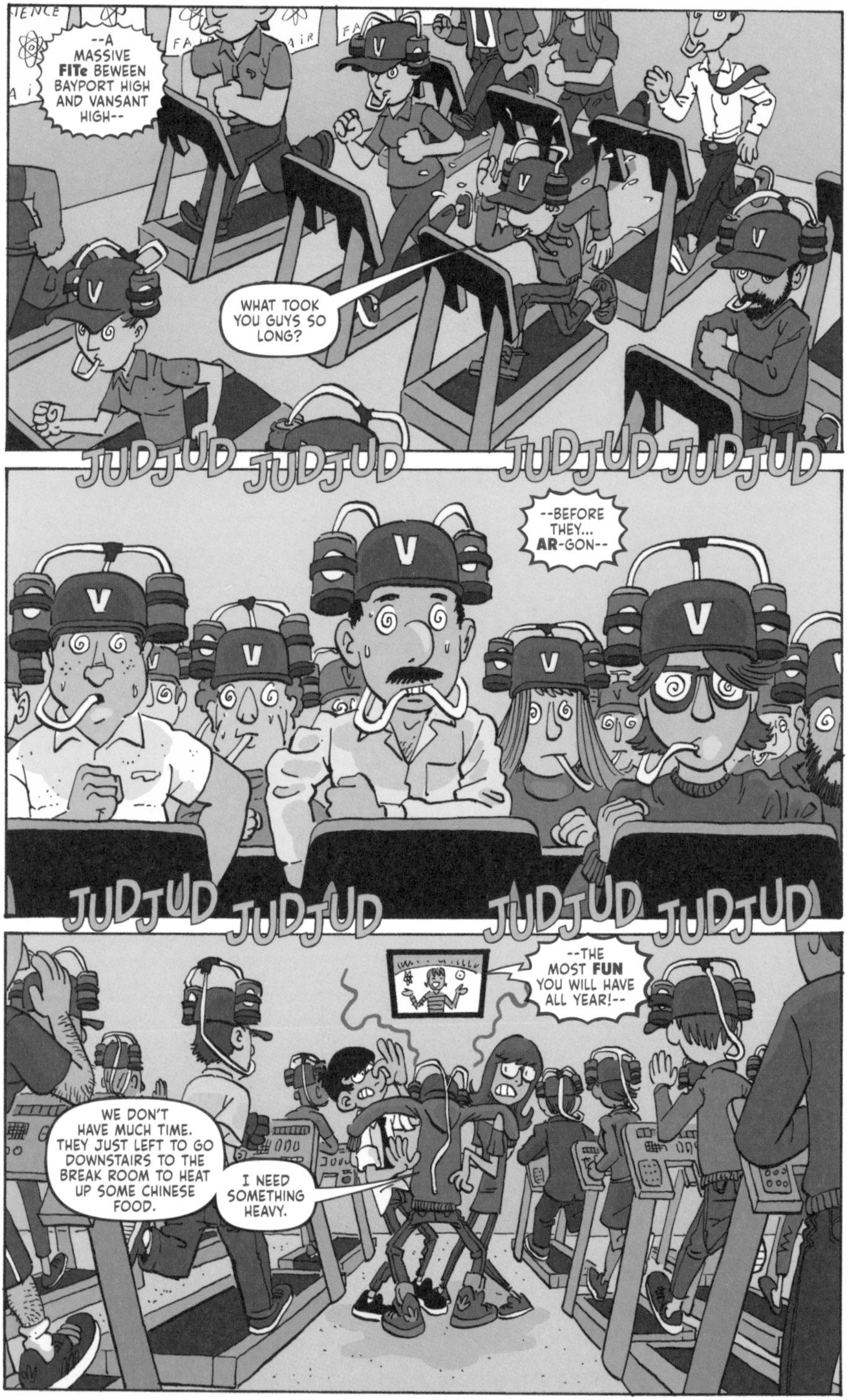
--A MASSIVE FITe BEWEEN BAYPORT HIGH AND VANSANT HIGH--
WHAT TOOK YOU GUYS SO LONG?
JUDJUD JUDJUD JUDJUD JUDJUD
--BEFORE THEY... AR-GON--
JUDJUD JUDJUD JUDJUD JUDJUD
--THE MOST FUN YOU WILL HAVE ALL YEAR!--
WE DON'T HAVE MUCH TIME. THEY JUST LEFT TO GO DOWNSTAIRS TO THE BREAK ROOM TO HEAT UP SOME CHINESE FOOD.
I NEED SOMETHING HEAVY.

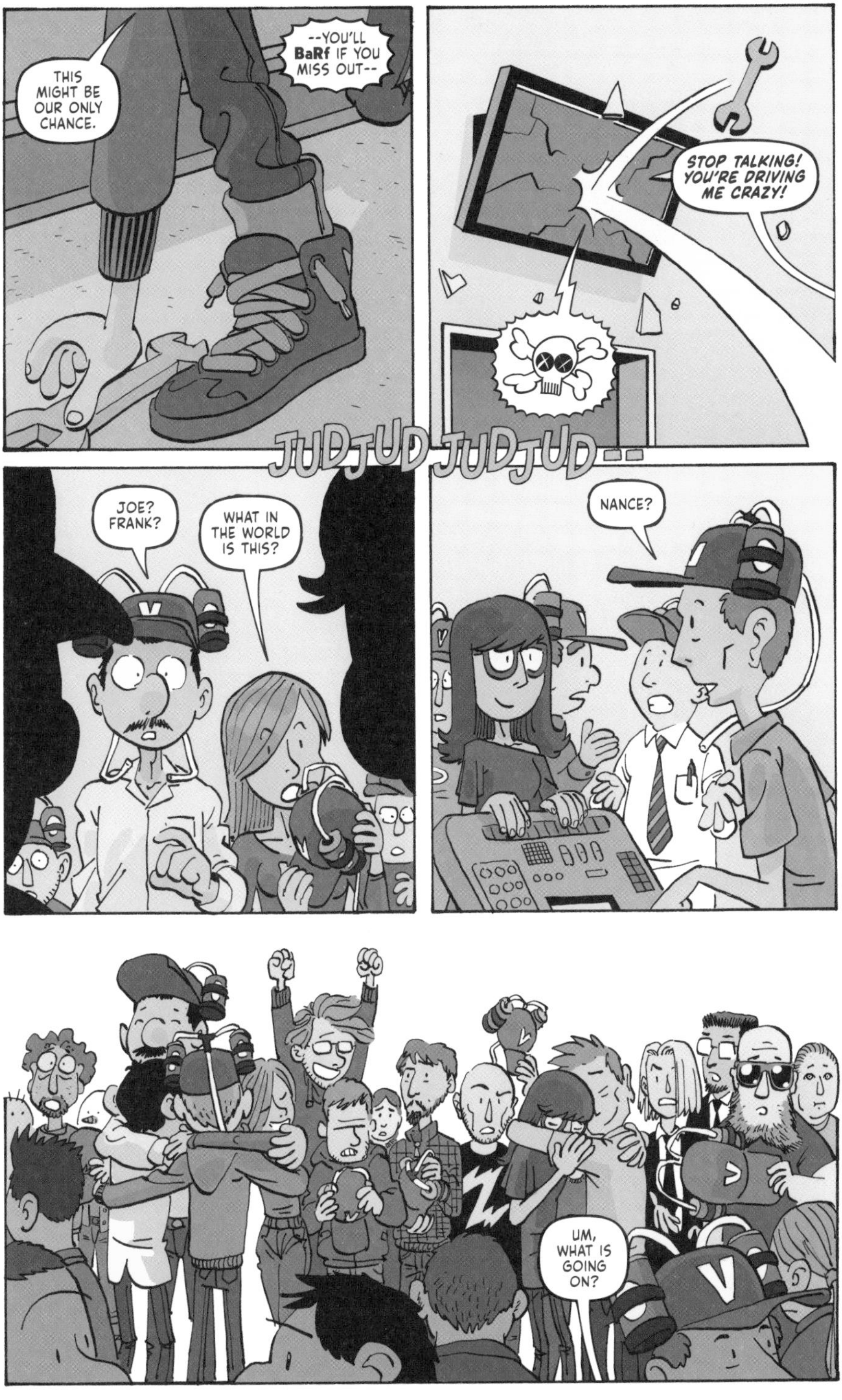
THIS MIGHT BE OUR ONLY CHANCE.
--YOU'LL BaRf IF YOU MISS OUT--
STOP TALKING! YOU'RE DRIVING ME CRAZY!
JUDJUD JUDJUD..
JOE? FRANK?
WHAT IN THE WORLD IS THIS?
NANCE?
UM, WHAT IS GOING ON?

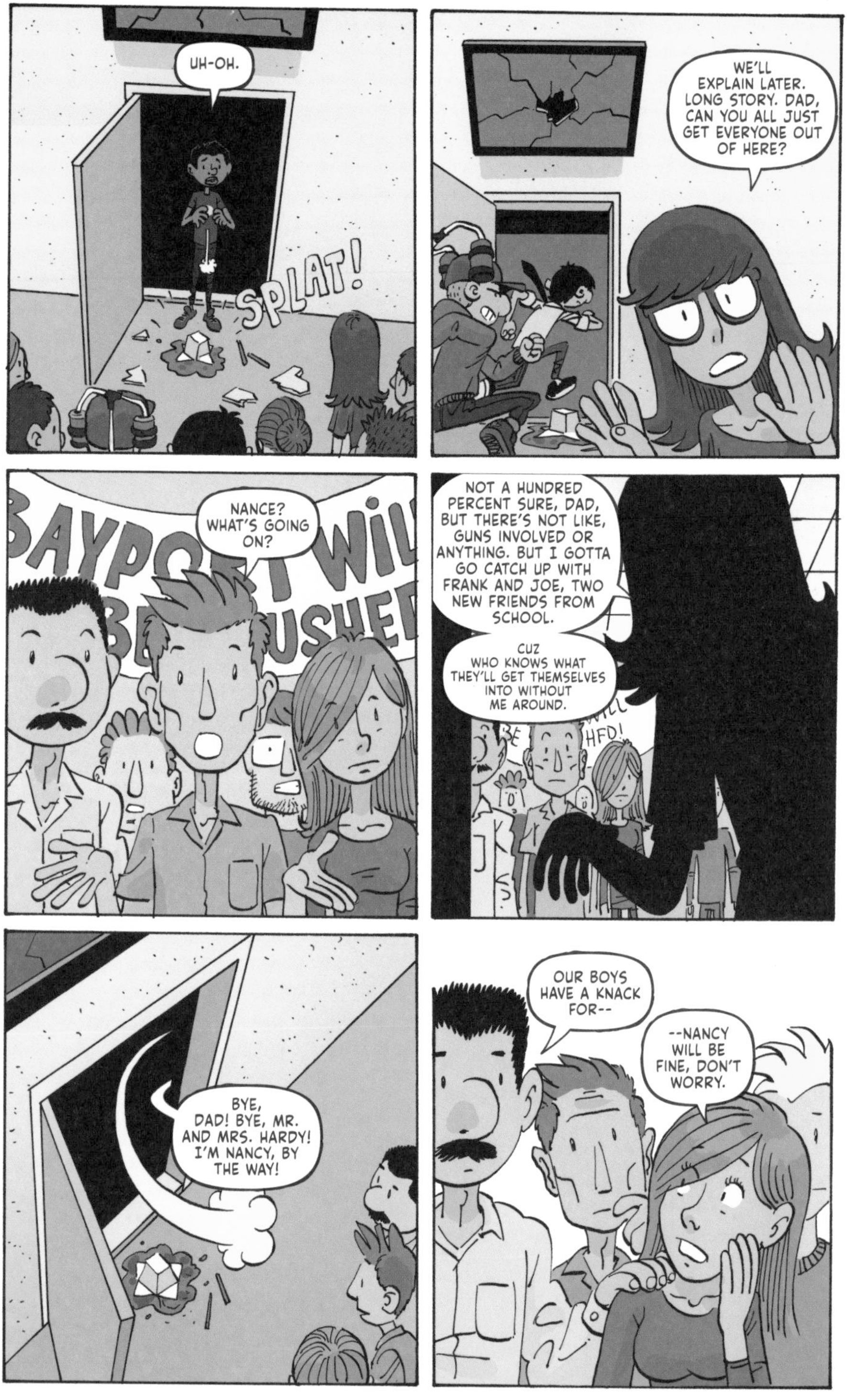
UH-OH.
SPLAT!
WE'LL EXPLAIN LATER. LONG STORY. DAD, CAN YOU ALL JUST GET EVERYONE OUT OF HERE?
NANCE? WHAT'S GOING ON?
NOT A HUNDRED PERCENT SURE, DAD, BUT THERE'S NOT LIKE, GUNS INVOLVED OR ANYTHING. BUT I GOTTA GO CATCH UP WITH FRANK AND JOE, TWO NEW FRIENDS FROM SCHOOL.
CUZ WHO KNOWS WHAT THEY'LL GET THEMSELVES INTO WITHOUT ME AROUND.
BYE, DAD! BYE, MR. AND MRS. HARDY! I'M NANCY, BY THE WAY!
OUR BOYS HAVE A KNACK FOR--
--NANCY WILL BE FINE, DON'T WORRY.

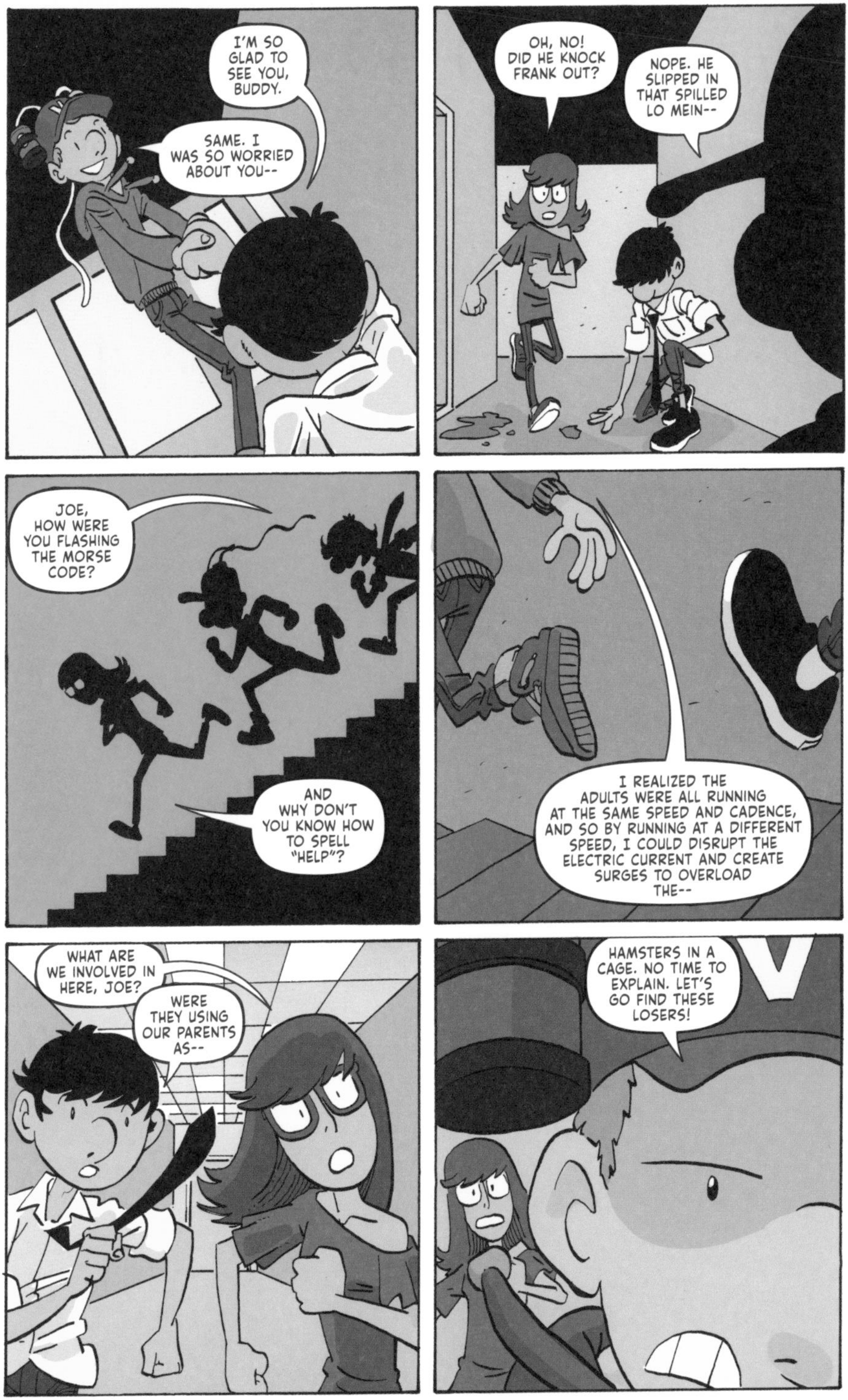
I'M SO GLAD TO SEE YOU, BUDDY.
SAME. I WAS SO WORRIED ABOUT YOU--
OH, NO! DID HE KNOCK FRANK OUT?
NOPE. HE SLIPPED IN THAT SPILLED LO MEIN--
JOE, HOW WERE YOU FLASHING THE MORSE CODE?
AND WHY DON'T YOU KNOW HOW TO SPELL "HELP"?
I REALIZED THE ADULTS WERE ALL RUNNING AT THE SAME SPEED AND CADENCE, AND SO BY RUNNING AT A DIFFERENT SPEED, I COULD DISRUPT THE ELECTRIC CURRENT AND CREATE SURGES TO OVERLOAD THE--
WHAT ARE WE INVOLVED IN HERE, JOE?
WERE THEY USING OUR PARENTS AS--
HAMSTERS IN A CAGE. NO TIME TO EXPLAIN. LET'S GO FIND THESE LOSERS!

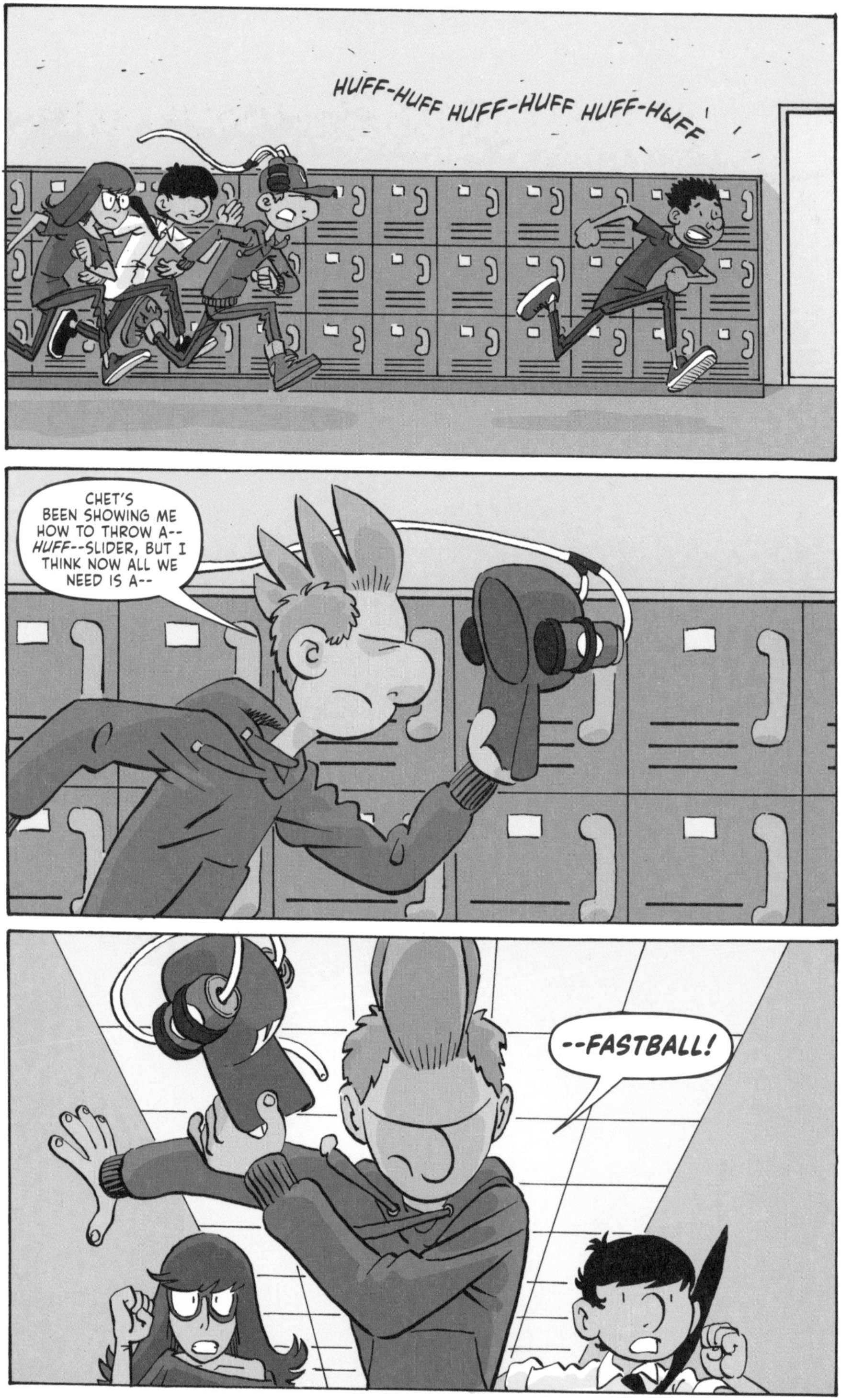
HUFF-HUFF HUFF-HUFF HUFF-HUFF
CHET'S BEEN SHOWING ME HOW TO THROW A-- *HUFF*--SLIDER, BUT I THINK NOW ALL WE NEED IS A--
--FASTBALL!

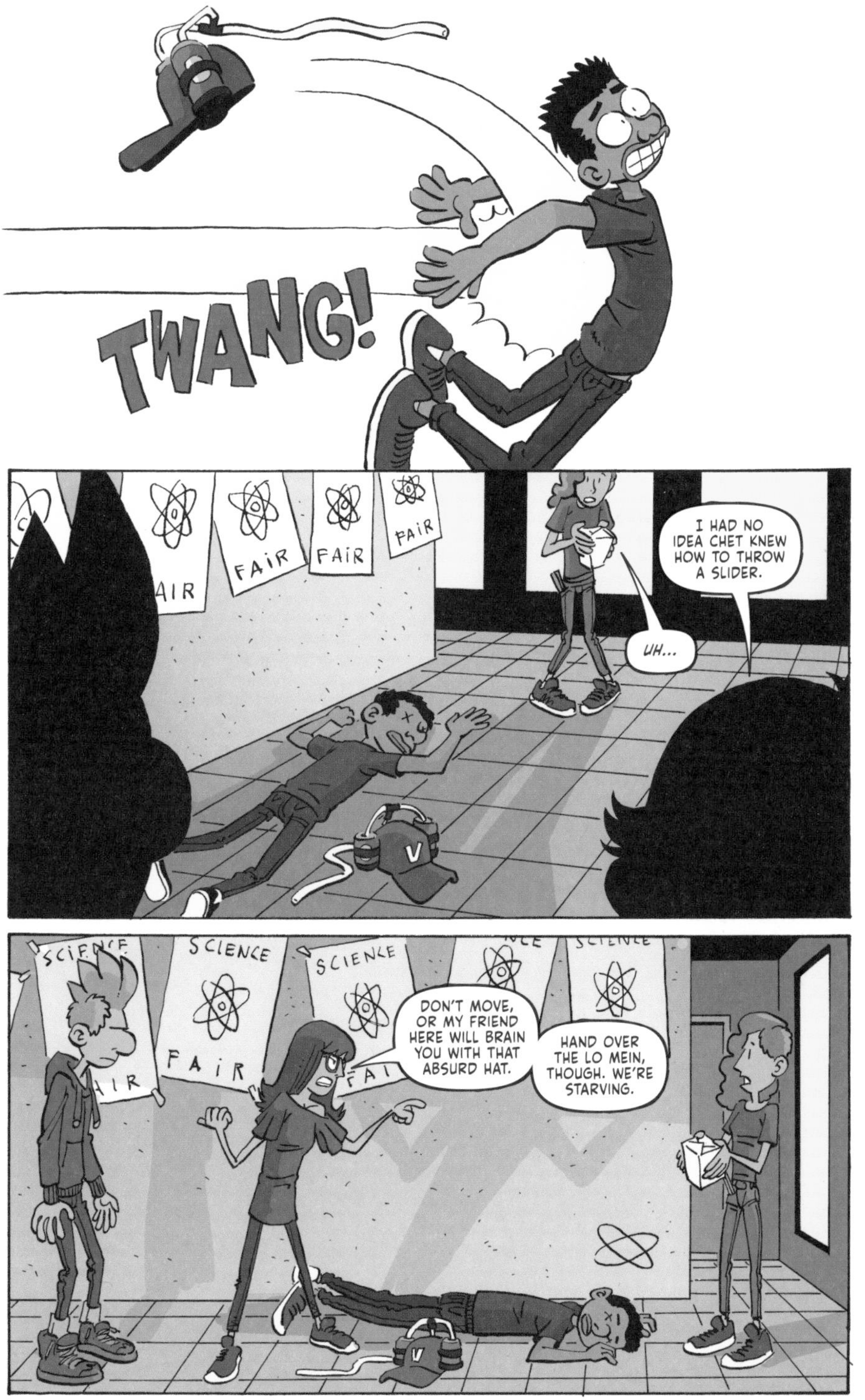
TWANG!
SCIENCE
FAIR
UH...
I HAD NO IDEA CHET KNEW HOW TO THROW A SLIDER.
DON'T MOVE, OR MY FRIEND HERE WILL BRAIN YOU WITH THAT ABSURD HAT.
HAND OVER THE LO MEIN, THOUGH. WE'RE STARVING.

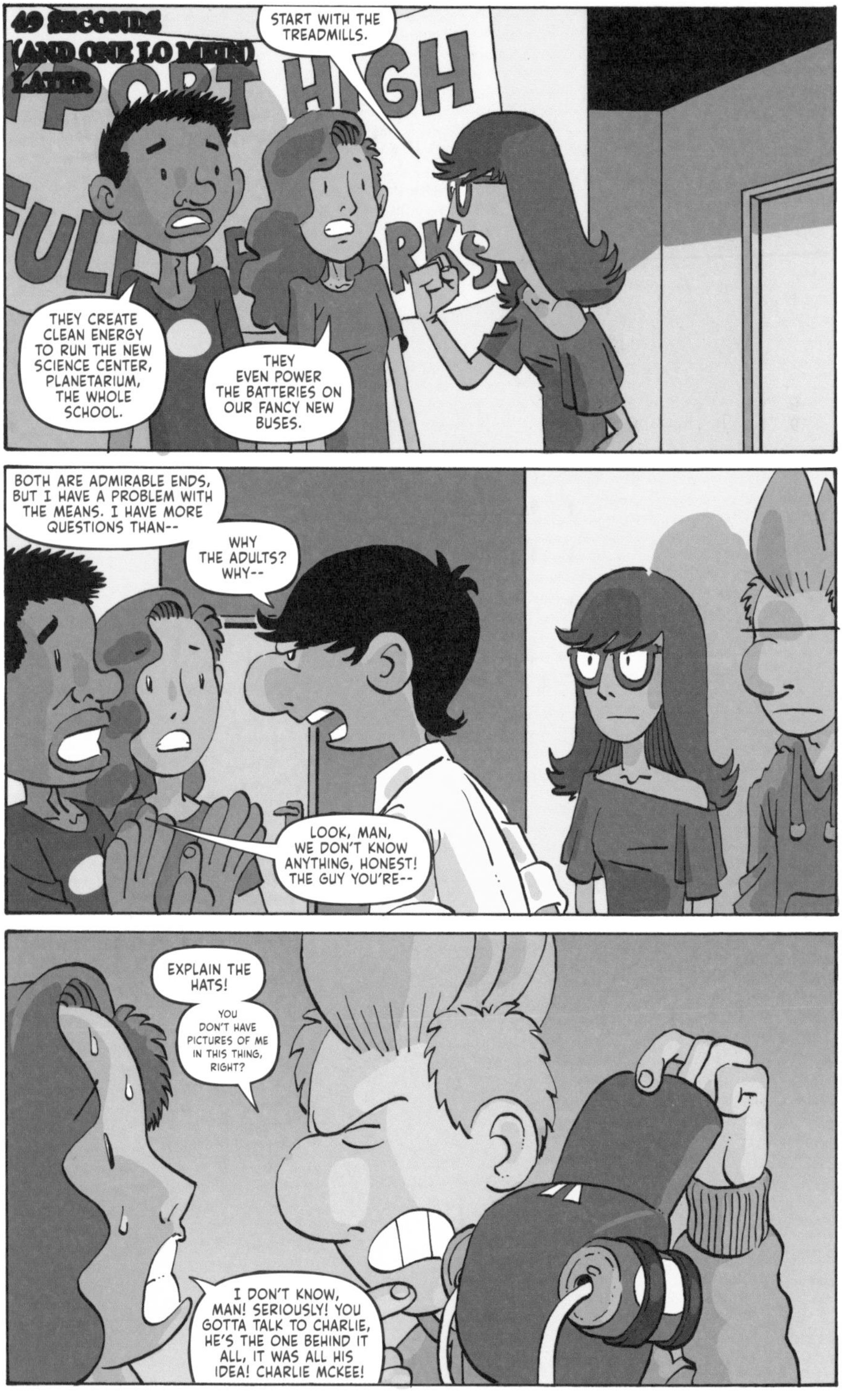
49 SECONDS (AND ONE LO MEIN) LATER
START WITH THE TREADMILLS.
THEY CREATE CLEAN ENERGY TO RUN THE NEW SCIENCE CENTER, PLANETARIUM, THE WHOLE SCHOOL.
THEY EVEN POWER THE BATTERIES ON OUR FANCY NEW BUSES.
BOTH ARE ADMIRABLE ENDS, BUT I HAVE A PROBLEM WITH THE MEANS. I HAVE MORE QUESTIONS THAN--
WHY THE ADULTS? WHY--
LOOK, MAN, WE DON'T KNOW ANYTHING, HONEST! THE GUY YOU'RE--
EXPLAIN THE HATS!
YOU DON'T HAVE PICTURES OF ME IN THIS THING, RIGHT?
I DON'T KNOW, MAN! SERIOUSLY! YOU GOTTA TALK TO CHARLIE, HE'S THE ONE BEHIND IT ALL, IT WAS ALL HIS IDEA! CHARLIE MCKEE!

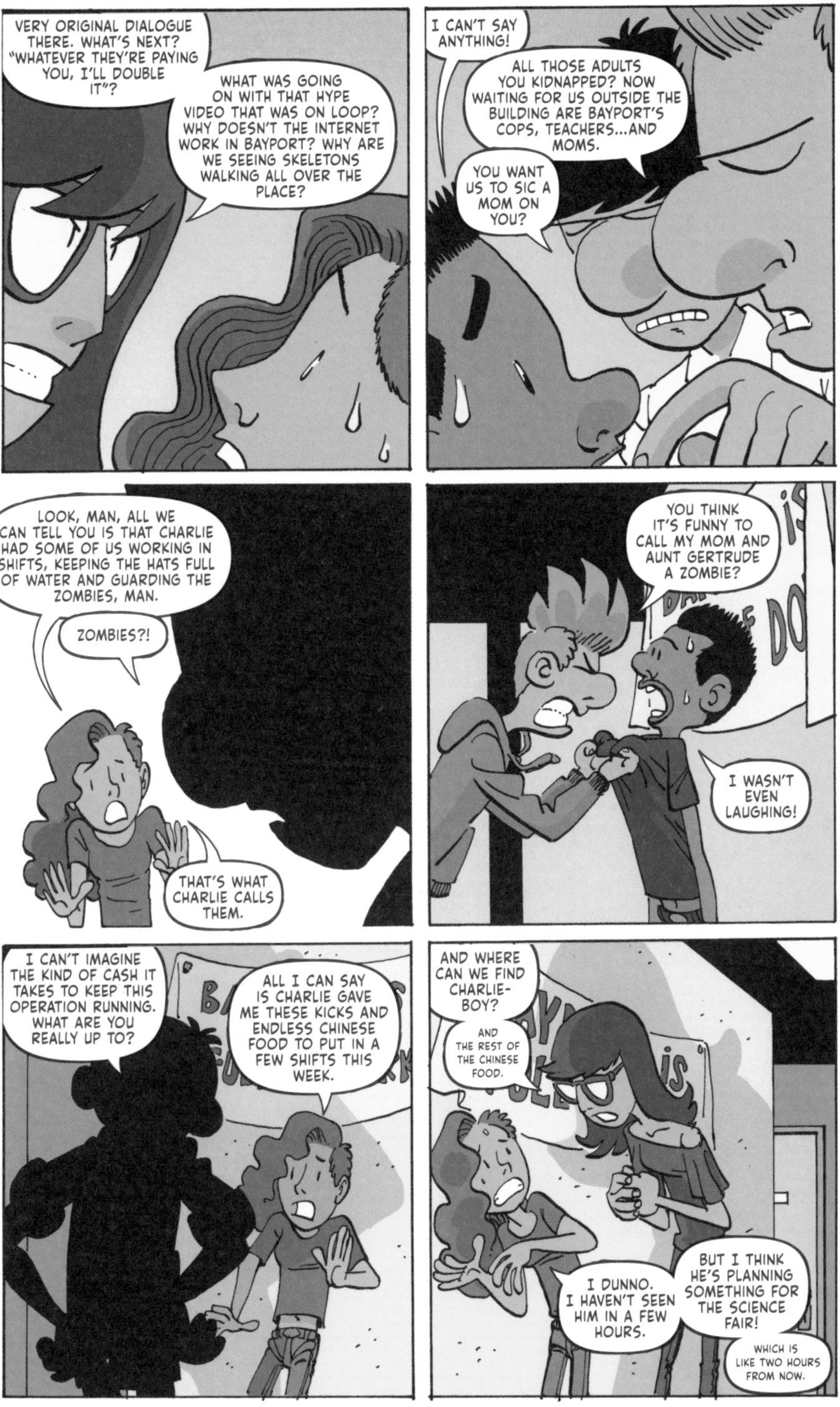
VERY ORIGINAL DIALOGUE THERE. WHAT'S NEXT? "WHATEVER THEY'RE PAYING YOU, I'LL DOUBLE IT"?
WHAT WAS GOING ON WITH THAT HYPE VIDEO THAT WAS ON LOOP? WHY DOESN'T THE INTERNET WORK IN BAYPORT? WHY ARE WE SEEING SKELETONS WALKING ALL OVER THE PLACE?
I CAN'T SAY ANYTHING!
ALL THOSE ADULTS YOU KIDNAPPED? NOW WAITING FOR US OUTSIDE THE BUILDING ARE BAYPORT'S COPS, TEACHERS...AND MOMS.
YOU WANT US TO SIC A MOM ON YOU?
LOOK, MAN, ALL WE CAN TELL YOU IS THAT CHARLIE HAD SOME OF US WORKING IN SHIFTS, KEEPING THE HATS FULL OF WATER AND GUARDING THE ZOMBIES, MAN.
ZOMBIES?!
THAT'S WHAT CHARLIE CALLS THEM.
YOU THINK IT'S FUNNY TO CALL MY MOM AND AUNT GERTRUDE A ZOMBIE?
I WASN'T EVEN LAUGHING!
I CAN'T IMAGINE THE KIND OF CASH IT TAKES TO KEEP THIS OPERATION RUNNING. WHAT ARE YOU REALLY UP TO?
ALL I CAN SAY IS CHARLIE GAVE ME THESE KICKS AND ENDLESS CHINESE FOOD TO PUT IN A FEW SHIFTS THIS WEEK.
AND WHERE CAN WE FIND CHARLIE-BOY?
AND THE REST OF THE CHINESE FOOD.
I DUNNO. I HAVEN'T SEEN HIM IN A FEW HOURS.
BUT I THINK HE'S PLANNING SOMETHING FOR THE SCIENCE FAIR!
WHICH IS LIKE TWO HOURS FROM NOW.

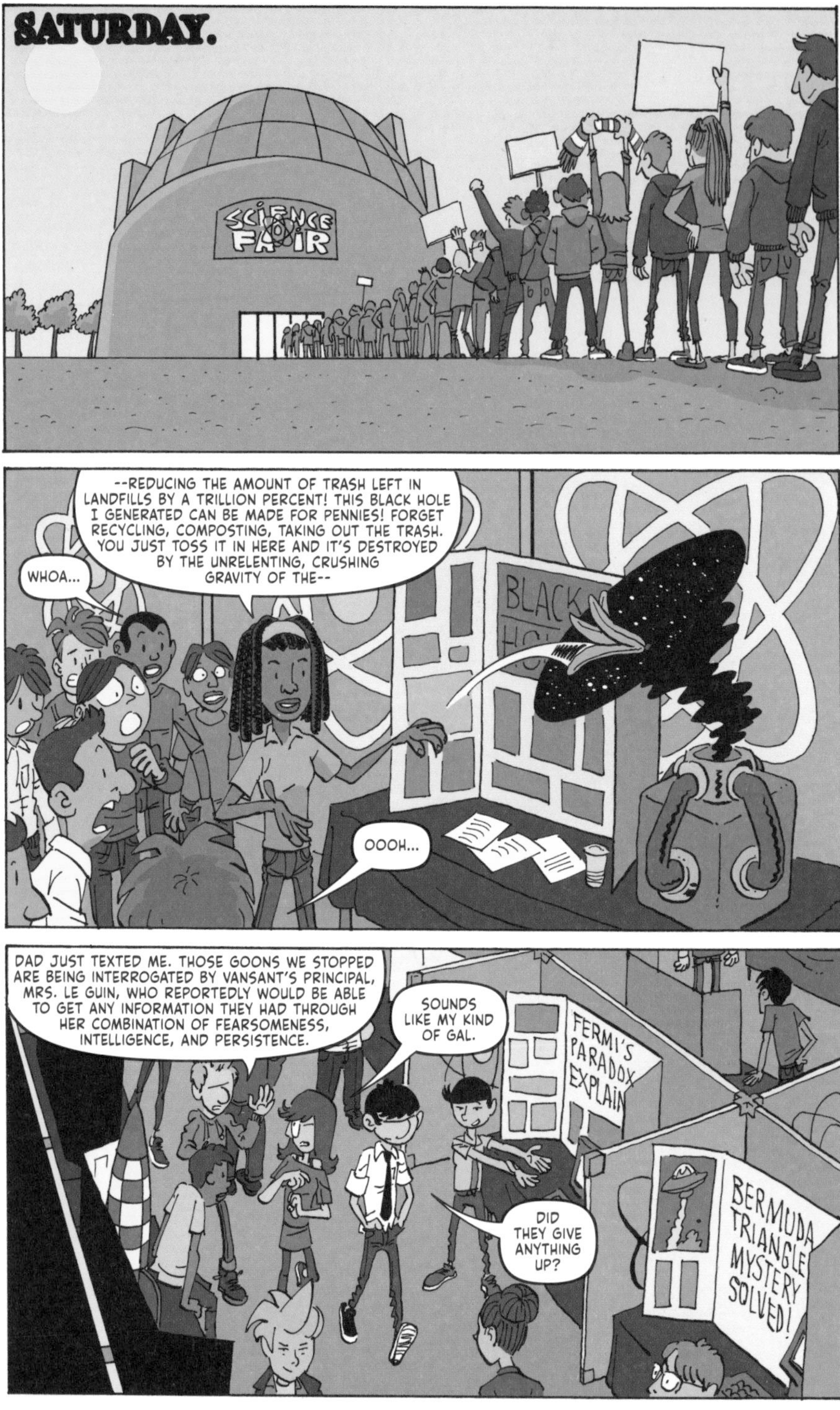
SATURDAY.
SCIENCE FAIR
--REDUCING THE AMOUNT OF TRASH LEFT IN LANDFILLS BY A TRILLION PERCENT! THIS BLACK HOLE I GENERATED CAN BE MADE FOR PENNIES! FORGET RECYCLING, COMPOSTING, TAKING OUT THE TRASH. YOU JUST TOSS IT IN HERE AND IT'S DESTROYED BY THE UNRELENTING, CRUSHING GRAVITY OF THE--
WHOA...
OOOH...
DAD JUST TEXTED ME. THOSE GOONS WE STOPPED ARE BEING INTERROGATED BY VANSANT'S PRINCIPAL, MRS. LE GUIN, WHO REPORTEDLY WOULD BE ABLE TO GET ANY INFORMATION THEY HAD THROUGH HER COMBINATION OF FEARSOMENESS, INTELLIGENCE, AND PERSISTENCE.
SOUNDS LIKE MY KIND OF GAL.
FERMI'S PARADOX EXPLAIN
DID THEY GIVE ANYTHING UP?
BERMUDA TRIANGLE MYSTERY SOLVED!

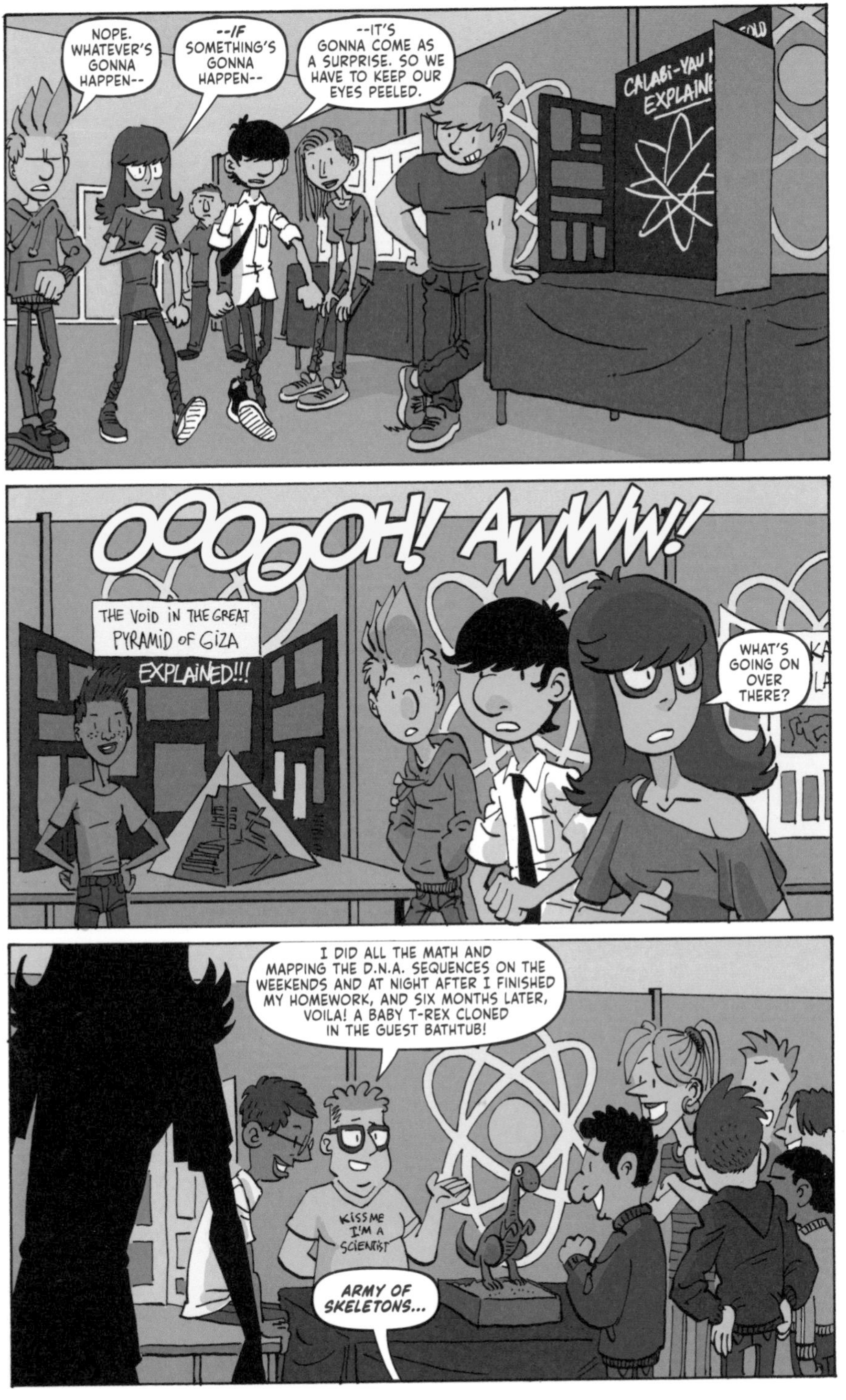
NOPE. WHATEVER'S GONNA HAPPEN--
--IF SOMETHING'S GONNA HAPPEN--
--IT'S GONNA COME AS A SURPRISE. SO WE HAVE TO KEEP OUR EYES PEELED.
OOOOOOH! AWWW!
THE VOID IN THE GREAT PYRAMID OF GIZA EXPLAINED!!!
WHAT'S GOING ON OVER THERE?
I DID ALL THE MATH AND MAPPING THE D.N.A. SEQUENCES ON THE WEEKENDS AND AT NIGHT AFTER I FINISHED MY HOMEWORK, AND SIX MONTHS LATER, VOILA! A BABY T-REX CLONED IN THE GUEST BATHTUB!
KISS ME I'M A SCIENTIST
ARMY OF SKELETONS...

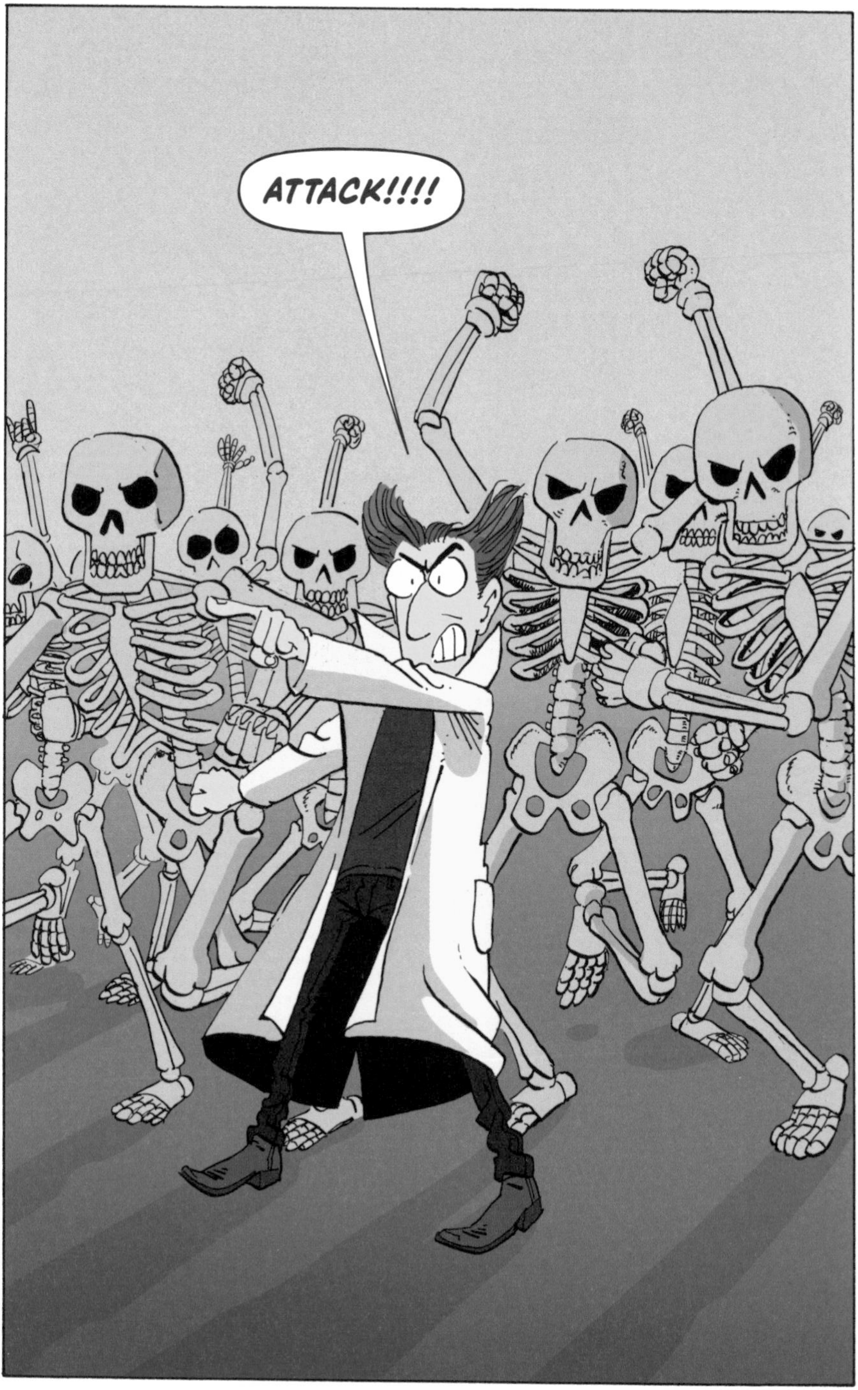
ATTACK!!!!

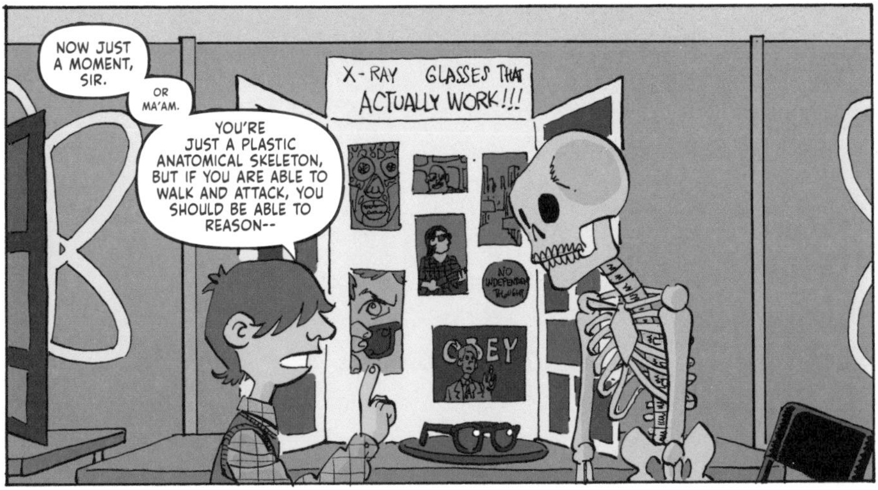
NOW JUST A MOMENT, SIR.
OR MA'AM.
YOU'RE JUST A PLASTIC ANATOMICAL SKELETON, BUT IF YOU ARE ABLE TO WALK AND ATTACK, YOU SHOULD BE ABLE TO REASON--
X-RAY GLASSES THAT ACTUALLY WORK!!!
NO INDEPENDENT THOUGHT
OBEY

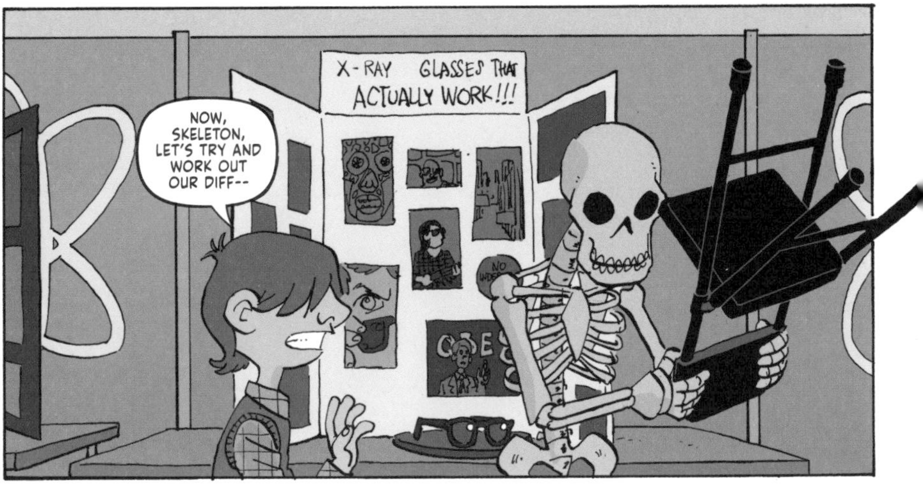
X-RAY GLASSES THAT ACTUALLY WORK!!!
NOW, SKELETON, LET'S TRY AND WORK OUT OUR DIFF--

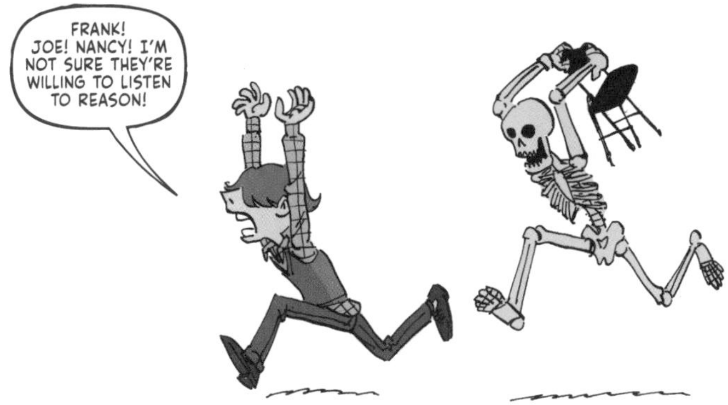
FRANK! JOE! NANCY! I'M NOT SURE THEY'RE WILLING TO LISTEN TO REASON!

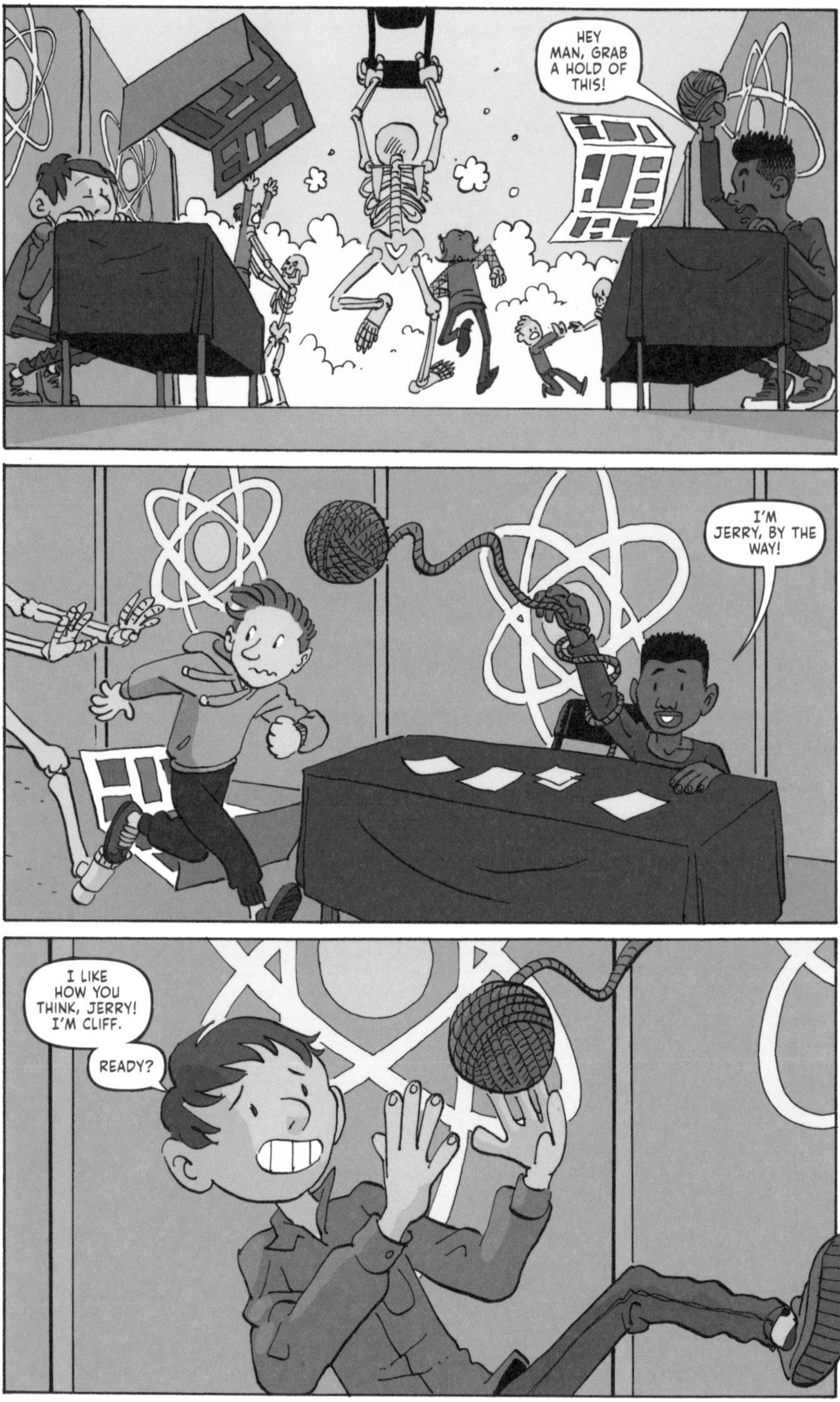
HEY MAN, GRAB A HOLD OF THIS!
I'M JERRY, BY THE WAY!
I LIKE HOW YOU THINK, JERRY! I'M CLIFF.
READY?

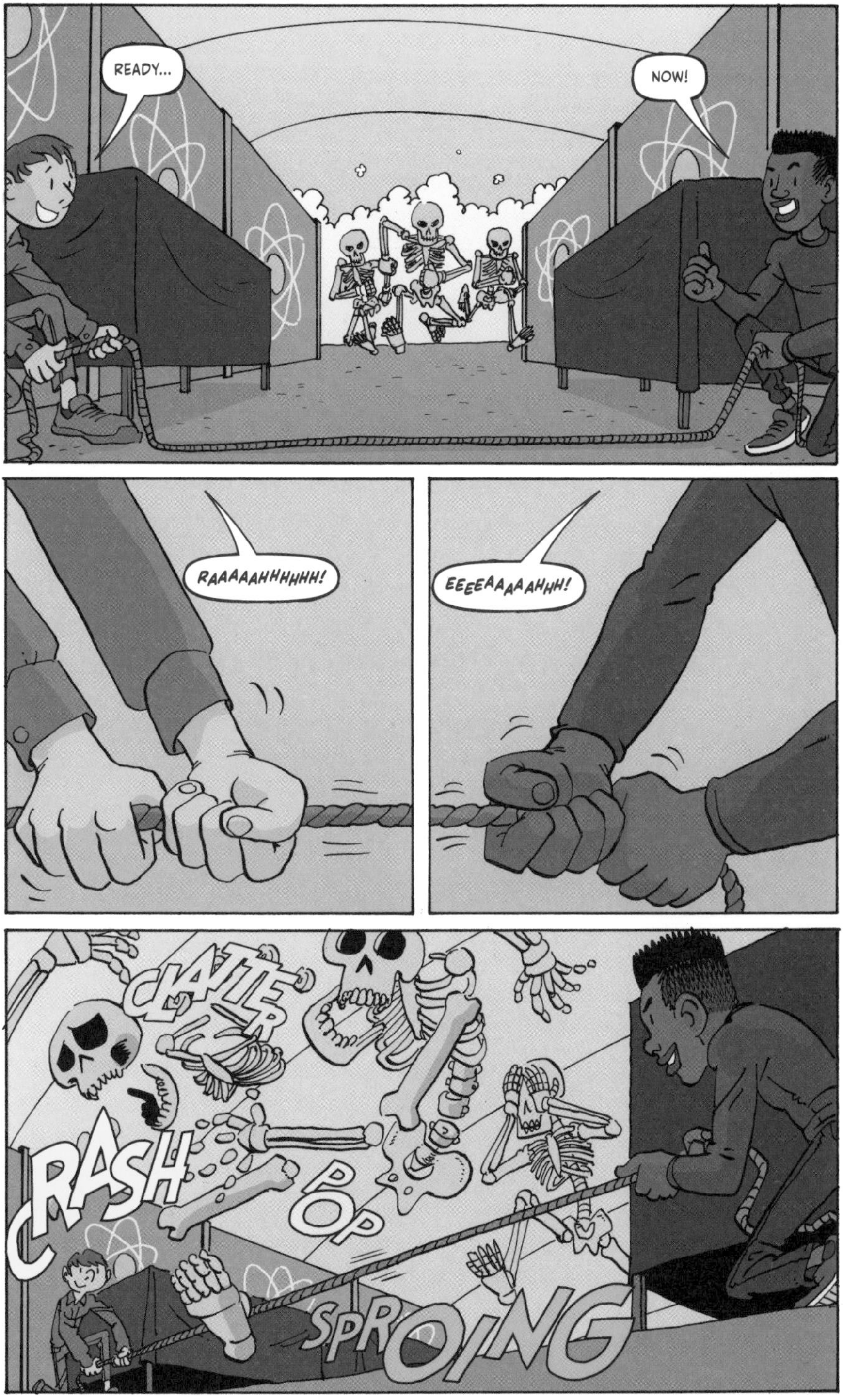
READY...
NOW!
RAAAAAHHHHHH!
EEEEAAAAAHHH!
CLATTER
CRASH
POP
SPROING

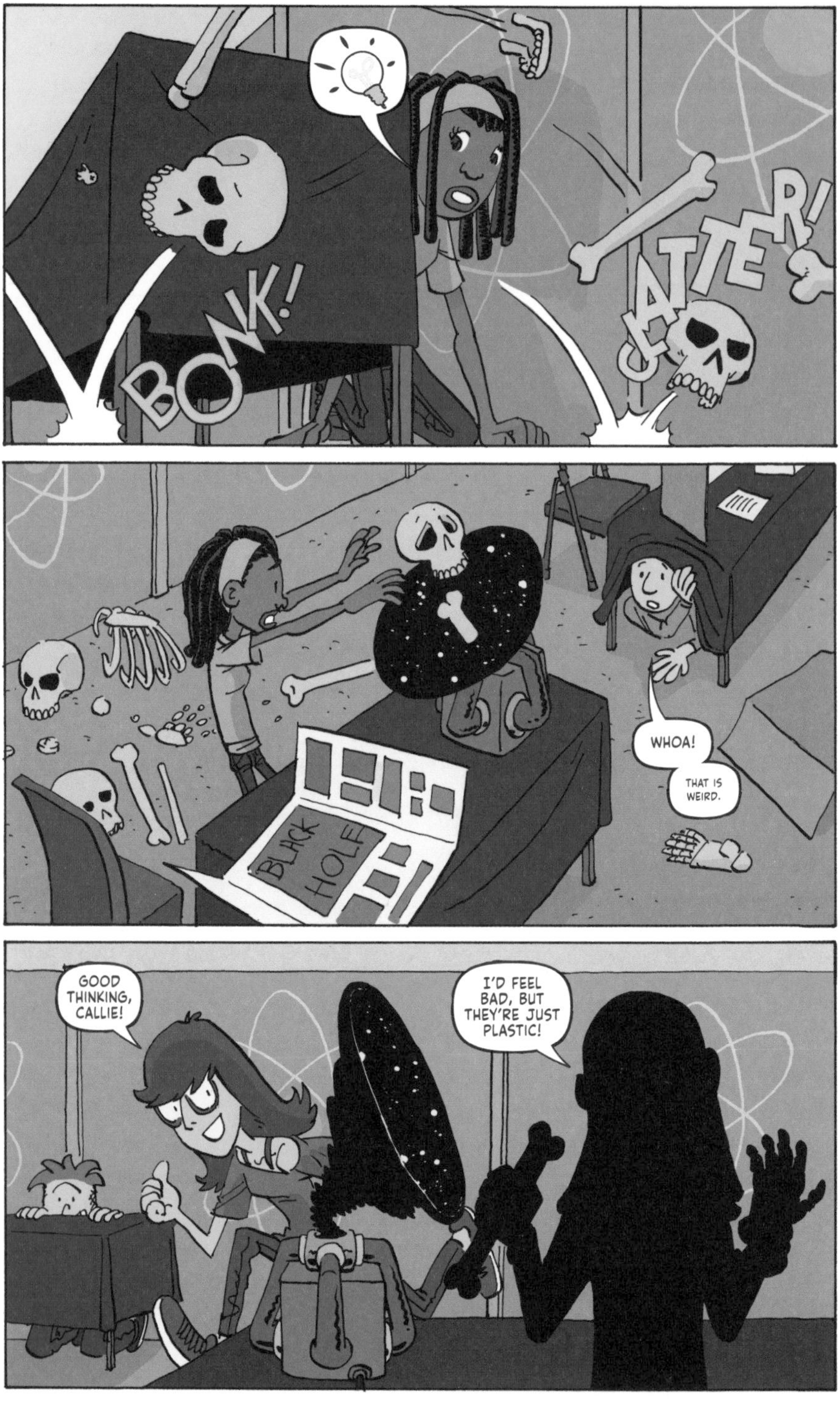
BONK!
CLATTER!
WHOA!
THAT IS WEIRD.
BLACK HOLE
GOOD THINKING, CALLIE!
I'D FEEL BAD, BUT THEY'RE JUST PLASTIC!

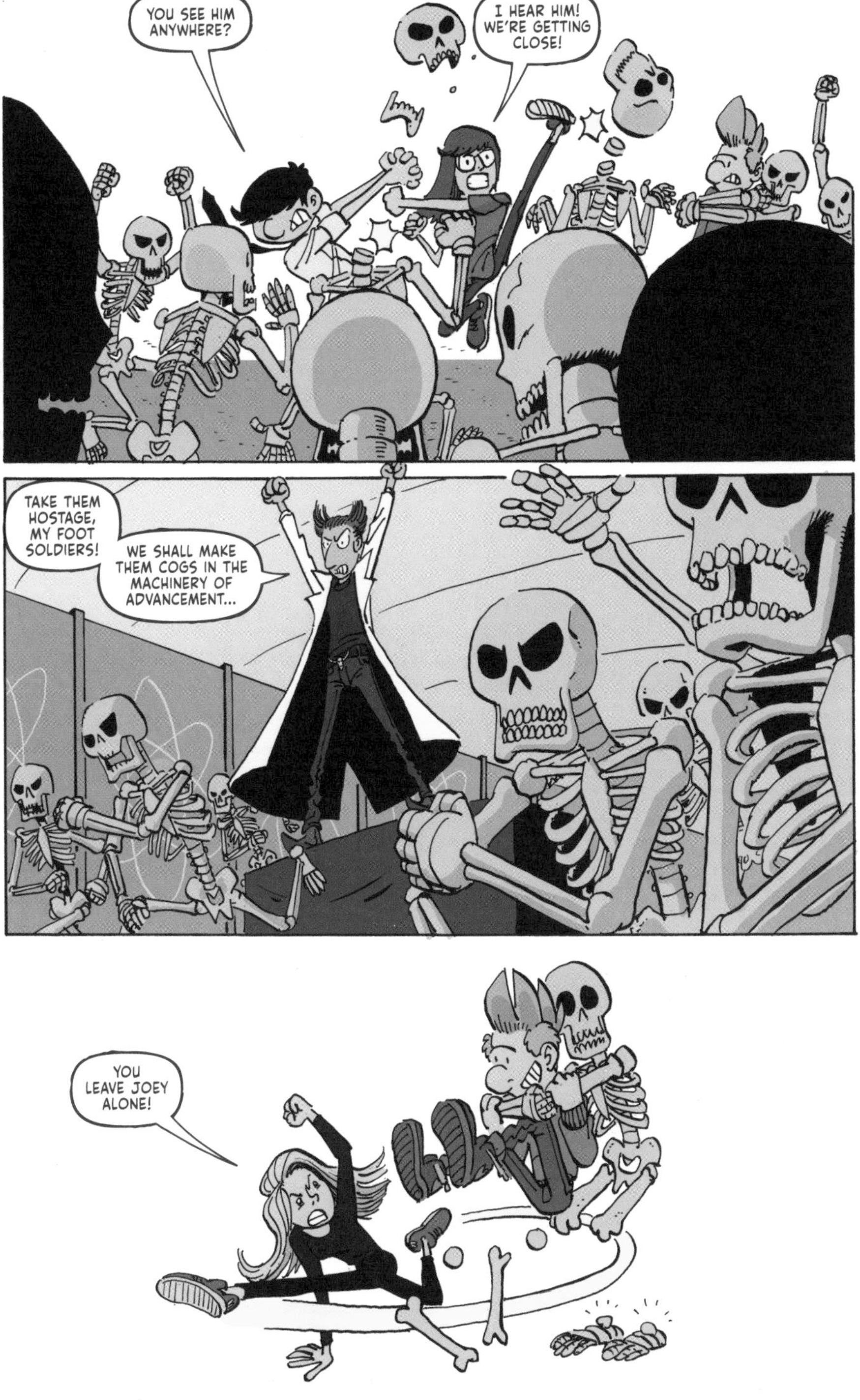
YOU SEE HIM ANYWHERE?
I HEAR HIM! WE'RE GETTING CLOSE!
TAKE THEM HOSTAGE, MY FOOT SOLDIERS!
WE SHALL MAKE THEM COGS IN THE MACHINERY OF ADVANCEMENT...
YOU LEAVE JOEY ALONE!

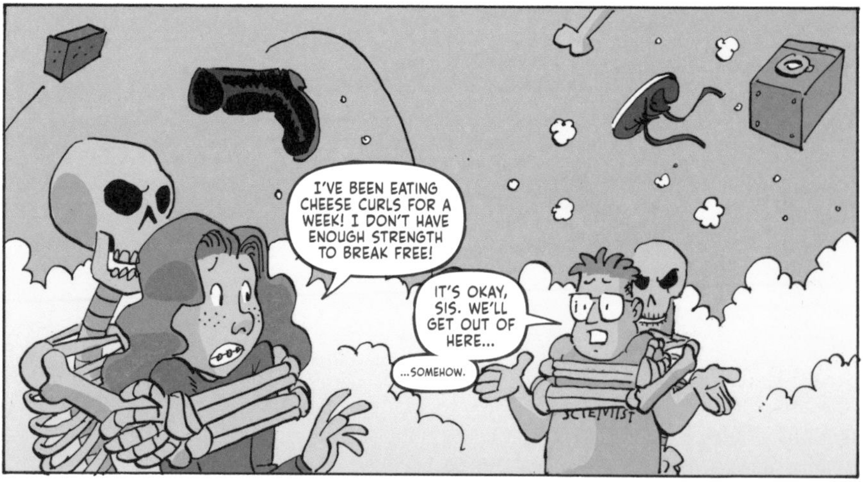
I'VE BEEN EATING CHEESE CURLS FOR A WEEK! I DON'T HAVE ENOUGH STRENGTH TO BREAK FREE!
IT'S OKAY, SIS. WE'LL GET OUT OF HERE...
...SOMEHOW.

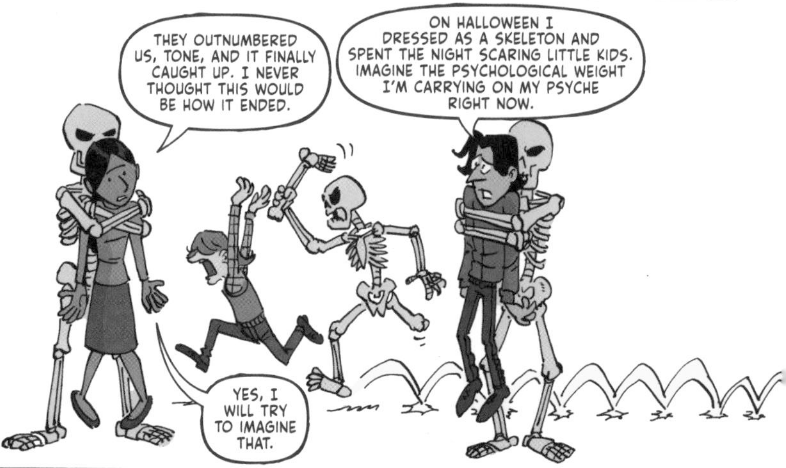
THEY OUTNUMBERED US, TONE, AND IT FINALLY CAUGHT UP. I NEVER THOUGHT THIS WOULD BE HOW IT ENDED.
ON HALLOWEEN I DRESSED AS A SKELETON AND SPENT THE NIGHT SCARING LITTLE KIDS. IMAGINE THE PSYCHOLOGICAL WEIGHT I'M CARRYING ON MY PSYCHE RIGHT NOW.
YES, I WILL TRY TO IMAGINE THAT.

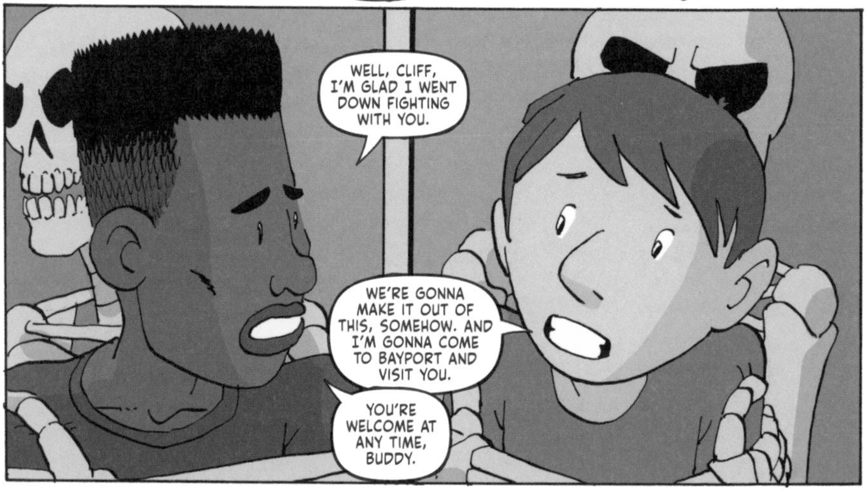
WELL, CLIFF, I'M GLAD I WENT DOWN FIGHTING WITH YOU.
WE'RE GONNA MAKE IT OUT OF THIS, SOMEHOW. AND I'M GONNA COME TO BAYPORT AND VISIT YOU.
YOU'RE WELCOME AT ANY TIME, BUDDY.

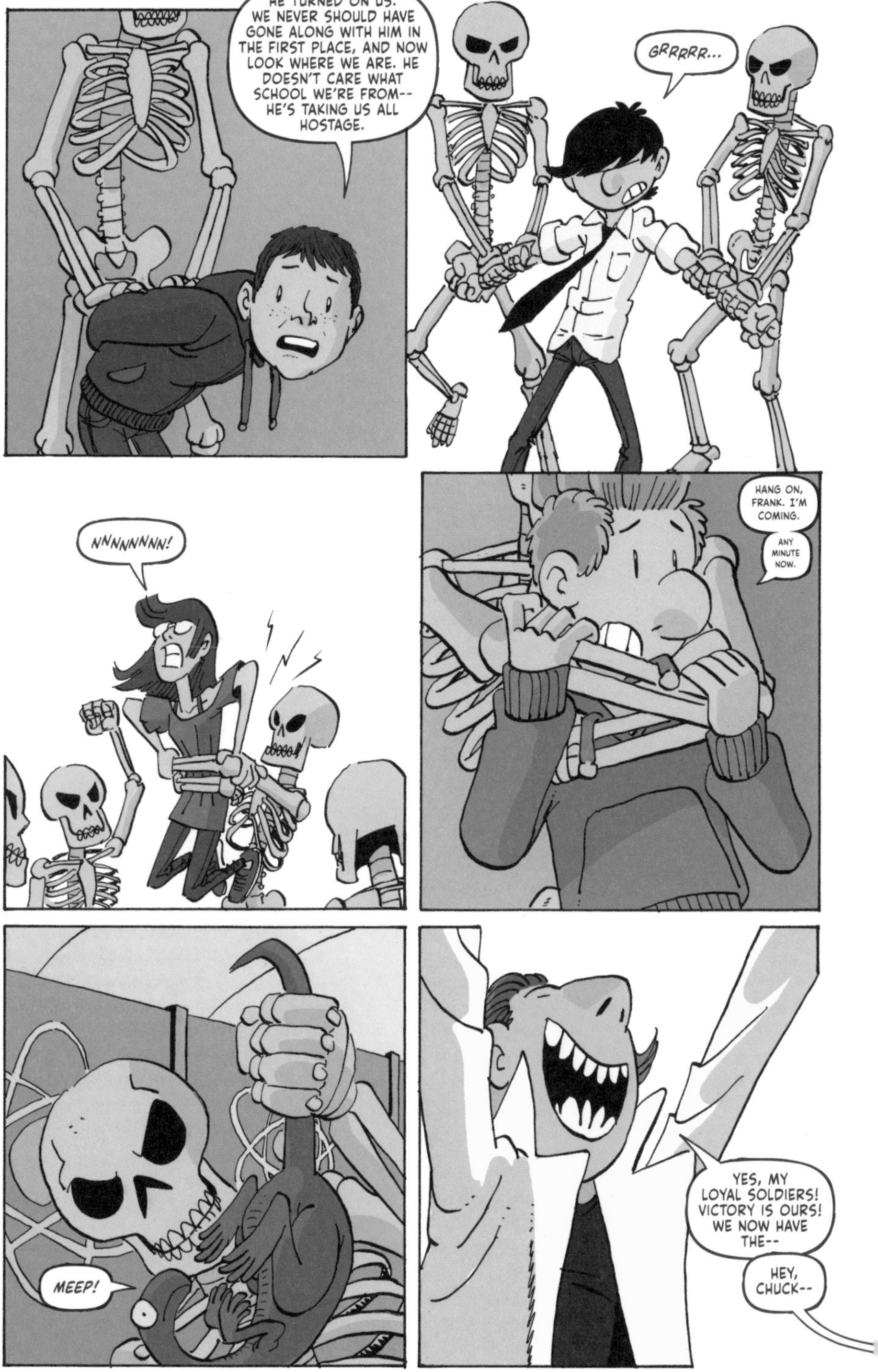
HE TURNED ON US. WE NEVER SHOULD HAVE GONE ALONG WITH HIM IN THE FIRST PLACE, AND NOW LOOK WHERE WE ARE. HE DOESN'T CARE WHAT SCHOOL WE'RE FROM-- HE'S TAKING US ALL HOSTAGE.
GRRRRR...
NNNNNNNN!
HANG ON, FRANK. I'M COMING.
ANY MINUTE NOW.
MEEP!
YES, MY LOYAL SOLDIERS! VICTORY IS OURS! WE NOW HAVE THE--
HEY, CHUCK--

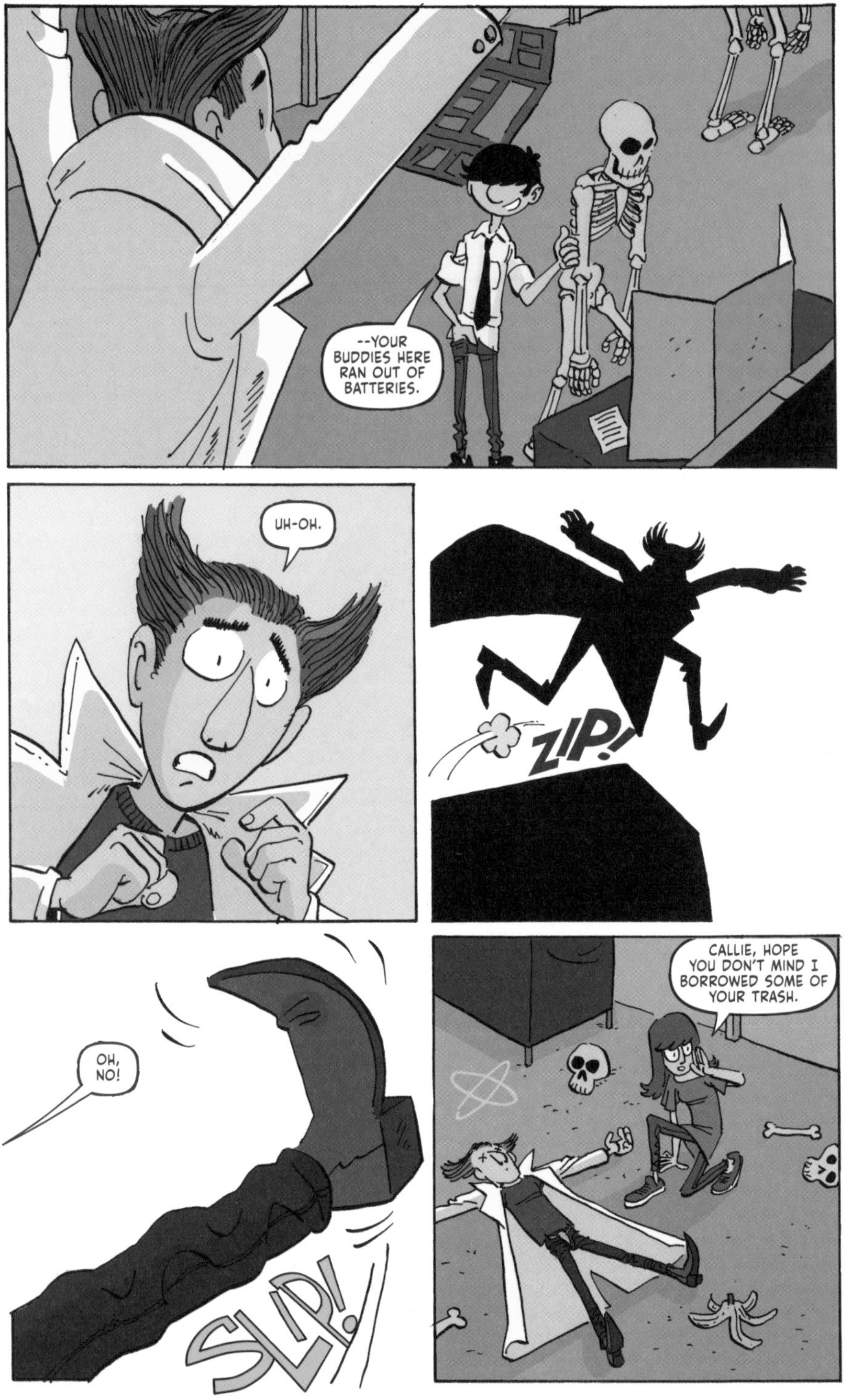
--YOUR BUDDIES HERE RAN OUT OF BATTERIES.
UH-OH.
ZIP!
OH, NO!
SLIP!
CALLIE, HOPE YOU DON'T MIND I BORROWED SOME OF YOUR TRASH.

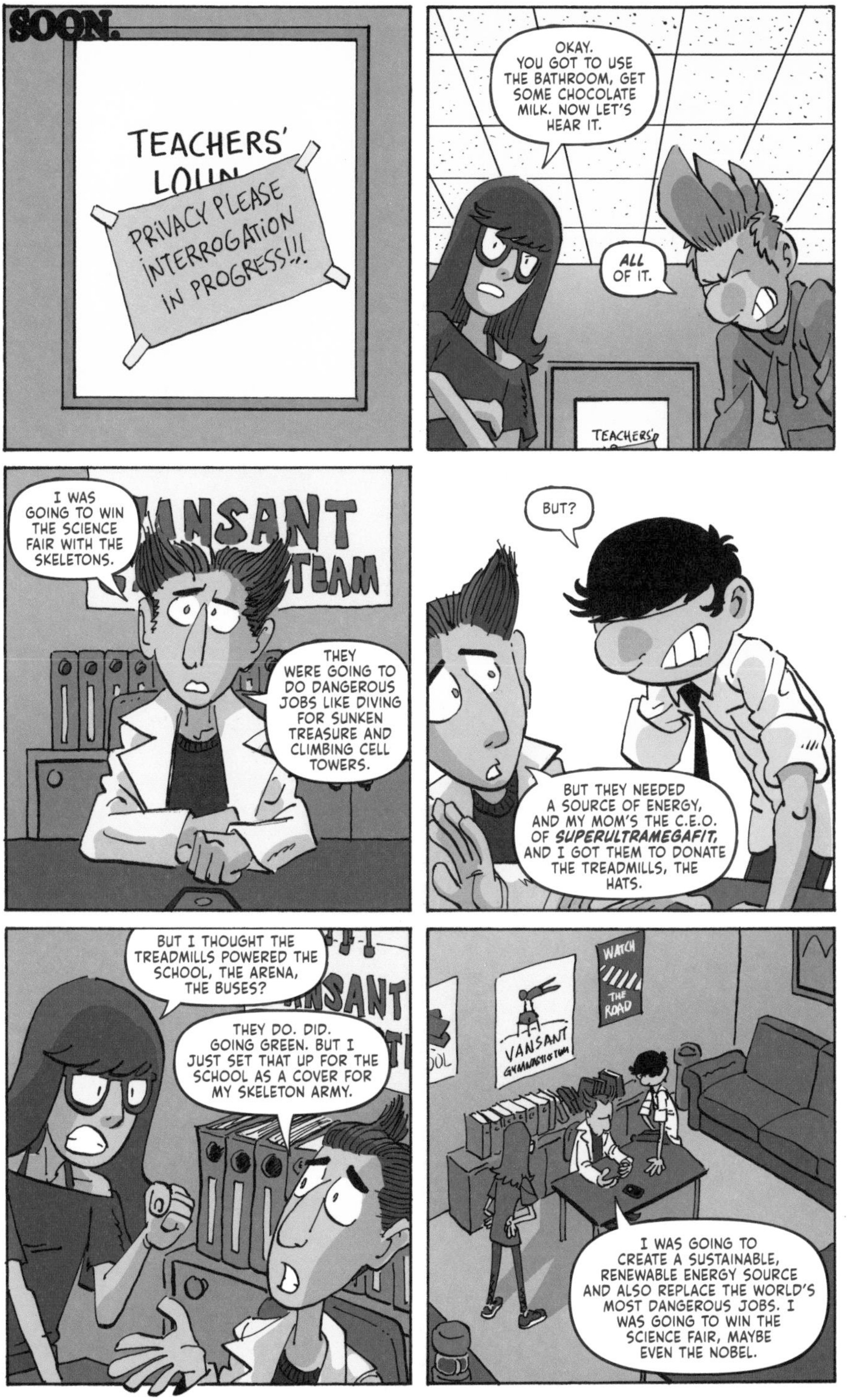
SOON.
TEACHERS' LOUN
PRIVACY PLEASE INTERROGATION IN PROGRESS!!!
OKAY. YOU GOT TO USE THE BATHROOM, GET SOME CHOCOLATE MILK. NOW LET'S HEAR IT.
ALL OF IT.
TEACHERS'
I WAS GOING TO WIN THE SCIENCE FAIR WITH THE SKELETONS.
THEY WERE GOING TO DO DANGEROUS JOBS LIKE DIVING FOR SUNKEN TREASURE AND CLIMBING CELL TOWERS.
BUT?
BUT THEY NEEDED A SOURCE OF ENERGY, AND MY MOM'S THE C.E.O. OF SUPERULTRAMEGAFIT, AND I GOT THEM TO DONATE THE TREADMILLS, THE HATS.
BUT I THOUGHT THE TREADMILLS POWERED THE SCHOOL, THE ARENA, THE BUSES?
THEY DO. DID. GOING GREEN. BUT I JUST SET THAT UP FOR THE SCHOOL AS A COVER FOR MY SKELETON ARMY.
WATCH THE ROAD
VANSANT GYMNASTICS TEAM
I WAS GOING TO CREATE A SUSTAINABLE, RENEWABLE ENERGY SOURCE AND ALSO REPLACE THE WORLD'S MOST DANGEROUS JOBS. I WAS GOING TO WIN THE SCIENCE FAIR, MAYBE EVEN THE NOBEL.

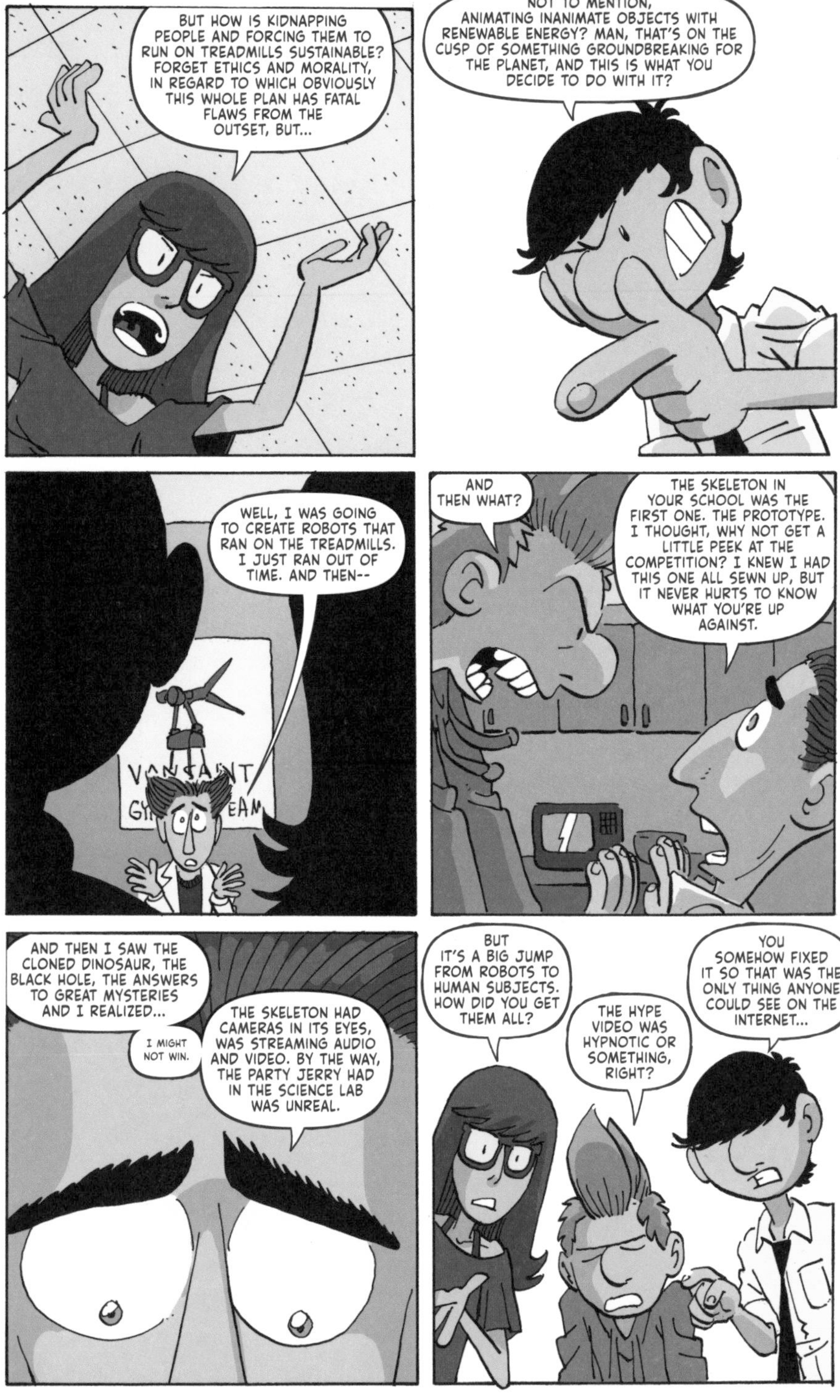
BUT HOW IS KIDNAPPING PEOPLE AND FORCING THEM TO RUN ON TREADMILLS SUSTAINABLE? FORGET ETHICS AND MORALITY, IN REGARD TO WHICH OBVIOUSLY THIS WHOLE PLAN HAS FATAL FLAWS FROM THE OUTSET, BUT...
NOT TO MENTION, ANIMATING INANIMATE OBJECTS WITH RENEWABLE ENERGY? MAN, THAT'S ON THE CUSP OF SOMETHING GROUNDBREAKING FOR THE PLANET, AND THIS IS WHAT YOU DECIDE TO DO WITH IT?
WELL, I WAS GOING TO CREATE ROBOTS THAT RAN ON THE TREADMILLS. I JUST RAN OUT OF TIME. AND THEN--
AND THEN WHAT?
THE SKELETON IN YOUR SCHOOL WAS THE FIRST ONE. THE PROTOTYPE. I THOUGHT, WHY NOT GET A LITTLE PEEK AT THE COMPETITION? I KNEW I HAD THIS ONE ALL SEWN UP, BUT IT NEVER HURTS TO KNOW WHAT YOU'RE UP AGAINST.
AND THEN I SAW THE CLONED DINOSAUR, THE BLACK HOLE, THE ANSWERS TO GREAT MYSTERIES AND I REALIZED...
I MIGHT NOT WIN.
THE SKELETON HAD CAMERAS IN ITS EYES, WAS STREAMING AUDIO AND VIDEO. BY THE WAY, THE PARTY JERRY HAD IN THE SCIENCE LAB WAS UNREAL.
BUT IT'S A BIG JUMP FROM ROBOTS TO HUMAN SUBJECTS. HOW DID YOU GET THEM ALL?
THE HYPE VIDEO WAS HYPNOTIC OR SOMETHING, RIGHT?
YOU SOMEHOW FIXED IT SO THAT WAS THE ONLY THING ANYONE COULD SEE ON THE INTERNET...

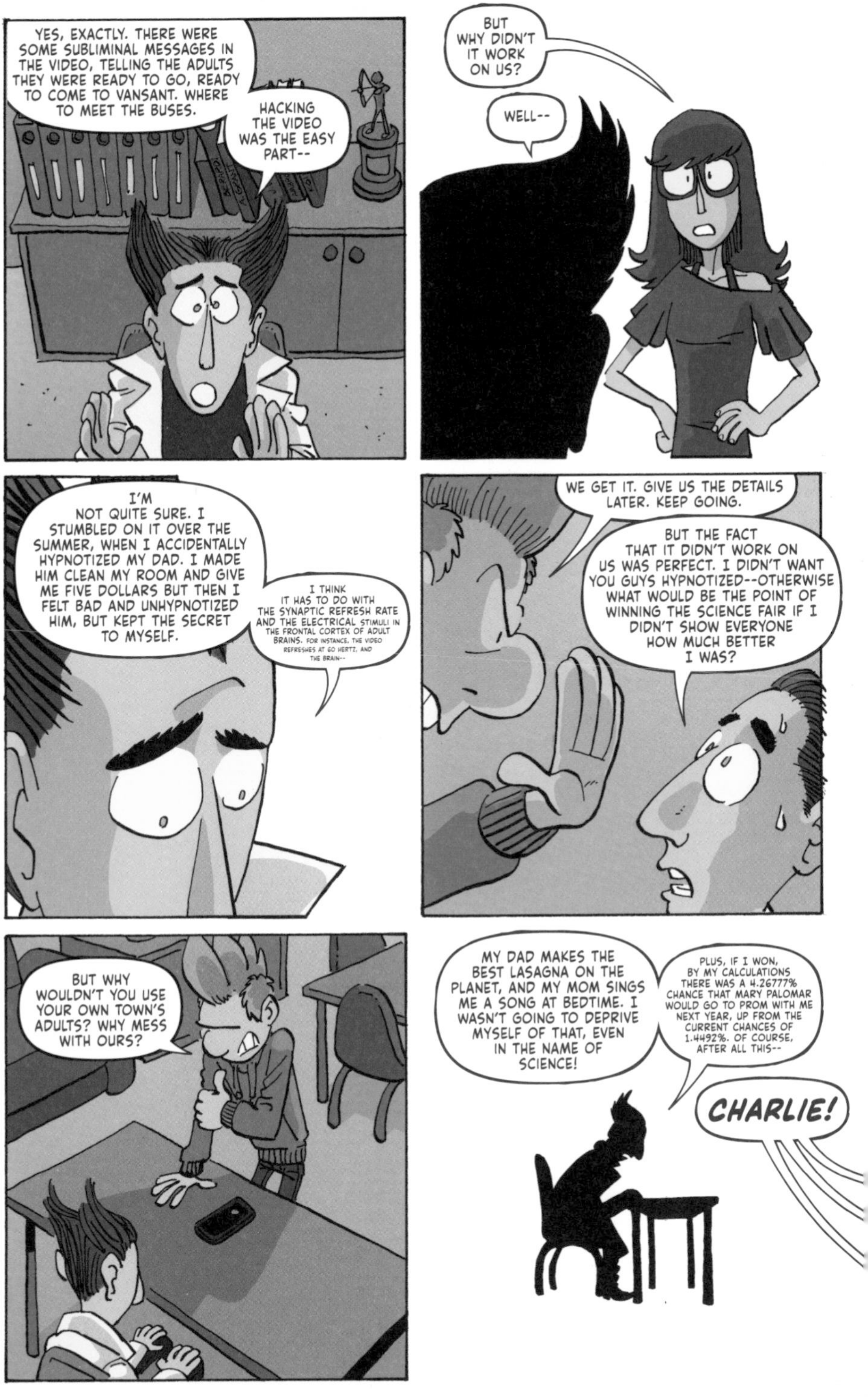
YES, EXACTLY. THERE WERE SOME SUBLIMINAL MESSAGES IN THE VIDEO, TELLING THE ADULTS THEY WERE READY TO GO, READY TO COME TO VANSANT. WHERE TO MEET THE BUSES.
HACKING THE VIDEO WAS THE EASY PART--
BUT WHY DIDN'T IT WORK ON US?
WELL--
I'M NOT QUITE SURE. I STUMBLED ON IT OVER THE SUMMER, WHEN I ACCIDENTALLY HYPNOTIZED MY DAD. I MADE HIM CLEAN MY ROOM AND GIVE ME FIVE DOLLARS BUT THEN I FELT BAD AND UNHYPNOTIZED HIM, BUT KEPT THE SECRET TO MYSELF.
I THINK IT HAS TO DO WITH THE SYNAPTIC REFRESH RATE AND THE ELECTRICAL STIMULI IN THE FRONTAL CORTEX OF ADULT BRAINS. FOR INSTANCE, THE VIDEO REFRESHES AT 60 HERTZ, AND THE BRAIN--
WE GET IT. GIVE US THE DETAILS LATER. KEEP GOING.
BUT THE FACT THAT IT DIDN'T WORK ON US WAS PERFECT. I DIDN'T WANT YOU GUYS HYPNOTIZED--OTHERWISE WHAT WOULD BE THE POINT OF WINNING THE SCIENCE FAIR IF I DIDN'T SHOW EVERYONE HOW MUCH BETTER I WAS?
BUT WHY WOULDN'T YOU USE YOUR OWN TOWN'S ADULTS? WHY MESS WITH OURS?
MY DAD MAKES THE BEST LASAGNA ON THE PLANET, AND MY MOM SINGS ME A SONG AT BEDTIME. I WASN'T GOING TO DEPRIVE MYSELF OF THAT, EVEN IN THE NAME OF SCIENCE!
PLUS, IF I WON, BY MY CALCULATIONS THERE WAS A 4.26777% CHANCE THAT MARY PALOMAR WOULD GO TO PROM WITH ME NEXT YEAR, UP FROM THE CURRENT CHANCES OF 1.4492%. OF COURSE, AFTER ALL THIS--
CHARLIE!

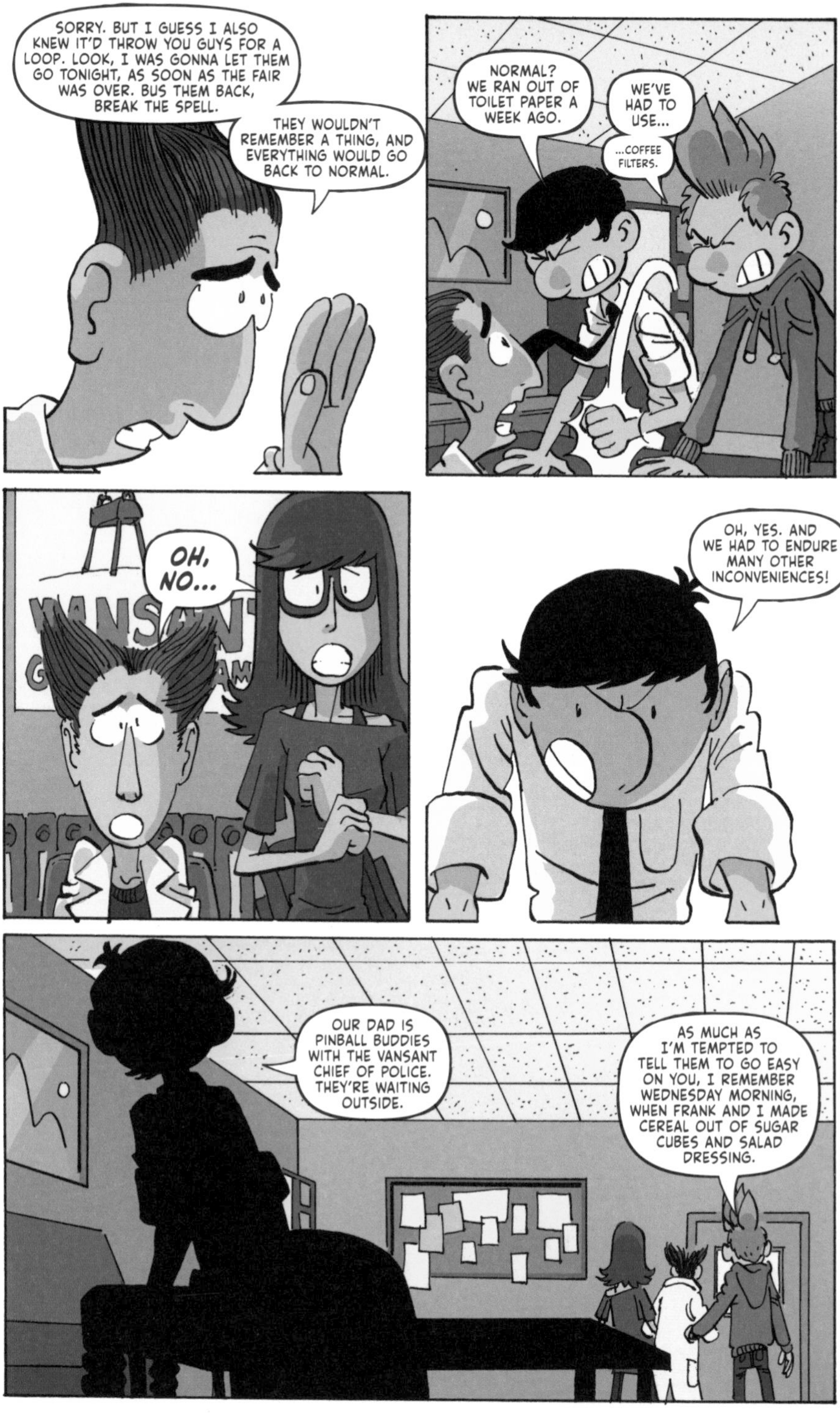
SORRY. BUT I GUESS I ALSO KNEW IT'D THROW YOU GUYS FOR A LOOP. LOOK, I WAS GONNA LET THEM GO TONIGHT, AS SOON AS THE FAIR WAS OVER. BUS THEM BACK, BREAK THE SPELL.
THEY WOULDN'T REMEMBER A THING, AND EVERYTHING WOULD GO BACK TO NORMAL.
NORMAL? WE RAN OUT OF TOILET PAPER A WEEK AGO.
WE'VE HAD TO USE...
...COFFEE FILTERS.
OH, NO...
OH, YES. AND WE HAD TO ENDURE MANY OTHER INCONVENIENCES!
OUR DAD IS PINBALL BUDDIES WITH THE VANSANT CHIEF OF POLICE. THEY'RE WAITING OUTSIDE.
AS MUCH AS I'M TEMPTED TO TELL THEM TO GO EASY ON YOU, I REMEMBER WEDNESDAY MORNING, WHEN FRANK AND I MADE CEREAL OUT OF SUGAR CUBES AND SALAD DRESSING.

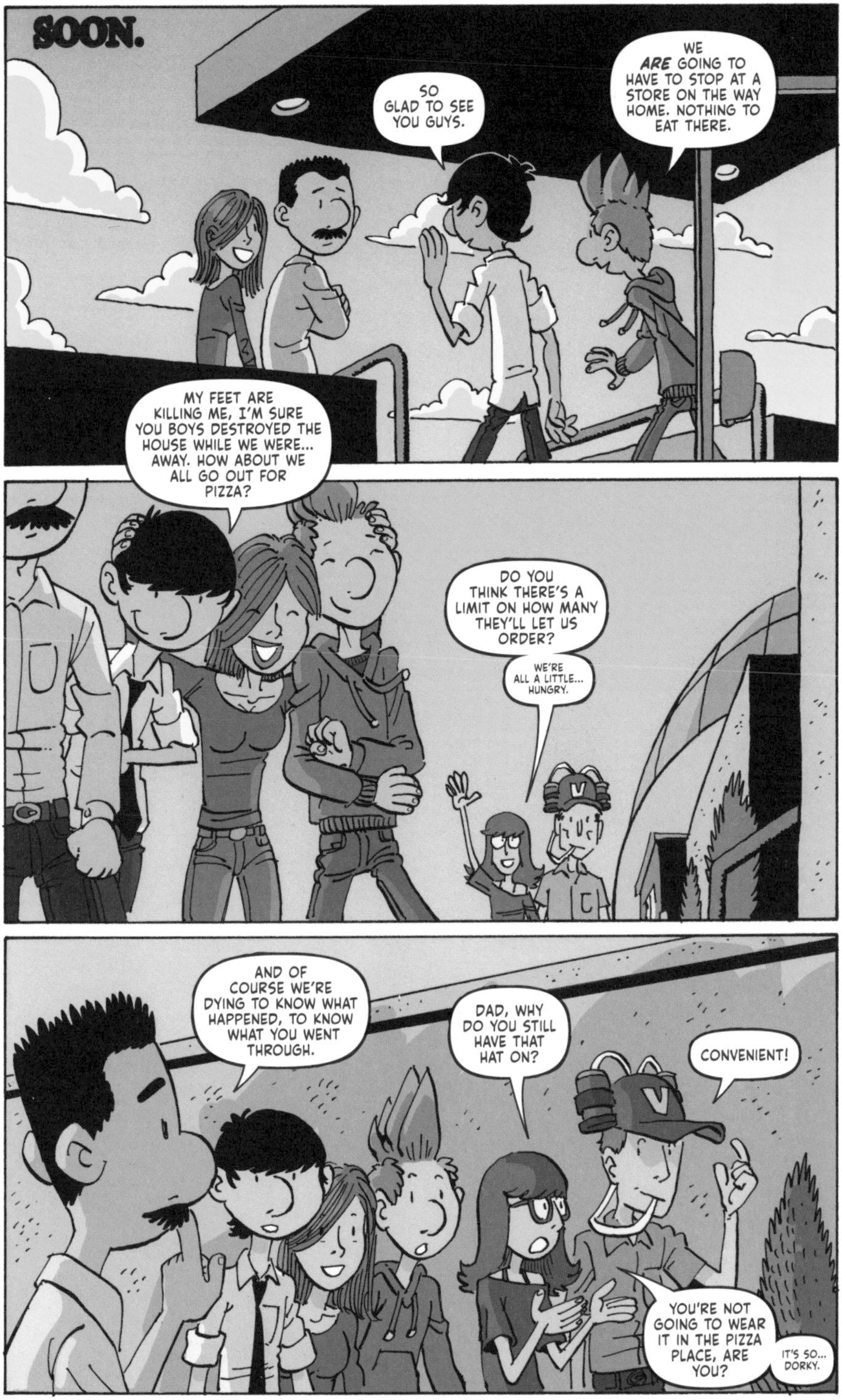
SOON.
SO GLAD TO SEE YOU GUYS.
WE ARE GOING TO HAVE TO STOP AT A STORE ON THE WAY HOME. NOTHING TO EAT THERE.
MY FEET ARE KILLING ME, I'M SURE YOU BOYS DESTROYED THE HOUSE WHILE WE WERE... AWAY. HOW ABOUT WE ALL GO OUT FOR PIZZA?
DO YOU THINK THERE'S A LIMIT ON HOW MANY THEY'LL LET US ORDER?
WE'RE ALL A LITTLE... HUNGRY.
AND OF COURSE WE'RE DYING TO KNOW WHAT HAPPENED, TO KNOW WHAT YOU WENT THROUGH.
DAD, WHY DO YOU STILL HAVE THAT HAT ON?
CONVENIENT!
YOU'RE NOT GOING TO WEAR IT IN THE PIZZA PLACE, ARE YOU?
IT'S SO... DORKY.

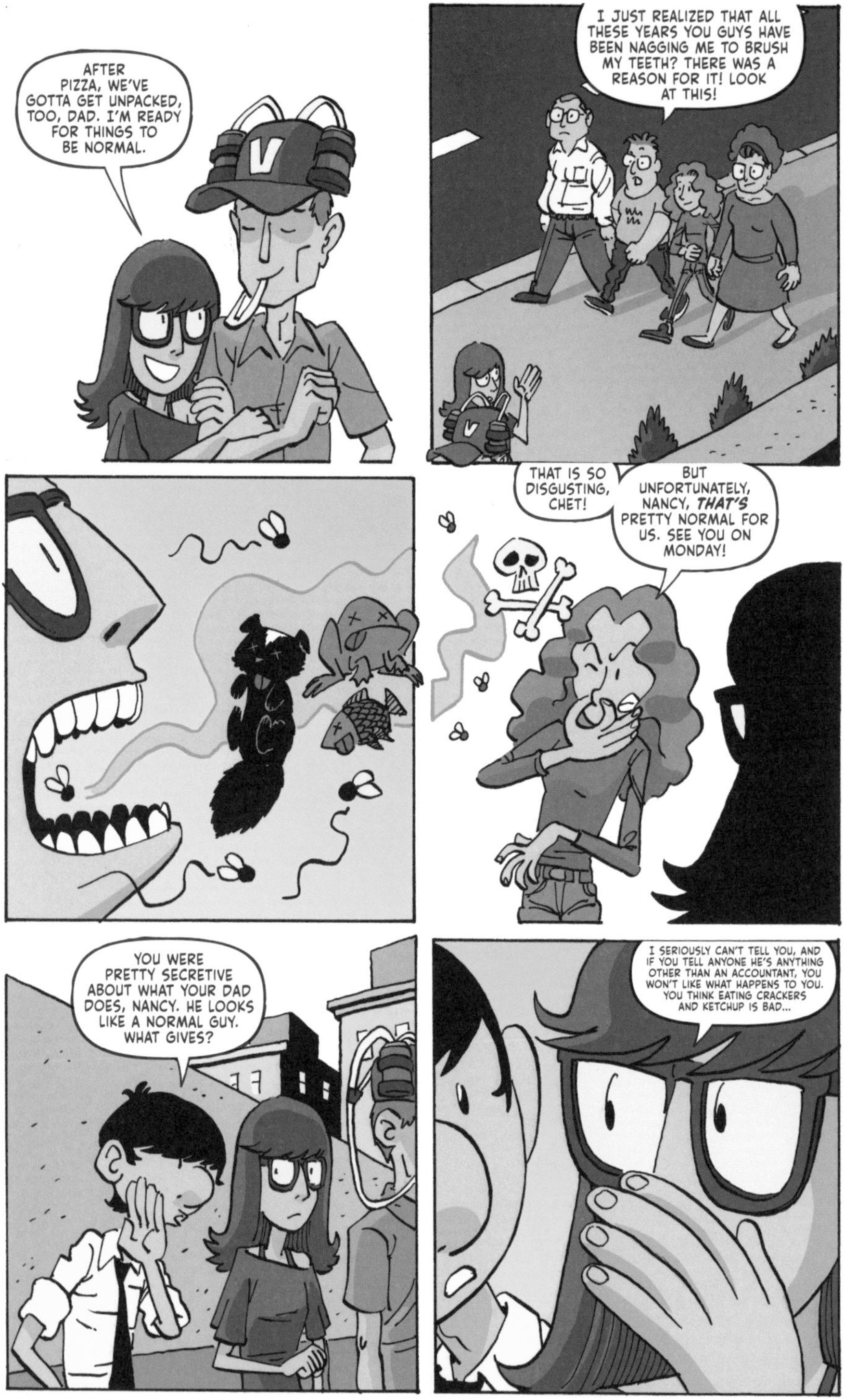
AFTER PIZZA, WE'VE GOTTA GET UNPACKED, TOO, DAD. I'M READY FOR THINGS TO BE NORMAL.
I JUST REALIZED THAT ALL THESE YEARS YOU GUYS HAVE BEEN NAGGING ME TO BRUSH MY TEETH? THERE WAS A REASON FOR IT! LOOK AT THIS!
THAT IS SO DISGUSTING, CHET!
BUT UNFORTUNATELY, NANCY, *THAT'S* PRETTY NORMAL FOR US. SEE YOU ON MONDAY!
YOU WERE PRETTY SECRETIVE ABOUT WHAT YOUR DAD DOES, NANCY. HE LOOKS LIKE A NORMAL GUY. WHAT GIVES?
I SERIOUSLY CAN'T TELL YOU, AND IF YOU TELL ANYONE HE'S ANYTHING OTHER THAN AN ACCOUNTANT, YOU WON'T LIKE WHAT HAPPENS TO YOU. YOU THINK EATING CRACKERS AND KETCHUP IS BAD...

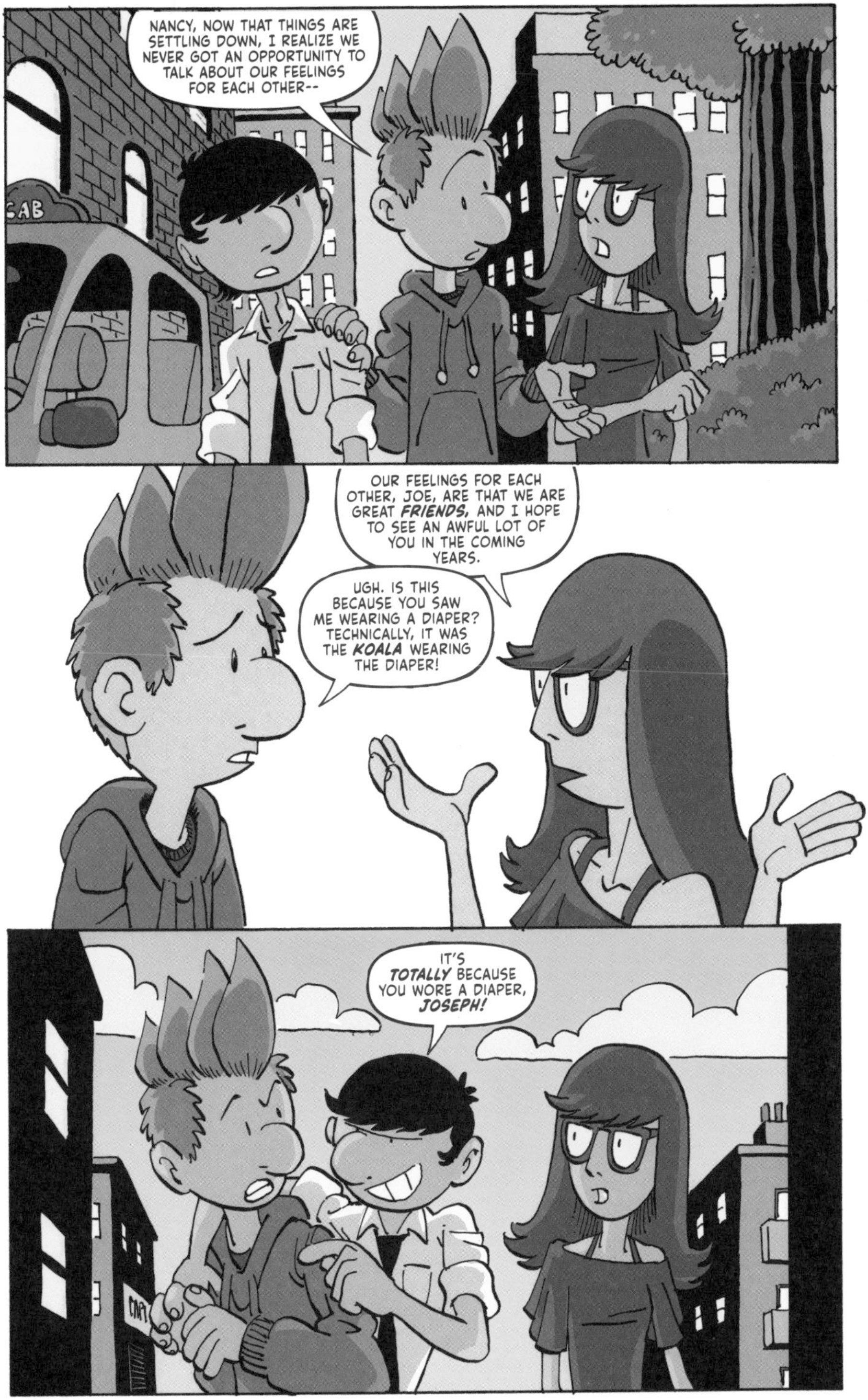
NANCY, NOW THAT THINGS ARE SETTLING DOWN, I REALIZE WE NEVER GOT AN OPPORTUNITY TO TALK ABOUT OUR FEELINGS FOR EACH OTHER--
CAB
OUR FEELINGS FOR EACH OTHER, JOE, ARE THAT WE ARE GREAT ***FRIENDS,*** AND I HOPE TO SEE AN AWFUL LOT OF YOU IN THE COMING YEARS.
UGH. IS THIS BECAUSE YOU SAW ME WEARING A DIAPER? TECHNICALLY, IT WAS THE ***KOALA*** WEARING THE DIAPER!
IT'S ***TOTALLY*** BECAUSE YOU WORE A DIAPER, ***JOSEPH!***

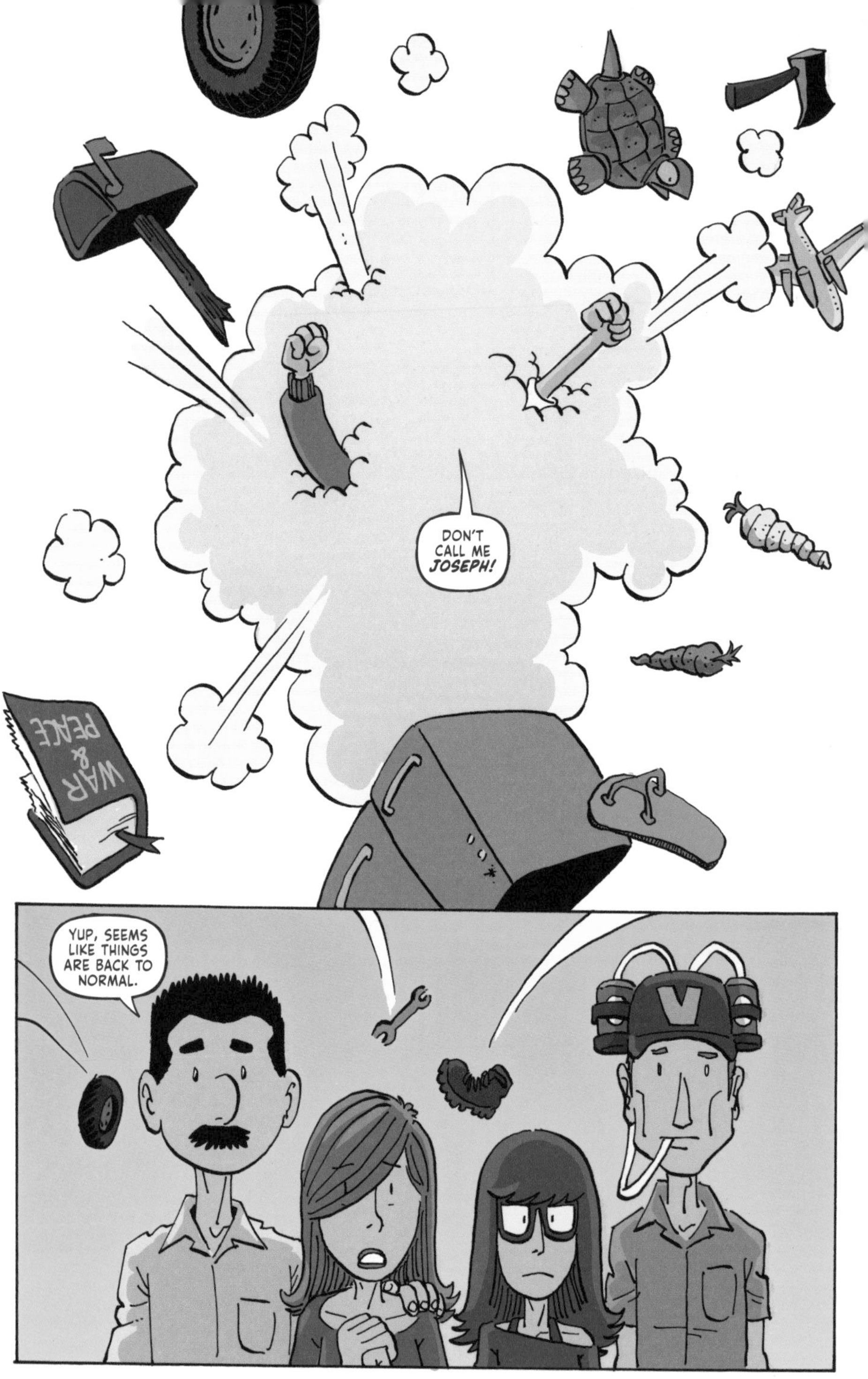
DON'T CALL ME JOSEPH!
WAR & PEACE
YUP, SEEMS LIKE THINGS ARE BACK TO NORMAL.
V

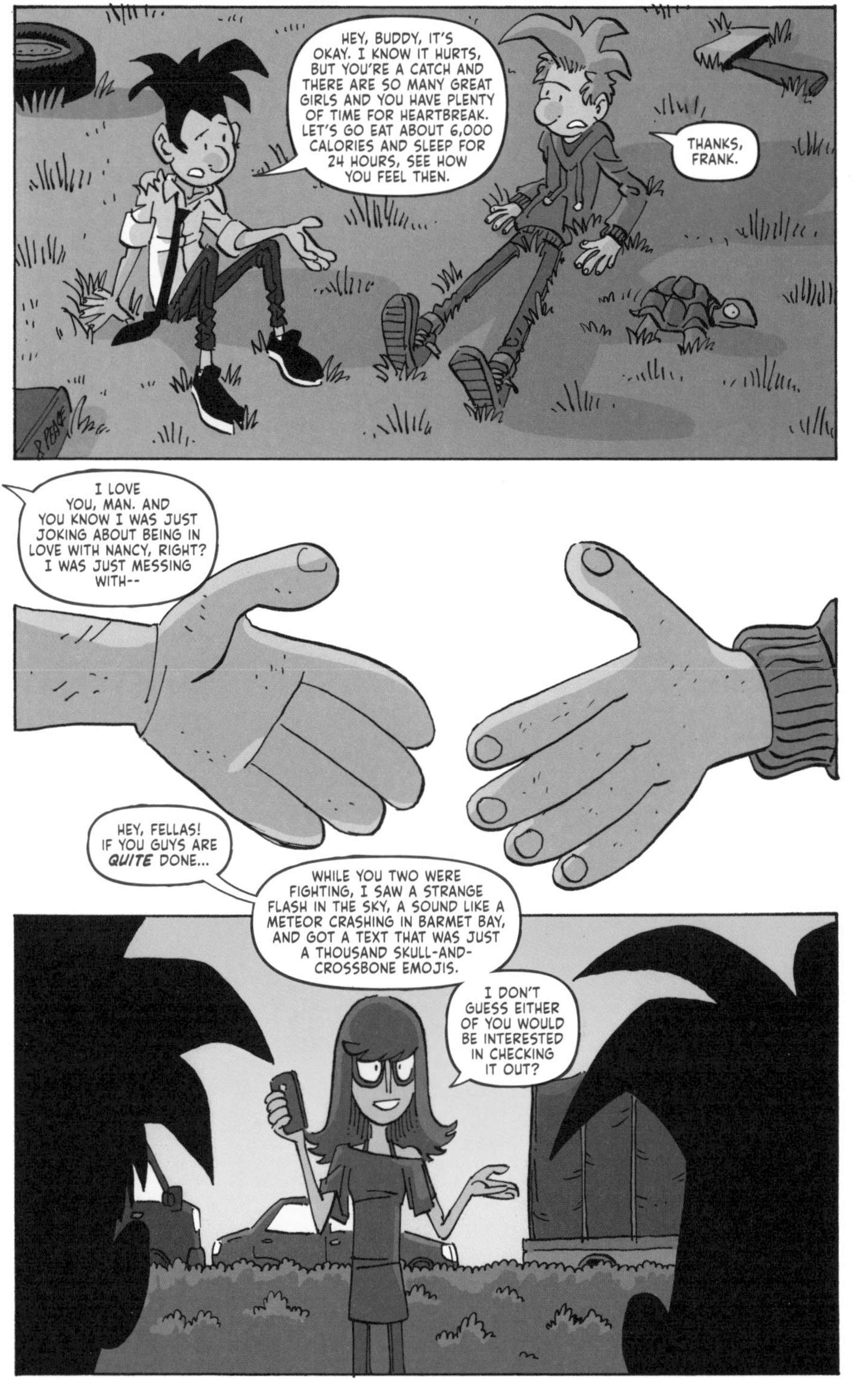
HEY, BUDDY, IT'S OKAY. I KNOW IT HURTS, BUT YOU'RE A CATCH AND THERE ARE SO MANY GREAT GIRLS AND YOU HAVE PLENTY OF TIME FOR HEARTBREAK. LET'S GO EAT ABOUT 6,000 CALORIES AND SLEEP FOR 24 HOURS, SEE HOW YOU FEEL THEN.
THANKS, FRANK.
I LOVE YOU, MAN. AND YOU KNOW I WAS JUST JOKING ABOUT BEING IN LOVE WITH NANCY, RIGHT? I WAS JUST MESSING WITH--
HEY, FELLAS! IF YOU GUYS ARE ***QUITE*** DONE...
WHILE YOU TWO WERE FIGHTING, I SAW A STRANGE FLASH IN THE SKY, A SOUND LIKE A METEOR CRASHING IN BARMET BAY, AND GOT A TEXT THAT WAS JUST A THOUSAND SKULL-AND-CROSSBONE EMOJIS.
I DON'T GUESS EITHER OF YOU WOULD BE INTERESTED IN CHECKING IT OUT?

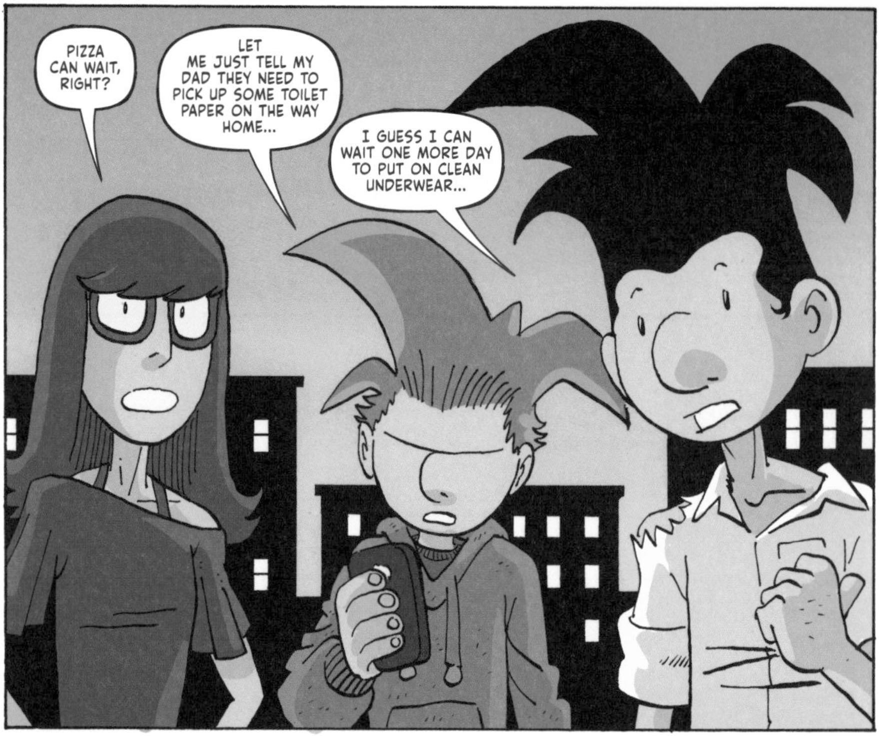
PIZZA CAN WAIT, RIGHT?
LET ME JUST TELL MY DAD THEY NEED TO PICK UP SOME TOILET PAPER ON THE WAY HOME...
I GUESS I CAN WAIT ONE MORE DAY TO PUT ON CLEAN UNDERWEAR...

NANCY DREW & THE HARDY BOYS WILL RETURN TO CRACK CASES, DO HOMEWORK, AND BREAK HEARTS

Bonus Materials

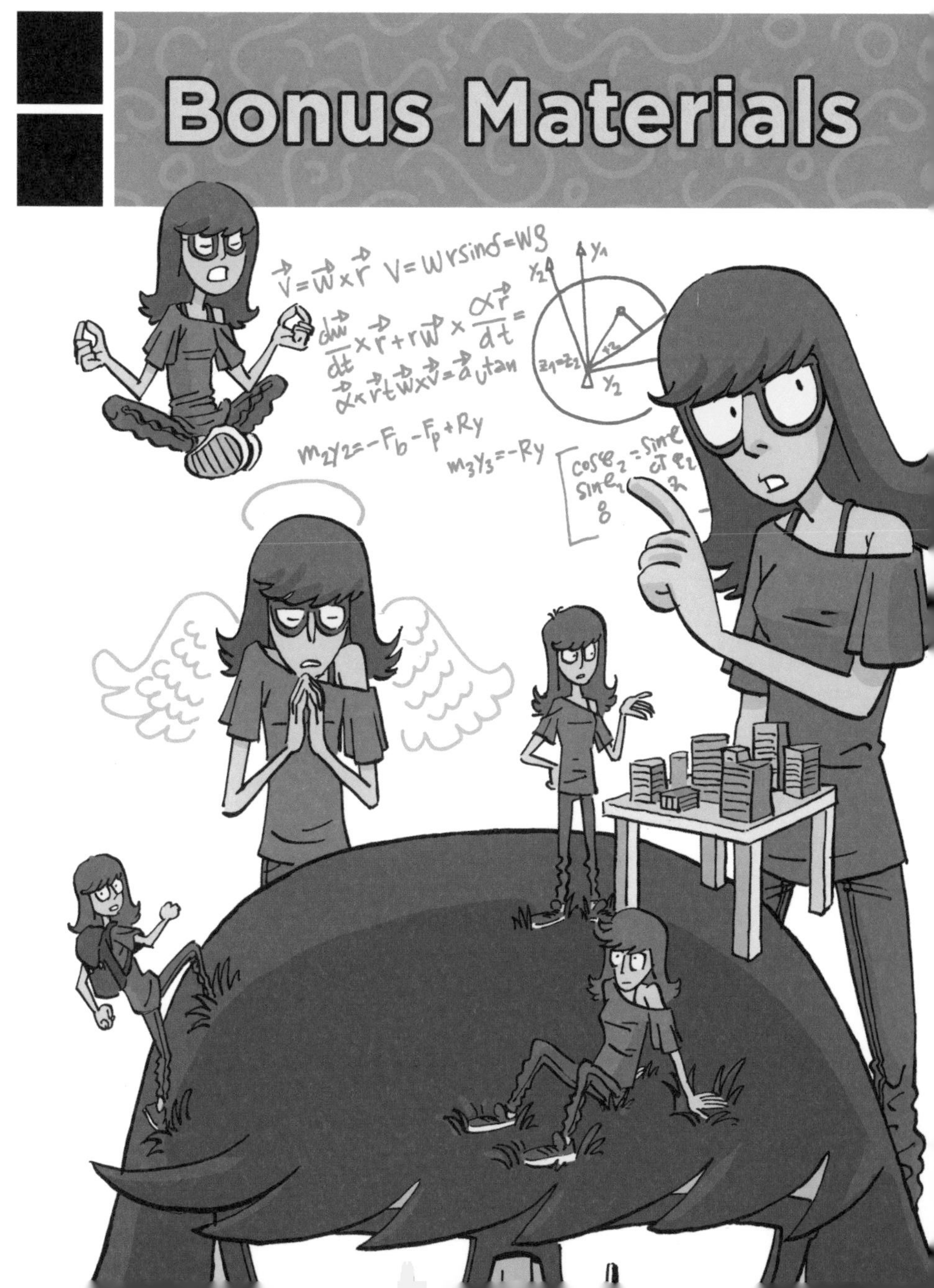

m2y2=-Fb-Fp+Ry
m3y3=-Ry

HEY, KIDS! YOU CAN'T EAT CANDY AND WATCH TV ALL DAY LIKE THE CHARACTERS IN OUR STORY—YOU GOTTA KEEP YOUR BRAIN SHARP! THE FOLLOWING PAGES CONTAIN SOME ACTIVITIES TO KEEP YOUR MIND QUICK!

CAN YOU SOLVE **THE CROSSWORD** BY FILLING IN THE NAMES OF THE KIDS IN THE BOOK?

HINT: IF YOU NEED HELP, REFER TO THE YEARBOOK ON PAGES 6-7!

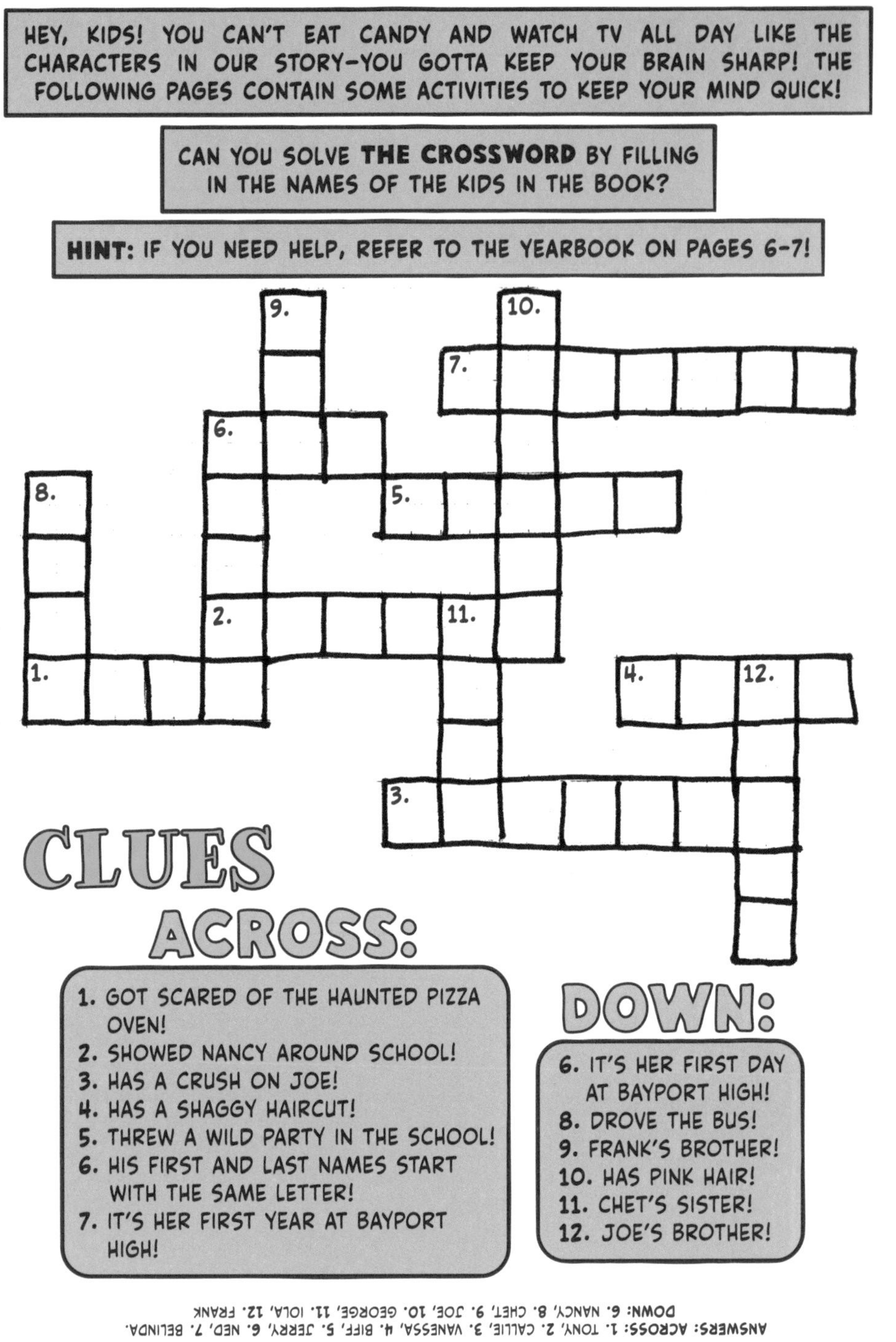

9.
10.
7.
6.
8.
5.
2.
11.
1.
4.
12.
3.

CLUES

ACROSS:

1. GOT SCARED OF THE HAUNTED PIZZA OVEN!
2. SHOWED NANCY AROUND SCHOOL!
3. HAS A CRUSH ON JOE!
4. HAS A SHAGGY HAIRCUT!
5. THREW A WILD PARTY IN THE SCHOOL!
6. HIS FIRST AND LAST NAMES START WITH THE SAME LETTER!
7. IT'S HER FIRST YEAR AT BAYPORT HIGH!

DOWN:

6. IT'S HER FIRST DAY AT BAYPORT HIGH!
8. DROVE THE BUS!
9. FRANK'S BROTHER!
10. HAS PINK HAIR!
11. CHET'S SISTER!
12. JOE'S BROTHER!

ANSWERS: ACROSS: 1. TONY, 2. CALLIE, 3. VANESSA, 4. BIFF, 5. JERRY, 6. NED, 7. BELINDA.
DOWN: 6. NANCY, 8. CHET, 9. JOE, 10. GEORGE, 11. IOLA, 12. FRANK

WHICH CHARACTER IS REVEALED WHEN YOU CONNECT THE DOTS?

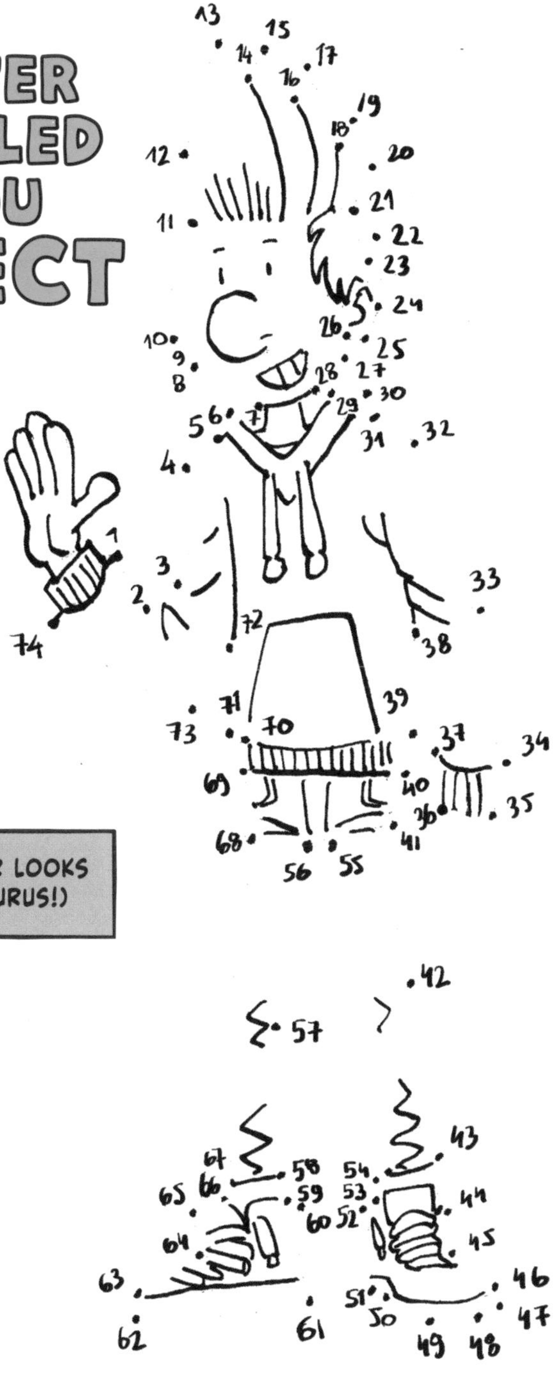

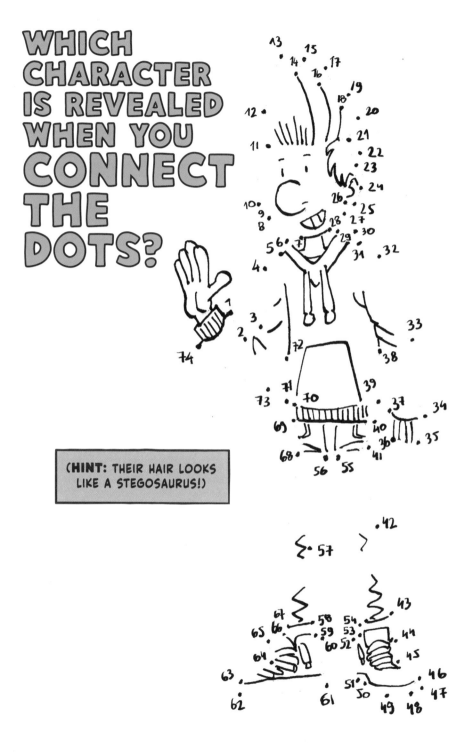

(**HINT:** THEIR HAIR LOOKS LIKE A STEGOSAURUS!)

SPOT THE DIFFERENCES!

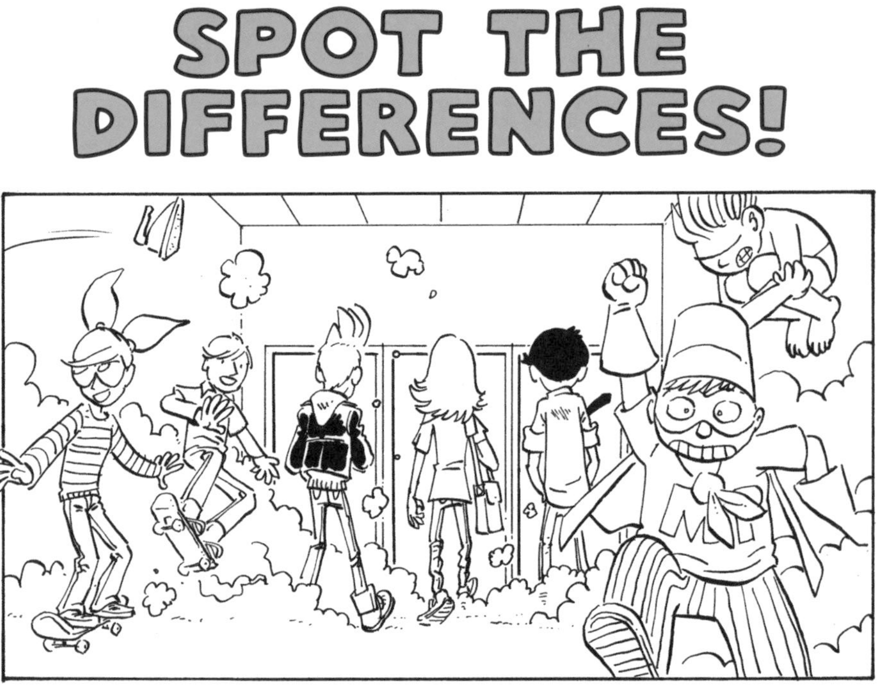

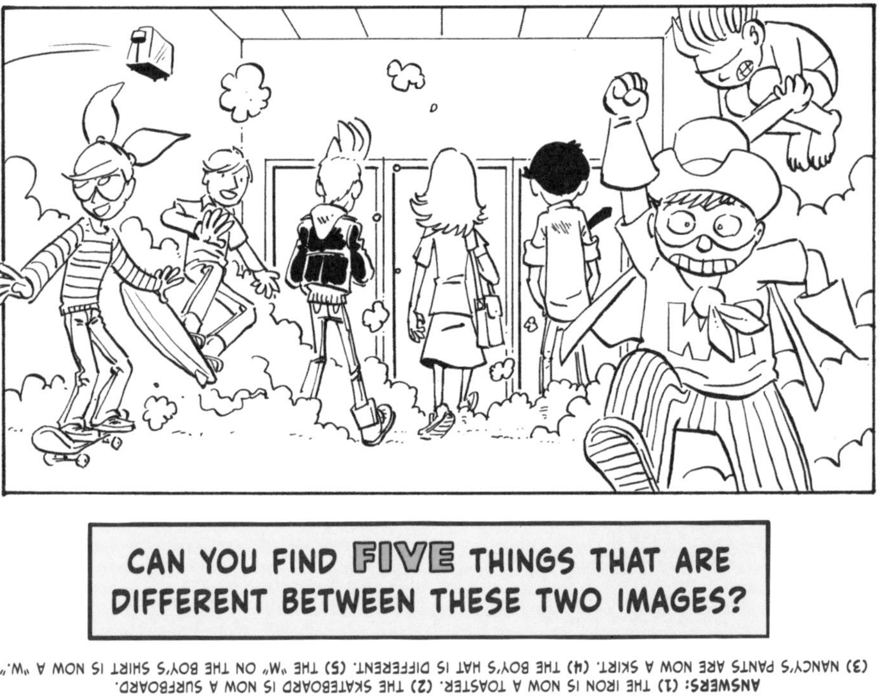

CAN YOU FIND FIVE THINGS THAT ARE DIFFERENT BETWEEN THESE TWO IMAGES?

ANSWERS: (1) THE IRON IS NOW A TOASTER. (2) THE SKATEBOARD IS NOW A SURFBOARD. (3) NANCY'S PANTS ARE NOW A SKIRT. (4) THE BOY'S HAT IS DIFFERENT. (5) THE "M" ON THE BOY'S SHIRT IS NOW A "W."

SEARCH-A-WORD

S	K	E	L	E	T	O	N	D	V
O	J	Z	L	Q	I	P	A	E	A
L	C	R	I	M	E	H	N	T	N
V	S	U	Q	E	U	L	C	E	S
E	M	Y	S	T	E	R	Y	C	A
Y	F	G	B	K	K	B	W	T	N
V	K	O	N	E	P	S	W	I	T
X	B	A	Y	P	O	R	T	V	E
A	R	U	M	H	E	C	F	E	O
F	O	O	T	P	R	I	N	T	J

HOW MANY OF THESE WORDS CAN YOU FIND?

BAYPORT
CLUE
CRIME
DETECTIVE
FOOTPRINT
FRANK
JOE

MYSTERY
NANCY
SCIENCE
SKELETON
SOLVE
VANSANT

GREAT DETECTIVES HAVE GREAT MEMORIES.

LOOK AT **PAGE 86** FOR **30 SECONDS** AND TRY TO REMEMBER **EVERYTHING** YOU SEE—

THEN COME BACK HERE AND TRY TO ANSWER THESE QUESTIONS **WITHOUT** LOOKING BACK!

1. NAME **THREE** OBJECTS FLYING OUT OF THE FIGHT BETWEEN JOE AND FRANK.

2. WHAT LETTER IS ON NANCY'S DAD'S HAT?

3. WHAT ANIMAL APPEARS ON THE PAGE?

SHARPEN YOUR CRAYONS– IT'S TIME TO COLOR!

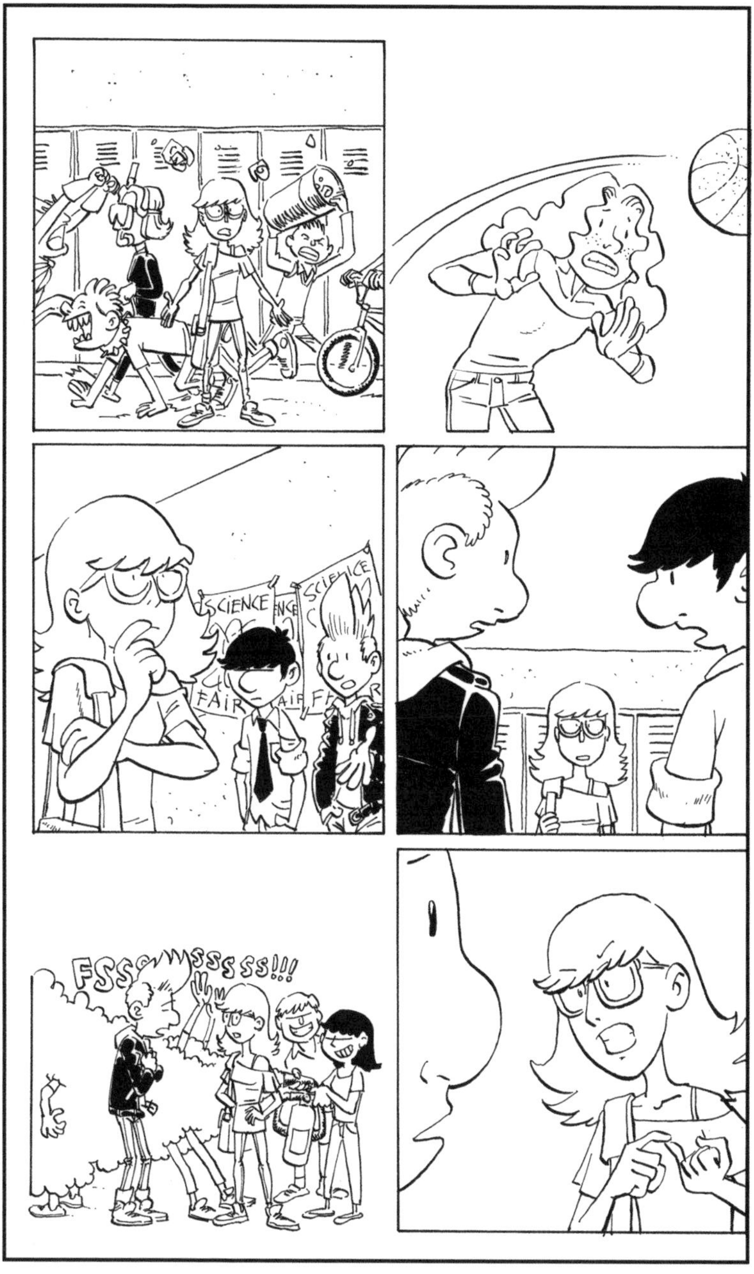
SCIENCE
FAIR
FSSSSSSSSS!!!

CHARACTER SKETCHES

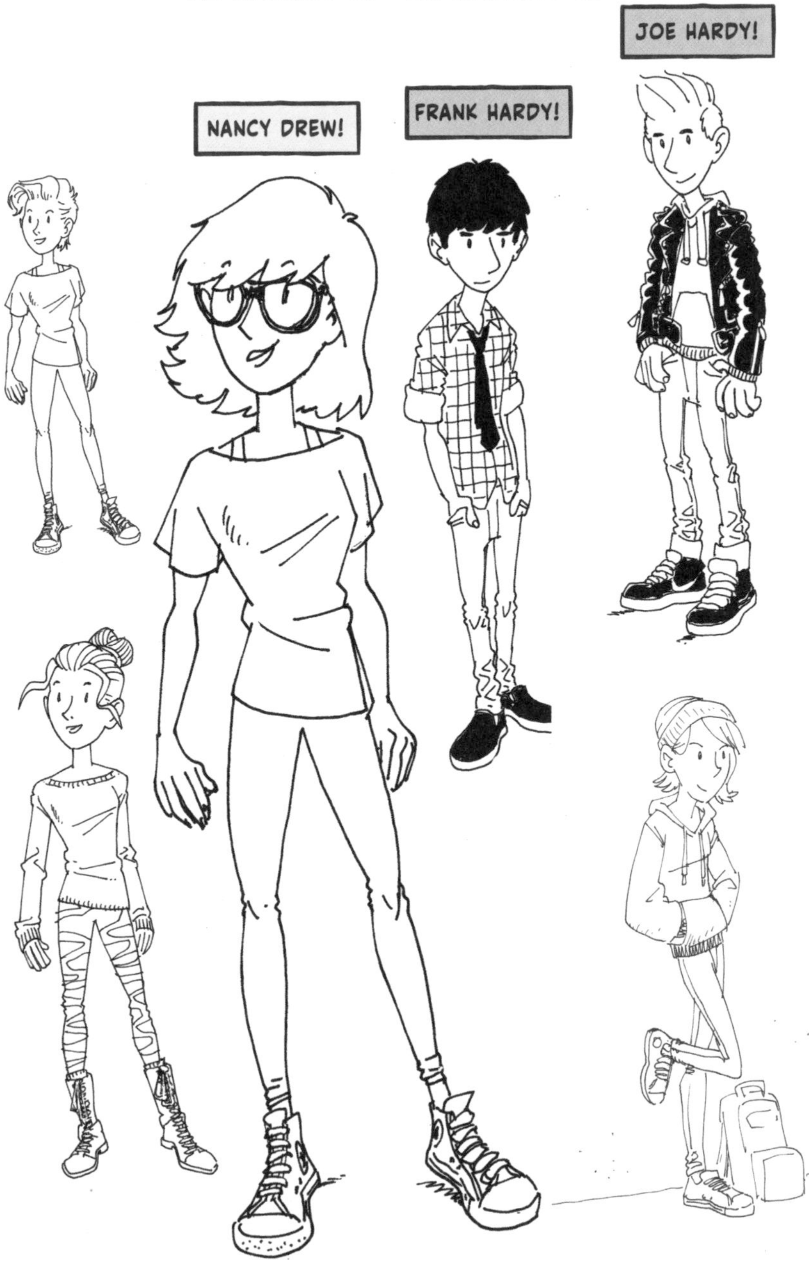
JOE HARDY!
NANCY DREW!
FRANK HARDY!

COVER SKETCHES

THE COVER IS ONE OF THE MOST IMPORTANT PARTS OF A BOOK, BECAUSE IT'S THE FIRST THING YOU SEE!

BEFORE BOB SOLANOVIČZ DREW THE COVER, HE MADE QUICK SKETCHES OF A FEW IDEAS TO SHOW SOME OPTIONS.

HERE ARE A FEW OF HIS INITIAL IDEAS.

NANCY DREW & THE HARDY BOYS

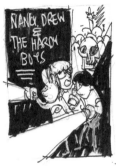

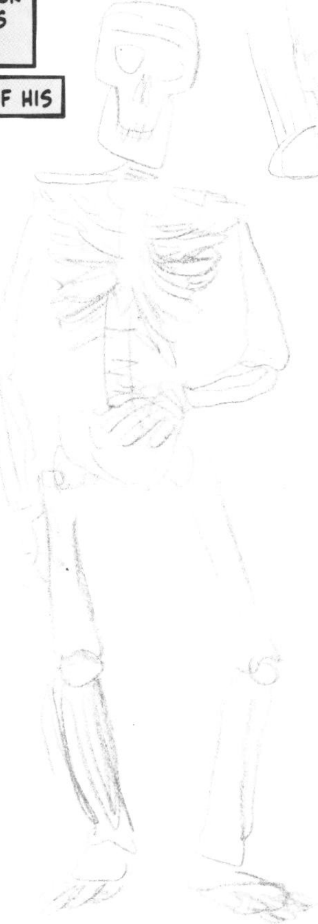

MY PERSONAL FAVORITE. OUR 3 PROTAGONISTS STUMBLING THROUGH THE DARK, BUT NANCY'S FLASHLIGHT REVEALS AN ARMY OF SKELETONS STANDING BEHIND THEIR BACKS!!!

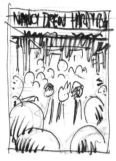

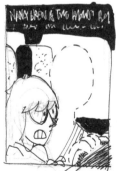

OUR HEROES SURROUNDED BY AN ARMY OF SKELETONS IN A HIGH SCHOOL HALLWAY

Nancy Drew & The Hardy Boys

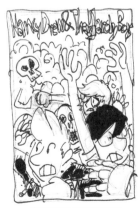

COMPLETELY SURROUNDED BY SKELETONS. NANCY PUNCHES ONE OF THEM IN THE JAW WHILE THE BOYS ARE SCREAMING.

I KNOW, IT'S A STRANGE ONE. MAYBE STUPID. BUT IT WAS ONE OF THE FIRST IDEAS THAT CAME INTO MY HEAD.

HOW A COMIC IS MADE!

1. WRITE THE SCRIPT—THIS TELLS YOU WHAT HAPPENS ON EACH PAGE, AND WHO SAYS WHAT!

PAGE SIXTY-THREE (6 panels)

Panel 1: In the hallway, FRANK is on the floor. JOE is helping him up. A nice moment between brothers.

JOE:	I'm so glad to see you, buddy.
FRANK:	Same. I was so worried about you—

Panel 2: NANCY comes flying out.

NANCY:	Oh, no! Did he knock Frank out?
JOE:	Nope. This idiot slipped in that spilled lo mein—

Panel 3: They head down the stairs, running.

FRANK:	Joe, how were you flashing the Morse code?
NANCY:	And why don't you know how to spell "help"?

Panel 4: On the stairs.

JOE:	I realized the adults were all running at the same speed and cadence, and so by running at a different speed, I could disrupt the electric current and create surges to overload the—

Panel 5: FRANK and NANCY turn around.

NANCY:	What are we involved in here, Joe?
FRANK:	Were they using our parents as—

Panel 6: JOE.
JOE: Hamsters in a cage. No time to explain. Let's go find these losers!

2. SKETCH OUT THE PAGE— THIS WAY YOU CAN MAKE SURE EVERYTHING FITS!

3. LAY OUT THE PAGE— THIS IS TO GET EVERYTHING EXACTLY WHERE YOU WANT IT BEFORE YOU START DRAWING!

4. DRAW THE PAGE IN PENCIL–
THIS WAY YOU CAN ERASE IF YOU MAKE A MISTAKE!

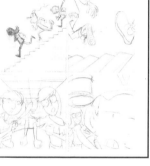

5. FINISH THE PAGE IN INK–
THIS IS HOW YOU ADD DEPTH AND MOOD!

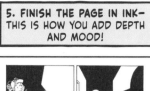

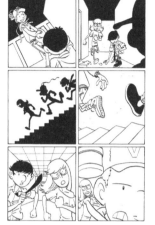

6. ADD COLORS–
YOU'RE ALMOST DONE!

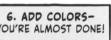

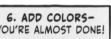

7. ADD LETTERS–
HOORAY!

I'M SO GLAD TO SEE YOU, BUDDY.
SAME. I WAS SO WORRIED ABOUT YOU--
OH, NO! DID HE KNOCK FRANK OUT?
NOPE. HE SLIPPED IN THAT SPILLED LO MEIN--
JOE, HOW WERE YOU FLASHING THE MORSE CODE?
AND WHY DON'T YOU KNOW HOW TO SPELL "HELP"?
I REALIZED THE ADULTS WERE ALL RUNNING AT THE SAME SPEED AND CADENCE, AND SO BY RUNNING AT A DIFFERENT SPEED, I COULD DISRUPT THE ELECTRIC CURRENT AND CREATE SURGES TO OVERLOAD THE--
WHAT ARE WE INVOLVED IN HERE, JOE?
WERE THEY USING OUR PARENTS AS--
HAMSTERS IN A CAGE. NO TIME TO EXPLAIN. LET'S GO FIND THESE LOSERS!

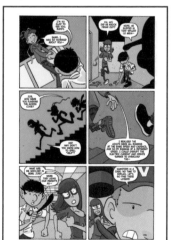

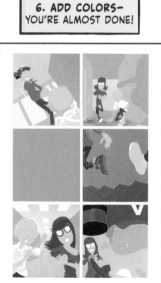

YOUR COMIC IS FINISHED! SHOW YOUR FRIENDS!

About the Creators

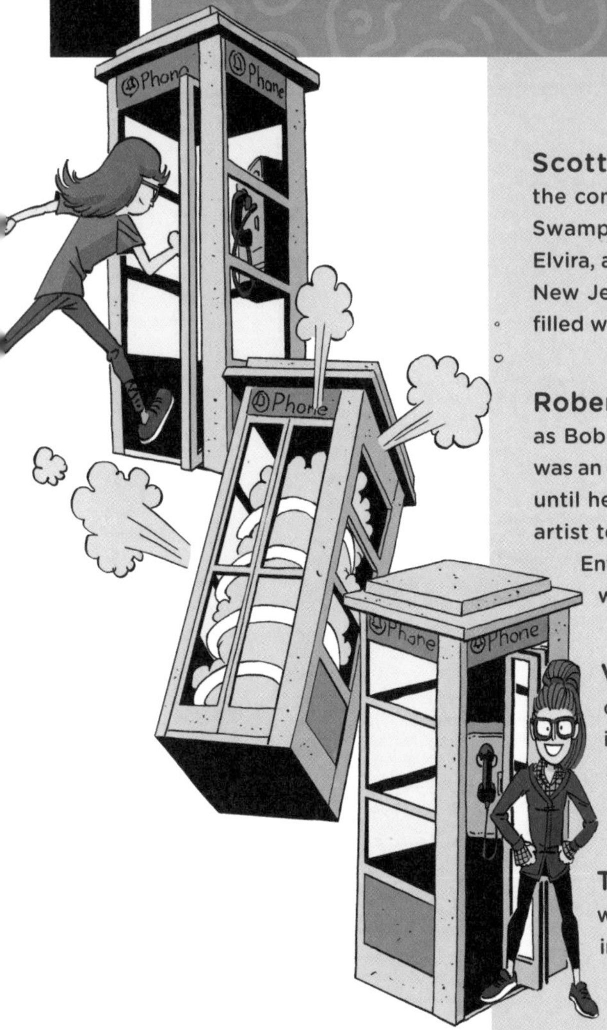
Phone
Phone
Phone
Phone
Phone

Scott Bryan Wilson has written the comic book adventures of Batman, Swamp Thing, Star Trek, Shadowman, Elvira, and others. He lives in Bloomfield, New Jersey, where he writes in a room filled with books.

Robert Solanovicz, better known as Bob in his native country of Croatia, was an unappreciated comic book genius until he forced his friend and colleague artist to send his portfolio to Dynamite Entertainment. The rest is history. Or will be. Or not.

Valentina Briški is a freelance comic book artist, colorist, and illustrator from Zagreb, Croatia. She likes cats, comics, and old movies.

Tom Napolitano is a letterer who's chained to a desk somewhere in Brooklyn, forever lettering many titles for Andworld Design, DC Comics, Dynamite, and others.